The Darknot

Book 3

of the Nethergrim Trilogy

Also by Matthew Jobin

The Nethergrim

The Skeleth

www.nethergrim.com

The Darknot

Book 3

of the Nethergrim Trilogy

Matthew Jobin

For my daughter

Prologue

Five years before

"Please, Father." The boy reached out to tug at the fur-trimmed sleeve. "I don't want to go."

The father's mouth twitched, his brows drawn low. The boy's heart leaped for an instant, one shiver of hope, then it dropped again. The father urged his horse onward, sliding past the boy without reply.

A troop of royal guards rode their broad-chested cobs in close guard around the boy. He knew them all, for they had come with him from the Spire at Paladon, where he had lived his whole life. They had been his protectors for as long as he could remember—but they had torn him from the hands of his mother a week before, dragged him from the hall and bundled him away into the cold. They would not look at him anymore.

"Please, Father." The boy looked about him. Dawn had not yet come. He rode with his father and the guards through wild and broken country. He shifted in his saddle. Perhaps, just perhaps, if he chose the right moment—

A heavy hand grabbed him by the back of his shirt. "Steady, my lord prince." The gray-bearded guard who shared his horse pulled him in tight. "You looked about to slip from the saddle."

"I don't want to go up there!" T boy had gotten a few beatings in his life for crying. "Please don't make me go." He could not stop, though, and no longer cared what the guards thought of him for doing it.

"Oh, will you quit blubbering!" The father trotted his horse farther out ahead. The boy watched him round the next turn, up high into the mountains, up and up to—he cowered down. He could not look at it.

The royal guard held the boy in an easy grip. "There now, my lord prince. There." He patted his shoulder. "It's a great honor to do this for your family and your kingdom."

"I don't want to go." The boy said it at the ends of his breath. "Don't make me!" He got no reply, no words from any of the guards around him. A hollow ball of terror swelled in him until it felt as though it might burst from his belly. There came another, darker moment, when the train of horses strung out single file along the rising walls of the mountain, when he nearly summoned the courage to fling himself off, off and down to bleed out broken and dead on the snowy rocks below. He hesitated, though, and the guard grabbed him tighter.

"Death's not better." The old guard snaked a mailed arm around the boy's waist and held it there. "Not so I've ever heard."

The boy hung his head and gave himself up to crying until he went hoarse. "I want Mama." It was his last plea and last revenge. "I want my mama." If his father thought less of him for it, what could it matter anymore? His last sunrise came, pink and yellow on the snow of the pass above.

The father waited at the junction, at the place where the trail could either run along the side of the mountain or turn upward for the summit. "Come on, curse it all. I want this done with." He pulled down the furred cuffs of his shirt and beat his arms together.

"Coming, Your Grace." The guard spurred his horse, which gave a snort and did its best to speed the pace up the treacherous road.

The boy gripped the horse's mane, twining the coarse chestnut hairs in his hands. Of all the things that had pleased him, in the days when he thought he was going to grow up to be king after his father, it was the thought of riding on a great horse of war that had made him happiest of all. Sometimes he had thought about riding to battle or charging in to save people from evil monsters, but mostly he had thought about the horse.

The descending wind pushed his tears down his face in cold streaks. The year before, when he turned six, he had gotten a wooden sword for his

Matthew Jobin

birthday. He loved swinging it around almost as much as he loved learning to ride on horseback. But then came the day when his father had returned to the Spire and taken away the sword. Since then, every day had been another step up into the mountains.

"Don't see why the king needed to drag the whole pack of us up here." One of the other guards hawked and spit over the side of a cliff. "Could get killed by a snowslide—and what's the boy going to do, run away?"

"Shut your mouth." The guard behind the boy bristled and pushed his fellow back. "Just you ride apart, if you can't hold your tongue around the prince."

The other guard snorted. "What's it to you? You'll never see him again."

The boy looked up again—and wished that he had not. They had come in full view at last. The place where they were going looked even more frightening than his nightmares had hinted, in all the weeks since he learned that he was bound to be sent there. It stood out like a diseased finger thrust toward the thin sky, a dark and ugly tower standing alone at the top of a pass. It seemed enormously, sickeningly tall, but it was not until the boy caught sight of the men waiting at the foot of it that he understood just how tall it truly was.

The father rode into the pass where stood the tower. The waiting men knelt in reverent greeting, then as the boy watched, more shuffled out from a cluster of huts built in the long shadow of the tower. Snow had not yet come down from the peaks, but the wind told tales of its approach.

The boy shivered. Such things could not matter to him—not anymore. He would not have to worry about the wind.

"Hail, King Bregisel!" One of the men beneath the tower came forth and made a bow as he approached the father's horse. "I am the master of novices. We laymen brothers of the *Eredh* greet you and honor you for the great sacrifice you make. You arrive on an auspicious day."

"Oh?" The father stayed astride his horse, though two other lay brothers rolled back the sleeves of their cassocks to help him dismount. "What sort of day is it? Is this one of those moon-conjunction things, then?"

The master of novices coughed. He pointed to the boy. "His seventh birthday, Your Grace. We obtained the date by correspondence with his royal mother."

"Oh yes. Good." The father seemed able to look everywhere in the world but at the boy. "Well—get your folk to cooking. We'll want a hot meal."

The master of novices hesitated. "Before or after?"

"After."

"Please, Father. Please." The boy tried to reach out for his father's horse, but the guard would not let him. "Don't make me go. I'll be better!"

The father turned his horse away, his teeth grit. "It's got to be done, boy." He seemed to be saying it to himself as much as anyone. "Got to be done. Might have more sons, anyway—queen's still young enough."

The boy sank down in the saddle, cowering in the shadow of the tower. The wind stroked the hairs on the back of his neck.

"Come on, then." The guard lifted him from the saddle, putting him bodily down into the arms of a pair of burly lay brothers. "You will have time yet—and none of us know how long we have in life."

The lay brothers wore mantles of undyed wool over their cassocks that chafed at the boy's face. They handed him along as though he were a sack of barley, maneuvering him over toward the tower, their footsteps crunching down the meager grass. The boy gave up struggling. He gave up everything.

There were no gates. More lay brothers waited in silence, on either side of a hole in the dark wall. They carried bricks, trowels and mortar. The boy could not hold back his screams.

The master of novices looked back to the father. "Your Grace? Anything you would like to say before we start?"

The father turned his horse. He stared at the boy, his forehead creased as though trying to remember something. For an instant of hope that hurt far worse than despair ever could, a look of remorse crossed his face. Then he blanked it away, shook his head and grunted.

The old royal guard leaned in over the boy. He wept, the tears running down into his graying beard. "It's not fair. It's not right. He's just a child."

The father rounded on him. "What was that? How dare you—what did you say?"

The guard brushed his face and roughened his voice. "I told him to remember his duty to his father, the king, and to remember that this is a great honor for his family." He bowed. "Your Grace."

The father unclenched his hands. "Ah. That's good, then." He turned to the boy. "Yes—be a good lad, now. Mind your duty and the honor of your family. That's what matters."

The shadow of the tower fell full across the boy. He twisted and wriggled again, trying to look back one last time. The father turned away, unwilling to

Matthew Jobin

meet his gaze, but it was not for a final plea that the boy looked east. It was for one last look at the rising sun.

"Chlodobert, only son of King Bregisel, I consign you in oblation to the tower of Eredhros." The lay brothers pushed the boy through the hole in the wall. It was not a long drop, but with so little light the boy could not help but trip and tumble to the unyielding stone floor.

"Please!" The boy hugged his knees. "Please don't." He reached into his shirt and pulled out something that none of the guards had noticed he was carrying—a worn and ragged stuffed toy dog. He clutched it close.

The bricks came quick and sure, slapped.into place with practiced skill. "There will be no light for you save the light of truth. You are laid upon the altar of truth, the lamb bleeds for truth—*Eredh, Eredh*, the thrice-opened eye. In time, you will come to see and accept the rightness of your fate. May the truth be of comfort to you."

"Father!" The boy leaped to his feet. No amount of despair could wash away his terror at the disappearing light. He scrabbled to the wall, reaching up for the vanishing hole. "Father, don't make me! Please, Father—Father, let me out!"

He got his hand over a brick, but a lay brother slapped it away. He tried again, reaching up to thrust his head out. He caught one image, one sight— his father lit by the rising sun, face in his hands, and the old royal guard weeping without trying to check his tears. Then a lay brother shoved the end of a pole through the hole in the wall, catching the boy in the chest and shoving him firmly back.

The boy sucked in a breath. "Father! Father, please, I love you! Don't make the light go!"

The hole got smaller and smaller still. Hope got smaller, smaller still.

The boy got up onto his knees. "Please, don't! I wanted to be better! I wanted to be good! I will be! If you let me out, I'll be better!"

"I cannot stand it." The father's voice got farther away. "Where is that meal? Hop to it, curse you, move!"

"Chlodobert, son of King Bregisel, you are consigned to the tower of Eredhros, to be brought forth only on the day of your death." The master of novices looked through the last open space, space enough for one brick. "Do you understand why you are here?"

The boy stared up at him. He could see only a pair of eyes. "Is it because I was bad?"

The eyes blinked. "Er, hmm. No. Not really."
The last brick shoved in. The darkness began.

Chapter 1

The Day Before Yule

E dmund plucked the pastry from his tray and set it down in front of Katherine. "This is on the house." A scent rose, steam and spice, nutmeg and honey with just a hint of rare and precious cinnamon.

Katherine looked up from where she sat, leaned head-to-head with Tom at the little table in the corner. Had she been so near to any other boy in the world, the sight of it would have made Edmund's guts clench in, but it was only Tom.

"Oho, look at this!" Katherine drew the cake near. "I'm not sure I can eat it all in one sitting." She called out her thanks across the tavern to Edmund's mother, Sarra Bale, who wiped her hands on her apron and ducked back through the kitchen door.

"It's for all of us. It's a Yule-cake." Edmund set down a pair of apples, sliced and dripped in honey. "And these are from the Twintrees. They call 'em eat-right-nows, so eat 'em right now."

Katherine drew back the chair to her right, just as Edmund had hoped she would. "Sit with us awhile. I'm telling Tom the news of the kingdom."

Edmund shot a look over his shoulder, searching for any sign of his father and a summons back to work. Instead he found the folk of his village smiling his way, lit orange-dark through the low expanse of the tavern. Henry Twintree raised a mug in silent toast; Mercy Wainwright waved her baby's hand as she bounced him on her knee. Nicky Bird and Horsa Blackcalf played rounds on flute and fiddle by the fire, winding up the frantic finish of a song about a bull that had gotten out of his paddock. The young men by the door made noisy echoes of the last refrain. Two of them locked arms; one raised his mug to sway in song but the other thought they meant to start a dance. Down they both went across the floor; a chorus of "Oh!" rose all around them, then it turned into a wave of laughter.

"What sort of news?" Edmund set down his serving tray and flopped into the offered chair. "About the king? I've heard five different tales of how he died, and two of them involve a vat of boiling oil."

"Can we eat first?" Tom leaned over the Yule cake, breathing in its scent with such rapturous lungfuls that it looked as though he were about to eat it through his nose. Even while sitting, he was almost a head taller than Edmund, and standing he was taller still. He moved in closer over the food, shifting his rawboned frame and giving Edmund the disappointing knowledge that it was his skinny leg that had been rubbing up against Edmund's own, and not Katherine's.

"We've got to eat it all together, Tom." Katherine held out a hand to keep Tom from diving into the cake face-first. "It's a Yule cake. Edmund, is it done proper?"

Edmund could hardly contain his giddy hope. "Of course. Mum cooks everything proper." He had one chance in three, and on the eve of that particular Yule, with all that he had suffered in the year just drawing to its close, he felt as though the world owed him some luck.

Tom passed a look of confusion from one friend to the next. Edmund guessed the question, but Katherine answered first.

"There's a bean buried in this cake somewhere." Katherine never slouched—her posture on a hard tavern bench was the same as it would be in a saddle. "If a man finds the bean, he owes the man beside him a day's work, but if a woman finds it, she has to give the man beside her a kiss." She was nearly Tom's height, which meant that she already stood taller than half the grown men in the village, though like her friends she was still but fourteen. The firelight reflected pinpoints in the depths of her oak-brown eyes, inner worlds where Edmund could lose himself and never wish to leave.

"That's not a fair game," said Tom. "I'd rather owe anyone a kiss than work his land an extra day."

Matthew Jobin

Edmund raised an eyebrow. "What, you'd kiss old Robert Windlee rather than plow his field for a day?"

"I would." Tom said it without an instant's hesitation. It was not that Tom was lazy—no one who knew him could possibly accuse him of that. He had been an orphan purchased at market by his master, Athelstan, and until the autumn of that year had lived a life of ceaseless labor working field, barn and pasture. Tom had been a bonded slave, and even though he had come under the protection of Katherine's father, the Marshal of Elverain, no one was really sure whether he was yet truly free.

"Tomorrow." Katherine turned a hopeful smile on Tom. "Harry's the lord of the land, now. We'll have it all settled tomorrow, you'll see."

Tom returned the smile without the hope. Edmund raced to think of something happier to say, something to turn them back to the promise of the cake between them, but felt a hard shove at his back before anything came to him.

"You donkey face! What do you think you're doing?" The voice behind the shove broke and piped high with every few words, then dove down once again, nasal and tuneless. "We're packed to the ceiling in here—everyone says the brown ale's gone off, someone spilled porridge by the door and everybody's stepping in it, and Henry Twintree wants change for a gold mark! I can't keep up!"

Edmund spun and shoved his little brother, Geoffrey, right back. "Go away. I'm resting for a bit."

"Resting?" Geoffrey wrinkled in his freckled face. "Who said you could be resting? It's the last day of Deadmoon—Yule's eve! This is the busiest night of the year!"

"Except for all the other busiest nights of the year." Edmund turned his back on his brother. A team of oxen could not pull him away from the Yule cake before him and the promise it contained. A silence stretched—Katherine and Tom exchanged a look—and after a few more shouts for ale across the room, Geoffrey stomped away, muttering curses under his breath.

"I get up before dawn to study and practice." Edmund felt an embarrassed prickle under the gazes of his friends. "Don't tell me you think I should be brewing ale and hauling sacks of barley instead of learning magic."

Katherine picked up her mug to take a drink of mulberry posset. She shook her head. No one in the village, no one in the whole barony could possibly say that, not after all that had happened that year.

"Now, when's it time for your song, hey?" Short and shaggy Nicky Bird clapped Edmund's side as he hopped along between the tables. "The song of Edmund and Katherine!"

"And Geoffrey." Katherine set down her mug. "And Tom."

"That's right, Tom and Geoffrey!" Nicky hopped up on a chair. "Come on, Horsa. We'll make something up!"

Horsa Blackcalf played his fiddle at the knee, cross-tuned to make a leaping harmony when he played two strings at once. Nicky Bird had perhaps less skill upon the swan's-wing flute, but what he lacked in precision he made up for in dash, always dancing as he played, singing out couplets from songs they all knew wherever they might fit into the tune. Together they made as good a pair of bards as could be expected of men who farmed for their living, men who only got to play their music in the evenings when they were often weary half to death. There was no sign of weariness on either man that night, though—a hard year had turned and passed on, and it was time to sing for hope of better years to come.

"So." Edmund leaned toward the Yule cake. "On three?" He counted, and on the count of three they each scooped a hand into the cake and started eating. He could not help but note that it did not taste quite as good as his mother's cooking usually did—still quite edible, to be sure, but lacking in something he could not define.

"Listen to that." Katherine spoke with her mouth full. "Just listen." She paused, just long enough to watch the wind slam the shutter of the nearest window so hard that it nearly came off its leather hinges. A whirl of snow arced into the room, glittering for an instant before melting down into water on the rush-strewn floor.

"I can hear it without really listening to it." Edmund shivered at the howls from outside—they sounded far too much like screams for his liking.

"May we stay here tonight? Papa can pay." Katherine was not eating nearly fast enough. At the rate she was going, Tom would eat so much of the cake that he was nearly certain to find the bean, and Edmund would rather not have the guilt of a day's owed labor from his friend the former slave. Edmund merely grunted in reply and made a show of reaching over to

Katherine's side of the cake, which caused her to scoop down in competitive hunger, and—

"Ah!" Katherine crunched down on something and drew it from her mouth. "The bean!"

Edmund felt a flush of excitement so strong that he could not help but drum his feet on the floor, even though by doing so he accidentally kicked Jumble, Tom's rack-ribbed, brush-tailed dog, who had lain peacefully asleep by the fire most of the night. Jumble got up and shook himself out, but instead of taking the handful of cake Tom offered him, he wandered off toward the front door of the tavern with his black-and-white ears pricked high.

"Well, then." Katherine seemed not to mind too much that the burden of the bean had fallen upon her. "I am chosen." She drew back her long dark hair over her shoulders, turned and—

"Wait, no!" Edmund gaped, but it was too late—Katherine had already planted a kiss on Tom's cheek. "Tom's on your left!" There was no point in saying also that the kiss was supposed to be on the lips.

Tom did not even seem to blush. He simply nodded, as though Katherine had done no more than punch him on the shoulder, then he scooped up the dregs of the cake while peering across the smoky expanse of the tavern at Jumble.

Katherine pushed half the honeyed apples in front of Edmund, perhaps as some sort of consolation. "What do you mean? It's always to the left, in odd years."

Edmund knew that he sounded like he was sulking. "I've never heard of that."

"The king's been on the throne for fifteen years, so it's to the left." It was impossible to tell whether Katherine was simply inventing a barefaced lie. Her dark eyes had depths indeed. "That's how it's always done."

Edmund crossed his arms. "The king's not on the throne at all, he's six feet underground—that is, if there's even anything left of him to bury."

Tom turned back to his friends. "So if the king is dead, who's the king now?"

Edmund gave up on his bad mood before it could really get going. After all, Katherine had only kissed Tom. "Well, that's the interesting part." He looked around him, then spoke softly under the din of the dance. "The wine merchant came through last week to fill his winter orders, and he brought a passel of news. He said that Princess Merofled hasn't been seen since the day the king died. He said the queen's gone stark mad, she's shut herself up in the highest tower in the Spire and folk can see her on the battlements high above them, pacing back and forth and wailing like a—"

"Get back to work, boy." Edmund's father, Harman Bale, walked stiffly past, one hand held pressed at his side. "Your brother can't handle this place alone."

Katherine watched Edmund's father cross over to join with the other men of the village council on their way out through the front door of the inn. "He's walking much better these days. He's almost back to his old self."

"In more ways than one." Edmund smacked his hands clean of crumbs. "The better he feels, the meaner he gets. He's gone back to calling me a fool for reading books. It's as though all the things we went through this year never happened."

Katherine shook her head. "I guess some people never change."

"I've changed." Edmund felt the bitter sting of it. "You've changed, Katherine. Why not him?"

"So are you going back to work?" said Katherine.

Edmund snorted. "No."

Martin Upfield stopped at their table, a heavy-bearded young man with a bear's frame of body but a draft horse's gentle heart. "Now, cousin—" He found nowhere to sit, so he knelt next to Katherine, though even so he was head and shoulders above the tabletop. "Now. About Uncle John."

Katherine followed his glance across the tavern at her father, John, the Marshal of Elverain. John Marshal sat alone, his hands drawn up clenched together over a mug that had sat untouched all night. He stared at the blank surface of the table before him, his grizzled hair and beard grown out longer than Edmund had ever seen it.

"Are you all right for food up at the farm?" Martin leaned on his thick forearms. "I'm your kin, Katherine, the only other kin you've got in the world. Let me help you."

Edmund tried not to let his brows raise. Martin was a cottar, a man without land enough of his own to feed himself, and so one who had to turn to day labor to make ends meet. It was a question whether Martin had laid in enough food to last himself the winter, let alone to feed three.

Katherine smiled. "I'll manage, cousin. Tom's helping."

Martin scratched his beard. "I could get some piecework at the mill. Jarvis has been letting things go a bit, since—" He shot a glance across at Alice Miller. "Since Tilly didn't come home."

Edmund followed Martin's gaze—Alice Miller slumped in her chair, alone among the revelry, forgotten for the moment by her neighbors and friends. Her three-year-old son played at her feet, seeming to enjoy all the extra attention folk were giving him without quite understanding what it was for.

"We'll be fine," said Katherine. "Papa's better than this, most days."

Martin stood up. "All right, then, cousin. But you know, if it comes to it, that you can call on me."

"Same for you," said Katherine.

Martin smirked across the table at Tom and Edmund. He pointed a thumb at Katherine. "Just like her mother, you know. Seemed like she was all grown up at twelve." He stepped back into the crowd. Edmund turned away from his friends, his attention drifting over to the Millers, then the Overbournes, and then Bella Cooper, each of them somewhat apart from their neighbors, each of them wracked with loss.

Katherine caught Edmund's gaze with a wave of her hand. "You saved my life—and your brother's, Tom's, and those kids from Roughy. You put the Skeleth back in their casket before they could lay waste to all the north. Don't lose yourself in a maze of might-have-beens."

Edmund came back to himself. "Nothing's the same anymore." He twiddled with the last slice of apple, then spun it with the flick of a finger. "Sometimes I think I still hear *her*."

The merriment around the three friends fell back muted, something made for others, a feast for the joyful, the ignorant.

"The Nethergrim?" said Tom.

"It's loudest just when I wake up, but I can't make out the words." Edmund leaned in, ducking as a gang of young folk started dancing just behind his chair. "Sometimes when I try a spell, I hear her call my name."

"Edmund, maybe you should stop trying to learn magic on your own," said Katherine. "You don't know what you might be risking."

Edmund looked around him, at folk whirling ever faster in the dance, chattering loud and happy. "Nothing's the same. Even here, back home, I don't feel safe anymore. The world isn't what we thought it was." He turned back to Katherine. "What if I need to learn things that might hurt me, so that they can keep dancing?"

Katherine had no answer to that, or at least none that she wanted to say aloud.

"Remember last year's Yule?" said Tom. "It hadn't snowed at all by then."

"Last Yule, we really were just kids," said Katherine. "No one had ripped our village half to bits. No one had tried to invade us yet. No one had stolen seven children and tried to murder them under a mountain."

Tom stared at the rushes on the floor.

Edmund kicked his heels into the legs of his bench. "Last Yule, me and Geoffrey hid all the mistletoe so that Lefric and Luilda couldn't find anywhere to kiss. Back then, the monsters were supposed to be all gone. Back then, Tilly Miller was still alive, and so was Wat Cooper. Back then, the Nethergrim was still supposed to be dead." A lance of wind slipped in around the shutters and touched the back of his neck, as though it had come in on purpose to find him.

Tom raised his head. "Back then, I was still a slave and had no hope of ever getting free. Back then, we were no threat to lords or wizards—but now we know we can beat them, because we already have." He smiled at Katherine. "Back then, Lord Wolland could not have dreamed in a thousand years he was about to be bested in battle by a peasant girl."

Edmund felt the solid bottom of his fear and stood firm upon it. "Or that a former slave might single-handedly free the great hero Tristan and save his whole barony from wreck and pillage."

Katherine got to her feet. "Up." She dug her elbow at Edmund, then at Tom. "Come on, up. Let's join the dance."

Nobles often danced in pairs, but peasants liked to dance in crowds, swinging partners one to the next with every few stamping measures. Katherine led Edmund in, then passed him on to Missa Dyer, and then made a point of pulling Geoffrey Bale into the whirl with the ale pitcher dangling from his fingers. Hugh Jocelyn's cap fell off—his bald head gleamed in the firelight—but the lively look on his face made him seem closer to fifteen than fifty. Lefric Green and Luilda Twintree contrived to come around into each other's arms again and again, but no one minded it much. Katherine passed by Edmund on the inside, then the outside. No time to brood—so passed the

Matthew Jobin

look between them—life is for living. Edmund wondered if all the lessons of life were the same. They had to be learned over and over again.

"Make a lane, make a lane there!" The opened front door let through a blast of winter air, making Edmund feel how warm the tavern had become. The village council marched in, first Edmund's father at a stagger, one hand to his side, then Jarvis Miller and Henry Twintree. The dancers parted to stand on either side of the room. Horsa Blackcalf put away his fiddle, and Nicky Bird let off one last tweet from his flute.

"Hail to the fallen sun." Henry and Jarvis carried a wooden carving between them of a wagon drawn by six oddly matched creatures—a horse beside a cow, a dog with its ribs exposed and other, stranger things. "Praise to the sun reborn." In the wagon stood the carving of a boy, his hands on reins made of twine. Behind him, at the back of the wagon, was a mount for an unlit candle, a real beeswax candle, not the smoky, smelly ones made of tallow that folk most often used if they needed to get around at night. Streamers of red and green decorated the little wagon, with garlands of holly that spilled down the sides. The councilors set it on the middle table, then drew back.

"We never got to pick a new boy for this year." Henry Twintree opened his hands toward the Overbournes. "It was meant to be Peter."

"That's true." Telbert Overbourne spoke with a heave of breath. "We didn't have a chance to think about it, after all that's happened since."

Henry scratched his beard and looked about him. "Well, it's got to be someone, some boy of the village."

It did not take long for everyone's gaze to drift in the same direction, toward the two boys standing side by side next to Katherine. Edmund was not sure whether he wanted the task or not, but he still felt just a little disappointed once the final decision had been made.

"Me?" said Tom. "But—but I'm not even—"

"Come here, Tom, come here and quit your stammering. You're chosen." Henry took a burning brand from the fire and handed it to Tom. "I did this, back when I was fifteen. Don't think for a moment that it means nothing. Yule comes tomorrow, five days without a moon, five days when the sun teeters and looks about to fall. Bring the sun back for us, Tom. Bring him back."

Tom stepped within the circle. "I don't really know the words." He lit the candle and stood back.

"The wheel stands low." Edmund started the words so that Tom could remember and finish them. "Hail to the dying sun, hail to the year turned on its round. Praise to the rising sun, the new year to come in its turn."

The candle guttered and almost died at birth. Everyone held their breath, for a dead candle at Yule was the worst sort of omen. The fire in the hearth seemed to flicker down with it, and everyone sucked in a breath at once. The flame dimmed to a spark—and then sprang back to sudden life, sun-yellow, the new year promised to come.

"So spins the wheel." Edmund said the words with everyone else.

Folk met eyes, smiled and awoke, and then left the circle they had formed. Nicky took up his flute and trilled a few notes on his way over to the hearth. Jarvis Miller and Telbert Overbourne, one as well-to-do as a peasant could be and the other naught but a four-acre serf, crossed the floor to meet as two fathers bereft.

"That was well done." Edmund moved through the splintering crowd to join Tom. "We usually make a bigger to-do about it, but—Tom? What's wrong?"

Tom snuffed the candle. He craned all about him, staring under the treading feet of his neighbors. "Where's Jumble?"

"That fool dog of yours ran outside when we went to fetch the wagon from the woodshed." Harman Bale spoke it in passing on his way over to the cellar for more ale. "He's been running all about barking himself hoarse ever since. Haven't you heard him?"

Tom turned and threw back the shutters of the nearest window, letting in a swirl of snow and an icy lance of wind. Everyone raised their voices in protest, but he paid them no mind.

"Jumble?" Edmund stuck his head out next to Tom's. "What are you doing out there?"

The wind died back just long enough for Edmund to make out other sounds, and when he heard them, they froze him more deeply than the cold ever could. Jumble was indeed barking—in ragged, desperate terror. The wind howled, it roared and rushed down field and lane, but that was not the source of the screams.

Chapter 2

A look passed between Katherine, Tom and Edmund. Katherine stepped to the corner of the room and reached for the tooled leather scabbard of a great sword-of-war, then jammed her feet into a pair of heavy boots. Edmund took up his work-blade and found an iron kitchen knife for Tom, though Tom did not seem to want it.

Bella Cooper sat down shaking on a bench. "What is that? What's out there?"

"Oh no." Mousy little Miles Twintree hugged his knees. "Please, no, please, not again."

"Stay here." Katherine strode for the door. She turned on Geoffrey, who had gotten up to follow. "You too."

Geoffrey scowled. "You're not my mother."

Edmund pointed at Geoffrey. "You heard her. Stay here." He reached for Geoffrey's horn-handled bow and quiver of arrows, ignoring his brother's red-faced protests. After all, both bow and quiver had once been his own, and he had never really agreed to give them up.

Katherine picked up her round wooden shield from where it leaned against one wall and joined Tom by the window. "What did you hear?"

"Shouts, muffled by the wind." Tom grabbed a double-knit cloak off the peg for himself, then another for Katherine. "Too high-pitched to be a full-grown man." He grabbed for the handle and drew the front door wide.

Edmund's father turned from the hearth with a scowl. "Now, where do you three think you're going with all that getup on you?"

"Tom and Edmund heard something outside," said Katherine. "We won't be long—we just want to look about." Jumble slipped back into the tavern, his coat dusted heavily with snow, and rushed barking over to Tom.

"Heard what, child?" John Marshal roused himself from his lonely huddle in the corner. "You can't mean to go out in this!"

"Just for a moment, Papa." Katherine paused at the door. "We won't go far."

John's graying brows drew upward, then down. "You will not go anywhere if I do not give you leave."

There were three dozen folk snugged close in the tavern, and thus no shortage of witnesses to the struggle of wills that ensued. John Marshal stepped out from his table. Edmund's father joined him—it was the first time Edmund could recall seeing the two men standing side by side.

"Just because you've been running about with your—your books and whatnot all year, that doesn't mean you're suddenly your own man." Harman glowered at Edmund and thudded a finger into the palm of his hand. "You live in my house, boy. You'll heed me when I tell you where to go, and stay home when I say stay!"

Edmund spluttered. "I went up into the Girth and back—I've been to the lair of the Nethergrim!" He pointed at Katherine. "She faced down an army and won!"

"An experience I hope neither of you will ever need to repeat." John Marshal drew himself up into the arrow-straight carriage of a man long drilled in war. "You are my daughter yet, Katherine—and Edmund, you betray the first signs of the arrogance so fatal to a young wizard."

Edmund flushed hot, but even so, he could not help feel just a little flattered. John Marshal had named him wizard. Not apprentice—wizard.

John looked over Edmund's shoulder. "Tom!"

Tom turned from the threshold of the door.

"You forget yourself—you are my ward and in my care." John could not seem to stop the note of happy pride when he said the words. "I must ask you where you think you are going without my permission."

Tom let go of the handle. "I heard voices on the wind. I do not like the sound of them, and neither does Jumble."

John shot a closer look at Jumble, who stood in tense guard by the door with his ears cocked high, tail out straight and a faint growl rumbling in his narrow chest.

Edmund's father pursed his lips "No doubt someone fool enough to try coming in for a winter ale after dark."

John Marshal shook his head. "The ale you brew is good, Harman Bale, but not that good." He looked about him at the villagers. "Very well, will some of you come with me? I will break you into parties that can search as you walk home. If you find nothing, carry on to your doorsteps, and good night to you."

"Hey, ho!" Short and shaggy Nicky Bird might have been nearing thirty, but he dropped his flute and hopped up to volunteer with the bounce of a boy. "I'm your man, John Marshal. If it's bolgugs, we'll give them a proper drubbing, just like Katherine did up on Wishing Hill."

"If it's bolgugs, or anything like them, you'll run back here as fast as you can and ring the village bell." John reached for his shield and sword. He assembled his neighbors into gangs with flicking gestures, grouping them by the directions of their dwellings from the front step of the inn. When all had been prepared and everyone had bundled up against the cold, he opened the door, then braced it against the wind to let his neighbors plunge outside.

Katherine made a face. "And you're going to run off into the winter night on your own, and keep me snug inside fretting about you?"

John smiled. "Of course not, child." He beckoned her over with Edmund and Tom. "I'm not such a fool as that."

Edmund thrust his way through the door behind Katherine. Outside, the wind threw snow sideways across a pewter sky, its violence dampened somewhat by the fall of new snow, which took every sound and smothered it dead.

"Brr, look at this." Bella Cooper drew her shawl up tight around her shoulders. "I knew we should have left before dark."

Baldwin Tailor stumped away toward the square. "It's to be a bad Yule, this year. You know what they say about a storm at the start of it."

"That's enough of that." Edmund's father waved his neighbors away, even though they were already leaving. "We've had a hard-enough year without you calling down doom on the end of it."

"You're no lord, Harman Bale, and I'll speak as I please." Baldwin's querulous voice cut across the wind, even after he had passed out of view behind one of the yew trees planted haphazardly throughout the village square. "You know what's said—storm at first, ending's the worst. This year's not done with us yet. Dark days coming, you mark me."

Harman rolled his eyes.

John Marshal led their party down the Longsettle road, past the Twintrees' house, then Hugh Jocelyn's pigsty and on between some of the outlying cottages and the village's common green—which was anything but green just then. "Mind those—let's go around." John waved Edmund away from the humped drifts of snow before them. "We haven't fixed the road yet."

Edmund gave the road a wide berth, trampling down Hugh Jocelyn's front garden as everyone had been doing for the past two months. There, just by Hugh's front step, had stood a woman who had nearly killed them all, who had led a pack of monsters riding in the skins of innocent men. He had no trouble remembering where the barricades had stood on that desperate morning, or where the dead of his village had fallen to the Skeleth.

A growling woof woke Edmund from his thoughts. Jumble woofed again, then hopped over the snowy verge of the road. Just as he did, the wind brought the sound of a shout, though so distorted by the keening gusts that neither word nor mood could be guessed from it.

John drew his sword from its scabbard. "That's coming from Henry's orchard." The call to action seemed to straighten him up again. "Let's divide ourselves here and have a sword in each party. Katherine and Tom, you go with Harman. Edmund, with me. Katherine, take the far side and I'll loop out to meet you."

"Be careful, Papa." Katherine did not give Harman Bale the chance to lead her detachment. She drew her sword and strode off behind Jumble, disappearing into the snow almost at once.

Edmund followed John along a bank of apple trees stripped bare by winter winds. "Is Baldwin right, Master Marshal? Will it be a bad Yuletide this year?"

"Let's worry about the prophecies of grouchy old men once we're home and safe by the hearth." John paused to look and listen, peering in between the barren branches of the orchard.

Edmund cupped a hand to the side of his head to listen, and found that it only tunneled wind into his ear. "Someone must have wandered off the road, like Father said."

"Perhaps. Still and all, keep your wits about you." John watched left and right as they descended to meet the river. Under the drifts of cloud and snow its waters looked nearly black, and without a moon in the sky the motion of

Matthew Jobin

its current was so hard to see that it seemed to meld with the rising moors beyond it.

John stopped ten yards from the banks. "Edmund, do you hear that?"

The wind died back, and Edmund caught the sound of screaming again.

"Edmund!" A child's voice cried out from somewhere in the orchard. "Edmund Bale! Down!"

Edmund turned to John. "Master Marshal, who was—" He did not get to finish. John seized him and hauled him down into the snow. Half a heartbeat later, something thudded into the tree where they had been standing.

Edmund coughed and spat out snow. "What—"

"Move!" John reached out to drag him to the opposite side of the tree— just in time, for there came another thud. Edmund risked a glance up, and saw two long, spiny barbs stuck side by side into the trunk. Something dripped from the tips, glistening a syrupy black in the moonlight.

"Oh, *sister*." A second voice—a man's, though oddly singsong—drifted on the wind from the opposite direction to the first. "You missed. Your silly pet completely missed them both, you absolute and utter goose!"

"Well, he hasn't fed in *days*, brother." A third voice, this one female, came from the same direction as the second. "He's all stroppy and nervous."

Edmund reached up toward the barbs. "I've seen these things before— and read about them. These come from a *uhaari*."

"A full-grown *uhaari*." John grabbed Edmund's hand away. "They're much more deadly than the young one you saw in the mountains. Stay down."

The first voice, the one that had spoken from deep within the trees, dropped in volume, twisted in what sounded like pain. "I would not mind some cider, if you have some." He sounded like a boy no older than Geoffrey. "I've only ever had it once."

The second voice, the singsong man, spoke again, only just audible over the howl of the wind. "Hear me, men of—wait, now, where is this, again? Oh yes, Moorvale. Men of Moorvale, I hereby warn you. Leave this orchard and run along home to your crafts and mending and so forth. My sister and I will have our quarry, and any who stand in the way of him will die."

John leaned around the trunk just enough to shout back. "On whose order?"

There was a long pause. "Well. The order of the king, I suppose."

"The king?" John peered carefully about him, squinting into the snow-laced dark. "The king is dead."

"Indeed, the king is dead," spoke the third voice, the woman. "Long live the king."

Edmund swallowed. Even buried in the snow, he felt the warm flush of fright. He did not dare stick up his head. "I could try a spell."

"You start a spell and you'll be dead before you get the third word out." John pushed him deeper into the drift. "Wait."

"John Marshal!" The boy was a good deal louder and closer than his attackers, somewhere in among the trunks of the orchard to Edmund's right. "John Marshal of the Ten, help me, please!"

John tapped Edmund's side. "On my mark, move." He waited — Edmund was not sure what for, until he felt the change of wind. "Now! Into the trees!" He started running. He heard John's huffing breath as he followed, then a whistling in the air, then a thud.

Edmund looked behind him, fearing the worst. "Master Marshal—"

"Keep going!" John shoved him onward.

Edmund smacked through the branches with his arms raised over his face. He would have run straight out the other side of the orchard if John had not caught up and stopped him.

"Come aside." John dodged behind another trunk. Edmund dared to look about him and found them so deep into the trees that he doubted any attacker in the world could see them, let alone strike at them. He glanced at John and saw the spiky barb sticking out of the shield he wore upon his back.

"Papa? Edmund, are you hurt?" Katherine's voice rose on the wind from somewhere across the orchard. "What is going on?"

John cupped his mouth to shout a reply. "This way, child! Come into the trees, hurry!"

Edmund felt the cold much less out of the wind and could hear much more. "Master Marshal, over here." He plunged off eastward before John could stop him, dodging through the trunks toward the sound of whimpered moans.

"Father." From the sounds of it, the boy in the trees was failing quickly. "Father, don't. I'll be good. Don't."

Edmund pushed between the branches and found him—a scrawny kid roughly Geoffrey's age and Miles Twintree's size, in a cloak and an ill-fitting tunic, facedown in the snow with a barb in his back.

"Master Marshal, I found him!" Edmund knelt beside the sprawled, shadowed figure. The boy wore rough boots that looked too large for him. His outstretched hand had a smoothness that told of a life free of work.

Edmund pulled back the boy's hood, then recoiled. The boy's face was similarly soft, despite the contortions of pain, though ill favored and oddly out of proportion, as though his right side had been molded with no clear memory of his left. Apart from that, he would have reminded Edmund of one of Harry's milky-faced, highborn page boys, were it not for the gemstone that protruded from the middle of his forehead.

"Don't take the sun from me." The boy sank his head. "I want to see him. Don't make him go."

Edmund leaned down to inspect the barb. It had struck along the boy's side, and from the look of it the point had gone all the way through. It writhed and wriggled, as though some force of life remained in it and it was trying to find a way to do the boy some deeper injury.

"Don't shift, don't move it, or you'll make it worse." Edmund stopped the boy from turning over. "There's not that much blood."

The boy sucked in a breath and stared off in the direction from which Edmund had come. "Edmund! Down!"

Edmund leaped to the ground, fearing the punch of a barb through his back even as he struck face-first in the snow. He twisted over, feeling no injury. He looked around him, wondering where the barb was, but saw only John Marshal stepping from the dark.

John knelt beside the boy. "We'll need a good healer, and quickly."

The boy stared in the other direction. "You're an odd one. Where did you get that sword?" His voice had the thick, faraway sound of someone slipping into sleep.

John Marshal moved around to the boy's face. "I've had this sword since I was not much older than you, child." He felt his forehead, touching the scar tissue around the gem. "Tell me, now, why are you looking for me? Who is chasing you?"

The boy swallowed and spat blood. "John. John Marshal of the Ten. Help me, please." He stared straight up, past John's face at the stars between the branches above.

Katherine led Tom and Harman into Edmund's view, sword and shield at the ready. "Who is that, Papa?"

"I wish I knew." John cradled the boy's head. "I think he is in delirium." Tom knelt beside him, his face but inches from the boy's side. He sniffed at the wound. Jumble did the same, then sat back growling.

Edmund's father came last from the dark. "Ugh, look at that!" He regarded the gem in the boy's forehead. "Is that the fashion away south these days?"

"We must help him." Katherine strode forward. "We can't let him die." She reached for the barb stuck into the boy's side.

"Don't!" Tom slapped Katherine's hand away with sudden and uncharacteristic violence. He pulled her back from the barb. "Poison."

Matthew Jobin

Chapter 3

"Raise him onto the bed, there." Tom cleared away the tattered remnants of Edmund's mother's sewing. "Gently. On his stomach."

John and Katherine lowered the boy stomach-down onto the bed in the inn's only private guestroom. The warmth had yet to wholly escape the place; Edmund turned to shift the log, coaxing the blaze alight on ready wood. He beat his hands together, taking his chance to warm them. Such had been his fright on the way home that he had not truly felt the cold until he was safe inside again.

The boy let out a moan as he came to rest upon the mattress—the sound had the delirious character of someone who was only dreaming of his suffering. Edmund took his chance to examine him more closely in the light. The boy's hair spilled out long and poorly kempt, a middling brown that stuck in sweaty bands across the gemstone and its setting of scarred flesh. It was not easy to discern his build under his heavy and oversized clothes, not least because he appeared to be carrying something bulky in a sack slung under his cloak. The pallor of his skin might have been the result of a life of ease out of the sun, or it might simply have been due to the wound and loss of blood. He kept his eyes screwed tightly shut, wrinkling eyebrows somewhat thicker than the average with every few labored breaths, breaths that waggled the spikes of the barb stuck into his side.

Edmund's mother stood at the threshold of the door, her work-reddened hands wrought together through her apron. "Shouldn't we bleed him?"

Tom shook his head. "He's got hardly enough blood left as it is." He stooped to inspect the wound in better light, his face running wet with the melting snow in his hair. "May we have some water, warmed but not hot? And milk, if you have it—sheep's or cow's, it doesn't matter."

Edmund's mother clutched her apron. "Oh, the poor dear." She bustled off, pushing Geoffrey away down the passage in front of her. "The poor dear thing."

Geoffrey could not be kept away for long. "Should we go to Lord Harry?" He stuck his head back through the door. "We need a healer, don't we?"

"Tom's healed half the sheep and oxen in this village, in his time." John Marshal stood back, giving Tom space to kneel in close at the bedside. "Let's give him a chance to look first."

Edmund's father let out a snort and spat into the fire. "I hope this boy's worth the trouble, whoever he is."

"Say good-bye, John Marshal." The boy rolled his face in the bolsters of the bed. "Four, one, two, three, six, five. Understand? Good-bye, good-bye, good-bye."

"He must be delirious." Edmund spent a long while watching the wounded boy on the bed before him. The wind screamed at the window, juddering it half off its hinges.

"It's almost Yule." Katherine leaned over the bed to loop the window shut, tying the cord as tightly as she could. "Funny things happen this time of year."

Edmund shivered. "They don't usually start until Yule does, though. The moon's still up."

The boy rolled over. His gaze focused on Katherine. "You're an odd one. Where did you get that sword?"

Edmund stepped closer to the boy. "What was that? What did you say?" The boy did not answer, seeming instead to slip back into delirious mumbling with his eyes fixed on nothing.

Edmund's father shot a dark look across the room. "You took an awful chance, John Marshal, dragging us back here with that—whatever that thing was—in the woods."

"Not so," said John. "I have encountered *uhaaris* before, many times in my campaigns with Tristan in the Girth. Their barbs fly fast and true, but they can be blown off course as easily as any arrow. Such a creature must wait for a lull in the wind, just like an archer. Once the storm started to pick

Matthew Jobin

up to its full strength, I deemed that we were safer out in the teeth of it than we were in the trees."

A superior smile curled Harman's lip. "That's because you were guessing there was only the one . . . *oo-hairy*, if that's the name of it." His voice took on the hectoring tone it always got when he told Edmund or Geoffrey off for mistakes they had made in their daily rounds of chores. "There could have been a whole pack of them—we could have gotten ambushed!"

John beat his cloak, knocking its dusting of snow into the fire. "And would you rather that a party of such creatures should find us cowering together in Henry's orchard, with nowhere to place our backs and make a stand? I took a chance, yes—the safest course I could see. If you knew anything of war, Harman Bale, you would know that a captain does not tell his men what is risked, when all the courses before them have risks."

Harman sneered. "And so you think you're our captain, then."

"You followed me, didn't you?" John Marshal picked up his discarded shield and left the room.

Harman's face turned sour, the sort of sourness Edmund could sometimes feel in himself and hated himself for feeling. "Just a moment, there, John Marshal—you can't just stride about my inn like you own the place." He did not seem to see the irony of following John from the room, after what had just been said. "We have a matter to discuss, you and I." He slammed the door behind him.

Edmund felt a twinge of hot embarrassment for his father. Wishing he had different parents had been near to a nightly ritual for as long as he could remember—and just when he started to feel guilty about it, out would come Father, doing something pushy and stupid like trying to tell off an old war hero for how he acted in a moment of danger.

"Sometimes, Edmund, I cannot believe that you're his son." Katherine raised up Edmund's spirits, then swatted them down again: "But then, you look so much alike."

Edmund sat back, feeling doubly miserable, but the sight of the boy's face contorted in agony, delirious and maybe dying, stopped him from wallowing too long. He knelt next to Tom and marked the look of grave concern on his friend's face. "Can I help?"

Tom bent over the bed, examining with slow care the place where the point of the barb protruded from the boy's side. "I could use some better light."

"That I can do." Edmund turned and rustled through the leather satchel he had tossed beside the bed. "I've been practicing this one." He felt past his bag of charms, past his twine-bound workbook and his bottles of ink. He rummaged about, back and forth—where was the stupid thing?

"Aha." Edmund's fingers closed around something hard and cold. "Got it." He sat back with the glowstone in his lap. He willed his mind to clear, and started thinking on the Signs of Making and of Light.

Tom beckoned Katherine to the bedside. "Why is he here, do you think?" He spoke in a murmur, though in such a small room Edmund could still hear them without the slightest trouble. "And how does he know your father, if your father doesn't know him?" No one knew, so no one answered.

Light is a crack in the darkness. Light was Edmund's favorite Sign, the crowning Sign of the Wheel of Essence, the one he had understood first and still understood best. *It is a sound, a harmony. It is white, but only in the manner that white can contain all colors within itself.* The words of his books came to him despite his cold fingers, despite the fact that he was hungry, despite his father and despite even Katherine. Light came to him as an idea from which proceeded all the light the world had ever known. It waited for its call.

John Marshal's voice rose in sharp anger from the tavern: "Just tell me now, if you wish to turn him out. Curse it all, man, come to it, if that's what you mean to say!"

Edmund's father replied in a tone half barking and half pleading. "We don't know who's after him, or what sort of force they might have! What if they come after us for keeping him?"

John Marshal had a soft voice, like his daughter's, but that only gave his shouted retorts more power for their effort. "He is a defenseless little boy, Harman Bale! Have you no heart at all?"

Edmund winced and nearly lost his spell. The Sign of Making was not an easy one for him—it was hard to hold on to the strangeness of its ideas. A magical Making was not nearly so simple as making a wish come true, for it involved knowing the difference between what a thing is and what it seems to be. He recalled words he had read dozens of times in *The Fume or the Flicker*, doing his best to drink in the knowledge, to feel it far below the surface of his mind: *The idea of a thing is mother to the thing itself. For the sculptor to make the statue, he must first imagine it. The sculptor displays his mastery in shaping the stone he finds. Were he a greater master still, he would not even need to find the stone. He would imagine the statue, and the statue would be.*

Matthew Jobin

"LET THE LIGHT OF THE STARS DESCEND." Edmund knew he had it—saying the words only helped him give firm shape to the thought he had already summoned. He moved his left hand through the Signs of Making and Light, with his right hand cupped over the crystal. He twisted all his body through the postures of the Signs as well, though the motions, the words, and even the glowstone were nothing but props upon which to hang a thought: "I MAKE A STAR UPON THE EARTH. LET THE LIGHT OF THE STARS DESCEND."

Blue-white light shot out between his fingers. He heaved a ragged breath, then withdrew his hand. The crystal shone bright enough to make him blink.

"You're getting really good at that one." Katherine grabbed the crystal and held it up—then looked about her, blanching. "What's happened to the shadows?"

"It's Wheel-magic—*dhrakal*—you know, wizardry," said Edmund. "Darkness has to balance light somewhere."

The shadows in the room took on the character of ink dropped in water. They seemed to whisper to him when they got near—and from the look on Katherine's face, to her as well.

"Ugh." Katherine shuddered. "Sometimes I hate magic. Couldn't you just have—what do you call it—drawn it through the center? Made yourself part of the spell?"

"I could have, but I didn't much feel like dropping half dead on the floor." Edmund crouched up beside his friends. "Drawing through the center pays for a spell with bits of the wizard's own life. We don't like doing that unless we have no other choice."

Tom gestured that Katherine should hold the light directly over the boy's back. He squinted down at the spiky barb again, with a look on his face that filled Edmund with foreboding.

The boy seemed to come awake under the steady and alien glow. "I want the sun. Please don't take it from me. Please, Father. Father, don't."

"I'll need to cut some of his clothes away," said Tom. "Should I ask his leave?"

"Yes, John, it must be now." The boy mumbled to himself, one eye open, sweating and drooling on the bolster. "You do have a choice. I only tell you what comes of your choices."

"I don't think he'll notice." Katherine picked up Edmund's work knife and, with deft care, widened the hole that the barb had made in the boy's rough tunic.

"Mama loves me." Some of his sweat might, in truth, be tears. "Father does not love me. Father thinks I'm stupid and useless. Don't make the light go, Father. Don't."

"That's good," said Tom. "Keep speaking. I want you to speak, anything that comes to your mind. We will talk with you."

The boy tried to twist his head to look at Tom. "Are you *Ahidhan*?"

Tom gazed at the boy in surprise. He turned back to his friends, and lowered his voice. "How does he know what that is?"

"He's dressed roughly, but he doesn't look rough." Katherine touched the boy's hand. "Not at all." Edmund felt odd for doing it, but he reached out and took the boy's other hand. The boy clutched to both him and Katherine and held tight.

The boy grimaced. "Why are shadows laughing at me? They say come closer. Will they hurt me?"

Edmund hoped his smile did not look as false as it felt. "They're just shadows." His skin tingled—he could feel the Wheels of Change and Essence swinging wildly about him, upset by the force of his will. His friends had yet to notice, but the fire had taken on a very strange cast, losing its wild flicker and starting to look more like a painting of a fire. Light and Darkness bounced on their axis, dragging Order and Chaos into a wobbling rhythm he had yet to learn how to fully control.

"I see two suns." The boy shut his eyes. "Which sun? Which is the one? It cannot be me who chooses. Four, one, two, three, six, five. Remember, John Marshal, remember." He hummed something to himself and let his head slide down the bolster, so that the furred hat he wore covered most of his face.

"Cut that free." Tom pointed at the satchel bag hanging from the boy's back. Katherine leaned out with the knife, raised the boy's cloak and cut the straps. She gave the satchel to Edmund. He could tell just by holding that it contained something flat and heavy. He reached in and felt, to his surprise, that what he had guessed would be some sort of book was instead a disk made out of metal, rough with carvings on both sides.

The boy's eyes flew open again. "I'm going to die. They're going to come. They're going to come and kill me."

"They will not." Katherine reached out to brush back the boy's hat and hair, so that he could see out again. "I will not let them."

Matthew Jobin

"Edmund, I will need three pairs of heavy gloves." Tom sat back on his haunches. He brushed the sweat from his forehead. "We are going to break the shaft of the barb."

Edmund gave the shaft an appraising, doubtful look. "It won't break easily."

"The poison's in the tip," said Tom. "We must break it so we can draw the front end of it through without letting the point slip back inside the wound. It will take all three of us, and we will have to work together."

Edmund let out a breath. "If you say so." He rushed outside and found pairs of leather gloves his family used when cording and splitting wood for the hearth. He handed them around, one pair each for himself, Tom and Katherine.

"You hold the barb steady around the wound, Edmund." Tom shouldered in beside Katherine. "The two of us will snap the shaft, right there in the middle."

The three friends leaned close together, each taking up a position along the barb. In doing so, they all clustered right beside the boy, who watched them with bleary, distant interest, as though they were not about to touch something stuck in his own body.

"Don't touch the point, Edmund, and keep your hands well above his back," said Tom.

Katherine tried to squeeze in beside him, then shifted up and put her arms around him to grasp the barb. The bristles along the barb poked at Edmund's hands, still somehow alive and trying to penetrate the heavy leather of his gloves.

The boy wet his lips. "Are you all friends?"

"We are." Even there, with his hands around a spiny, poisoned barb, Edmund still felt a warm tingle at the feeling of Katherine's encircling arms. "Just lie still, now. This won't take but a moment. What's your name, by the way?"

The boy blinked rapidly, trying to push away a mixture of tears and sweat. "I don't remember my right name, anymore."

"Oh," said Edmund. "Well, then—what do your friends call you?"

The boy simply stared at him.

"Ready?" Tom squashed himself between Katherine and Edmund, and took a grip on the shaft of the barb. "Now!"

The barb bent against Edmund's hands. Its spines came alive, thrashing out and grabbing. He did not think it would snap before he lost his grip— but then it did.

Tom let out a sigh of relief. "There. Almost done." He nudged his friends aside, drew the shaft through, then wrapped the opened wound with a poultice.

"If you kill me, you'll never know." The boy sank onto the bed. "Don't lose the light."

Geoffrey shouldered back into the room with a bowl of milk in his hands. "What was that screaming about?"

"We got the barb free." Katherine took a stick and shoved both ends of the barb into the fire. "Where's my papa?"

Geoffrey brought the milk over to Tom. "He's gone." He spoke over Katherine's startled questions. "He took his horse and left, just after the storm blew itself out."

Edmund darted a glance at the shuttered window and saw that it no longer shook with the wind. "But what about that creature? It's still out there, somewhere."

Geoffrey helped Tom arrange the bowl near the boy's face. "That's what I said, but he just shoved right past me."

Edmund grabbed for his glowstone and quelled its light, now that Tom no longer needed it, for he did not like the mocking tone the shadows around him were starting to take. The fire gave off much less light than its heat would suggest, and what light was there seemed only to outline the shadows. He had cast but the simplest of spells, one ranked for a novice in a book like *The Fume or the Flicker*, but even simple spells had costs. He doubted there would be good lighting in the room where he sat for a day or more, as the shadows slowly trickled out between the gaps in the slats and stole back to a place where Darkness reigned eternal.

"Drink just a little." Tom cradled the boy's head and raised the bowl to his lips. "You must build your strength again."

The boy tried to drink, but retched and choked, and sank back in a pasty sweat on the bolster.

Geoffrey looked from Tom to Edmund. "Will he live?"

"You twit!" Edmund dragged him away from the bed. "Don't talk like that where he can hear it!"

Matthew Jobin

Tom stood up beside them and lowered his voice. "If the point had not gone right through, he would already be dead. Even so, he got half the dose."

Geoffrey's red brows shot up. "What—you mean he's been poisoned?"

"Will you stop it?" Edmund glared at him, then turned to Tom and lowered his voice to a whisper. "What are his chances, with the dose he got?"

Tom heaved a sigh. "The toss of a coin."

"Can we give him better odds?" said Katherine.

"We can, but it means going outside." Tom looked at the shuttered window.

Edmund watched the barb catch fire, blazing up with a smell like a moth that had flown in too close to a summer lantern. He thought of the other barbs that had arced straight and sure out of the dark. "Outside where?"

Tom exchanged an odd look with Katherine. He turned back to Edmund. "To the Dorwood."

Chapter 4

The Day of the Plow, The First Day of Yule

E dmund prodded his horse with his heels. "The Dorwood." He drew in beside his friends. "This is madness. This is stark and utter madness."

"Then why did you come with us?" said Katherine. Tom clung to her back, perched behind her in the saddle. Katherine did not seem to mind their closeness. She never did—with Tom.

The storm had abruptly dropped dead and the clouds had blown themselves clear out of the sky. The river Tamber ran swollen but glassy calm, gorged on cold and seeming to flow more slowly than water truly should. The horses followed the river's eastern banks—the wild banks, a lonely strip between broad water and desolate moor.

Edmund felt a memory rising in him, one he had been trying to keep down for weeks. It lay there just below him always, that chamber in the tower on the moors where the Voice of the Nethergrim had pressed in and nearly broken him. Sometimes it felt as though he had lived all his days since then only just out of reach of that swallowing presence, and when he fell into it he wanted only to shrink down and be small.

"Do I need to remind you that folk who go in past the eaves of the Dorwood never come out again?" He looked north toward the distant line of trees, then east over the rolling breadth of the moors. "And do I need to tell you both again what happened to me out here?"

"Believe me, I remember." Katherine followed Edmund's gaze. "That was far out on the moors, though, in the tower of that old king. We're not going anywhere near that place—we'll hug the riverbank, all the way to the forest."

"Oh, good." Edmund drifted away from his friends and over toward the river. "So we'll only be going to one place of deadly peril tonight."

Tom's voice had nothing of harshness in it, but even so it jolted Edmund upright in the saddle: "Don't worry—I've been to the Dorwood before."

Edmund steered his horse back next to Tom, staring at him in confusion. "What? Into the Dorwood—when?" He waited for an answer—when none came, he asked another question. "How far in will we need to go?"

"Not far," said Tom. "We can't lose sight of the edge, or we really will never come out again."

Edmund waved about him at the freshly-fallen snow. "It's the thick of winter. How can we expect to find a growing plant this time of year?"

"I will find it." Tom could be truly infuriating sometimes, in his quiet, stone-faced way.

Edmund looked to Katherine.

"I trust him," was all she said.

Edmund's horse walked with reluctant strides, dragging his hooves through the shifting drifts of snow and falling well behind the muscled young charger that carried Tom and Katherine. Edmund found himself forced, time and again, to urge his horse onward with jabs from his heels, especially once the looming line of trees bristled up black across the whole of the northern horizon.

"Slow down a bit." Edmund did not want to raise his voice too loud, though he did not know who—or what—he feared might overhear him. "We're not all riding Indigo, you know."

Katherine tugged the reins. Her horse raised his massive gray head and shot an impatient look behind him. To Edmund's mind, Indigo never behaved as a horse truly should. Most horses quite sensibly shied away from danger, but Indigo often had to be restrained from charging into it headlong. When Indigo was summoned from his stall at the stable, he strode forth like a battle-hardened king ready to defend his cowering subjects. When there was trouble, Indigo threw back his ears and raised his great hooves as though battle was the whole point of life. Edmund was a peasant, and no judge of horseflesh, but even to his eyes Indigo looked the perfect warhorse, the sum of every knight's fondest dreams, with a haughty temper to match his martial power. Indigo seemed to like Katherine's company, and everyone else in the world could go hang, as far as Edmund could tell.

"Easy. Easy, now." Katherine murmured, and with some coaxing brought Indigo back to a walk at Edmund's flank. "He's nervous."

Edmund eyed Indigo's muscled back, his firm gait and dauntless gaze. "You could never tell by looking." His own horse, a fat-bellied pony of a far milder demeanor, walked somewhat the easier with such a fiery companion at his side.

Katherine shivered and took a hand off the reins to draw her cloak more tightly shut. She looked over at Edmund. "I don't suppose you know a spell to keep us warm, do you?"

Edmund let forth a laugh that puffed white vapor into the air. "If I did, don't you think I would have cast it by now?"

The snow of the storm lay in high, loose drifts that shouldered up along the riverbank, mantling the grass and smothering what little sound there was to hear. The hooves of the horses pushed through the fluff without crunching it, so cold and so lightly laid as it was, and even the jingle of their harness seemed muted, as though made by something duller than metal.

Katherine reached out to stroke the flabby neck of Edmund's pony. "He's keeping up well. What's his name?"

"Bluebell," said Edmund. "Father bought him at the castle last week. One of Lord Aelfric's clerks ran away to join Lord Wolland's army, so they sold off all his property, and of course Father was first in line at the auction."

Katherine ruffled Bluebell's mane. "Well, I like him. He's tougher than he looks." She flicked a smile up at Edmund. "I could say the same for his rider."

Edmund felt another blush, one that was stronger than the cold. He would have gladly ridden into and out of the Dorwood a hundred times to hear Katherine speak so.

"Edmund, I've been thinking about you lately." Katherine seemed to struggle for words. "Worrying, I suppose. Are you . . . have you been well, since—"

"Did you see that? Did you see it?"

The tone of Tom's voice snapped Edmund back to where he was and where they were going. "What's wrong?"

Tom looked about him, left and right in open fear. "Shades. Shadows." He shook. "This feels bad."

"The moon's down." Edmund checked the whole of the horizon to make sure. "It's later than I thought."

"Then it's Yule." Katherine pulled off her gloves. "The first day—the Day of the Plow." Her hand drifted to the hilt of her sword. The hairs stood up on the back of Edmund's neck. It seemed as though the same thing happened to Bluebell's mane, and if not for the steady, forward clomp of Indigo's hooves, Edmund felt sure that Bluebell would have turned to bolt.

Movement caught the corner of Edmund's eye. He squinted, he stared— he saw nothing but snow and stars and a reaching line of branches clutching at the sky ahead. Eastward, starlight fell feeble on the snow-decked moors. Across the northern horizon ran the bristled line of the Dorwood; Edmund knew that it was he who was moving toward it, but in the dim of the night he could almost think that it was the other way around. The Tamber slurried dark as death to the west, its surface a second sky.

"The lights, the shadows." Katherine's words came thick and slow. "Your spell won't go away."

"I'm not sure it's my spell doing this." Edmund stared out and down at the river. Then he looked up at the sky, because he found himself unwilling to see what his eyes wanted to tell him. He forced himself to stare back down again—and once he saw it, he could not look away.

Tom leaned forward—Indigo snorted—then he gasped. "Edmund, I see it."

Edmund steered Bluebell toward the banks. He stared into the black below.

The black opened up.

"See what?" Katherine's voice seemed to move from left to right behind Edmund. "I see water."

"The stars." Tom said it. "They're not the same, above and below."

Katherine gasped for fear.

Hope drained from Edmund, as though it dripped out of him and into the river. He clutched his middle—he would not have been surprised to find himself bleeding to death from the belly. The water ran and rushed past, time running by, time making babies into corpses, time running down the banks of endless, thoughtless, faceless change. The stars reflected in the water were not the same stars as the ones in the sky. The stars below began to move.

When the Voice came, Edmund knew that he had been expecting it. **Edmund Bale.** The Voice was not a sound—it was a presence. **Again we meet, but next time we meet, we will not meet like this.**

Edmund pressed his hands to his ears. "I don't want to meet you again—not ever."

"Who is he talking to?" Katherine's voice sounded far away. "Tom, what is happening?"

When next you see me, Edmund, you will see me with your eyes. The stars became a face. The face grew a smile. **Do you not feel it? My faithful servant makes his magic in my name.**

"We beat you before, you and your servants." Edmund shut his fists. "We can do it again."

Oh, child, you have already lost. The Voice of the Nethergrim betrayed no trace of anger. **You lost before you were born.**

Edmund raised his voice to a shout. "I am not your child!"

You are. You know it in your inmost self. The stars in the river melded together, picking out a ghastly pair of eyes and a cruelly smiling mouth in ever greater detail. **You know that you can twist and turn as you like but, in the end, you will always face toward me.**

Katherine spurred Indigo to the water's edge. "You leave him alone." She waved her sword. "Curse you, leave him alone!"

Does she intend to cut the river in half? The Voice sounded a little like Katherine, but a Katherine who had lost her innocence, a Katherine who purred and gave knowing winks. **Are you sure this girl has a mind sharp enough to keep you satisfied?**

"Don't you talk about her," said Edmund. "Don't you dare!"

Katherine lowered her sword. "What is it saying? Who is it talking about? Tom, can you hear it talking?"

"I should have come alone," said Tom.

The Voice grew closer to Edmund. **Child, everything that you have done against me amounts to earth piled up against the rising flood. Water will flow downstream, Edmund, one way or another.**

"Stop it." Edmund plugged his ears, but he knew that it would not stop.

There is nothing you can do to halt what is to come, said the Voice. **There never was.**

Matthew Jobin

"I will stop you," said Edmund. "I will fight you and I will stop you."

If you carry on against me, I will be your death, said the Voice. **That is the one and only choice you can make.**

Edmund felt something touch him. He pulled away, but then he felt fingers close around his own.

"My friend." It was Tom. "Why do you always think that the Nethergrim is telling you the truth?"

Edmund forced himself to look away from the river. He saw Tom with one arm around Katherine's waist, seeming to hold her up. With his other hand, he gripped Edmund's.

Tom spoke slowly, every word distinct: "How do you know that it is not lying to you, to get you to do the things it wants you to do?"

Edmund snapped awake. He turned back to the river with a snarl. "Tom's right. You're a liar."

Let us put that to the test, child. The Voice grew fainter again. **The spell that brings me into the world is nearly complete. You know what that means.**

Edmund shuddered—he knew exactly what it meant. Somewhere in the world, at that very instant, seven children were dying in the most horrible agony, and there was nothing he could do to make it stop.

"Edmund. Edmund, what is happening?" Katherine's voice grew muffled to Edmund's ears, even as it grew more frantic. "Tom, can we help him?"

"The spell." Edmund thought, just for a moment, that he could feel it, could see it, deep in the reflection of the water, past the stars. "Vithric's casting the spell that makes him younger, the one that lets the Nethergrim into the world." When he stared into the water, he saw a seven-pointed star, but then he saw the victims and could not make himself see anymore.

When next we meet, you will see me with your eyes. The stars pulled apart. The face in the river unwove itself. Until then, Edmund Bale.

Edmund curled down over the pommel of his saddle. The silence that followed came, as it always did, like a gap in his thoughts. An emptiness swelled in him, a dread, a feeling that there was nowhere to go, nowhere to run or hide, and there never had been—never in his life or in the life of anyone who had ever drawn a single breath.

"We should go home," said Katherine. "We've come too far."

"No!" Edmund forced himself up again. "No."

He tugged his reins, turning an unwilling Bluebell north. "I should listen to Tom more often. Everything the Nethergrim tells me, everything she has ever told me, it all might be a lie. We go on. We do what we came here to do."

"What does fear buy us, in the end?" said Tom. "Come, it's this way, up along the stream."

Katherine brought Indigo around beside Edmund and steered them toward the trees. The clomping of hooves on snow made the only sound that Edmund could hear, save for the creak of saddle and harness, and the sound of his breath puffing steam into the dark. Tom guided them to the bank of a stream that flowed from under the trees to join the river. They followed it up toward its source, away from the river, away from open sky and the world they knew. The black line of the Dorwood grew before them, grew until its hanging branches took them in.

Matthew Jobin

Chapter 5

K atherine could not remember how long she had been riding in the forest. She might have just stepped in under the boughs at that very instant, and then again, she might have been wandering there for days. Birch stood with alder, oak with spruce, their limbs laced together in a blur and then distinct again. The air held still between the bare and spreading branches, the stillness that comes right after thunder—but she could not remember hearing any thunder.

Tom slid to the ground behind her. "Let's walk them from here. Down this way—it's safest right along the stream."

Katherine dismounted at the bubbling, laughing edge of the brook. It seemed to take far too long to come to earth, but even so, she landed so softly that it felt as though she had done no more than bounce up and down on her toes. She looked over her shoulder. Edmund, lit by starlight, leaped down from his fat pony as though he had been riding horses all his life.

"You've been hiding things from me." Edmund led Bluebell up next to Tom. When he smiled with the whole of himself, something seemed to light within him, and Katherine knew how he could have faced down the Nethergrim and won.

Tom reached out and touched the branch of a willow. He did it as though he were greeting someone he loved. The feeling came again that thunder had just passed, that Katherine lived in the silent space between the beats of a gigantic heart. She trembled. She felt at her own face, just to remind herself who she was.

Indigo nuzzled his nose into Katherine's side. She jumped—she had forgotten she was leading him.

"Come, now." Tom stepped on ahead, and it felt to Katherine that her fear grew in bounds for every pace he took away from her. "Let's not linger."

Katherine took up Indigo's reins. "Where are we going?"

"Don't be afraid." Tom took her hand. "We can leave the way we came." He offered his other hand to Edmund, who hesitated, then grasped it.

Katherine felt Indigo's breath on her neck. "Should we leave the horses behind?"

"They are better off than we are, in here." Tom gave her a gentle tug and drew her on.

He led her through a wood with no trail, through night, through the bottom of her fear. She forgot for a long, long while what it was that she wanted there, why she had come to that place, or even whence she had come. She could not think of whose hand held hers. The hand led her over root and hollow—down, it seemed, always down, descending clefts that could not be guessed at from above, down into a place of still air, down until the sky disappeared.

"Mama." She could hold it in no longer. "Mama."

She clutched at her rag-doll horse. Her father rocked back and forth beside her— weeping, his hands gripped in the folds of his cloak.

"She is gone." *Lord Tristan knelt at her side. His kindly face blocked out all else.* "Katherine. Child. You must be brave now. He needs you."

"Katherine." A closer voice came, one near at her side. "Not her. Not her. No."

Katherine searched for the owner of the voice, and found Edmund. He walked with his big blue eyes shut, led by Tom's other hand.

"Not her, please no." His voice quavered. "I won't let you have her."

"Edmund," said Katherine. "I'm right beside you."

He opened his eyes. He looked at her. When had he grown up so much?

"We are here." Tom let go. Katherine panicked and flailed out for his hand, but then she felt the absence of her fear. Indigo brushed past her, lowered his head and started munching the grass at her feet.

Katherine threw her cloak over one shoulder. "I don't feel cold anymore." She looked about her. "The trees—they still have leaves."

Tom stepped into the open and down a row of tended herbs. "It's not winter here. It never is."

Matthew Jobin

Katherine glanced at Edmund and found him looking as stunned as she felt. They stood side by side at the edge of a clearing, a circle of open sky bounded by crowding trunks and branches. Before them lay a nighttime garden in the full tide of summer growth. Plants that Katherine had never seen in her life coiled on hazel-twig trellises to either side of a tended path. Fruits whose shapes were new sights to her eyes bent the broad crowns of unfamiliar trees.

"This place." Edmund followed Tom into the open. "It isn't real, is it?"

"We're here within it," said Tom." That's all I know."

"How often have you been here?"

"Not often. Whenever I could find a way." Tom brushed along the rows of herbs, feeling his way in the starlit dark. Even the rustles he made seemed cozy, the soft hush of a day well ended. Katherine felt as though she could simply lie down on the earth and go to sleep; come to think of it, perhaps she already was asleep.

"I want to say things." She left the horses grazing along the garden's edge. "I want to say stupid, happy things."

Tom raised his head over the trellisses. "They're not stupid."

Katherine walked the garden path. "Doesn't it feel like we are whispering in one another's ears?" She let her fingers trail over curling shoots, then felt along leaf and branch. She stooped to smell a flower.

"If you could come in this far, Tom, why go back?" said Edmund. "It's better here than it is outside."

Tom bent down beside a plant that bore berries of a bright and curious blue. "Sometimes I think that I am bound to the world, that folk need me and there are things I need to do in life." He plucked four berries with deft care and held them on his palm. "Other times, I think I'm just afraid."

He led them in between the trellises and out the other side of the garden. Beyond it, the trees held a cottage in a sheltering guard—a tiny hut of wattle and daub, with two round windows and a low, narrow doorway, all in darkness.

"Whose is this?" Katherine turned at the step. She looked out over the garden curled in its many shadowed shapes. "Who keeps this place?"

Tom pushed back the narrow wooden door and entered the hut. "I wish I had Edmund's big thoughts and big words. Maybe then I could explain."

Katherine ducked in behind Edmund. Flint scraped on steel, then a rushlight blazed up in Tom's hand. Dried herbs hung from every available space on the walls and ceiling. The fire pit held cold ash. The pallet beside it was as neatly made as any bed in a castle. Across from the door stood a trestle bench of oak and iron.

"It's as though whoever lives here left just a moment ago." Edmund knelt by the tiny hearth. "The embers are still warm."

Tom pulled back the chair and sat at the bench. Katherine crossed the tiny room in two strides and looked over his shoulder. A varied array of clay vials and jars stood in rows down one side of the bench, and next to them measuring bowls, stacks of bundled herbs and strange implements of iron, wood and bronze. Measured rows of medicines took up most of the rest of the surface, some in loose piles of leaf and powder, others stuffed into parchment envelopes and still others boiled down into thick salves and sealed into their jars with daubs of wax.

Katherine sat on the pallet next to Edmund and watched Tom assemble a collection of jars and herbs before him with sure and nimble fingers. Edmund curled himself back against the bolster, into the corner of the wall, and held out his hands over the fire. Tom picked up a vial and sniffed its contents. He poured the vial into a bowl, crushed in each of the four berries, then pounded at the mixture with a pestle.

"Is there somewhere we can go where the Nethergrim can't find us?" Katherine felt her fingers on the worked leather of her sword hilt. Neither of her friends answered. By turns that came with each of her breaths, by the rising of each hair on the back of her neck, she found herself growing afraid again.

There was no open window, yet a shadow fell across the room. There was no light save for the rushlight on the bench—it swelled, and yet its glowing point seemed to move farther away.

Tom raised his head and turned from the workbench. He stared at the windows, then the door. "Someone's coming."

Katherine felt her skin seize and tense. Tom grabbed the vial he had mixed.

Edmund sat bolt upright on the pallet. "Maybe it's just the horses."

Katherine threw back her cloak. "Not horses." She felt for the hilt of her sword and braced to draw.

Footsteps approached the door, stomping the earth in a thundering rhythm. The rushlight juddered in its holder. Vials bounced, then rolled off the bench. The three friends stood together, and then, as the earth-shaking

Matthew Jobin

impacts got closer and closer, they all three cowered together at the back of the room.

Breath steamed between the cracks in the walls, carrying with it a musky odor that stung the eyes. A bellow sounded, a groan so deep that Katherine felt it through her feet. She shot a desperate look at Edmund, hoping for some sign that he understood what was happening, but he simply shook his head, white with fear. Tom turned and doused the rushlight, plunging the little cottage deeper into darkness.

The door bent inward, prodded by something outside. Another bellow came so loud that it made dust fly from the walls. Katherine's hand shivered at her hilt, but she could not force herself to draw her blade.

"*Ränan riitu, hegi vit!*" A voice rose from outside, rounded and foreign. "*Toovhi, toovhi!*"

A heartbeat came and went. The musky odor receded. The thing outside moved off, shuddering the earth under the cottage less and less as it got farther away.

Another man spoke, with a deeper voice than the first and a hard Wolland burr to his speech. "How do you know it understands Vhakkat, Seb?"

"I'm sick of speaking your language, Roki—it's like gargling sand." The foreign man outside sounded young, with a snooty, cutting tone to his voice despite the lush vowels of his accent. "Now get over here and control this *küsa rekkel.*"

Edmund shifted over in the dark. Katherine was about to restrain him, to hiss a warning in his ear, but all he did was drop under one of the two round windows, then ever so slowly raise himself up to peer through the shutters.

"YOU ARE SUMMONED AND BOUND BY COVENANT." The man named Roki raised his voice in the chant of a spell. "ON PAIN OF THE CURDLING, OF DEATH FOR THAT WHICH YOU HOLD MOST DEAR, ATTEND ME. I YOKE YOU TO MY WILL."

Another bellow shook the cottage. Katherine found herself clutching her ears.

"Roki, are you quite sure you bound it properly?" said the snooty-sounding foreigner. "I don't want it getting loose."

"Course I did, Seb," Roki answered with an air of imperturbable disdain. "I went through her work-notes before we came—three times."

Katherine pulled her friends back together and dared a louder whisper. "What is it? What do we do?"

"It is very, very big." Edmund's reply was little more than mouthed words in the darkness. "I think it has horns. I would very much like to stay quiet until it leaves."

The pounding thuds of the big creature's footsteps receded farther still and then stopped.

"We're not going into that little hut over there?" The one called Roki approached the cottage. "Could be interesting. No one would know."

Katherine eased her sword from its scabbard. She flicked a look at each of her friends. Edmund curled his fingers and made an inward motion with his hands. Tom looked around him, then picked up a heavy-looking iron ladle from the bench.

"No one would know." Seb made a mocking, heavily accented imitation of Roki's voice. "Your master won't know? My mistress won't know? What if Vithric finds something you filched from in there once we're back in Rushmeet, and asks you where you got it? *Toovhi*—get over here, curse you for the son of a dung sweeper, and let's do what we must while we still can."

All three friends breathed out at once. Edmund returned to his vigil at the window.

"Over here." Roki's voice grew more distant again. "No, no, not that way, not right through the—ah, well. Come on, then."

Tom gasped. He almost got up, but Katherine held him back. The creature outside made a series of crunching, cracking noises as it pushed its way through the garden.

"Good riddance for now, *hegi vit*," said Seb. "So, who takes what from here?"

"I'll take this one and head east," said Roki. "Home country for me—I'll have some help. Are you all right with south?"

"*Tai, tai*—yes, yes," said Seb. "But how are either of us going to get there? It's winter past these trees, and we're far up north."

"We've got an ally not too far from here," said Roki. "One of Vithric's old friends, if you can believe it. He keeps a good stable of horses nearby."

It was Katherine's turn to gasp. She moved to the other window, but could not find a space to see out.

"Let's get on with it, then." Roki rustled off into the trees. "When we get to John Marshal's, make sure you take a fast horse—you're due for tomorrow, but I've got a day to spare. Then on the Day of the Ship, we meet in the city and hope no one figures out what we've been up to for the last few days. After that we have only a few more miracles to pull off and everything's daisies and roses."

Seb's voice got harder to hear as it grew more distant. "How far is this farm? We don't have to walk all night, do we?"

"Oh, don't be such a baby. This way. Stay on the path."

"But it's winter!"

"I told you to dress warm, Seb. Come on." The voices died away.

Katherine sucked in a breath. She pushed back the door, and in racing out tripped over a huge, steaming heap of dung.

"What was that?" Edmund sat back shuddering on the bed. "What on earth *was* that?"

Katherine staggered up and rushed into the garden—then stopped, staring about her in horrified wonder. A smear of smashed trellises cut at an angle through the furrows. Beyond that, broken branches showed the path of the creature's exit, down to the banks of the stream.

Edmund came out at her side, and gaped at the trail of ruin before him. Tom was worse—the sight brought tears to his eyes.

"Hurry." Katherine sprinted down through the garden and back the way they had come. "Hurry! They were talking about Papa. Let's find the horses and see if we can catch them."

Chapter 6

T he three friends found their horses without trouble, but they saw not a sign of either of the two young men or anything more of the shadowed creature that had shaken the earth back in the Dorwood. Bluebell would not settle down enough to let Edmund ride, so Tom and Katherine took the reins in hand and led the horses along the banks of the stream, through what had once felt like a dream but had turned to a sleepless and worrisome night. Once the three reached the eaves of the Dorwood, they had little time to spare in thought for what they had seen, for the storm had shown its second face, and the wind whipped white across the world.

It was all Tom could do to guide them at a stumble back along the snow-humped banks of the Tamber without treading too near and falling in. Such was the wind, such was the hard slant of sleet in the black of the night, that if he had run across the men he had seen in the Dorwood he might have tripped over them before he saw them. He thought he heard, from time to time, a low, rumbling bellow on the wind, but the howl of the storm robbed the sounds of all direction.

The snow left not a trace of trail. Moor, plain and riverbank looked just the same, all folds of ground smoothed out and hidden in the steely dark. No one spoke, no one needed to speak—they needed to do nothing but keep up their plodding march in the teeth of the wind. Their lives hung on Tom's sense of direction—that thought had passed between them without a word, not long after they lost sight of the Dorwood. If Tom were to lose his way, they might wander in a circle, freeze up and drop dead within a mile of home. There was no light in the village at that hour, not a single tongue of flame to guide them, nothing but the river and the bite of wind at Tom's cheek. Sometimes it seemed as though the river had vanished in the gray-white, shapeless world, and with his heart in his mouth, he would scrabble wildly about in search of it, losing them too much precious warmth and time.

Cold cut at Tom with axe strokes. It ran down his collar and stabbed his belly; it rushed in through his mouth and lanced his lungs. He had lived half of every year outdoors, all his life, tending to his master's sheep and oxen, but had never felt such a bitter night. Winter often uttered its threats to someone like him, someone who had never had good shelter or enough firewood, but on that night, winter got up and screamed at him—*dead, dead, I want you frozen and dead.*

"The wheel stands low." Edmund muttered it over Tom's shoulder, though Tom was not sure if he was speaking to himself. "Will it always turn?"

Perhaps, if they had twenty miles of snowy ground to cover, one of them might have fallen to the cold, but as it was, they were merely two miles from home; and though their journey seemed without end, at last it ended. Tom touched one of the great stone posts on the east bank of the river, then crossed the span in a clutch of terror, for a fall into the turgid water below meant sure death.

The horses' hooves clicked dull upon the stone. No one fell, no one froze—instead they stumbled through the square, dragged the horses to the stable, and fell all in a heap through the front door of the inn, right on top of a leaping, rambunctious Jumble and a frightened-looking Geoffrey.

"You pack of utter twits." Geoffrey shouldered the door shut behind them. "What was I going to tell Mum if you all died out there?" He wore the sort of clothes meant for going out in the cold, but he was inside, tending a small fire in the hearth with a cloak draped double on his shoulders.

None of the friends could form an answer. They spared just enough thought to pull off their cloaks, shake out the snow and let the relative warmth of the inn reach them more quickly. Edmund and Katherine stumbled to the fire and hunched on a bench, shivering and red at the cheeks. Jumble panted as he ran back and forth between them, happy but worried, then worried but happy, one ear cocked, unsure.

"Pull your boots off." Geoffrey stomped over to Edmund. "Warm up. Pull them off—I'm not doing it for you."

Edmund gave his brother a dull stare, too stunned even to retort. He sat in numb silence while Tom removed his boots.

Tom felt Edmund's toes. "No frostbite. You'll feel better soon." He did the same for Katherine. No frostbite, but a deep white chill. His own hands throbbed as they came back to life. It had been a near thing.

"Oh, ow." Katherine clenched her teeth, and then her fingers. She wrapped her hands together in her lap. "Warming up is the worst part. Ow."

"Well, it better have been worth it," said Geoffrey. "Father came downstairs for more firewood a while ago, and I had to lie and say you were in the other room with the boy."

Edmund seemed to be coming back to himself, for he looked upon his brother with a habitual frown marking his features. "You love lying to Father, so shut up about it."

"No, you shut up." Geoffrey returned the hard look in full. "I'm sick of always staying behind to look after things while you go and do whatever you like."

Edmund scowled. "Well, then, next time an evil wizard drags you into the mountains to kill you, I'll take your advice and stay home!"

"Let's leave them be, for now." Tom pulled Geoffrey aside, down the short corridor to the inn's private room. "Let's see if we can help our new friend."

"I've been looking in on him." Geoffrey picked up the smoldering rushlight from its loop by the door. "He's miles deep—just babbles when I talk to him. His eyes don't move."

Tom had been afraid that Geoffrey would say just such a thing. He quickened his step—absurd as that felt, for he had been gone half the night and might already be too late—and thrust back the flimsy door.

"Father, Father, no." The boy had his eyes shut. "Don't. Don't take the light." His smooth hands clutched at his bedsheet, but his heavy woolen covers had slipped off in the throes of his fever.

Geoffrey bent over him. "Who is he, do you think?"

"There are six." Spittle nearly choked the boy—whitish, flecked with the milk he had not been able to drink down. "That's the answer. Not five, not this time."

Matthew Jobin

Tom touched his forehead and felt the heat. "Will you fetch some more warm water?" He turned to Geoffrey, who shot a glare in reply, but did as he was asked.

"Our fathers always fail us, in the end." The boy gurgled. "That's just the way of things."

Tom cradled the boy's head. "Hush, now. Hush." He turned him so that he could breathe more easily. "You are safe. You are among friends."

Geoffrey returned with a clay bowl of water. "How bad is it? Will he die?"

Tom hoped that silence would let Geoffrey know why it was wrong to ask such questions. He poured out half the water, then mixed in the crushed berries he had made in the Dorwood. He placed his hand over the mixture, and placed his hope in it.

"Four, one, two, three, six, five." The boy turned his head in the crook of Tom's arm. "Master Marshal—it seems to me that my life is my own to risk."

Tom raised the bowl to the boy's lips. "You must drink this. Just a little. A little at a time."

It was hard going. The boy could only swallow in tiny sips, and more than once he spat up dark blue all over Tom's shirt. The door opened—Tom looked over, expecting to greet Katherine or Edmund, but instead John Marshal pulled up a chair by the fire, cloaked in shadow and crowned with snow.

"Drink some more." Tom felt John's gaze on him as he murmured to the boy, but could not pierce the dark well enough to make out the expression on John's face.

He could not stand the silence for long. "Where have you been, Master Marshal?"

John let out laugh of low pitch and little humor. "I never in my life thought I would have cause to accuse you of being cheeky, Tom."

"I am sorry that we left." Tom cradled up the drooping boy before he could slide down among his sweaty covers. "We feared he might die, and I knew of a way to help him."

John Marshal pulled back the hood of his cloak and smoothed down his graying, grizzled hair. "Tom, there is a doorway through which every boy will one day walk. That doorway is unmarked, without sign or warning of what lies beyond. Only when he crosses through and the door shuts firm behind him does he know what he has lost, what he can never return to see again. The path of manhood lies before him, a dark plain beset with pits and stunted trees—and then a cliff."

Tom took a pinky finger and cleaned out some bluish spittle from the boy's mouth. "That has already happened to me."

"It has not," said John. "I can see it in your face. You are yet a boy, despite all that you have suffered, and so is Edmund, and my beloved daughter remains a girl, if only for a little while longer. That little while is more precious to me than a wagon loaded down with gold. The days that you have yet to spend in childhood, in happiness and hope, they are everything to me."

"They should not be," said Tom. "Don't hold on to things that always fade away."

The boy shuddered in his arms. "I'll be good, Father. I'll do anything you want. Please don't make the light go."

Tom balanced the bowl in his lap, and cradled the boy's head to make it easier for him to keep the medicine down. "Master Marshal, you are no fool, and I do not think you were a fool when you were young."

John Marshal laughed again, though it seemed almost a cry.

"By the time children are my age, they can see the difference between what you think life is and what you want life to seem to be for their sake." Tom crushed in the last berry and stirred the mixture with a spoon. "If you lie to us, we know it, and that only makes our world all the darker."

John Marshal stared at the fire, stirred it with a poker and stared at it longer. "You will save that boy's life. You will not fail."

"I will do all I can, Master Marshal." Tom stole another glance across the room. Something about John Marshal, the only grown-up to have been truly kind to him and the nearest thing to a father he had ever had, seemed terribly frightening and wrong.

John stood up. He hovered there for a moment, his gaze fixed on the boy, then he strode away, opening the door and leaving without another word.

The boy did not die. By the deepest watches of the night he had stopped his raving and dozed with strong and even breaths. Tom laid him gently down upon the bed, wrapped the poultice tight around his wound and drew up the covers to his chin. He sat on the rush-and-dirt floor at his side, resolved to watch him through the night and feed him the last of his mixture should he need it.

Matthew Jobin

The door pushed back again, much later, creaking on its thick leather hinge and startling a rat away into a corner. Katherine had been crying, that was clear enough. She led Edmund into the room and sat down at the table with her arms crossed over her middle. Tom watched her in alarm, then glanced at Edmund.

"It's her father." Edmund slumped on the foot of the bed, palms pressed to his cheekbones. "I've never seen him like that."

Tom would have asked his friends what was wrong, but just then the boy stirred and choked. Tom took his wrist. He felt his pulse—weak but steady—and looked into his eyes. He had never yet seen him so awake.

The boy fixed on him. "Who are you?"

"My name is Tom." He traced the lines of the boy's palm. Just as he always did with the animals he helped, he got a sense, a feeling for the rhythms of the boy's life. He felt the boy gaining against the last of the poison, throwing off its power by the breath. He would live. There was no longer any doubt. "What is your name?"

The boy drew back his hand with a jerk. The effort of it left him collapsed on the bed. "I'm no one."

"No one?" Edmund answered in the silence of Tom's confusion. "You'll have to try a bit harder than that. I nearly got skewered by a poison barb in the Twintrees' orchard because of you."

The boy brushed at his drool-caked mouth. "Then—who are *you*?"

Edmund leaned over the boy. "My name is Edmund—but you already know that."

The boy hissed and sat upright, then grimaced and sank back again. "What did I say? What did you hear?"

"You called for me by name." Edmund leaned in closer, his bright blue eyes searching the face of the boy. "How do you know me?"

"I don't." The boy shrank away from Edmund. He made a feeble attempt to cover the hole in his tunic. "You must not have heard me right. It's cold."

Edmund turned to his friends. "At least he's answering our questions now, even if his answers don't tell us anything."

"Please." The boy made a weak gesture with his fingers. "I'm no one. I mean no one any harm."

Katherine stood and brushed past Edmund. She sat on the floor next to Tom, hollow at the eyes from weeping. "We mean you no harm, either. If you trust us, you will find your trust well placed."

The boy squinted at Katherine. "Why were you crying?"

Katherine made a hopeless gesture. "My father."

The boy gathered enough strength to raise his head. "Our fathers always fail us, in the end. That's just the way of things."

Tom shot a surprised look at the boy, who did not seem to understand the meaning of it. He turned to Katherine. "Whatever your father said, he cannot have meant it."

Katherine scanned some unknown place in the shadows by Tom's shoulder. "Papa spoke as though I'd betrayed him, as though I'd ruined something important, but I can't figure out what I did. Why won't he talk to me? Why is he skulking around as though he has something to hide?"

Before Tom could think of a reply, there came the sound of someone hurrying past their window, crunching through the newly fallen snow at a run. Tom turned to listen; whoever it was, he turned at the step of the inn, thrusting back the door to the tavern room with every audible sign of haste.

"You've got some nerve, John Marshal, stomping right back through my tavern without settling up your debts." Edmund's father raised his voice to a following shout from the kitchen. "Who's to pay for that boy in the room there? That's our best room, our only private room! Get back here!"

The door to the private room shoved back. "You will come with me now."

The boy recoiled, staring over Tom's shoulder at John Marshal, who had never seemed to Tom less dignified and trustworthy than he did just then. It was not just the stubble nor the unpleasant odor born of a night of hard effort while bundled tight against the cold. Perhaps he had lost some weight, since the Skeleth, or perhaps it really was the first hint of old age.

"Papa, are you feeling well?" Katherine reached out to pluck his sleeve. "I've been worried all night."

"Unhand me, Katherine." John stepped past her with a brusqueness that Tom had never seen him use with her before. He loomed over the boy. "You will come with me."

The boy shrank from him. "But I am wounded."

"Wounded or not, come." John held out his hand. "You came looking for me, and you have found me. We leave now."

"Papa, you have not told me where you were." Katherine recoiled, confused and hurt. "You don't know what we saw tonight—there's a creature in the forest, and wizards who—"

"Curse you, child, I know all that!" John rounded on Katherine with a waspish anger that made Tom jump. "I know ten things for everything you have ever learned. This is no time for the games of children!"

Katherine flinched. She nearly wept again, but held her ground. "You have not explained why you left tonight, Papa, or why you need to take this boy away."

John set his expression hard. "I am your father, Katherine, not your friend. You are to explain yourself to me and not the other way around."

This time Katherine really did start to cry. Tom heard the sounds of tramping feet upon the road, the clinking of harness and mail armor. He glanced at Edmund, but found his friend looking even more lost than he felt himself.

"Now." John turned back to the boy. "I know of a place far safer than this. There are those who would shelter you and give you aid. You must come with me now, or I will not be able to protect you."

He extended a hand. The boy trembled, but seized it.

Edmund got out of his chair. "You know what we have suffered, Master Marshal, what we've learned. Trust us. Don't throw us aside like we're ignorant children."

"Oh, but you are ignorant, Edmund." John gripped the boy with his calloused sword hand. "Ignorant of far too much." He brought the boy to his feet, bundled him up far more roughly than he should, and brought him to the door.

Katherine tried to follow. "Papa—"

"You have made enough of a mess of this already, Katherine." John shot a look back at her that could not fairly be called anything but a glare. "When all this is done, you and I shall have words."

Boots tramped into the tavern, the sort of hard boots worn by well-shod riders. The voice of Edmund's father raised in a surprised, wheedling hail from the tavern: "My lord, how kind of you to visit! Would you care for some—no, of course, my lord, of course, yes, make yourself right at home. I'm sure you know your business here."

John let out a curse and shut the door. "This way, this way, come!" He dragged the boy back into the room, kicked open the window and pulled him out over the sill into the screaming wind. The boy had time for just one last, pleading look at Tom before he disappeared into the white.

Katherine leaned back against the wall, hands to her face, looking as though she wanted to melt through the cracks in the plaster and disappear. Heavy footfalls approached down the passage from the tavern. Edmund and Tom exchanged a look, then sprang in opposite directions. Edmund grabbed the boy's abandoned pack and shoved it in behind the bed, while Tom shut the window just before the door could be thrust wide again.

"Hail to you, hail and greetings, your . . ." A head poked in, sandy hair cut in the latest noble style over a face of solemn, youthful, handsome features—no longer a boy, but not quite yet a man. A pair of burly knights muscled into the room behind the newcomer.

Lord Harold of Elverain scanned the room with gold-flecked eyes. "Where's he gone?"

Matthew Jobin

Chapter 7

E dmund Bale came first to breakfast. He ladled himself some cold porridge from the pot and set it down next to him at the largest table of the inn. He ate with slow, careful spoonings, turning aside as he did so to keep the glop from dripping onto the three books he had laid open on the tabletop, their pages held flat by the use of empty bowls from the kitchen.

"Twelve symbols around the edge." He touched his fingers to the curve of carved and ridged metal before him. "Inside that, a ring of thirty." He flipped through the pages of *The Sworn Book of Gunthacram*, unsure of what he was hoping to find.

Dawn made its first bleak introduction through the cracks in the shutters, heralding a morning as chilly as most winter nights. Dawn meant day, though, and day meant work. From the sounds of muffled chatter on the street, a few young men were stomping past, bewailing the cold as they marched off to the labors of the day. Oxen lowed, yoked and jangling in the harness. Someone drove stakes for Hugh Jocelyn's new pig fence, heave and hammer—Martin Upfield, most likely, for no one else could wield a mallet that long without a rest.

"Then, inside of those, six more, larger than the rest." Edmund murmured to himself in hopes that the sound of his words would strike at something in his memory and light a new thought. "Four of them in quarters, then at the very center, the last two."

The inner six symbols reminded him of something, but he could not quite think of what it was. He tried to read one, translating its complex shape out of Dhanic into his own language of Paelic as best as he could. "*Horse–Ocean. An ocean horse? Horse of the sea?*"

A shadow loomed over the pages. "What's that thing?"

Edmund glanced up at Geoffrey, then down at the metal disk on the table before him. "That's what I'm trying to figure out. I found it in the sack that strange boy left behind."

"Oh." Geoffrey took up a bowl, despite the fact that by doing so he freed the parchment pages of *The Fume or the Flicker* to turn and flip themselves over. "We're low on firewood. We've got rights to glean fallen branches from the lord's hunting chase until the end of Yule, so Father wants us out there early before the rest of the village grabs up the good stuff."

"Hmm." Edmund traced his fingers over the weathered incisions that ran in concentric rings on the disk. Even though the Signs of magic Substance sat at the center, he still could not be sure that what he was reading was a spell.

"We've still got to keep warm, Edmund." Geoffrey sat down across from him. "Whatever that boy was here for, whatever Katherine's father or Lord Harry might have wanted with him, we've still got to live. Do you want to freeze this winter?"

Edmund flipped the disk over to examine the other side. The reverse of the disk had been carved in what looked like a view of the sky, with limbs of the horizon to let the viewer know it was a view straight upward. The constellations looked nothing like any configuration of stars he had ever seen. The other strange thing about the scene was that it bore two suns, facing each other in mirror image across the sky, though surrounded by stars. In between the suns was a last Dhanic symbol, carved deep and small so that any shift in the shadows seemed to warp its shape and change its meaning. After squinting at it for a while, Edmund thought it read, *Crowns– Over–All, Man–Child–Circle* and *Death–Days–Endure.*

"Edmund, did you hear me?"

"Heard you, yes." Edmund scratched a note in his workbook, a sheaf of loosely bound parchments purchased for far too much coin from a merchant at the winter fair in Longsettle. "Got to live."

"Edmund, look around you." Geoffrey dropped the volume of his voice but raised its intensity. "This place is falling apart."

"What?" Edmund spared half a glance at the wall. "Looks fine."

"It's not." Geoffrey jammed his wooden spoon into his bowl so hard that some of his porridge flecked onto *The Fume or the Flicker*. "Father's wound is still not fully healed, and you're always too busy to help. Me and Mum have to do everything these days."

Edmund shot his brother a hard look, then used his sleeve to remove the porridge. "Would you rather that I didn't study, then? Would you rather that Vithric had killed you, or Warbur Drake had, or the Skeleth? You'd have no worries about the inn then, would you?"

Geoffrey crossed his arms. "You and Father were really good at brewing ale. The new stuff I'm making's not half as good, and Mum's too busy helping me to cook at her best. The locals aren't enjoying themselves in here as much as they did, and the lord's men wouldn't take our ale as the winter tax until Mum threw in some chicken stew to bribe them."

"Hmm." Edmund rubbed his temples, willing the object before him to give up the secret of its meaning. What was it? Who had made it and why? Why would a babbling, odd-looking boy with a gem in his forehead be carrying it while under pursuit and in peril of his life? He hoped Tom and Katherine had managed to find John Marshal and learned why he had stolen the boy away without explaining where they were going, for Katherine's sake as much as anything.

"Edmund, are you listening?" Geoffrey raised his voice. "I said that we are going deep in debt and it's only getting worse. We got fined last week because you skipped off your duties mending Lord Harry's pasture fences, and Mum's been too busy doing both Father's chores and yours to make some extra money selling her cooking preserves at market. We couldn't even afford to thatch the roof this year, even though it's due and Nicky Bird was going to give us a good deal on the price. If this keeps up, we'll have rain in here come spring."

Edmund could not hear himself think with all the jabbering from across the table. "You're twelve years old." He set his elbows on the table and shot a sharp look at his brother. "Since when did you care about stuff like that?"

"When you *stopped* caring!" Geoffrey glowered at him. "Edmund, we're peasants. We have to work! Mum's running herself into the ground."

Edmund waved a hand. "Oh, Mum's fine."

"She's not!" Geoffrey dropped to a whisper, for footfalls had sounded on the stairs from above. "Take a look at her some time. Take a good look."

"Hmm." Edmund returned to contemplation of the disk. "Right. Take a look at Mum." He traced his fingers down the lines that cleaved the ring second closest to the center into four equal parts. Across from *Horse–Ocean* stood *Heart–Home,* while across from *Snake–Battle* was a symbol that he could only read as *Land–Blade.* What could they mean?

Another shadow loomed, larger than Geoffrey's. "Boy, get on with you. Time for the gleaning."

Edmund looked aside, but not quite up, at his father. "I'm not finished with breakfast yet."

"You are now." Harman Bale picked up Edmund's bowl of porridge and turned away. He walked over to the pot, his stiff, dragging limp more obvious in the morning, and dumped the porridge back in. He let the wooden bowl clatter down dirty on the table.

Edmund curled one hand around his quill, but not so hard as to break it. "This is important, Father." He stabbed a finger down on the disk. "I have to figure out what this is and why that boy had it with him."

"That boy's wrapped up in the sort of things folk like us don't need to know about." Edmund's father sat at the table, his left elbow resting right on top of the only complete copy of the *Paelandabok* in the entire known world. "Sooner he was out from under my roof, the better."

Edmund kept his eyes on the disk and parchment before him. He felt a prickle up his neck, the certain knowledge that his father was staring at him. He flipped the disk over and stared down at the doubled sun.

"Sarra, get down here, will you?" Harman called up the stairs. "I'm starving."

Edmund jotted a note. "Your arms still work just fine, Father."

"What?" Edmund's father turned back to him and barked. "What did you say?"

Edmund kept his gaze on his work. "I said that your arms work just fine, Father, so why don't you get some breakfast for yourself?"

In the following silence, a late flock of geese flew past outside, honking as they raced south overhead. Edmund's mother crept downstairs and pattered on toward the kitchen, then started fussing with her crockery. Geoffrey ate in noisy, hurried gulps, then rushed over to the door to dress for the cold. Edmund looked closely at the outermost twelve symbols and noted that the symbol for *Curved–Gathering–Blade* looked rather like a sickle, while *Purify–*

Double–Stick could look, if he turned his head just so, somewhat like a jointed threshing flail.

Aha! Edmund turned to make a note in his workbook. So very simple.

"What are you still doing here, boy?" Harman Bale spoke with such abrupt loudness that Geoffrey jumped and Edmund could not help but flinch. "I said get on to the gleaning!"

Edmund calmed himself, blotted the ink he had spilled and kept writing. "Same answer as before, Father," he said. "Your arms work just fine, so if there's work to be done, why don't you go and do it?"

There came a stunned gasp. "What was that?"

"You heard me."

Edmund looked up at last. His father sat in arm's reach, stubbled, foul of breath and spoiling for a fight. His mother stood rooted to the spot by the kitchen door, her hands clutched and working in her apron.

"You truly think you're something, don't you?" Edmund's father fumed at him over the parchment of his books. "You think that just because you've waved your hands about and done your fancy spells that you're better than the rest of us. You're letting this place fall apart."

Edmund folded his hands across the disk. "So are you." He could hardly believe how calm he felt. "The difference between me and you, though, is that I have a good reason to do less around here."

Harman scowled, darker than Geoffrey's scowls in every sense of the world. "You live in my house, boy, under my roof."

"That's all you have over me now, Father." Edmund faced Harman full on. "Just the roof."

Harman set his teeth and leaned closer. Edmund wondered why people never really seemed to change. His father had nearly died, nearly lost both his sons, had struggled up from his deathbed to the promise of a new and better life, but as the weeks had passed he had sunk back down into his old self, grouchy and sour whenever he felt that he was not given the respect he was due. Why could he not stay changed? Maybe, Edmund thought, people simply are what they are, and never really learn anything.

"I've had bolgugs slavering over me, ready to tear me up and swallow me in bits," said Edmund. "I've had the greatest wizard the world has ever known looming over me with his hands at my throat. Do you really think you can scare me?"

Harman Bale clenched a fist. He leaned toward Edmund, then looked down at the parchment before him.

"Do not touch my books." Edmund felt not a trace of fear. "I warn you."

"You warn me." Harman rolled the words, chewed on them and spat them back. "*You* warn *me.*"

"I do, Father."

Harman seized up the *Paelandabok,* turned and strode for the fire. He had not made two strides before Edmund struck.

"FATHER, I NAME YOU. FATHER, I GRIP YOU." Edmund made the Sign of Closing with his right hand. He extended his left arm. "YOU ARE CONFINED."

He folded space around his father, just as he had done to trap the Skeleth two months before, but such was his anger that he used the folded space like a claw, and before he knew it he had picked his father up and held him dangling, clutched in what looked like nothing but air, but through which could be seen broken angles of the ceiling and walls, as though there were no straight lines anywhere.

Harman's hands fell open. The book dropped to the floor.

"Maybe you'll never change, Father, but I have." Edmund stood up and advanced, one hand held out to keep the folded space of his claw pressed in. Through his cold anger, he felt some surprise at how well the spell had worked. The best he had ever done with such magic on short notice was to make left temporarily right—he had expected to do nothing but spin his father around and confuse him for long enough to make a grab for the book. Instead, he had his father in his clutches, and though he felt the cost of the spell rippling through the spaces of the world, deflecting the travel of innocent folk on the roads and making paths fail to come out of the woods where they should, he still felt nothing but the grim satisfaction of finally, finally showing his sneering, bitter, brittle father that—

"Edmund!"

Edmund could not help but glance aside at the sound of the voice, for it was the first voice he had ever heard. His mother stood across the table, shaking and pleading, her hands held out to him.

"Put your father down, Edmund." The look on Sarra's face struck Edmund sick, for it was not the sort of face she had ever turned to him before. He suddenly wanted nothing more than to see her smile at him, but she simply stared, tight and trembling, looking upon him in just the same way she had always looked at his father when his temper flared and raged.

Edmund's skin went clammy. Maybe people never change. Worse yet, maybe they grow into just what they hate.

Edmund looked up at his limp, dangling father. The last time a spell had been cast in the tavern of the inn, it had been his mother who had been seized in an invisible claw, and his father had nearly died trying to free her. It had been Vithric, betrayer and murderer, who had cast the spell.

"You're right, Edmund. You have changed." Geoffrey advanced from the door with his fists up. "Put Father down."

Edmund had no idea how to gently move his claw of folded space. He could do nothing but end the spell, which dropped his father a few feet to the ground. Harman struck the edge of the table in his fall, then rolled face-first onto the floor. Edmund's mother rushed to tend to him. Edmund grabbed up his books and the disk, shoved past his brother and ran outside.

He stopped just past the front step, his heart in his mouth. He looked up, eastward over the Twintrees' roof, over the moors and between the lace of running clouds.

The Nethergrim smiled down upon him. **And so we meet again, Edmund Bale.**

Chapter 8

Katherine was never sure how she always knew when the farm she and her father called home was empty. She called out anyway. "Papa?" Her voice fell dead in the snow that covered pasture and field. "It's us! It's Katherine and Tom. Are you here?"

Tom stopped and knelt by the turn at the gate. "See those tracks? Two men on foot, coming up the road just as we did. I've seen them here and there all the way from the village." He stood and turned. "It was harder to tell, but I think I saw the tracks of at least two horses going the other way."

Katherine ignored the gate and hopped the fence, as she had been doing ever since she was tall enough to clear it. "Why didn't you tell me that on the road?"

Tom did what he always did when Katherine asked him a question whose answer she already knew. He did not so much look away from her as simply go on doing what he was already doing, which just then meant tracing the footprints up to the path that led between the stable and the little cottage where Katherine lived with her father.

"Yes, fine, very well—I was stewing, wasn't I?" Katherine followed Tom, taking care not to tread ahead of him and ruin the tracks. "You've been waiting to ask me what Harry said to me last night, when I followed him out of the inn."

Tom stood up straight and abandoned his search once he reached the well-trodden path that led out through the garden. "If you want to tell me, I will listen."

"Harry took me aside, kissed me on the lips, then told me nothing of any use." Katherine strode to the door of the stable. "He stroked my hair, touched my chin and told me not to worry, that he had things to do just then but he would see me at the moot today and might have a chance to explain. Then he rejoined his knights, got on his horse and left—and I let him go."

Tom ducked into the stable behind her. "Does kissing make people feel differently about things?"

"That's a careful way to put it." Katherine reached for the lantern down on its hook by the door, took up the flint and tinder and sparked a flame to life. "I think it turns me into an utter fool sometimes."

She walked the central passage of the stables, basking in the warmth from the furred bodies in their stalls even as she found what she had feared she would find. "Three horses missing—two of the mares and Papa's own riding horse." She turned back and forth. "Papa did all the night chores before he left. He was waiting here—he knew those two wizards were coming."

Tom came to her side. "He's often gone, isn't he?"

Katherine pulled back the door to a stall at the far end. "Papa always said he wanted to stay home and live quiet after his days with Tristan and the Ten, but every now and again he would just disappear for a while. I would have to take care of things or get my cousin Martin to come up and help."

"You've got my help, too, whenever you want it." Tom took up a lead and halter. "I'll always be more use sweeping horse dung than holding a sword."

"Don't be so sure of that." Katherine got another halter over the muzzle of the young warhorse in the stable before her. "I've seen your fire, Tom. I saw it under the mountain of the Nethergrim. You can grow up to be a man-at-arms, if that's what you want."

Tom smiled a little, but lowered his head, so that his ill-kept bangs masked his eyes. "I'm just a slave."

"You're not a slave anymore," said Katherine. "You're free now."

"We don't know that yet," said Tom. "We find out today. It was your father who was supposed to speak for me in court."

Katherine felt a knot in her belly. "Papa will come back in time for the hallmoot. He loves you, Tom. He'll come back, he'll make his case, and I promise you Harry will set you free. This much I swear—Harry won't be getting so much as another peck on the cheek from me until you're free as the air."

Tom buckled his halter under the chin of his horse. "And then what? I've never had to think about it. I expected to work on my master's farm until I dropped dead. Now I don't know what to do."

"Can't you become an—what are they called—*Ahidhan*, you know, a healer?" Katherine picked up the lunge line in its coil by the door. "You could go back to Quentara and seek out Thulina Drake again. I'm sure she'd take you in."

Tom shook his head. "I don't know. I still feel as though Elverain's my home."

"Then you really can become a man-at-arms, if that's what you want," said Katherine. "I'll train you with sword and lance."

Tom's shoulders went up and down. "I don't know."

"Don't just throw the thought aside," said Katherine. "You should find a pool of water and look at your reflection some time. You're getting bigger."

Tom led his horse out into the passage. "Bigger?"

"Now that you're free and eating well, you're starting to gain some muscle." Katherine punched him on the shoulder as she followed him out, horse in tow behind her. "Don't be surprised when the girls start making eyes at you."

Tom did not seem to know what to do with such words. "But then there would be kissing, and I might turn into a fool."

Katherine shot him the friendliest of scowls. "Are you making fun of me?"

"I'm only saying what you said." Tom led his horse out to the nearest paddock. Katherine had something of a struggle with her horse, for though he was little more than a colt he had gained a good deal of the bulk that would one day make him a warhorse, and he knew of only one place where he could stand out of the wind.

"Buttercup—Buttercup, come." Katherine tugged the lead, not hard enough to hurt, but hard enough to make it a command. The horse—his birth name of Buttercup was unlikely to be kept—threw back his ears but complied, stomping at a sulk into the paddock. Katherine and Tom turned back to retrieve another pair of horses, and then another, pulling them out of their warm but dung-covered stalls and into the hard cold of Yule. They kept watch on Katherine as they huddled together in the paddock, all of them gone shaggy for the winter and all of them looking as miserable as Katherine felt, though she would argue that she had many more reasons for it than they did.

Tom maneuvered another reluctant colt into the paddock, then closed the gate. "Let me help you, Katherine. I can muck out the stalls."

"Thank you," said Katherine. "I'll go get us a bite to eat."

Tom led his horse in through the stable door. Katherine turned the other way on the path, tramping up through the snowed-under remains of her garden to the little wood-and-thatch cottage she shared with her father. She touched the notches on the doorpost, cut at her height on her birthday every year. She traced them higher; she had begged Papa to stop when she turned twelve, but he just laughed and told her to be proud. Be proud, my daughter.

"Papa, come home safe." How many times had she said it, through the years? "Come home soon."

Katherine coaxed the cooking fire back to life and hung a pot above it. Memories arose, unbidden in the smoke. She was not much of a cook, to be sure, though she was a mile better than Papa. All he could make was an awful black broth he called soldier's stew, something from his homeland in the south. Blood and pig's trotters, vinegar and salt—she retched just to think of it. The memory of trying to gulp it down under Papa's watchful eye made her laugh—and the laughter somehow nearly turned to tears.

"Why, Papa?" Katherine chopped up a few roots and vegetables and threw them into the water. "Why won't you trust me?" She looked down at her reflection, watching the thick curtains of her hair sliding down to frame her face. She tried to see the parts of her that were not her father. She cast a glance aside, to the tiny bedroom where her mother had died trying to give birth to her stillborn little brother.

The pot boiled over. "Enough. Enough." Katherine pulled it from the fire and ladled out helpings for herself and for Tom. She could wallow deeper in the mire of her worry, or rejoice for all that had proven good. She set one bowl of stew atop the other, held them in one hand and opened the door to step outside.

"Katherine!" Tom's voice sounded from somewhere behind the stable, muffled by the snow. "Katherine, help!"

Katherine leaped back inside, dropped the bowls of stew on the table and snaked out a hand for her sword. She ducked into her father's bedroom—like hers, hardly big enough for a cot and a small trunk—and pulled up

Papa's shield from where he stored it under the bed. "Tom?" She sprang back out into the snow. "Tom, what's wrong? Where are you?"

"Please, Katherine!" Tom's voice got more frantic as it got farther away. "Help me!"

Katherine burst into a sprint. She vaulted the paddock fence, startling horses that were already pacing in a tight, worried clump. Past the opposite fence stood a copse of birch and alder over the stream that separated her father's farm from the farm run by Tom's old master, and it was there, in between the white and gray trunks, that she found Tom, alive but pale with fear, being marched up to the footbridge that joined the two plots of land.

Tom's old master, Athelstan Barnwell, whirled around. "Stop right there, girl." He took a few paces backward, so that he could aim his loaded crossbow at either Tom or Katherine. "You should have played it smart and stayed in your house. This I swear, I will plug you in the gut if you ever come between me and my property again."

Katherine forgot both her fear and her confusion in the rage that took her. "I warn you, old man." She advanced, shield raised. "Leave Tom alone."

"He's mine by the laws, and I'll be keeping him!" The lines around Athelstan's wrinkled mouth drew in to a snarl. "I paid for him and I'll have my profit from him in work or in coin!"

Katherine met the glare of the old man's ice blue eyes. "He's being made free today by those very same laws, so he'll be yours no longer." She took a good grip on the sword.

"Pah." Athelstan spat. "He'll be no such thing. I paid for him square down in Rushmeet when he was but a babe. He's mine!"

Katherine circled to her right, placing Athelstan directly between herself and Tom. "You know full well that Lord Harold will make him free today, and that's why you've come to steal him away first. You were going to drag him off somewhere to sell him before it could be made law."

"You're a bright one, you are." Athelstan turned this way and that, bent of back but gripping his crossbow steady and straight. "Now run along home, girl, and I'll be taking this boy with me."

Katherine took her chance to come a step nearer when Athelstan swiveled the crossbow back to Tom. "You go near him and I'll cut you down. You mark me, Athelstan Barnwell. I will do it."

"You come near me and I'll put this bolt right through that shield of yours and through your belly, you great, thick strumpet." Athelstan curled

Matthew Jobin

his lip. "You play the man, so I'll put you down like a man. I've always said you've got ideas beyond your place."

Katherine felt nearly sure that it was all bluster. She had half a mind to just walk up and snatch the crossbow from Athelstan's hands, but there was something in his hard blue eyes that made her wonder whether he might just pull the trigger.

"They say your farm's fallen on hard times." Katherine wove back and forth, shield up straight at Athelstan, ready to take the bolt on the metal boss and then charge. "They say your wife and daughters ran off one day, while you were out in the field doing the work Tom used to do for you. They say your livestock have fallen ill, worked half to death without Tom to keep them healthy. No wonder you'll risk getting hanged for murder to make some quick coin."

Athelstan turned full on Katherine. "You're nothing but a gossiping harpy, aren't you? Like every other woman born."

It worked just as Katherine had hoped it would. She had drawn Athelstan's ire and his full attention. What Athelstan did not know was that his former slave had seen some battle in the last few months and crept up noiselessly behind him with his fists balled tight.

"Kill me, Athelstan Barnwell, and Lord Harold of Elverain will hunt you to the ends of the earth." Katherine took another step nearer, making sure her bluff carried force. "He'll have you drawn and quartered. You talk of gossip—everyone knows what's said about Harry and me."

Athelstan pivoted, standing Tom off with his leveled weapon, then swung back to Katherine before she could make a move. "What do you care what happens to this boy? He's nothing but an orphan, a slave, just a worthless little—"

He stopped, mouth open. Katherine thought for a confused instant that he had seen something behind her, or that something had popped inside his hateful little brain. Instead, he backed up a step, turned to Tom and said:

"What do you care what happens to this boy?" He swung back toward Katherine, crossbow at the ready like before. "He's nothing but an orphan, a slave, just a worthless little—"

He stopped.

Katherine kept her father's shield up. "You already said that." She flicked a glance at Tom—he looked as confused as she was.

Athelstan turned back toward Tom. "What do you care what happens to this boy?" It was then that Katherine noticed the snow—it seemed to swallow up the treads of his feet every time he started his accusation over again. "He's nothing but an orphan, a slave, just a worthless little—"

"I am terribly sorry," spoke a voice. "I had no wish to intrude—but you see, I have no time."

Katherine backed up a step. She kept her shield raised to Athelstan, but risked a glance aside. A man stood between the trunks of alder on Katherine's side of the stream—old and frail, with a thinness that had never swelled into a middle-aged paunch. His heavy furs hung on his narrow shoulders as though a larger man had asked him to try them on for a joke. White hair thicker than that of most young boys stood out higgledy-piggledy from all sides of his head—and his ears and nose, for that matter.

"How like your mother you look." The old man's voice rolled and dove. He shuffled forward, either too weak or simply unused to walking in thick snow. "How proud she would have been to see you now."

Athelstan shuffled and turned from Tom to Katherine. "What do you care what happens to this boy? He's nothing but an orphan, a slave, just a worthless little—" He stopped, backed up and reversed yet again.

Katherine stepped out of the arc of Athelstan's aim. She lowered her sword and faced the old man. "I can only guess that you are some sort of wizard."

"Those of my kind would maintain that the word *wizard* has no meaning." The old man had a face like the crescent moon, curved and cragged from brow to chin. "To our way of thinking, we all affect what is to come by our actions, and thus we all perform a kind of magic with every day of our lives. I will grant, though, that some of us have more skill at it than others."

He blinked and squinted at Athelstan, snow-blind or perhaps merely short of sight. "I do wish I had stopped him on a less spiteful set of words."

Katherine sheathed her sword. "If you had wanted to wait for Athelstan Barnwell to say something kindly, we'd all have frozen to death first."

Tom stepped around in front of his master, peering at Athelstan's face as he spat the accusation he never finished. He started laughing, more loudly than Katherine had ever heard him laugh.

The old man did not have a walking stick, but he looked as though he needed one. "My path is named *Eredh* in the old tongue. We study the order and the harmony of all that is." He stumbled on his way over; Katherine offered him her arm. "Thank you. I am an old friend of your father's, though I doubt you would recall."

"I do," said Katherine. "I was ten years old—I remember it was the night that Indigo was born. You came and spoke with Papa, then paid him a penny."

"Yes." The old man reached into his furs. "I come to do so again."

He held forth a silver coin. "Will you give this to your father, when next you see him?"

Katherine glanced down at the penny in the old man's palm. "Papa is not here just now."

"I know that," said the old man. "I expect you to find him."

When seen up close, there was something about the old man's gaze that made Katherine want to look away. "Why do you think I will go to find him?"

"You will go because you are his daughter and he is in the greatest danger." His gaze appeared kindly and terribly patient, which only made the sight of what poked from beneath his thick white bangs all the more alarming. A gem protruded from his forehead, just like the boy's, though where the boy's had had a bluish cast to it, the old man's was diamond-clear. That only made it all the uglier, for through its clear facets Katherine could see how deeply it had been driven into the old man's skull.

"I can see through it, if that is what you are wondering." The old man smiled. "I see better through this gem than I can through my eyes, not least because I have spent nearly my whole life in utter darkness. We *Eredh* track the paths of the future as the hunter tracks the deer, and see the places where the tracks separate. Katherine Marshal, I see your father both alive and dead by the end of Yule. It is your action—you who love him most—that will settle him one way or the other."

Katherine took the coin. On one side, the hunting hound, emblem of the royal family, had been slashed three times in parallel. On the other, the head of the king had been crossed out.

"Find him and show him. Tell him to take heed. He will understand." The old man turned to go—then turned back. "He is a good man, Katherine."

Katherine closed her hand around the coin. "I know."

"The greatest sorrow in life comes when a good man, by trying to do good, does a great evil." The old man flicked a glance at the sky, westward into the empty gray opposite the thin and weary sun. "It makes me wonder whose world this really is." He turned to walk away, struggling through the drifts of deep snow.

"He's nothing but an orphan, a slave, just a worthless little—" Athelstan went through another round of his looping dance of hate. Every time he stepped backward, the snow seemed to heal up around his footsteps.

Tom stepped out to call after the old man. "What are we to do with him?"

The old man turned while fumbling for a wide-brimmed hat of a type Katherine had never seen, one that was of little practical use in a winter wind. "You could easily kill him, but it would sadden me to learn that you had." He walked on with one hand clamped down on his head to stop the hat from blowing off. "He will rejoin our present moment before too long, and if you leave this place before then, he will think you have become wizards yourselves." It occurred to Katherine that she could easily run after him, catch up with him, draw her sword and demand an explanation. Then it occurred to her that the reason he was so calmly walking away was that he already knew that she was not going to do it.

"Come on, Tom." She thrust the penny into her belt. "Maybe Edmund can help us sort all of this out." She strode up to Athelstan one last time, waiting for the pause at the end of his broken sentence. She stuck out her tongue at him, then turned with Tom and made her way back through the snow to the stable.

Chapter 9

T he lights of Yule burned high upon the mantels, in the sconces and loops of the hall of Castle Northend. The tapestries that hung upon the walls had been newly cleaned, and some of them recently replaced, so that scenes of stern valor hung cheek by jowl with bright images of ladies riding through groves of trees in full bloom. As was custom on the first day of Yuletide, the lord of the land sat in judgment over all the suits and squabbles that had collected since the midsummer fair. As was custom also, precious few of the folk in attendance that day were paying the case at hand the slightest bit of attention.

"My lord." The chief clerk of the court coughed sharp and loud, waiting for something like silence to descend. He drew his bushy white eyebrows together and glowered down at the assembled peasants seated on the crooked pairs of benches below him, then tried once again to make himself heard over the gossip, the laughing games of dice and the bawling of a small child by the entrance to the buttery.

The clerk held up a parchment roll to the light of a lantern. "My lord, I will repeat the charge . . ." He raised his voice yet louder. "I say, I will repeat the charge, and pray the court be silent so that it may be heard in full!"

Young Lord Harold of Elverain did no more than nod his head in response. He sat beside his clerk, facing his people on the raised platform at the far end of the hall. He drummed his fingers on the arms of his heavy chair of carven oak, the many silver rings he had inherited from his father catching gleams in the surrounding light. His clerks and jurors attended him, the former group drawn from the literate townsmen who kept his accounts, the latter mostly folk from his villages, all chosen to give him counsel for the judgments of the day. They all wore looks of august gravity that were not in the least way justified by the case at hand.

Harry sighed and bestirred himself. "Did you say 'pigs'?"

The chief clerk looked down at the parchment. "Aye, my lord." He snapped the edge of it with his fingers. "Pigs."

An enormous log of beechwood lay upon its side in the hearth, its fire making the hall warm and cheery, but choking and close at the same time, with a resinous tang to the air that stung the eyes. Edmund could not begrudge it, though, for within the hall, in the midst of smoke and firelight and among the talk of many folk, he could almost forget the light from outside.

Why do you hide from me, Edmund? It came slanted through the arrow-slit windows above, the light and the Voice. **Come out into my light.**

Edmund shuddered and buried himself farther into the darkest corner of the hall. He had only barely made it to Northend with his mind intact—in fact, he had lost his wits for a while and wandered off the road, stumbling right into the path of the annual plow races done that day every Yule and nearly meeting his death under the hooves of Henry Twintree's team of draft horses. He cast frantic looks up and down the aisles, at the benches laid out in cramped and crooked rows, where sat folk from all the villages and hamlets of the barony—Longsettle and Quail, Roughy and Dorham, his own village of Moorvale and the artisans of Northend town. Where was Tom— where was Katherine? They had to come soon, for it was the day that Tom had to make his case to be set free. They would understand; they would help.

The days dwindle. The tone of the Voice in Edmund's mind matched the lifeless gray of the light. **I am rising. Come out and feel the warmth of my glow.**

Edmund drew in a shuddering breath. There was nothing for it but to try a spell, there in the midst of the Yuletide moot. If he did not do it, he might go raving mad right there in front of everyone.

"I AM MYSELF WITHIN MYSELF. I REIGN ALONE OVER MY THOUGHTS." Edmund made the Signs of the Wheel of Thought in twos—left and right for Babble and Communion, then forward and back for Perception and Obscurity. He felt the rim of the wheel form like an invisible guard around him as he drew

Matthew Jobin

the axis up and down for Truth and Lies. "I STAND WITHIN THE FORTRESS OF MY MIND AND SHUT THE DOOR."

I am everywhere, Edmund. The Voice got quieter, but lost not a bit of its sibilant certainty. **You cannot hide from me forever.**

"I SHUT THE DOOR." Edmund locked the Voice of the Nethergrim out of his mind. He breathed in relief, only to find the family of Longsettle shepherds on the bench beside him staring his way, while at the same time shifting aside to get as far away from him as they could.

Harry did not seem to have heard Edmund's spell up at the front of the hall, for he waved for the clerk to continue. "Very well, then." He let his hand drop back to the arm of his great chair of state. "Call the complaint."

"My lord, I will so." The clerk coughed again. "Hugh Jocelyn, who is your tenant and farmer of your village of Moorvale, and who you may find seated there—" He pointed at Hugh, who fairly leaped up on his bench, hands wrought in clutching anticipation of righteous justice done. "Hugh does accuse one Nicholas Bird, also your tenant and poor cottar, and also of Moorvale, who you may find . . ."

The clerk trailed off. He searched the hall with a squinting, book-ruined gaze.

Harry heaved another sigh. "Nicholas Bird, attend court." He waited, then sat up in his chair. "Nicholas Bird of Moorvale, get in here!"

"Eh?" A voice piped up from the back of the hall. Edmund, like everyone, turned to look and caught Nicky Bird in the act of trying to impress one of the castle scullery maids with a juggling routine. Nicky did not miss a beat. He dropped the leather balls one by one into his pouch and strode up the rows with a grin that would have seemed impish on a little boy.

"Ah no, not Hugh Jocelyn again!" Nicky struck a pose of comic suffering. "What have I done this time?"

"Come down here, Nicholas." Harry put on an air of deep solemnity, perhaps because he held court over people many times his own age. "You stand accused."

The clerk scanned his roll, glanced up at Hugh Jocelyn and began with an air of resignation. "My lord Harold, men of the jury, Hugh Jocelyn accuses Nicholas Bird of vexing his new prize pig, Daisy-belle, and demands redress of one-quarter of the pig's worth, as Daisy-belle's piglets look poorly and likely won't taste very good."

A swift titter of laughter ran through the room. Nicky wandered down the aisle to the front, taking his time and waving cheerily to his many friends.

Harry shot an incredulous look at Hugh. "Vexing."

"Yes, my lord!" Hugh cried back in his reedy chirp of a voice. "Vexing!"

The light behind Nicky Bird fell to a flat gray as the grand double doors of the hall slid wide behind him. Light from outside streamed through, past the farther doors that served to guard the entrance to the keep but were kept open on the day of the moot. Edmund shrank away from it, but could not get far enough.

You can only hide in the shadows because my light casts them. The Voice seeped in over Edmund's spell, carried on the horrible light. **The days draw down, Edmund, down to their end.**

"Shut up! Shut up!" Edmund clutched his head. "Whatever it is that you are doing, I will put a stop to it!"

You tried to stop me coming into the world when first we met under my mountain. The Voice purred its contentment into Edmund's mind. **Yet here I am, shining down above you, greater now than I was then. Do you truly not yet understand? Against me, Edmund, there can be no final victory.**

Edmund took a hard grip on his mind. "I SHUT THE DOOR." He was Edmund Bale; he was the cause of his own thoughts. "I SHUT THE DOOR!"

"What door?"

Edmund jumped. Katherine stood beside him in the aisle, dressed in her heaviest tunic, breeches and riding boots, carrying a cloth bundle much longer than it was wide.

"Door?" Edmund shook himself. He wanted more than anything to explain to Katherine, but not here, not with the shepherds of Longsettle listening in. "Oh. I was sleeping—dreaming." A castle guard drew the double doors of the hall shut. The Voice dropped to a wordless buzz at the edge of his perception, and through his relief Edmund felt the fall of silence in the hall.

Edmund looked up over the benches and watched Harry watching Katherine. Their gazes met, young lord and hero's daughter, for a long moment before they both looked away. Not a few of the villagers glanced from Harry to Katherine, then leaned over to whisper to their neighbors.

"Do you think he'll just keep her on the side, like?" One of the Northend shopkeepers either has less tact than his neighbors or simply did not care who heard him. "He's got to find a proper wife, or this whole barony's bound for trouble. Can't just go on fiddling about with peasant girls all his life."

Everyone heard it—even Harry, who coughed into his sleeves, knit his brows and pretended that he had not. Katherine turned to stare over the heads of the folk of Elverain, searching for the source of the words. Edmund had never in his life seen her look so weak.

Edmund made space for his friends to sit beside him. "I thought you'd never get here in time." He searched their faces. "Katherine, where's your father? We've already had Tom's case delayed once. I doubt we can do it again."

Katherine sat down with an unwonted heaviness, seeming to have lost all of her natural grace. Tom took the seat beside her, trembling from head to toe. Edmund had been wondering for weeks where Katherine stood with Harry. He could not help feel a twinge of hopeful joy to learn that Katherine did not know, either, though as soon as the feeling struck he felt guilty for it.

Edmund glanced around him to make sure no one was listening in. "Katherine, Tom, listen, did you hear anything strange on the way here? Hear, or maybe see anything?"

"We did." Katherine placed something on the palm of Edmund's hand. "I found this."

Edmund looked down in confusion at the worn silver penny in his hand.

"A strange old man gave it to me, a man with a gem in his forehead," said Katherine. "I'm to give it to Papa."

Edmund turned the coin over. It bore three slashes across the emblem of the hunting hound, while the head of the king on the reverse side had been crossed out. "What for?"

"I wish I knew," said Katherine.

Harry wrestled Hugh's case to a conclusion, though by then most of the people were paying it no attention at all. Nicky made a pledge never to vex Hugh's pigs again while Hugh stormed out unsatisfied that no fine had been levied. The villagers joked and gossiped among themselves while the clerk scanned his parchments and conferred with the councilors.

The clerk returned to his place before the people. "We will now hear the case of Tom, the bondsman of Athelstan Barnwell."

Tom stood up at this, then sat down, then, at the silent urging of his friends, stood up again. Katherine stood up with him, then so did Edmund. Harry glanced their way across the hall, though it was clear to Edmund that he was looking at Katherine, not Tom.

The clerk of the court raised his parchment. "My lord, a free farmer of your village, one Athelstan Barnwell, is the accuser. You may find him—" He stopped to scan around, as did everyone.

"Hmm." The clerk turned this way and that. "Athelstan Barnwell, are you here?"

There came no reply save for hushed whispers.

"Any of his kinfolk, then?" said the clerk.

The silence held. Edmund glanced over at Katherine, wondering at the cryptic smile on her face.

"Very well." The clerk carried on at a sign from Harry. "Athelstan Barnwell demands the return of his bonded slave, Tom, who you can see there at the back of the hall. Speaking for Tom, my lord, is your servant and court officer, John, the Marshal of Elverain, who is . . ."

The clerk looked around the hall, waiting for John to stand up. He sighed. "Does anyone come here to have justice done?"

"No, we come for the free food!" The carefully anonymous voice was Hob Hollows, but Edmund was not about to give him away.

Katherine stepped out into the aisle. "If it please the court, may I speak for my father?"

"You may not." The clerk snapped at her without waiting for Harry. "You are but an unmarried girl, and have no standing in the eyes of the law. Sit down."

"I beg you to hear me!" Katherine strode up toward the front. "My father brings something to buy Tom's freedom, given to him by Lord Tristan himself for this very purpose."

Harry held up a hand to stop the clerk from barking Katherine back into her seat again. "What is the offered payment?"

"This, my lord." Katherine laid down the bundle she had been carrying and drew back the cover.

Everyone breathed in a gasp.

"This is my lord Tristan of Harthingdale's own sword-of-war, the one he carried in his campaign against the Nethergrim years ago." Katherine stepped away and turned to Harry. "It is worth the price of a slave many times over. My lord Tristan offers this sword to Athelstan Barnwell in exchange for Tom's freedom."

Edmund shot an encouraging smile at Tom. "Well played." At the sound of Lord Tristan's name, most of the conversation died away. There were precious few among the folk of Elverain who could hear it spoken without an air of reverence descending upon them, and Katherine played on that reverence for all it was worth.

"We thus beseech you, my lord." Katherine turned to Harry again, pleading with him, daring him to deny her and look harsh in front of his people. "Accept this payment in safekeeping for Athelstan and judge Tom to be free."

Harry shifted in his grand chair, glancing aside for advice from his jurors. "To make Tom free, Athelstan should be here to accept payment himself."

Katherine made an imploring gesture. "My lord, consider what Tom has done for our land. Consider his plight, my lord, and consider the bond of good friendship you have made with Lord Tristan. Would you spurn his generous offer?"

Harry hesitated, pinned in the gazes of his people.

"Come on, Harry, come on," Edmund muttered. "Are you really that spineless?"

Harry opened his mouth to speak, but before he could answer, the double doors of the hall swung wide again. The name called forth by the startled guard had half the barony up on its feet and Katherine reaching for the sword she had laid out in offered payment.

"I say again—Sir Wulfric of Olingham!" The guard rapped the butt of his spear twice on the flagstone floor of the hall but could command no silence. "Wulfric of Olingham does request audience with my lord Harold."

Wulfric strode up between the aisles as though a sea of folk had not risen to block him. "You will forgive this intrusion, my lord." At his approach, they parted, leaving him a clear path. "My mission to you will not wait."

Tom leaned in close at Edmund's side. "Can you do a spell, if we need one?"

Edmund shot a glance at the filtered light from outside. "I can try."

Harry stood from his chair of state, his features wrought in what he must have hoped looked like stern anger but to Edmund looked like barely concealed fear. "Two months ago, sir knight, you and your father waged war upon my lands. What business could you possibly have here today?"

"I come from the south, my lord, with a writ and summons." The tread of Wulfric's heavy boots upon the flagstones beat out a steady confidence. Wulfric was not much older than Harry was himself, but had already reached a size and bulk that most men never attained. He wore chain armor, under which his muscles bulged as though the chains might soon need to be let out to contain them. His surcoat, muddy at its trailing hem, bore the emblem of his father, the head of a ram faced as though charging, tongue out, eyes on fire with the rage of war.

Harry sat back in his chair. If he had meant to look stately and unconcerned, he failed. To Edmund, it looked as though Wulfric's approach had made his knees go weak. "Writ and summons? You have no power to summon me anywhere."

"Of my own, I have no such power." Wulfric bore his heavy-bladed sword in its scabbard and a windlass crossbow over his back. He reached for his belt—the guards at the doors sprang forward—but it was only to draw forth a tube of leather, bound in ribbon and sealed in wax. "Herein the power lies. Read, my lord."

The captain of Harry's guard stepped up and snatched the tube from Wulfric's grip. He turned, and with a gesture of reverence that looked too much for show, placed it in Harry's obviously trembling hands.

Harry fingered the waxen seal attached by a bit of ribbon to the bottom edge. "This—this cannot be."

"It can." Wulfric raised his voice, speaking as much to the assembled villagers as to Harry himself. "My lord Harold, baron of Elverain, you are summoned forthwith, to make with all due haste to the city of Rushmeet, there to do homage and swear fealty to His Grace, our glorious king."

Harry read the parchment. He looked up at Wulfric. "But the king is dead."

"Indeed so, my lord." He turned on his booted heel, striding past Katherine, past Edmund and all the folk of Elverain, unimpeded to the door. "The king is dead. Long live the king."

Chapter 10

The voice sounded from too close by for Edmund to ignore it any longer: "What do you mean frozen? All of it?"

Another voice spoke in reply. "All of it, my lord, from bank to bank, as far downstream as Longsettle and maybe farther still." The second speaker was a guard who had a voice better suited to shouting out the hours of the watch than whispering in the upper stories of a castle at night. "No one has ever seen the like."

Edmund shook himself from the trance of his thought and found that he was cold. He sat huddled under blankets in Lord Aelfric's old study, a small room dominated by a round council table and shelves stacked with more books than he had seen anywhere else in the world. The relief he had felt at sunset had long ebbed away, for the more he had learned in his studies that night, the more confused and despondent he had gotten—and the closer to the following dawn.

"Folk say that they hear great cracking booms from out on the ice. One man says he heard a bellow or a roar from the banks." The guard turned back to follow Harry through the wardroom, his heavy tread leaving Edmund in no doubt that he approached the door to the study. "Sounds like work for a wizard, my lord."

Lord Harold of Elverain let out the sort of curse than none of the girls who loved him from afar would believe that he could make. "We have no wizard, so we shall have to make do with the next best thing. Rouse all the men and send them out along the riverbank on swift horses. Tell them to report back at the first sign of trouble."

Edmund threw his blanket over the strange metal disk on the table before him. He turned to make a doodle in his workbook and feigned surprise when Harry booted back the door.

"Still awake, I see." Harry stepped into the room. He looked out over the tabletop bedecked with quills and candles, rolls of parchment and books laid out open in rows. "I expect that a night in here must be your fondest dream come true."

Edmund rubbed his eyes, then rose from his seat in a show of reverence. "Yes, my lord. I thank you again for the chance."

"You and I have never spoken much." The wound Harry had taken in a joust that autumn showed itself only by a momentary wince as he lowered himself down into his carved and cushioned chair. "I think it is time that we did."

Edmund bowed and sat down again. "My lord." He hated using the title, but it was only truth. Old lord Aelfric was dead, brought down by an assassin's arrow, so now his son Harry ruled Elverain. At least, that was how Edmund thought it worked. He made a mark in his memory to study the laws of inheritance, just in case.

Harry folded his elegant, smooth-skinned, many-ringed hands. "Do you know the history of our kingdom?"

"Somewhat, my lord." Edmund reached out to touch the *Paelandabok.* "Long ago, a tribe of men crossed the Girth mountains from the plains of the west, and—"

"No, no." Harry flicked his fingers. "Not that old stuff. I mean the history that matters here and now."

Edmund dried his quill and stoppered his inkwell. He preferred, whenever he could, to keep a patient silence before the sixteen-year-old boy who was owed the yearly taxes on his family's inn, who took his fee for every marriage, every birth and every funeral in Elverain, and who had the power to do anything short of hanging the peasants who lived on his land. Harry had always affected an air of tolerant kindliness toward Edmund, but Edmund saw right through it.

Harry reached out and seized the silver coin on the table between them. He held it up to the candlelight. "Do you know what this means?"

Edmund blanched—he had forgotten the coin. He cursed himself for leaving the stupid thing out in plain sight. He raced for the right lie, having not the faintest idea who or what he might expose by speaking what little truth he knew about the strangely marked penny Katherine had been given. "It means a night at a cheap inn, my lord, or a supper with no meat."

"Don't try to be clever." Harry handed the penny across to Edmund. "Do you know why there is a hunting hound stamped on one side?"

Edmund turned the coin over. He was not sure whether he was already in trouble just by having it. The firelight picked out the grooves of the triple slash across the hunting hound on one side and the cross through the head of the king on the other.

Harry started talking again before Edmund could decide what to say. "In the days when your father was a boy and mine a man of middle years, in those days before the Nethergrim rose in the mountains, our kingdom was nearly torn apart by a war for the throne." He took up a goblet from the table and poured out sweet cider from the jug a kindly page had brought for Edmund. "You must know at least that much."

"I do, my lord," said Edmund. "Thirty years ago, old king Clothar the Mad died without an heir. The succession passed among his cousins, but no one could decide whose claim was the stronger."

"Just so." Harry drank, then poured himself the rest of the cider. "One side of the family claimed the crown by descent through Ketta, the elder sister of Clothar, who was married off to the grand *Mrekos* of Ausca half a century ago. After the *Mrekos* died, Ketta married again, to Huda Houndesthorn, who was nothing but a petty knight from Sparrock town. That side of the family chose the hunting hound for their token, the emblem of Huda, a man whose love of the hunt was matched only by his love of war. The other side decried the claim of the Hound, arguing that the Great Charter of wise King Andhun, by which the laws of our kingdom were set in times long past, barred the passage of the crown in so scandalous a manner."

Edmund did his best to follow Harry's reasoning. "Scandalous?"

"No king in all our history has ever before claimed the crown by descent through a woman, much less one who had her children by a man of such low birth," said Harry. "To the twinned kings of far Üvhakkat, our throne has been considered vacant ever since. Worse yet, in Ausca, not only do they never bother to use the title 'queen' for the wife of a king, but poor Ketta was only the third wife of the *Mrekos*."

Edmund still did not understand the problem—but then, he did not know why Harry had chosen to lecture him on politics, either.

"Third wife at the same time." Harry waited for the meaning to sink in. "By Auscan law, their *Mrekos* may be married to as many as seven women at once. It must be some compensation for the fact that each *Mrekos* seems to last about five years in power before someone knifes him in his bed or puts poison in his favorite sweets. It's usually one of the wives that does it, in fact. Sending poor old Ketta off to the *Mrekos* was just a way of getting her out of the clutches of that grubby little wall-climber Huda Houndesthorn, and if the *Mrekos* had lived past Ketta's birthing years, our whole kingdom would be in a good deal less trouble. As it was, when she returned to our lands, she was still in the prime of her years. She married Huda and gave birth to Bregisel, the man who until two months ago we hailed as His Grace, our glorious king."

Edmund blinked. "Then . . . what about the other side?" He had always assumed that since he had trained his mind in the abstractions of magic, he would easily be able to grasp anything that someone like Harry could understand. It turned out that in the question of tangled family trees, he had nothing on Harry.

The winter wind banged the shutter open, tickling the pages on the table and flattening the tongues of the fire in the hearth. Harry waited for Edmund to get up and close it before he spoke again. "That branch of the family took for themselves the emblem of the Stag, from the banner of Eberulf, who claimed the throne by descent from Rigunth the Fat, younger brother to King Clothar's father, King Hartmut the Squinty-eyed. They have argued for years that since Rigunth was born after his own father had taken the throne his claim was always stronger than that of his elder brother Clothar. The trouble there, of course, is that accepting the claim of the Stag means saying that even Clothar, who might have been mad as a spring ram but had reigned in peace for twenty years, should never have sat upon the throne in the first place. The Hound, for their part, argued from the same Great Charter of Andhun the Lawgiver that succession to the throne came by strict order of birth, and that whether the child was born before or after the father took the throne was of no consequence, but the Stag, for their part, argued that the copy of the Great Charter kept in Paladon Spire had been magically altered in secret by the Lord High Mystical seventy years ago, and that their own copy of the Charter, which they kept in Westry, was the one that preserved wise King Andhun's intentions in their purest form, and that anyway

Andhun had never even mentioned the idea of the crown passing through a daughter. You see?"

"I . . . I think so, my lord." Edmund's head had begun to spin. "It's the claim of the children of the second marriage of a princess to a . . . lesser man, which is against the ancient law, versus the claim of the cousins descended from a younger brother, which is also against the ancient law, assuming that no one has secretly changed the ancient law. Is that right?"

"More or less." Harry settled back into his great council chair, from which still hung his late father's fur-trimmed robe. "Well, as should be plain, there was no avoiding war. It was a close-run thing, that war, dragging on for years and sending many men to early graves, but in the end the Hound won out."

"Everyone knows that much, my lord." Edmund sometimes wondered to himself whether caring about who was king was simply something missing in him from the start, or whether reading too many books that told of too many lazy, foolish, or evil kings had cured him forever of adoration for the crown.

"Now, do you see the symbol there, trampled under the paws of the hound?" Harry reached out to tap the penny in Edmund's hands. "That is an antler, a torn-off piece of the Stag, a message to all who see it—we have won the war, and so we claim the peace."

Edmund set down the coin, unsure of whether Harry was trying to lay a trap for him, for he kept talking about it without mentioning the cryptic marks that defaced it. "Is there something for which you need my particular aid, my lord?"

Harry sat back, far enough into the shadows that Edmund could no longer read his face. "We should trust each other, you and I. We are on the same side."

Edmund could not help but bristle. "And what side is that, my lord? Who has summoned you to the city of Rushmeet?"

Harry drank, then set his goblet down, pointedly ignoring Edmund's question. "I want your aid, Edmund Bale. I want a court wizard."

"But, my lord." Edmund threw Harry's overheard words back at him. "You know that I am not in truth a wizard."

"You have done much for Elverain." Harry came forward, favoring Edmund with a winning, wheedling smile that made Edmund want to punch him square on the nose. "No one can deny that."

Edmund did not know how to guess his way to safety and knew he could do nothing to escape Harry's gold-flecked gaze. He decided to try shifting the ground. "Who was that boy, my lord? The mad, babbling one you came to find at my parents' inn."

Harry leaned his elbows on the table. "I will tell you who he is, if you tell me where he has gone."

Edmund found himself shifting away. Harry stared down at the penny, then picked it up.

"Yes, Edmund, I noted John Marshal's absence." Harry fingered the penny, clacking it between his many rings. "He was not only meant to stand before me today to sue for Tom's freedom. He is an officer of my court—only recently reinstated, I might add—and he is duty bound to give me an account of my stables every year on the Day of the Plow."

"Katherine doesn't know where he went, my lord." Edmund let his dislike for Harry stiffen his back. "And before you ask—neither do I."

"I am not asking whether you know where he is," said Harry. "I am asking you whether you can find him and the boy he took with him. You trapped the Skeleth, Edmund. I have no doubt the stories are true. You also broke Vithric's spell beneath the mountain of the Nethergrim. Can you compass this task, as well?"

Edmund let his gaze drift down to the covered metal disk, then away before Harry noticed where he was looking. Ideas spun in his mind, spells he had read about but should have needed years of training to try. He wished despite himself that Katherine was there, not only to soften Harry's manner but to answer questions that Edmund would never even think to ask. Whose side *was* he on, anyway?

"I might be just sixteen, but I am lord of Elverain." Harry stared at the dwindling wick of a candle. "My father gave me my lessons on statecraft. I know that a kingdom is never weaker than the moment when a king dies."

Edmund thought back through the histories he had read. He could not help but acknowledge such a truth.

"There is worse still," said Harry. "Huda Houndesthorn had power enough to conquer in the old wars, but not power enough to purge. Many of his old enemies still hold their feudal lands. Ever since the Hound took the throne, the power of that throne has diminished, and lords have risen in private wars again and again, only barely restrained from pulling the whole kingdom apart. The sons of Eberulf flew into exile, begging shelter in the

Matthew Jobin

distant Exarchate of Üvhakkat. In the years since, lord has plotted with lord, each of them maneuvering to secure his footing on shifting sands and to topple his rivals if he can. Not even the rumor of the Nethergrim disturbed them, for it was a rumor that came and went, leaving them safe in their castles to plot and connive. Our kingdom, Edmund, has remained one while a single man's heart continued to beat. It beats no longer."

Edmund shook his head. "To us peasants, my lord, who sits as king does not really matter much. We pay our taxes every year—what difference does it make whose face is stamped on the coins we hand over?"

Harry opened his hands. "Do you know what happened to the lands that refused to make their peace and bow to the Hound at the end of the old wars? They called it the Harrowing. You are free to look it up in your books, but I will give you the essence of it. Many peasants who did not care who was king still dangled from a noose or writhed on a lance-point because their lord harbored the wrong loyalties. If you care for nothing else, surely you care at least for that."

Edmund pictured his father suspended from the claws of his spell. It was not difficult to picture him hanging instead from a gallows. He felt a squeeze in his guts, a wish to run home and beg forgiveness, but at the same time a wish to run and keep running.

"I travel south tomorrow to the city of Rushmeet, to support I know not whom, and to face dangers I do not yet know." Harry raised his voice to break into Edmund's thoughts. "I require your aid."

Edmund shot a hard look across the table at his lawful lord.

Harry flicked his long bangs back behind his ear. "Katherine's coming, if that helps."

Edmund bit his lip so hard it nearly bled. He took back the penny from where Harry had dropped it on the table. "Let us put together what we know, my lord. I overheard you saying that the river Tamber has frozen over."

"In a single night," said Harry. "The Tamber has not frozen in all the memory and record of Elverain. Do you understand what that means?"

"No, my lord."

"It means that Wolland can cross the ice wherever he chooses." Harry pounded one fist in the other. "If he's behind the summons down to Rushmeet, I won't know what he's planning until I am far out of position.

He could strike at me anywhere—I do not have one tenth of the men needed to guard such a long border."

"Wolland?" Edmund had not, in truth, understood what Harry had meant. "Then you still fear attack."

"You know as well as I do what Lord Wolland had planned for these lands," said Harry. "He was defeated but with his army intact. He has lived to run home, lick his wounds and plot his revenge. In the meantime, the king has been murdered, as I am sure Wolland knew would happen all along, and now he has another chance to gain his desires. For all I know, this summons is nothing but a ruse to get me someplace where I can be killed with ease."

Edmund did not like Harry, not one bit, but he could not bring himself to wish him dead. "Then do not answer the summons."

"If I do not and the one who summons me gains the throne, then I will be taken for a traitor and thus forfeit," said Harry. "I am not yet married. I have no heir. If I die, Edmund, Elverain will fall into chaos, and your family will suffer with it."

Edmund rubbed his chin. "Then—you go to support the claim of this new king, if his claim is sound."

"That's the trouble." Harry shook his head. "It is not sound. Not yet."

Understanding came to Edmund in a flash. "The boy from the inn."

Harry flicked a look at Edmund. He nodded, just once.

Edmund laid one hand on the canvas that covered the disk. "Very well. I will help you, my lord."

"Good." Harry rose at once. "We ride tomorrow at dawn." He turned to go.

Edmund halted him as he passed. "What about Tom?"

Harry sighed. "Yes, yes. If you pledge to serve me, I will make him free tomorrow. It must be done at a crossroads, anyway."

"Thank you, my lord." Edmund returned to his books. Harry paused for a moment, perhaps to say something more, but then turned and left, closing the door behind him.

Edmund drew back the canvas covering from the disk. He picked up his quill and dipped it in his inkwell. The image of his mother came and went from his mind, replaced by an image of the wounded, nameless boy. He turned the disk over and stared down at the picture of the sky carved upon its other side, a sky full of unfamiliar stars though yet in daytime, a sky with two suns.

Chapter 11

The Day of the Sword, The Second Day of Yule

Katherine pushed back the trapdoor that led to the top of the tallest tower of the castle. "Edmund?" She spied him on his knees beneath the battlement, one hand on something flat and round, his gaze fixed on the stars above. "What are you doing up here? It's freezing!"

Edmund wore a bundle of blankets over his shoulders and an absent expression on his face. "Cold, yes." He scanned the sky from edge to edge. "Glad you're here."

"I had to ask every guard in the castle before I found one who knew where you'd gone." Katherine reached back to help Tom up the ladder behind her, then crossed the roof to join Edmund in the meager shelter of the battlements. "What is that you've got?"

"This is what that boy we found in the Twintrees' orchard was carrying." Edmund leaned away from the metal disk at his feet, letting starlight carve shadows on the rings of symbols that covered its face.

Katherine knelt down on the flat roof of the tower. "Is it some sort of spell?"

"No," said Edmund. "It's a calendar."

Tom, in his turn, pulled Jumble up onto the roof, then strode over to the battlements and looked out across the world. The heavy clouds of the day had parted, letting starlight through but also the hardest, blackest chill. Jumble followed him, tail down but ears perked up.

Edmund turned to Tom. "You can feel it, can't you?"

Tom reached down to touch Jumble's forehead, to stroke and to soothe. He let out a steaming roil of starlit breath. "Even the air smells different than it did. It is horrible and wonderful, both at once."

Edmund traced his hand around the rim of the disk. "The world is not what we thought it was."

"It never is, so it seems." Katherine undid her belt and laid Lord Tristan's sword aside, next to the heavy wooden case used by the castle guards to store their crossbow bolts. "I wish at least one of you would talk sense with me."

Tom sat down with his friends, so that they formed a triangle around the metal disk. Katherine looked from Tom to Edmund. They did not resemble each other—one tall and one short, one dark of hair and the other almost too fair and pale—but there beneath the stars they had a kinship in the way they moved, the way they sat and in what passed across their faces whenever their gazes drifted to the horizon.

Katherine accepted a blanket from Edmund. "You're afraid of the sky." She wrapped it around her shoulders; the knowledge of their fear sparked fear in her. "You both are."

Edmund ran his hands around the outer rim of the disk. "These are Dhanic symbols of the oldest kind." He stopped on a symbol that looked to Katherine as though someone had wanted to draw a sheaf of wheat, but then got bored and started scribbling doodles all around it. "It took me a while to work things out because I was thinking about it too hard, but the numbers twelve, six and five should have been a hint."

He traced out the symbols nearest Katherine. "*Curved–Gather–Blade. Sky–In–Anger, Purify–Double–Stick.*"

Katherine looked down. The meanings of the symbols came to her all in a rush. "*Curved–Gather–Blade*, that's a sickle. *Sky–In–Anger* is thunder, and *Purify–Double–Stick* is a threshing flail. Sicklemoon, Thundermoon, Threshingmoon—three of the months of the year, summer to autumn."

"Yes, exactly. Now, watch." Edmund held the rim of the disk while he pushed at its face. With a grinding whine it turned, so that rings of six and five began to spin, one faster than the other.

Matthew Jobin

Katherine touched one of the symbols on the ring just inside the ring of months. "What are these?"

Edmund's eyes flashed in starlight. "A ring of six, inside a ring of five, inside a ring of twelve."

"Oh, of course," said Katherine. "The days and weeks of the year."

"Right. Our calendar has five weeks of six days each for every month." Edmund spun the rings farther on. As every cycle of thirty days completed, a mark on the first day shifted over to the next in the ring of twelve. "Every year is made up of twelve months, each of exactly thirty days, new moon to new moon. Three hundred and sixty days in perfect harmony."

Tom made a space for Jumble to lie across his lap. "Then your calendar is not complete. After the twelve months come the five days of Yule."

Edmund turned the days through the weeks and then the months — Milkmoon, Harrowmoon, Haymoon. "Isn't it odd, now that you think of it? The year, I mean — so nearly perfect, but then it's not. Five days left over at the end, like . . . a crack in the sky, words left unsaid, a fiddle that can't be tuned. Doesn't it make everything feel a bit broken, somehow?"

Tom rubbed his chin. "Maybe your numbers only make the world seem odd to you. Maybe everything does not have to work like this funny disk."

"But you feel it, don't you?" Edmund held his gaze on him, blue eyes on green. "You can almost see it."

Tom's shoulders, less skinny than they once had been, still folded up when he got scared. "The sky today looked strange, and the stars — they've never looked like they do tonight. Everything is drifting. Something's wrong, this year."

Katherine gazed upward again, looking with greater care at the stars above. The feeling seized her hard — she might not have Edmund's book knowledge or Tom's long experience sleeping under the open sky, but she still knew the round of constellations that ran their course through every year of her life. The stars she saw above had changed, sliding out of their places, as though the shapes they made — the Archer and the Chariot, the Maiden and the Boar — were all melting away.

Edmund turned the wheels of the disk on and on — Threshingmoon, Gatheringmoon, Woodmoon. "It might seem wrong to us only because it's something that hasn't happened in time out of memory." Some hidden internal mechanism squealed. "Each day has a color and a shape: Red Birchday follows Blue Birchday, and so on through Yellow, Black, and

White, and then Blue Horseday, Red Horseday and on through month after month. So spins the wheel."

"Then what about Yule?" Katherine huddled closer in under the battlements, thankful that Edmund had chosen the side in the lee of the wind. "Three hundred and sixty days, then five days without a moon, every year—The Day of the Plow, then The Day of the Sword, the Day of the Hearth, the Day of the Ship and lastly the Day of the Wind."

"I've always thought those were funny names," said Tom. "Do you know what they mean?"

Edmund shook his head. "No one knows. Their meanings are out of all memory now, whatever they meant long ago."

Tom stuck the tip of his tongue out the side of his mouth, as though thinking was for him a form of physical effort. "Maybe the stuff in the middle of the disk is Yuletide. Those symbols, there, the bigger ones. You haven't explained those yet."

"Just coming to them." Edmund slowed the turning of the disk as the days of Deadmoon, the last month of the year, rotated beneath his fingers. In the very center of the disk was a final set of symbols, four set in quarters around two in halves. When he reached the last day before Yule, something happened to the symbols in the center of the disk that made Katherine blink in surprise.

"Go back." She waved her hand. "Do that again, more slowly."

Edmund spun the rings of the disk in the opposite direction, moving it back into the final week of Deadmoon. He turned around and advanced time once again. At the end of the month, one of the four symbols moved inward by the work of some cunning mechanism, followed toward the center by the one across from it, then the one to its left, and so on.

"The first one says *Land–Blade*." Edmund counted them one by one as they moved inward. "Then *Battle–Snake*, then *Heart–Home*, then *Horse–Ocean*. The inner two say *Crow–Road* and *Man–Mountain*." When all four had reached the center, the inmost pair rotated until all six joined to form a single symbol.

Katherine felt the dislocating sense of witnessing a revelation that she could not understand. "What does that middle symbol mean, all joined together?"

"*Courage–Upward*." Edmund shrugged. "It's such a tangle that I can't begin to make out what it might mean in our tongue."

Katherine sat back. "Those symbols in the middle of the disk can't stand for Yule, though." She pondered for a while. "That's six symbols, but Yule has only five days."

"I know." Edmund unwound the disk. "I wish I understood it better. I wish that boy had told us what he knew of it."

"I don't know if he knew anything at all," said Katherine. "He seemed utterly lost."

Tom shook his head. "He knew many things. He knew things before other people knew them." He met Katherine's questioning look. "He said things that only made sense long afterward."

"He knew my name, but then pretended that he didn't," said Edmund. "He knew your father's name, too."

The mention of her father's name stirred what Katherine would have rather let sit. "I wish we at least knew who he was."

"Harry knows, and told me," said Edmund. "That boy is the last prince of the Hound, heir to all the kingdom."

"Prince?" Katherine gave him a look. "Don't be silly, Edmund. The king and queen only have one living child, little Princess Merofled. Their sons all died as babies."

"No," said Edmund. "One survived."

The world seemed to tilt and shift under Katherine. "Then why didn't King Bregisel name him as his heir? He looked like he's been half starved or worse all his life—and why on earth would they put a gem in anyone's forehead, let alone a prince of the realm?"

"I don't know about any of that." Edmund turned the disk over. "I only know what I have here before me."

Katherine looked down at the reverse side of the disk. "It's a picture of the night sky."

"That's right." Edmund started turning the rings of the disk once again, making its internal mechanism grind softly forward through its account of time.

Katherine leaned in to examine the disk more closely. "Why are there two suns?"

Edmund gave her a hollow, hunted look. "You couldn't see it at all, then. In the sky yesterday."

"See what?"

Edmund touched the larger of the two suns on the disk. "The Nethergrim."

No blanket would be warm enough for Katherine just then. Jumble wormed his way out of Tom's lap and snuggled up against her.

"The Nethergrim will rise tomorrow, just there in the west." Edmund pointed at the shadowed peaks of the Girth. "Closer tomorrow to our own sun that she was yesterday. Her light will flood the world, stronger and stronger as the light of our sun grows weaker."

Tom's face went gray. "Yes. That's it. That's what I feel."

Edmund bent back down to turn the disk. The suns approached each other until one, the one he had named the Nethergrim, covered the other.

"What does that mean?" Katherine knew how her voice sounded, knew how badly she wanted to be told that it was nothing, just an ancient calendar that told no one anything of use, but the look on Edmund's face gave her no such comfort.

"Katherine. Tom. I don't know how else to tell you this." Edmund sat back. "No one else seems to know it, no one seems to understand, but I think that time is about to come to an end."

Chapter 12

K atherine checked the reins and brought Indigo to a stop, though it felt to her that any halt upon the road was nothing but a chance for the vicious wind to seize hold of her and chill her bones. At least there was no danger of her falling too far behind; the canopied, decorated wagons she followed might have been hauled by teams of hard-striding draft horses, but even so the snow on the road often brought them nearly to a stop. Harry and his knights rode in a tight formation around the wagon, shields up and ready, scrutinizing every tree and barnside for signs of an ambush. Grooms and servants marched in a clump just behind, leading mules while being mules themselves, for they carried almost as much on their own backs as the beasts of burden that they dragged along on rope leads. A pack of greyhounds followed at the heel of their trainer, wearing brass collars in the shape of crowns, studded with gems that glittered without warmth in the dead winter light. The whole procession moved at a pace of a comfortable walk, though its pace was the only comfortable thing about it.

Katherine looked abreast along their line at Tom, who kept turning back and forth in the saddle of the easy-walking riding horse she had chosen for him.

"What is it, Tom?"

"The light," said Tom. "It's still *wrong*. It's even stranger today than yesterday."

Katherine turned to Edmund, hoping for some help, but he sat rigid in the saddle of his horse, the hood of his cloak pulled down over his face and his eyes shut to slits, muttering something over and over while making an inward-pulling gesture with his hands.

"The colors." Tom stared at the stalk-stubbled, snow-decked fields, then the frozen surface of the Tamber, then straight up at the cloudy sky. "Wrong. I've never seen a day like this."

Jumble yanked an ice-coated stick from the brush along the road and tried each of the three friends in turn, offering it up to play tug-of-war. Tom was too busy staring at the sky and Edmund was too busy mumbling into his hood, so Katherine leaned down to pick it up and give it a throw. It turned out that the real game Jumble wanted to play was offering the stick, then growling and playing tug-of-war with anyone who took a grip on the other end.

"As you like, then." Katherine curled in her arm, raising an alarmed Jumble high into the air. Jumble's growl turned into a whine. He unclenched his jaws, falling with a muffled thump into an icy rut of road. He did not seem to begrudge Katherine's trick, though, for he happily chased the stick once she took good aim and threw, racing and barking through the snowy fields between the road and the river.

"Hoy, back there, stop that!" The dog trainer bolted after his charges, but there was no catching greyhounds once they had leaped to a sprint. The trainer shot a bitter look at Katherine, then raced across the hedgerow in pursuit. "These dogs are meant as a gift to our new king! Do you have any idea how much they're worth?" The greyhounds might have been worth half the price of a good riding horse apiece, but they did not seem to think themselves above a game of tug-the-stick with Jumble in the snow.

Katherine thrust her gloved hands under the extra cloak she kept folded in the saddle for warmth. It looked like a grayish sort of day to her, no question of that, with a lifeless sun seeming barely able to pierce the wisps of cloud to the southwest. She wished that she could see what Edmund could see—and then again, she truly did not wish it.

"Let's sing a road song." She nudged Indigo in close to her friends' horses. "Edmund, you've got the best voice—you start."

Edmund swayed back and forth in his saddle, out of time with the steps of his horse. He wore no gloves, but he gripped the pommel of his saddle as though his hands could not feel the frigid lances of wind that ran between

Matthew Jobin

the fields. Katherine caught Tom's eye, then took up a position on Edmund's left side while Tom took up the right.

"Edmund, are you feeling well?" Katherine got near enough that she could see her friend's face more clearly than she had since they set out from the castle. Edmund's blue eyes stared straight ahead, seeming to fix on nothing. He held his teeth clenched under parted lips, his breath steaming hard between them.

"Leave me." Edmund clenched his reins. "Go away. I hate you."

Katherine recoiled. She took up her reins and was about to turn away before Tom caught her with a look.

"Stay," said Tom. "He's not talking to you."

Edmund wrung his hands around the reins so hard that Katherine wondered what would break first, the leather or the skin of his hands. "You can't scare me anymore. No—stop it. Stop!"

Katherine took off her glove despite the cold. She reached out and put her hand on Edmund's. He hissed, stopped swaying and sat up straight in his saddle. He glanced at Katherine with a look that made her want to find someplace to hide him, made her want to do anything to see the old, clumsy, hopeful little Edmund again.

"You can hear me?" She let go. "What is it? What's wrong?"

Edmund stole a look up at the sky as though it were the roof of a cave about to collapse and crush him. "It's worse, much worse than yesterday." He came back to himself. "Please. Please stay with me. Please talk to me. It's hard to hear myself thinking."

"All right." Katherine reached into the saddlebag beside her. "Here—I have a present for you."

Edmund fixed on her with what seemed to be great effort. "A present?"

"Your sword." She drew it forth and placed it in his hands.

Edmund held the blade in its wood-and-leather scabbard, looking down at it as though he did not know what it was. A belt dangled from the loops, its work-hardened leather retaining the shape of the waist that once had worn it.

"Harry told me to make use of his armory." Katherine arranged her saddle blanket so that it would serve to better warm her legs. "Beautiful, isn't it? You don't see many like that anymore."

Edmund drew the blade. "It's a strange sort of sword, I suppose. I don't know much about them but I've never seen one quite like it." Gray light found glints upon the hilt, on the bronze plaques hammered on the cross guard and the band of silver wire twisted into the lobed and flattened pommel.

"But why me?" Edmund shot the blade home again. "Why me and not Tom?"

"Katherine got me a sword, too." Tom put a hand to the hilt of the slender arming sword Katherine had chosen for him. "I've been wearing it all day."

Edmund traced a finger on the cross guard of his new sword. A row of tiny animals reared and fought with one another around the edge—stags, bears and boars picked out in skilled detail, marred here and there by the blows of unknown enemies. The edges ran wide and nearly parallel until they rounded in just before the point, battle-nicked all along the length. Whorls of gray twisted down between the shallow fullers, as though a wisp of smoke had been caught and forged into the steel. Along this strip of swirled metal ran two words, incised just past the hilt—KING CHLODOBERT.

"Turn it over," said Katherine.

Edmund turned the blade. ". . . had me forged," he read on the other side. "King Chlodobert had me forged."

A flake of snow struck the blade. The leather grip held the discolored impressions of the hand that once had wielded it. Edmund slid his fingers to match them—but then shook his head. "I shouldn't keep this."

Katherine reached down to straighten the girth of Edmund's horse, wondering how he could make such a mess of his saddle and tack just by riding at a walk for a few miles. "You should."

"I'm the son of innkeepers."

"Put it on." Katherine picked up the scabbard and handed it to him. "Let's see how it fits."

Edmund threaded the sword belt at his waist. Katherine reached over and moved the belt higher on his opposite hip.

"There." She sat back in her saddle and smiled at him. "It looks well on you."

Edmund stared at the blade. "I don't know how to use it."

Katherine reached for the bridle. "I would tell you that sword's too short to wield from the saddle, but you can't really ride, either."

Edmund half smiled. "If it comes to it, if I do need to use this, tell me one thing I should remember."

"Swords like that are weighted to the point." Katherine let down a stirrup to better match Edmund's height. "Check your swing and don't overreach, or it will throw off your balance and leave you open to a counter."

Edmund put a hand to the hilt. "I can remember that."

"Good." Katherine took up her reins. "And here we are. Three heroes on our steeds of war."

Edmund laughed. "Bluebell, a steed of war?" He touched the mane of his horse, then nudged Tom. "So, sir knight, how are you with a lance?"

"You must learn to fight," said Katherine. "The two of you must learn, and if no one else will teach you, I will."

"Tom." A voice called out from the head of the column. "Dismount. Meet me up ahead."

Katherine felt a surge of hopeful joy. "Oh, Tom, this is it!" She took the reins of his horse. "Go on, go!"

Tom hopped down from his saddle. He adjusted his belt, then his cloak, then his belt again. "What do I say?"

"Harry says everything." Katherine nudged him with her boot. "Off with you!"

Cries came from along the halted line of wagons. "Hurry up, will you? We're all freezing out here!"

Tom obliged, loping along past the procession to join Harry out in front of the line. Halfway along, he was stopped by a castle guard and surrendered the sword he had forgotten he was wearing.

The importance of the moment seemed to hold Edmund's attention on the world around him. "Why at a crossroads, do you think?"

"Just the custom, as old as the mountains." Katherine could hardly hold down her excitement. She led Edmund around the wagons and up to the front of the line to get the best view. "Can you believe it? Tom is being made free. He's going to be free!"

A warm look spread across Edmund's face—but then his gaze drifted up, high into the clouds. His expression changed back to fright, to despair and hatred. He made the funny inward motion with his hands again while muttering something about shutting a door.

Harry strode ahead, up to the place where the Roughy road crossed the road that led south from the castle. "Approach me, Tom."

Tom stepped forth, his rail-thin height making Harry look oddly short and compact beside him. Katherine shaded her eyes to watch, for though the sun did not shine, its filtered light still caught in the drifts of snow between the fields.

"Now then, in my right as lord of Elverain and peer of the realm, I grant unto you, Tom . . ." Harry hesitated. "No second name?"

Tom shook his head. "No, my lord."

Harry raised his hand. "Very well, then, I grant unto you freedom of the roads and villages of Elverain. You are a slave no longer. By this act do I make you free, Tom of—"

"Tom!" Edmund's voice rose to a sudden shout, startling Katherine and making Bluebell dance beneath him. "Tom! My lord! Look out!"

Katherine whirled to stare at Edmund, who had snapped from his mumbling trance and was shouting at the top of his lungs. She did not know what he feared, but she drew Tristan's sword from its scabbard along her saddle and pulled her shield off her back, ready for anything.

"Get out of the crossroad, now!" Edmund spurred Bluebell forward, past braying pack mules and bewildered servants. "Move!"

Katherine could not understand what it was that she saw, but she knew that it boded no good. "Harry, Tom! Get out of the crossroads!" She sucked in a frigid, frightened breath. "Now!"

Harry looked up, then down, rooted to the spot. Tom tried to grab him and pull him aside, but in doing so only seemed to turn abruptly and run straight into the ground, disappearing into the ice-rimmed dirt without a trace. Jumble rushed up barking frantically and fell straight through behind them, through a hole that did not seem to be there.

"Oh, *sister*." A singsong voice sounded from high above. "Now we'll have to chase after them!" A shadow widened across the joining of the roads—waving, jointed arms that blocked the sun.

Chapter 13

"What is happening?" Harry grabbed for Tom's arm. He fell to his knees. "What is happening to the world?"

Tom swayed, feeling as though at any moment he might fall without knowing which way was up or down. His guts knotted and lurched. There was nothing about the pieces of the scene before him that should have made him feel so sick and strange—not when taken separately, at least. Before him ran a road in winter, hedged in by rows of trimmed and leafless bushes. Beyond that he saw thick forest on the other side of a wide, half-frozen river.

The problem was that the road ran right onto the water, some of the trees seeming to sit right atop the rippled surface. A hare ran past in panicked flight at the sight of Jumble. It fled by Tom and into the trunk of the largest tree he had ever seen in his life, then disappeared.

"I'll just pop in after them, sister." The voice seemed to come from behind Tom and beside him, both at once. "I doubt they'll get far."

"Harry!" Katherine's voice cried out from the same confused morass of impossible directions. "Tom, where are you?"

Tom sank down. He felt mud and dry dirt, both at once. The rock he touched was there, and then not there, and then there again—then it was grass, then ice. After that, for an instant, the roadway was cobbled, but then it was mud again. Jumble swayed and pitched over beside him.

Harry rolled into a ditch and retched. "Where are we?"

"I think…I think we're in more than one place at the same time, my lord." Tom staggered over to Harry, though with every step he felt as if he had suddenly pivoted toward the ground or the sky. "It's as though left and right are the same direction, and that new road is somehow both upward and forward at once." Jumble roused himself in the roadway and managed to make it as far as Tom's side before he collapsed again, whining in frightened confusion.

"Stand up." Tom grabbed for Harry's tunic, but only succeeded only in pulling off his fine cloak. "My lord, please, you must stand up! We must find a place to hide!"

"You're so *impatient*, sister dear." A young man approached at an ambling walk on the road behind Tom, which meant that he somehow walked straight downward out of the sky. He took one last step, then seemed to right himself with disorienting speed to stand level on the ground. "You threaded through far too many crossroads at once. I swear I can see all the way to Westry from here!"

"It will save time, brother." A slightly younger woman stepped lightly out of the air behind him, taking his hand on the turn to touch her soft-booted feet to the ground. "We can go straight through to Lum's Graves once we've finished our business here." She turned to stand back to back with her brother, but at the same time she stood above his head, turned at a perfectly square angle. Just past her, insomuch as direction still meant anything at all, Tom could see Katherine and Edmund astride their horses in front of a column of Harry's knights. The waving, jointed shadow grew in width above them—or perhaps that which cast the shadow grew nearer.

The brother had a mouth that cut in a V-shaped angle, the point of it too far down toward his cleft chin and the edges too far up toward his cheekbones. "If we find the boy here, sister, we won't need to go to Lum's Graves at all." The mouth marred an otherwise handsome face, dark eyes evenly set under a smoothly rounded brow and over a straight, somewhat delicate nose. "Mother's grace, you've got the whole of the north tangled up! This is the Hundredthorn!"

"Oh, stop complaining, will you? The rivers count as a crossroad," said the sister. "That way if we don't find the boy, we can either go forward or back to try the other part of the plan."

Tom stared above him at the knotted, reaching branches of the enormous tree that was there, and then not there, and then there again. It had a trunk that a dozen men could not reach around with linked arms. The place where it stood seemed to be the very same place as the river—the longer he looked, the better the place resolved itself as an island set where three rivers joined into one to flow downstream. From the branches hung swords, dozens of swords in various stages of rust, tied with ropes that ran the gamut from rather new to so weathered that they seemed likely to snap at any moment.

The brother looked about him, seeming entirely at ease amidst the broken angles of the crossroads. "Now then—my lord Harold of Elverain, is that you in the ditch over there?" When he opened his mouth to smile, teeth that looked like sharpened stakes moved apart, and Tom spent an awful instant wondering what such a man might like to eat. "I entirely promise not to kill you if you just hop on out and toddle over to me. You are a hostage, you see."

The captain of Harry's guard sounded the charge from beyond the twisted crossroad. "To my lord Harold! Cut those two down! Knights, advance!"

"Advance where?" cried one of the knights. "Captain, where *is* my lord Harold? Where is *anything*?"

The many-armed shadow grew larger still, casting darkness from above, from all sides, and somehow from below. The knights recoiled and halted their charge. Katherine grabbed for the bridle of Edmund's horse before it could rear and throw him in a panic. A thing crawled out of the spaces whose direction had no name, a thing like something Tom had seen up in the Girth mountains on his journey to the lair of the Nethergrim. This particular creature, though, was far larger than the one that had reached from the dark to throw its deadly barbs in Vithric's service, waving jointed limbs of a sunburn red instead of a mottled greenish black.

"This won't take but a moment, brother." The sister, twenty at the oldest, stood near Edmund's modest height—slender, fine of feature and dressed with more elegance than anyone Tom had ever seen. "I'm just going to kill a few people first, so they know not to be contrary with us." The *uhaari* moved past her, driving back the knights and sending the rest of Harry's procession into screaming flight across the roads and fields. It waved its jointed limbs from the dizzying vanishing point where they approached one another without ever seeming to meet. Barbs flew, then folk screamed, pierced through from back to front. Most of the others fled—some of them, caught in the shifting directions of the crossroads, seemed to emerge near Tom and Harry and wander in desperate confusion through places far from home.

"Oh, well, *that's* not fair at all!" The brother turned around and stepped through the junction point at the center of the crossroads, so that he came to his sister's side. "If we're to be killing people, I want to do a bit. You know it's my favorite thing in all the world."

Jumble shoved his nose under Tom's arm, as though begging him to gain his feet. Tom struggled up, trying to ignore the feeling that by doing so he was instead moving sideways.

"Can't." Harry almost threw up again. "Can't move. Can't." He resisted all of Tom's attempts to drag him out of the ditch and farther into cover, curling instead into a shaking ball in the muddy, frigid water of the ditch. Tom drew his sword. If he could not bring his lord to safety, he would have to think of another way to help.

A new voice turned Tom's head. *"Riian!"* A dark-featured young man approached from the opposite direction to the battle, shouting something at him in a language Tom did not know. He wore thick clothes, overbundled as though he had no one thing warm enough for winter. *"Riian, hevhittar*—get lost, foreigner, if you know what's good for you!" He set down a decorated bag and rummaged through it, in an action that reminded Tom of Edmund.

Tom backed away, holding his sword out level. "Who are you? Where are we?"

Harry struggled up. He took one look at the dark young man and ducked back into the ditch.

The dark young man's hair curved down straight around his chin, thick and black. "My name is none of your business—and if you don't know where you are, that's your problem." He curled in his fingers. "WHAT IS THE NAME OF STONE THAT CAN BEND?" With a sudden jerk, Tom's sword flew from his hands to stick itself into the ground, just by the base of the huge tree.

Jumble growled and tried to stand up. Tom seized for him and leaped around behind the tree. He tried to use the massive trunk for cover, even though it was only between him and the newcomer some of the time. It dawned on him then that he recognized the voice from the night he, Katherine, and Edmund had traveled into the Dorwood. "Wait—is your name Seb?"

The battle back in Elverain had not slackened in pace or intensity. Tom turned to look behind him—which was at the same time above him—just in time to see Katherine take a barb from the *uhaari* on her shield.

"Everyone, hold together!" Katherine raised her sword and pointed it ahead of her. "Knights, regroup behind me! Archers, draw and fire!"

"Arrows? Silly girl." The sharp-toothed brother crossed his arms. "FOR THE ARROW TO REACH ME, IT MUST FIRST REACH HALF THE DISTANCE TO ME. FOR THE ARROW TO REACH HALF THE DISTANCE TO ME, IT MUST REACH HALF OF HALF THE DISTANCE, AND SO ON AND ON TO NOTHING. I CANNOT BE STRUCK, FOR THERE IS NO SUCH THING AS MOTION."

The volley of arrows arced high—but then they all stopped, hovering still in the air.

"Arrows." The brother snapped his fingers, and the arrows fell straight down toward the road, forcing Katherine and Edmund to spur their horses and scatter aside. "Really, now."

"Are you all listening?" said the sister. "Here is what we bargain. You know who we've come looking for. Walk him out, now, drop him right here, and we'll stop killing everybody, give you back your lord Harold and go along our merry way. Doesn't that sound all fair and lovely?"

The brother knit his brows. "Oh, dear. We didn't kill the one we're looking for, did we?" He looked around him. "That would be a shame, to kill him all in a rush, just like that."

Tom shot a glance over the rim of the ditch. Seb stood a short distance from the great tree, moving through stances and motions that reminded Tom yet more of Edmund.

"WHAT IS THE NAME OF STONE THAT CAN BEND?" Seb clasped his hands, then fanned them out. "COME FORTH, YOU WHO ARE SHAPED, AND BY THAT SHAPING, SHAPES THE WORLD. COME FORTH, SUBSTANCE OF THE SWORD, OF THE PLOW AND THE LOCK, SHIELD AGAINST THE FALL, EMBLEM OF THE AGE. COME FORTH! I PLACE MY YOKE UPON YOU."

Tom heard a snap above him, then another. He scooped up Jumble and only just dove out of the way of the swords that had started falling from the tree. At a gesture from Seb, the swords all leaped toward him as though about to pierce him through. Seb retained his calm, though, and made an action with his hands that reminded Tom of a potter at his wheel. The swords fell together, piling onto one another in a shape that grew ever more distinct—four legs, a tail, a rearing head.

Across the juncture, back in Elverain, the brother and sister had scattered most of the resistance with spell after world-twisting spell. The sister turned and favored the brother with a sweetly cajoling look. "Brother dearest, did you secure Lord Harold back there?"

"Eh?" The brother paused in the middle of a spell that raked hard fronts of wind through the crossroads, throwing knights from their horses and dragging fleeing peasants back and forth across the barren fields. "No, not as such. He's the one with the fancy cloak and the pretty hair, yes?"

The sister cast a spell that plucked one of the pack mules straight into the air, as though up had suddenly become down. "You might want to go and fetch him, or at least make sure he hasn't scampered off somewhere."

Tom steeled himself, one hand on the embankment of the ditch for balance. He got a good grip on Harry's sword and tried to remember everything Katherine had ever taught him about its use.

"It's your fault, sister." The brother turned back through the center of the crossroad. "I honestly could not resist. You *know* how much I love killing people."

Tom sprang forward, Harry's blade at the ready, but even as he did so, some unseen force snatched the sword from his hand, yanking it away to join the others forming into the metallic shape on the other side of the tree. He grabbed Jumble by the scruff and staggered away from the brother. "We don't have the one you want."

The brother looked Tom down and up from boot to face. "Mother's grace, I thought someone like Lord Harold would have better taste in body servants!" He smirked. "Whippy bit of leather, aren't you?"

"We don't have the boy." Tom raised his hands. "John Marshal took him."

"Don't be a goose," said the brother. "We've been torturing John Marshal for a whole night down in Rushmeet. I'm sure if he had taken the boy along, he would have babbled it out by now."

Tom charged the brother, fists up—but then forward was upward, and upward was sideways, and all of a sudden he was on his back in mud that was dry hot sand and then cold mud again.

"There, now." The brother smiled. "Just lie there for a while, there's a good boy. We'll be back in just a moment—maybe kill a few more peasants, just for fun, and then you, probably, and—oh."

He looked up past Tom, through the wide trunk of the tree that was there and then not there, at Seb and the creature that had formed out of the swords.

"Oh." The brother stepped back from Tom. "Sister, may I borrow the *uhaari* for just a teeny tiny moment?"

"Of course, brother," said the sister. "I think these folk have just about got it through their heads that they should do what we ask of them."

The *uhaari* moved on a carpet of its countless legs, closer and closer to the point where the roads all crossed. Once it reached the middle, it seemed to expand, unfolding into the angled space where up was down, left was right, and forward was backward. Tom at last saw what lay within the vanishing point of the inward-spiraling legs. He clutched his head and looked away, which meant looking through the angles of the crossroad at the assault the pretty sister was carrying out on his friends and neighbors back in Elverain.

The sister threw her silken hair back over her ears, standing in the icy center of the crossroad south of castle Northend. "Oh my. Oh *my*, this is good fun. Happy Yule!" She twisted in her hand, smashing the mule back to the ground and splattering its body wide across the crossroad. "Happy Yule to one and all!"

"Edmund!" Katherine only just dodged out of the way of the falling mule in time. "Edmund, help!"

Tom looked back across the crossroad. He had witnessed magic of various kinds over the last few weeks, but nothing prepared him for what met his eyes then. Seb had mounted himself up on the back of a massive horse that seemed to be made entirely from the merged and melted swords that had hung from the tree, woven together as though they were reeds for making a mat. He had fashioned the last few swords into a lance, which he held couched under his arm like Katherine did when she rode at the targets back on her farm.

"Well, hello there, Seb." The brother interposed the *uhaari* between Seb and himself. "A bit odd meeting you here, I must admit. Fairly sure Vithric gave you a different job to do."

Seb leveled his lance. "I decided not to do it."

"I always thought you were hiding something," said the brother. "The Clave should have done to you what they did to me out on the moors."

"Maybe they should have," said Seb. "But they didn't."

Tom got his bearings and gained his feet. "Jumble, stay." He circled wide around the *uhaari*, dodging behind the stone tower that was there and then not there. He turned to look behind him. "I said stay!"

Jumble padded along behind Tom, hackles up, lips bared to the gums. Tom had no choice but to let him follow. He heard the sound of rolling hoofbeats, the scuffle of footsteps and the sound of three voices raised in varied chant. He rounded the tower and leaped forth onto the road at angles to the one where he had landed, then stopped in utter shock.

It looked just as though Edmund had called forth a great wave of fire out of thin air, blown from a single torch. The sister held Edmund's spell at bay with fronts of summoned wind, but only barely.

From the other direction there came a trumpeting roar, then a squelching crunch, then an unearthly squeal.

"Oh, dear," said the brother. "Oh, dear, dear."

Tom turned to see Seb plunging his lance deep into the vanishing point between the jointed legs of the *uhaari*. The *uhaari* lurched back, oozing from an infinitude of wounds. Organs gushed and spouted, spurting in every direction and spilling steaming fluid all over the road and into the join of the river.

"Time to go, sister!" The brother leaped past Tom and drew the sister back toward the crossroad. "This is all rather *much*, don't you think?"

The sister flashed Edmund a doe-eyed look. "My dear little thing, we are going to tell Vithric *all* about you."

Edmund let his spell drop, scattering the last of his fire into the raging winds. "Vithric already knows about me." He drew his sword and charged.

The sister threw her summoned winds aside, clearing a path back to the *uhaari*, while the brother split the earth under Edmund with a word of power and a slice of his hand. Edmund recoiled, staggering this way and that in an attempt to dodge the opening pits around him. Katherine charged in on Indigo, spurring him to a leap over the broken ground. She scooped up Edmund in one arm and carried on toward sister and brother with Lord Tristan's sword-of-war raised high.

From the other side, Seb spurred his metal mount to a clanking gallop, splashing through the twitching form of the *uhaari* and racing toward the center point of the crossroad. Tom thought for one horrible moment that he was about to be trampled into the earth, so he grabbed Jumble and rolled back into the ditch by the roadside.

Matthew Jobin

Harry rushed past, fleeing back toward the crossroad, back toward Elverain, without seeming to notice Tom at all. The brother and sister retreated to the place where the road came down from the sky, then seemed to turn at a perfectly square angle and walk straight down into the earth.

"After them, hurry!" Edmund made a gesture that looked as though he were trying to keep a door open with his hands. "They're going to—" The in-rushing winds swept the rest of his words from Tom's ears.

There came a *whoomph* noise. The rushing arcs of air fell apart, fanning out into fingers of ice-laced wind and melding into stillness. The road in the sky disappeared.

Just like that, it was over.

Tom got up on his knees. There was no sign of Katherine or Edmund, of Seb or his strange steed—or Harry, for that matter. The folk of Harry's party could just be glimpsed as dots in the snow, racing at a sprint toward the distant castle. The wagons stood abandoned. He was home, back in Elverain, but his friends were gone. All he had succeeded in doing was to trade places with them.

Tom clutched his head. What to do? In all the teetering madness, what to do?

The brother's words came back to him. John Marshal.

Tom leaped to his feet. He gave the crossroads wide berth, just in case, then rejoined the roadway once he had passed on southward. Jumble sprang ahead of him, seeming to want to head in that direction even more badly than Tom did himself. Tom brought his long legs to a sprint, keeping the pace until long after the crossroads had receded out of view behind him.

Chapter 14

"Wolland." Harry raised his head and looked about him from the snowy hillock where he had tumbled to a stop. "We're in Wolland."

Katherine staggered over to join him, but dizziness overcame her at the edge of the unfamiliar crossroads between the shepherd's huts. She splayed out her hands to lower herself to the frost-hardened ground, but could not trust the ground to stay firmly beneath her.

"Metal, made of swords." Harry tried to sit up. "Did you see it? It was made out of swords . . . and that other thing, it . . ."

Edmund got up from the place where he had been lying in the snow. Katherine waited for him to explain, to say something to clear the clouds of her confusion, but he merely turned to a point on the horizon opposite the sun and stared in silence.

Katherine felt a nudge at her back. She turned and put her arms around Indigo's neck. "We fell so very far, through so many places." She held him close, burying her face in his mane, stroking his neck to calm them both. "How can it be that we are still alive?"

Edmund sprang westward as though trying to attack the horizon. "You can't scare me with just words!" He raged, fists in the air, his voice a screech. "I will beat you! I will!"

Katherine led Indigo over to Harry, keeping to the verge all the way around the cross of the roads. She sat down heavily, still unable to trust her legs. "Did anyone see what happened to Tom?"

"Then I will do what I must, whatever comes of it!" Edmund raged at the sky. "Stop laughing!"

Harry shot a look at Edmund behind his back, then glanced at Katherine. "I've heard more than one tale about a wizard that loses his wits."

"Edmund." Katherine steered Indigo wide around the crossroad. "Do you understand what just happened? Do you know why we're here? Harry says this is Wolland."

Edmund said nothing in reply. When Katherine reached him, she found him standing with one foot in a half-frozen pile of sheep dung, making the inward gesture she had seen him make back in Elverain, his eyes pressed tightly shut.

Katherine prodded his back. "Edmund."

Edmund jumped. "I need you!" He whirled to face Katherine. "It's not working. My spell is not working. I need you."

Katherine took a step back from him. "I am right here with you." She forced herself to stop retreating from the wild look on his face. "Edmund, please, if there is anything you can do to explain—"

"A lock of hair." Edmund looked down as though reading something. He looked at her, his eyes a chiseling blue. "I need a lock of your hair."

It was Katherine's turn to tread in the dung. "What?"

"Please, Katherine." Edmund grabbed his head, squeezing so hard that it looked like he was trying to squish his brains out through his ears. "Please. I can't think. Your hair, just a little."

Katherine stared at him, ready to say what any girl might say to such a request made in such a manner. Then she remembered Edmund breaking the spell that would have killed her in the lair of the Nethergrim, remembered him sealing the Skeleth away from the world, remembered him snapping the blade of Lord Wolland's sword before it could descend to strike her. She took out her knife and undid her braid.

"Katherine, come here." Harry got to his feet and crunched away through the snow. "I think I see something over this way."

"Just a moment." Katherine freed her hair and raised her knife. She looked at Edmund. "How much?"

Edmund did not seem to have heard, but then his eyes darted to meet hers. "Just enough to hold."

Katherine cut near the tips, freeing a tress of two curls' length. She held it out to him.

"Thank you." Edmund took the lock of hair in his hands as though it warmed him.

Harry's voice took on the tones of someone who was not used to being ignored. "Katherine, I need you over here."

Katherine turned to see Harry going around the crossroad to its opposite corner. Indigo stood with his head cocked, breath steaming in a snort. Farther on past both Indigo and Harry, metal glinted from the distant roadway, focusing to blinding shards the light that rose reflected from the snow.

"I AM MYSELF WITHIN MYSELF." Edmund took the lock of Katherine's hair and looped it around one of his fingers. "I REIGN ALONE OVER MY THOUGHTS. I STAND WITHIN THE FORTRESS OF MY MIND AND SHUT THE DOOR." He made the inward motion again and again.

Harry cast a sickened glance from Katherine to Edmund. "What is he doing?" He came closer. "Is that some of your hair he's got?"

Katherine strode past him. "Who is that coming?" Farther off, down the southward road, the metallic glint resolved into the approach of men on horseback.

Harry joined her. His breath puffed out white in a gasp. "I suppose nothing should surprise me today."

Katherine tensed. "Why, who is it?" The longer she looked, the better the approaching party resolved in her view. She noticed the hard-striding gait of the warhorses at the same time as the rich colors worn by the riders.

"That is Grimoald, Duke of Westry, a lord richer than the king himself." Harry shaded his eyes. "Beside him rides Leukso, the grand *Mrekos* of Ausca, but by marriage also the count of Darrow. He is the one leaning half out of his saddle to talk to my uncle Magneric, the Earl of Anster."

Katherine had heard tell of such grand names in her life, but had never thought to see the folk who owned them. "Those are half the great lords of the kingdom!"

"A very important half," said Harry. "The men riding last are Balamar and Gundobad, the sons of old king Eberulf, he who was overthrown and killed in the wars when our fathers were young. It makes sense, in a way— this is the fastest route up to the city of Rushmeet from the south, and Rushmeet is where I've been summoned to meet them."

Katherine reached out and brought Harry down into a crouch. "They're riding without guards or retainers and moving at speed. We don't have long before they reach us."

Harry turned with Katherine back toward the crossroad. "You there!" He barked at Edmund. "You're the one who brought us here. Explain yourself!"

Edmund ignored him. He stepped out to the place where the roads joined with the stone disk in his hands. He laid the disk on the frozen dirt and knelt before it, turning its rings back and forth.

Katherine stepped to the edge of the crossroad. "If you sit there, how do you know that you won't fall through again?"

"I won't." Edmund beckoned her near. "That spell is ended. The cost is paid."

Indigo would go no closer to the crossroad. Katherine stood indecisive.

Edmund flipped the disk over. "I've read about such things. Crossroads have a magic all their own. The right sort of spell, cast at just the right time, can join them at strange angles, letting the wizard travel miles at a step. We got very close to catching that pair of wizards, but they must have gotten one crossroads ahead of us before the spell ended."

"You've spoken about paying costs for spells before." Katherine willed herself to follow Edmund out into the cross of the roads. "That's your sort of magic, isn't it? Wheel-magic, I think you call it."

"*Dhrakal*, in the old tongue," said Edmund. "Finding the balances of the world and learning how to tip them. A skilled wizard can make the world turn to his will, but unless he wants to burn himself up in paying for it, he must find a way to balance the spell's effect on the world. The fire spell I made, for example—there won't be a home fire in all Elverain that will light tonight. I hope no one gets too cold."

Katherine looked about her. "But why is all of this happening so fast? All my life, I had barely heard about wizards and magic, and now this. It's as though the world had come loose from its hitching post."

"It's Yule, Katherine," said Edmund. "The five days outside the months, the five days between the years. They're always strange, but this one is much stranger than usual. Magic is getting easier and easier to make. I can do things I could never have hoped to try even a week ago."

"Why?" Katherine could ride, she could wield a lance and swing a sword, but what use was any of that in such a world? "Why this year, why now?"

Edmund flicked a look at Harry, who stood in the trees by the nearest hut, facing the approaching nobles. "I've worked out a few more things since we spoke last night. When we're alone again, I'll tell you everything I've learned."

Katherine felt a flare of anger, the frustration of never seeming to know enough. "You should tell Harry all that you know, and right now! He is your lord by the law!"

Edmund curled his lip. "Law." He said the word like a curse. "The laws of men are nothing but a crust that forms around power." He turned away, looking to the horizon again.

"The nobles have sped their pace." Harry returned from the southern quarter of the crossroad. "They'll be here soon."

Edmund leaped up. "Then I say north. There's a line of trees in that direction. If we hurry, we can reach cover in time."

"We'll have to go on foot—Indigo can't carry all three of us." Katherine took the long scabbard for Lord Tristan's sword from her saddle and slung it around her waist.

"Katherine, come here." Harry fussed with his clothes. "Can you help me get this mud from my tunic?"

Katherine was not sure she had heard Harry properly. "Who cares about mud? We're about to run for cover!"

"Not at all." Harry smoothed back his hair. "We are awaiting an embassy."

Katherine found herself getting rather tired of recoiling in confusion from one boy, only to turn and find the other talking greater madness. "Harry, we are in Wolland, the homeland of the very man who invaded you not two months ago. Those nobles are a gang who plotted against the king, and likely had him murdered!"

"Indeed so." Harry reached down to adjust his boots. "The loyal lords of the Stag approach, but there are a few missing from their number. My late father, for example."

Katherine found herself taking a step away from Harry, just as she had done with Edmund earlier. "Lord Aelfric plotted against the king?"

"Of course." Harry removed the empty scabbard from his belt. "He saw nothing wrong in plotting to overthrow a usurper."

114   Matthew Jobin

Katherine caught Edmund smirking at her. She ignored it. "Harry." Not knowing what to do, she started beating the mud off his back. "You can't mean to join those men."

"I can and I will." Harry went over to take up Indigo's reins, only to find Indigo shying back from him with an angry snort. "Those are the very men I was going to Rushmeet to find. I inherited my father's lands and title—Lord Balamar will believe I inherited his loyalties with them."

Edmund snorted. "And they'll take you to Wolland's castle at Dorseford, where Wolland will have you roasted on a spit." He crossed his arms. "Your pardon, my gracious lord, but that is the stupidest plan I have ever heard."

Harry cocked a smile at Edmund that Katherine had to admit made him look just a little less handsome. "You are a peasant, and so you understand nothing. Nobles may make war upon each other, but they do not betray each other's hospitality. If I ride in with the sons of Eberulf, Wolland will have no choice but to treat me with honor."

"Honor." Edmund spat the word. "It rules your world, and it ruins everyone else's."

Harry turned to Katherine. "Trust me, this will work. We'll gain entrance at Dorseford, and if we are careful, we'll be able to figure out what they are plotting."

"And then what?" Katherine threw up her hands. "How do we get out, once we're in? Wolland's not just going to let us go."

"He will." This time Harry gave Katherine the sort of smile that tended to make her lose hold of her wits. "Do you trust me?"

Katherine found the truth slipping out despite her doubts. "I do." She turned to Edmund.

Edmund heaved a chilly breath. He looked at Katherine, then sighed and nodded.

"Good. Settled, then." Harry shot a hard smile at Edmund. "It is not for the court wizard to decide where to go, only to aid his lord in going where his lord wills. All quite simple, once you get used to it."

Edmund bowed to him, low and insincere. "My lord."

Katherine took hold of Indigo's reins. "If he is your court wizard, then what am I?"

Harry answered her with a look that promised everything and said nothing. He turned to face the road. "Hail!" He raised his hand to the approaching figures. "The lord of Elverain greets you!"

Chapter 15

"**A**nd I'm telling you, cousin, kin or not, rules is rules. You get all that inside by sunset or you'll have to sleep on it tonight, right where it is."

Tom tried to raise his head. He found it very hard to look anywhere but the road. One pace followed the next. One pace and the next. He opened his mouth to another gasping gulp of frigid, snow-laced air. Jumble loped beside him, tongue lolling. His front left leg had started to drag, forcing him to lope a little sideways to stay on course.

"Oh, come now! It's going to take me an age to move all this!" Two men stood at odds on the road ahead, between two carts, one full and one empty. One of them held his arms raised to plead. "Just give me till evening bell."

"I tell you I can't!" The other held a spear and wore a dirty surcoat of red and yellow.

The first man was by far the larger and heavier of the two. "It's not my fault that accursed knocksman sold me a bad cart!"

The surcoated guard banged the butt of his spear to the road. "It's not mine either, cousin. Rules is rules."

Lead had turned to charcoal in the sky. The road ran up past the carts to an open gate between two wide round towers. Banners on the walls matched the colors of the guard. It looked like a castle, just like the castle at Northend—though maybe bigger, it was hard to tell. Tom darted blurry glances all around him at the cottages lining the road, the gleaned barren fields, the watermill down by the river. Where had he turned wrong?

"You could drag it in piecemeal," said the guard. "Drop it inside the walls and come back for the carts tomorrow."

"And hand it over to every beggar on the street?" The other man tore at his thin dark hair. "This is six months' work!"

The guard shrugged. "Well, you'd better do something, cousin. They'll be sounding sunset bell soon enough, and then those gates will shut with you inside or out."

"You've gone hard, Clarance, cruel hard." The other man jabbed a finger at the crest on the guard's tunic. "Who was it that set you up in that finery you've got on, who spoke your name for a watchman even though you're half again too short and you were once a—"

"Rules is rules! That's what guarding is! I didn't take this job to do favors for my kin." The guard raised a hand at Tom without looking at him. "Just you slow down and wait a moment, stranger."

Tom slowed his pace, loped, stumbled to a jog and came to a halt a few yards back of the carts. He heard a keening. Jumble tottered over to the muddy water by the roadside for a drink, but his legs gave out beneath him before he could reach it.

"Hoy, Clarance!" Someone spoke from the walls above. "All well down there?"

"Well enough," said the guard over his shoulder. He turned back to his cousin. "Look, I can't help you, especially not now. Captain's heard some grim news lately and he's got us all on the jump. The bell rings, the gates shut—so you'd better work out what to do while they're still open."

"Where—" Tom framed the word without sound. Everything spun. He saw the ground coming but felt nothing when it hit.

"Here now—steady, my boy." The man with the carts hovered over Tom's view. He did not look old, perhaps thirty at most. Snow dotted his beard, melting near the skin of his face. A long cowl dangled from his neck. He held out a drinking horn. "Get some of this down you."

Tom reached up, but he trembled with weariness and could not hold the horn.

"Oho! Look at you, hey?" The cowled man pulled Tom up and sitting, then poured a mouthful of wine between his lips.

Tom gasped and choked. He rolled onto his side in the muddy snow.

"There, now." The cowled man slapped Tom's heaving back. "Now, you see, Clarance, charity, that's what you're lacking. If your mother'd lived to see you—"

"Don't you start about my mother," said the guard. "What's wrong with him?"

Tom crawled over to the ditch and threw up, though precious little came out. Pain shot through his gut. The melting snow seemed to run right through him.

"Where—" He heaved one more time. "Where can I find the city of Rushmeet?"

The cowled man barked a laugh. "You're there, my lad, and now you have my curiosity in double suits! How did you get here?"

"I ran." Sprinted, to tell the truth. Tom had never run so hard for so long in his life.

"I can see that. From where? Dunston?"

"Elverain."

The cowled man shook his head. "For all the earth why would you want to go and do a fool thing like that?"

Tom struggled to his feet—oh, they hurt. His legs could barely hold him standing. "I have to get inside."

The guard stepped back to block his way. "That's a farthing, then."

Tom swayed. "What?"

"A farthing."

"It costs money to go inside?"

The cowled man shook his head. "Where are you from, boy? Did you run straight out of the Dorwood?"

"I haven't got any money," said Tom.

The guard shrugged. "Then you're not getting in."

The cowled man raised his hands again. "Now, Clarance—"

"Look, I've had enough out of you." The guardsman glanced back at the darkening walls. "Old Iron Lungs might heave round that corner at any moment, and d'you know what it'll cost me for letting a stranger in without the toll? My hide, cousin. My hide and this job. You want him to go inside, why don't you reach into that purse of yours and give him a farthing?"

Tom turned to the cowled man. "I'll help you load your cart."

The cowled man raised thin brows. "You can hardly stand!"

"I'm a good worker," said Tom. "I'll load that cart."

The cowled man considered. "For a farthing?"

The guard made a disgusted noise. "Pay him fair, cousin."

The cowled man glanced at the guard sidelong, then held out his hand to Tom. "Fine, then. If we're in by sunset bell, half a penny."

Tom grasped his hand. He staggered past to the loaded cart, a large and sturdy construct with a harness for a pair of donkeys or horses, though there were no beasts in view. One wheel had come right off, broken at the joint of the axle. Tom raised quivering arms and pulled the cover from the slanting top of the load. He seized the first thing on the pile, hauled it up, and felt the long and floppy weight of a bolt of broadcloth. He lurched across to the other cart, a rickety contraption made to be dragged about by hand.

The cowled man reached for a bolt. "Pile them long and straight, now! Don't just dump 'em or we'll never fit 'em all." He followed Tom to the handcart. "Step quick—the longer these things sit in the snow, the longer I'll need to rent a tenterfield to dry 'em out again."

Tom laid down his bolt and smoothed it flat. He felt oddly lucky that his feet throbbed with such pain that the trembling in his arms seemed like no hardship in comparison. He shot a look at Jumble to make sure that he was merely resting and had not seized up in a convulsion from the long exertion of the run. Jumble lay nearly still, but flicked an ear toward Tom each time Tom passed him. That would have to do for now.

"There, yes, just like that. Good lad." The cowled man nudged Tom's side as they passed. "Huddy Fuller's the name."

"Tom."

They crossed each other, once and again, back and forth between the carts. Huddy Fuller cast a considering glance at Tom. "You're a slave, aren't you?"

Tom did not spare the energy to shake his head. "Not anymore."

Huddy Fuller heaved up another bolt. "I don't know what they tell you up in Elverain, but you're not free just because you made it to the gates. You've got to get yourself a trade, keep inside the walls for a year and day, show us it's worth keeping you."

"I'm free," said Tom. "I was freed today."

"Then what are you running for?"

Tom spoke the lie he had been working up over a dozen pounding miles of road. "Chasing a horse thief."

"Oho!" Huddy Fuller turned to call out. "Hear that, cousin? Tom here says he's running down a horse thief!"

"What's that you say?"

Tom spoke breathless enough that Clarance had to step close again to hear. "See anyone on a chestnut courser, white blaze on the nose?" He described John Marshal's grouchy old riding horse as best as he could. "Stallion, on the tall side, past his prime but not yet gone to seed."

Clarance shook his head. "I didn't start till high bell—it's my half day." He turned back to the wall. "Hoy, Bennet!"

A helmet rose up on the walls above, then part of a shadowed face. "What?"

"Did you see anyone come in riding a tall old stallion, chestnut with a white blaze?"

"That I did."

Clarance called up to the helmeted guard. "What'd he look like?"

"Thought he was a boy till he got close." The other guard leaned out over the parapet. "When he opened his mouth, though, I nearly reached for my sword. Reminded me of the stories about bolgugs with those spike teeth of his. He had another man on the saddle behind him—older, looking half dead—said he was his sick father come to find a healer. He slapped a penny in my hand, and when I said I'd have to run in for change he just rode on by."

"That's him." Tom reached for another bolt—they got harder to lift the farther down he got. "The stallion's good breeding stock."

"Sounds like it," said Huddy Fuller. "You've been done wrong, my boy, and just a day free into the bargain."

A bell rang out from across the city. Huddy Fuller hurled a curse into the air and rushed back for the last few bolts. Tom found some reserve of delirious strength and staggered back and forth between the carts, no longer bothering to be careful how he laid the cloth. Clarance stood watching for a bolt or two, then threw down his spear and joined in.

"Hoy, Clarance!" The helmet popped up over the wall again. "Are you deaf?"

"Just a moment!" Clarance grabbed the last bolt from the cart, turned and tossed it onto the pile. Huddy Fuller threw the cover over the top.

"Don't you give me your just-a-moment—Captain could be anywhere!" The helmet drew back from view. "Get in, curse you, we're closing!"

"I said just a moment and you'll give me one!" Clarance seized the lead of the handcart. "Come on, then. On three and pull!"

Huddy Fuller grabbed the other lead, and on the count of three the handcart slurped up from its ruts and started moving for the fast-closing gates. Jumble roused himself and, with a whine, started limping along behind. Tom tried to push from the back of the cart, but in truth he simply walked at a stagger, his head resting down on the bolts of cloth. The gates looked like they would close too quickly for the cart to enter, but they slowed halfway through their arc and left just enough of a gap for just long enough. They slammed shut right behind Jumble's dragging tail.

Tom drifted, the pain in his feet far away. The wet cloth made for a soft pillow, and beneath the broad arch of the gates he felt no sleeting snow on his back for the first time all day.

A door drew open in one of the towers and the helmeted guard leaned out. He wore colors like Clarance's over thick leather armor and bore a crossbow on his back. Up close he looked a sour sort. "All well?"

Clarance pushed his long hair from his brow. He nodded. He was beardless, much younger than his cousin, and missing the lobe of one ear.

The other guard jutted out his chin. "Who's your friend?"

"Just met him." Clarance stripped off his surcoat—he wore no armor beneath, just a quilted jack. He handed the surcoat through the door. "He ran here. From Elverain."

The other guard snorted. "And I'm the Duke of Westry." He turned back inside and shut the door behind him.

"Here, then." Huddy Fuller reached into his pouch. "A half penny well earned."

"Thank you." Tom pushed himself up from the cart. He took the offered coin. "Do you know where I can find an inn?"

Huddy Fuller spent a moment in thought. He looked to his cousin. "You want some supper?"

"I wouldn't say no."

"Follow me, then—both of you." Huddy Fuller nodded to Tom. "You can stay with us tonight."

Tom floated, head down on the back of the cart. He seemed to trundle through the same village square over and over. Streets turned onto other streets, lanes met other lanes between houses that seemed too tall and far too close together. He belatedly started full awake in worry, but found Jumble still pacing wearily along behind him.

"Evening, Huddy." A figure passed them by in shadow. "You're at it late."

"No choice of mine," said Huddy Fuller. "Evening to you."

Chickens squawked in abrupt chorus from a shadowed croft as they passed. Someone opened a door and peered out, torch in hand. A murmur rose over the strains of a flute. The men turned the cart onto a wider street— the sounds grew more distinct, high voices and low, a tune Tom could almost name. He caught a glimpse of something vast and dark upon a rise between the houses. It looked something like a castle, but in such poor light he could not be sure.

The cart passed a tavern, and Tom heard a chorus of shouts calling for Clarance to come in for a round. Clarance waved them off, then turned again a few houses on, down a narrow lane between the crofts. At the point when Tom could not imagine taking one more step, the cart stopped at last.

"That you, dear?" A voice floated out from the house on their left.

Huddy Fuller heaved off the cover from the load. "We've got guests— Clarance and one other."

"Well, you didn't tell me! I've only made enough for us."

"Then you'll have to think quick, won't you, my love!" Huddy Fuller turned to Tom. "You go on in, just through there. We'll be along."

Tom pushed back a timber gate and stumbled in through the back door of the house. Warmth and firelight rushed toward him and nearly dropped him to sleep on his feet.

"And who might you be?" A woman chopped turnips by the fire. She wore her long dark hair drawn through a kerchief, spilling out behind her in curls that made Tom think of Katherine. A girl of twelve or thirteen watched Tom come in, but the woman did not turn.

"My name is Tom." He let Jumble through and shut the door behind him.

"Go sit there, then." The woman pointed with her knife at a chair on the opposite side of the fire, where a small boy sat curled at play with a pair of toy wooden knights. The boy looked up at his mother, then returned to his game.

"Up—out!" The mother waved her son from his perch. "Go play on the floor." The boy set his lip but took his toys down to the rushes.

Matthew Jobin

"I don't mean to trouble you." Tom approached the fire with his hands spread to take the warmth. Jumble made it as far as the hearthstones before he collapsed again.

"It's no trouble." The woman nodded to the girl. "Emmie, get this man some ale."

"He's not a man, Mama." The girl frowned at Tom. "He's just a boy."

"On with you!"

"Do you have sweet cider?" Tom sat in the chair vacated by the boy. "Or just fresh water, maybe?"

"First time I've ever heard a man say that." The woman glanced up at him across the pot.

The glance held. It turned into a stare.

The woman looked the same age as her husband, with a soft chin and but a few lines on her forehead. She scanned Tom's face with hazel eyes. "Do I know you?"

"I'm from Moorvale, up in Elverain." Tom could not tell where his dizziness came from. He gave it up to weariness. The chair took his weight; he sank.

The woman shook her head and shrugged. "Then we're strangers, I expect. How do you know my husband?"

"We just met." Tom reached out to ruffle Jumble between the ears, to reassure him and give him leave to drop asleep. "I helped him get his cart in before the gates closed, then he invited me here."

The woman dropped the turnips in the pot and stood up. "Well, you'll have to wait a while for supper."

"I don't mind." Tom's stomach chose that moment to growl.

The woman gave a laugh. She moved across to the opposite corner of the room, where stood a tidy kitchen with a short table, two cupboards and hand towels hanging from a pole. "Bring some cheese, Emmie. Let's have the old stuff."

The girl made a face, for she had only just stepped into the room. She swung around and left again with the mug still in her hands.

Her mother set to some cabbage with her knife. "You want a husband of your own some day?"

"No!"

"You want a man of your own, stop pulling faces whenever one's around."

Emmie stepped in again. She held out the mug and a wedge of cheese on a short board.

Tom took them both. "Thank you." He raised the mug and drank half in a swallow, then wolfed down the cheese.

The woman glanced across her shoulder. "You look half done in, Tom from Moorvale."

"I've had a very long day." Tom set the cheese board on the floor. "Do you mind if I take off my boots?"

"Go on ahead."

Tom slid off a boot, hissing with the pain of it.

"Oh, your feet!" Emmie leaned in, stricken with open disgust. "They're horrible!"

Tom raised the foot to view in the firelight. They were indeed horrible; badly blistered, with one nail cracked down its length and looking ready to come off. The boy looked up from his imaginary battle and gasped.

Emmie climbed back into her chair. She fixed Tom with a look that started as hard suspicion but melted into simple curiosity. "Are you running away?"

Her mother turned. She looked at Tom's feet, then at her daughter. "Emmie, go kill a chicken."

"I just sat down again!"

Her mother pointed out the door. "Now."

Emmie heaved a sigh, then got out of her chair. She pulled a long knife from the kitchen table and shoved out through the back door.

"That fat gray one, with the white tips." Her mother opened one of the cupboards and reached in for a salt cellar. "And get the salves and some goose grease when you're done."

Tom slid off his other boot in slow agony. He sipped his cider to the dregs. The boy knocked the heads of his wooden knights together. One seemed to lose the contest; the boy turned him down onto his back in an elaborate, flipping arc. The victorious knight approached, hopping along the floor in the boy's dirty hand. He jumped again and again upon his opponent's prostrate form. "Hah-ha! Ha-ha, die!"

Tom's fears seemed to barge in through the door as though they had run down the road just a little slower than he. What had happened to Edmund and Katherine? Where, in all this maze of streets and masses of folk, could John Marshal be? He found himself wondering if the cures he had used on the strange little prince had even had time enough to work. Maybe he had simply died on the road, somewhere.

The woman scraped a chopped mass of turnip greens into the pot. She sat down in her chair and cast a long look at Tom's feet.

"I'm not running away." Tom nearly left it there, but then he looked up at her. "I've . . . come looking . . ." He hesitated, on the brink, then let the words hang.

"Emmie's gone for a chicken, I see." Huddy Fuller leaned in through the back door. "How long's supper, then?"

"A while. I'm starting over." The woman turned and nodded. "Evening, Clarance."

"Evening."

"Well, we're just going to run down to the Arms for a round, then," said Huddy Fuller. "Hey, Tom? Fancy an ale or two before the bell?"

Tom shook his head.

"Fair enough. Running here from Elverain would drop me stone dead." Huddy Fuller slapped the jamb of the door and turned away. "Back soon."

The woman stirred the pot. She flicked a look at Tom.

"I'm chasing a horse thief," he said.

The woman raised an eyebrow, half in the motion of looking down at her stew. She dipped in her spoon and took a taste. "Your horse?"

"No." Tom cursed himself in silence—the truth had slipped out before he knew it. He fought to turn from her gaze; she finally relented and let him go. They sat in silence for a time. The little boy reached out to stroke Jumble gently along his back, soothing him without waking him.

Emmie returned with a headless chicken under her arm. Her mother nodded to the kitchen table. "Gut it, will you, dear?"

Emmie sighed. "Yes, Mama." She dropped the chicken on the kitchen table and started plucking feathers.

Tom stared into the fire, his thoughts aswirl. He sat within a city teeming with people he did not know. He had no talent for talk—he could not even lie properly. He was lost, and if he was lost then so was John, and maybe his friends as well. What could he possibly do?

He felt weight in his hand. The woman had placed his mug there, full to the top once more.

"Only cider again." She sat down. "I'm like you, can't stand the strong stuff."

"I'm very sorry." Tom sat up straight. "I don't know how to be a guest. I never even asked your name."

"Theldry. The boy's name is John, after his grandfather."

Tom looked down. The boy looked up. He waved a wooden knight—the one who had lost had returned from his grave to fight on.

"That's my favorite name," said Tom. "If I ever have a son, I will name him John."

Chapter 16

E dgar, the baron of Wolland, stretched a pudgy hand toward the cage that hung suspended from a chain in his great hall. "What will you offer, my lords, for young prince Chlodobert, only son and heir of our late and much lamented king?"

"This was a terrible idea." Edmund waited in his chair with his arms crossed on his belly. "The very worst of ideas." The rich smells drifting in from the castle kitchen worked at his gut—fear and hunger churned in him and summed to something very much like a stomachache.

"We found the prince, at least." Katherine sat across from Edmund, on the low bench nearest the high trestle table where the nobles took their feast. No one else was seated in the rest of the lower hall. If Edmund concentrated and ignored the row of booted feet on the raised platform just beside him, he could almost imagine that he was eating with Katherine alone.

"We found him, all right." Edmund slid a glance up at the cage, in which sat the boy he had last seen in his parents' inn, streaked with smoke from the fires below, curled up with his head on his arms and one leg dangling out between the bars. "And now we're trapped in here with him."

"Harry will settle things," said Katherine. "You'll see."

Lord Wolland clapped his hands. "Come, my lords, be of good cheer!" His smile kept its customary curl, lifting the ends of his rounded cheeks and making him look as though someone had just told him a secret better left unsaid. "The very crown of the kingdom is within your grasp! What say you,

Grimoald, Duke of Westry? What say you, most serene and noble *Mrekos* of Ausca? What say you, my man of destiny, lord Balamar, son of—"

"Speak not my father's name." Balamar, the elder son of old king Eberulf, had all the look of a wild-eyed beggar stuffed into the armor of a noble lord. "Say not a word about the man you betrayed to his death in the old wars of our youth. We are here to deal in the hard truths of statecraft and war. We are not come to sample the suckling pig at your Yuletide feast!"

"Speak for yourself, *mrate*!" Leukso, the grand *Mrekos* of Ausca, was dressed even warmer than the weather demanded, swaddled in glossy fur up to his laughing, winking eyes. He took an offered goblet from a servant. "So, my lord Wolland, what revelry have you in store for us tonight?"

"Revelry of all descriptions and to suit all tastes, most serene *Mrekos*!" Lord Wolland flashed the sort of broad smile Edmund had learned to fear most from him. "But, my dear Balamar, where is your noble brother? He is a great favorite of my son, Wulfric, here, who had hoped to break a friendly lance or two with him upon the jousting lists tomorrow!"

Balamar took up his dinner knife in a grip that left it unclear where he most desired to stick the blade. "My brother rode on to join with our knights and fighting men, so that if I do not come out of here alive and whole tomorrow, he shall storm this place and stick your fat ugly head on a pikestaff."

Lord Wolland boomed a laugh. "You are as sharp a wit as they say! And how was your stay in the fair land of Üvhakkat?"

"You mean my thirty-year exile?" Balamar carved himself a hock of ham and started eating. "Well enough, if you don't mind having stewed dog's brains for breakfast every morning."

"Ha!" Lord Wolland bade his son, Wulfric of Olingham, to stand up with him. "Well, once you are king, perhaps we can invade the place and teach them better cooking!"

Magneric, the Earl of Anster, swept out one arm in presentation. "My lord, you have yet to acknowledge my sister's son, Harold, the baron of Elverain, who sits here beside me. He tells me he was summoned to do homage to my lord Balamar in Rushmeet, but we had the good fortune to meet him on the road."

"Yes." Lord Wolland blinked his deep-set eyes. "Yes. I see him." His gaze drifted from Harry down to Katherine. Edmund felt a chill.

"A very, very bad idea," Edmund muttered to Katherine. They both had their swords, but what good would that be against a whole castle full of guards? If they tried anything, they would be shot through before blade was out of scabbard or spell was out of mouth.

"Now, now, Edgar." Balamar raised his goblet. "Let's not have old scores come between us, eh? Just because this stripling trounced you in battle two months ago, that does not mean you cannot both be my faithful lords together in council." He drank to cover his hateful smirk, but his eyes carried the truth across the hall.

Lord Wolland regained his composure as though it had never been lost. "No, indeed! In fact, my lord Harold, your arrival here only speeds that which is already set in motion." He turned to Wulfric. "My son, I perceive that my lady is now prepared to greet our guests. She stands in the wings — will you see her in?"

Wulfric bowed low. He stomped out behind the tapestry at the back of the hall — he tried to be elegant about it, but such a one as he could have no hope of elegance — and drew back into the hall with a noblewoman on his arm.

Harry let out a gasp. So did Katherine. For his part, Edmund almost felt like laughing.

"My lady." Wulfric led a woman neither young nor old, neither fat nor thin, to her chair next to Lord Wolland's.

Harry found his voice. "Mother!"

Lady Isabeau of Elverain could not seem to hold her son in the grip of her gaze as well as she usually could. To Edmund's eyes, it looked as though she had hastily arranged her veil and dress. It was only when her gaze alighted on Katherine that she seemed to find her fire again.

"You recognize the one who gave you life, my lord Harold — what a dutiful boy you are!" Lord Wolland slapped the table. "Now, my good lady and lords, we are all assembled here for a common purpose, are we not? Let us speak to that purpose. Come, then, feast with me. I have an offer to make."

"Fie upon your offers and your bargains, my lord." Grimoald, Duke of Westry, had a demeanor to match his name and age. "You tried to betray us. You took the knowledge of our plot and manipulated it for your own purposes. You took the confusion we sought to create by the murder of the king and tried to use it to carve your own kingdom out of the north, and now you come to us with a promised bargain to fold yourselves back into our ranks and share the spoils of a victory you do not deserve. Come to it, man, make your offer, and by the cloven crown, it had better be a good one!"

Katherine clattered her pewter goblet to mask her words. "Edmund, what can we do?" She shot a look upward at the cage, suspended and slowly turning many feet in the air. "Can we free him?"

Edmund leaned forward to offer Katherine more cider. "You have a crossbow trained on your back. No, don't look around—don't notice him. He's over in the shadows behind the tapestry of the boar."

Katherine lowered her head to drink. She flicked a look over Edmund's shoulder. "You've got one, too. He's up in the gallery, behind a pillar."

Edmund felt a tingle of fright. "Harry's a fool. He's going to get us all killed."

"He knows what he's doing," said Katherine. "He is noble. This is his world."

Harry stood from the high table with his goblet raised. "My dear and noble mother." He bowed to Lady Isabeau, then turned along the row. "My esteemed lords and knights. We all of us know that the question of who should sit upon the throne is one we cannot allow to vex us for long. The prosperity of our lands depends upon a common peace."

"Indeed! Well spoken!" Lord Wolland held out a heavy-fingered hand in a gesture of approval to Harry, then swept it back toward his other guests. "Here, then, my lords, is the path to that cherished peace. If you bargain in good faith with me, then I shall but say a word and the boy who hangs above us will be yours. If, on the other hand, you do not give me precisely what I want, you may of course depart unmolested, as is honorable, but with the knowledge that a claimant to the throne yet lives and has the full support of the lord of Wolland in his bid to wear the crown his father left for him."

Lord Balamar cracked his knuckles. He fixed a wolfish stare upon Wolland. "Then, my lord, we will besiege this castle, storm this keep and have that boy down ourselves, and woe then to any who defend him."

Lord Wolland's smile only grew. "No, my lord. No. You see, I have a number of agents, trustworthy men, who await my word in the great cities of our kingdom. Should they fail to hear from me in a few days' time, they will whisper in the ears of the men who support the Hound that the true heir sits besieged within my castle. They will come in force, you will be trapped between them and my walls, and I will be hard pressed to spare the lives of any one of you traitors to the crown."

There was, of course, no way to tell whether Wolland was lying. Edmund knew that was what the eternal smile was for, to mask everything Wolland felt or thought.

Harry turned back and forth. "Now, my lords, please, let us not allow this august council to descend into threats."

The Duke of Westry slammed his tankard on the table. "Let it descend indeed into all the threats that anyone will care to make!" He shifted forward on his chair. "Let's have plain speech and quick speech. I cannot abide flower-talk."

Lady Isabeau reached over and grabbed Harry by the sleeve. "Sit down, my son. You embarrass yourself."

A train of men followed the chief steward of the castle between the tables bearing platter, cup and bowl. They laid a supper before the nobles such as Edmund had never seen: roast roebuck aglow in a rich glaze; griddled goose with thyme and coriander; quail's eggs and mutton stew. An old man set knives on the table, then goblets that he filled with wine from a cask marked in Auscan lettering.

"Ah, how I have longed for a taste of home!" The grand *Mrekos* lit up with anticipation at seeing the ruby liquid pouring from the cask. He picked up his goblet the instant it was full. "Your health, my lords!"

Katherine took another chance to speak to Edmund under the clamor of the service at the high table. "We must find a way to free the prince, or at least stop them from making their bargain for him."

Edmund watched Harry take his seat in a humiliated huff, enjoying the spectacle in full before turning back to Katherine. "I don't care who is king."

"If they hand the prince over to Lord Balamar, then Balamar will take out a knife and slit his throat, right here and now," said Katherine. "Do you care about that?"

Edmund looked up at the shivering boy suspended yards above his head. He had always imagined that being royal made for a life of ease and pleasure—but, then again, he had also read about many kings who died on the point of a sword.

Katherine gripped her goblet, fingers tight around the stem. "And if the prince is here, then where is Papa?"

Lord Wolland took up his dagger and carved himself more meat in one helping than most peasants ate in a month. "Let us have plain speech indeed, my lord duke, but let us have it over our feed. I find all such discussion more pleasing with a full belly." He made a lowering gesture with his hand. With a clanking noise, the cage descended on its sturdy iron chain. It stopped but a few feet from the ground, just down from the high table, close enough to Edmund that he could almost reach out and touch it. The cage wobbled and turned on its axis, spinning little prince Chlodobert slowly around in the space between the high table and the rest of the hall. Lord Balamar shifted a sidelong look at Wolland, then stood abruptly with his hand at the hilt of his sword, making to go around the table and toward the boy in the cage. He found Wulfric standing in his path.

"My gracious lord." Wulfric crossed his arms. "You have not touched your meat. You would make our castle cooks so very sad to learn that their future king scorned their labors."

Lord Balamar eyed Wulfric, then shot a sour look over his shoulder at Wolland. "You pick a strange way of making peace with those you have already once betrayed, my lord." He returned to his seat.

"My lord Balamar, I do not expect your good grace and favor." Lord Wolland opened his hands. "I am a practical man. The more a man talks of friendship and honor, the quicker I reach for my dagger. Let us discuss what we can trade for our mutual benefit, and leave all talk of loving unity for the womenfolk—your pardon, my lady Isabeau. You play politics so like a man that sometimes I forget."

A group of servants approached the cage and shoved food through the bars—the very same rich food that the nobles ate. The boy prince seized what he was served and placed it in his lap, then took the goblet shoved into his hands, though some of the posset it contained sloshed out through the bars below him.

Lord Balamar made a sneer. "You feed him well, for a prisoner likely soon to die."

"I feed him as befits his rank—which exceeds yours just at the moment, my lord." Lord Wolland carved himself another bite. He leaned out to look down at the prince. "Eat! Eat up, my lord prince. When a man has food before him he should eat as though it were his last meal."

The prince popped a slice of goose in his mouth and chewed.

Matthew Jobin

"Ah, excellent. You, too, are a practical sort." Lord Wolland tipped back his goblet. "My lords, this I tell you—meat has a power within it. When you eat it you know just what you are. Consider, my lords, that for all our titles, all our august names and honorifics, that we are made of meat ourselves. Look upon yonder boy, what is he without the name Prince Chlodobert? He is yet skin and eyes, a pumping heart, veins and suchlike. I am sure that he now wishes to have only these, for it is his name that marks him, his name that means his death."

The idea came to Edmund like a bolt of lightning. He sat back in his chair, turning from the gaze of the nobles.

"Say the word, Edmund." Katherine breathed it. "Say it, and I'll leap right onto that cage."

"No." Edmund shot her a warning look. "Wait." He took out his workbook, then his quill and ink. He opened to a blank page and set quill to parchment.

The boy—Edmund had to remind himself to think of him as a prince— seemed far more alert than he had back in Moorvale, grimy and battered though he was. "Dorwood, Hundredthorn, Lum's Graves, Harrowell. Sky above and pit below," the boy prince said while still rotating in his cage, over one shoulder and then the other, looking at Edmund all the while. "Plow, sword, hearth, ship, wind, tower. Turn, turn, turn."

The Duke of Westry curled his lip and shot a suspicious glare at the prince. "What was that about?"

"Worry not, my lord," said Wolland. "The mind of my lord prince has been addled from his years locked in the lightless labyrinth of Eredhros. He spent most of last night babbling what sounded like a housewife's shopping list for market day, interspersed with commands for silence so that he might hear the approach of the crows. Oh yes, and cries for his mother."

Harry got out of his chair again, ignoring the sharp glances from Lady Isabeau. "My lords, one and all, might we not find a way to get what we want without war?" He turned up and down the row in hope of support. "I say only that, to acknowledge the rightful claim of Lord Balamar, we need but press that claim before a full assembly of the nobles of the kingdom. There is no need to shed blood!"

Lord Wolland cracked his smile wide enough to show teeth. He made a rising gesture with his hand. The cage ascended toward its original position near the ceiling. The prince ate his goose while rotating slowly in the air.

"Enough of this bibble-babble, my lord." Grimoald, Duke of Westry, wiped his beard nearly clean of wine. "I said before that I despise flower-talk. Come to it! You have the boy, and we want him. What do you want in exchange?"

"A free hand in the north," said Wolland. "Everything north of the river Swale will be mine as overlord—Elverain, Overstoke, Quentara, Harthingdale—all of it. I will hold it in fealty from the king, but from him only, with no other lord able to interfere. You will create me Earl of the Northern Marches, and I shall have the right to bestow that earldom to my heirs as I see fit."

Katherine curled her fists. "So, Wolland will be king of all the north after all, in all but name."

Edmund looked up from his work, his hackles rising. Both he and Katherine had fought and nearly died to keep Lord Wolland from conquering the north only two months before, and here they were listening to their homeland being put up on the block for trade like a pig at market.

Lord Balamar recovered from his shock with a scornful laugh. "You ask far too much, my lord."

"Then I deem that you will never be king, my dear Balamar." Lord Wolland replied with such swiftness that it seemed to Edmund that he had already guessed Balamar's answer, and possibly a few answers ahead in their bargaining. "Your family lost the war for the throne thirty years ago, long enough that most folk think it the judgment of destiny. To rally enough support to topple the Hound, you must eliminate their claimant. I applaud your plan to marry yourself to Bregisel's maiden princess Merofled, thus uniting the claims of Stag and Hound, but your claim will not run with Sparrock, with Anster or Merensil or any of the other lands loyal to our late king, if they discover that an elder child yet lives."

Edmund leaned to Katherine. "How old is Princess Merofled?"

"Ten," said Katherine.

Edmund flicked a horrified glance at Lord Balamar, who looked fifty years old if he was a day.

"The way this can be done without war is by marriage," said Katherine. "But only if the boy above us dies. Edmund, do you have an idea?"

Edmund got back to work. "I do."

"Then what are you doing?" Katherine leaned in to look. "Is that a drawing of a horse?"

Matthew Jobin

"Yes."

Katherine leaned closer. "It's not a very *good* drawing."

Edmund started writing a word under the hooves of his sketched horse, making sure the letters were large and thickly shaped. "It doesn't need to be."

Wolland washed down his meat with broad gulps of wine. "There is more. Young lord Harold and I did not begin our days as fellow peers of the realm in a manner suited to long friendship. If I am to become earl of the north, then he will be under my power, and I want to make the best start of such an arrangement. I wish to prove that I bear him no ill will for his headstrong and youthful folly at the bridge of Moorvale. Lord Harold's mother, a wise and judicious woman, has proposed a way in which the discord between our lands might be ended, so that I may begin my days as his overlord in peaceful harmony."

Harry leaped up again. He curled his fist, but the effect was ruined by his smoothing back his hair first. "I did not fight you at the bridge of Moorvale, my lord, just to see you reign above me!"

"You did not fight us there at all, my lord." Wolland smiled on Katherine, with a smile that made Edmund's skin crawl. "She did."

Edmund cleared his throat. "Lord Harold slew the wizard Warbur Drake before she could bring her full power to bear against my village." He had to give Harry his due in that much. "We honor him for it."

"Did he?" Wolland turned a smile on Harry. "Well, well, all the better for that! You are more truly a man than I had guessed, Harry my boy, and so all the better suited for your part in our grand bargain."

Harry looked from Wolland to his mother. "And what is my part?"

Katherine seemed to guess it, for she gripped the table. "No. Please, no."

Lord Wolland folded his pudgy hands. "That you shall marry yourself to my daughter, Helisent, at the same time that my lord Balamar marries himself to the princess Merofled. Thus shall the kingdom be secured, as will the north."

Edmund felt as though a beam of sunlight had somehow pierced the night of the place, shining through the windows of the castle without a hint of Nethergrim to taint it. Harry married off, Harry out of the way! He could have hoped for nothing better in the world.

"A double wedding!" The grand *Mrekos* raised his goblet. "How splendid! Do you know that every nine years, in our grand city of Quolapet, sixteen maidens are married off at the same time to a willow tree, after which they are chained to its trunk and—"

"My lady Isabeau!" Lord Wolland pushed the grand *Mrekos* aside to call to her.

"Perhaps we shall take a turn in the dance at the wedding feast? We are both of us widowed, after all."

Edmund had not known that the lady Isabeau could blush. Katherine sank down on the table across from him.

Harry turned to Katherine, then his mother. "But—"

"Do not look so glum!" Wolland laid a playful punch on Harry's shoulder. "You will be my son-in-law! We will be family. We will sit at each other's hearths. You will give me grandchildren to bounce upon my knee! Once this is done, dear Harry, I shall never forsake you, for you will be kin."

The grand *Mrekos* washed down his meat with broad gulps of wine. "Well, well, my lord Balamar, what say you? Does Lord Wolland bargain in vain?"

"It is of no consequence to me who a petty baron marries." Lord Balamar stared up hard at the caged boy whose life was all that stood between him and the throne. He turned that hard look down to the nobles ranged along the hall. "For my part, I see no choice but to accept, but once I wear the crown, I warn you—cross me and die."

"Cross you?" Wolland could hardly smile more widely. "My lord, you will be king, crowned by destiny itself! Who would dare?"

Balamar did not seem to find the joke amusing. He nodded his head once, though, and Lord Wolland took that for a sign of his acceptance.

"Very well!" said Wolland. "I shall come with you to attend this most happy event, after which you shall create me earl of the north before my peers. When all of that is complete, I shall release the prince to you to do with as you will."

"My first command to you as king will be to spare me the trouble." Lord Balamar got up from the table and strode away through the hall. "Just send me his head."

Matthew Jobin

Chapter 17

T om picked up one of his thick leather boots from the place where
they sat by the fire to dry. He slid it on. Blisters and chafes jostled for
attention up his foot and over his ankle. He let out a grunt as his toes
touched the end.

He reached for his mug and found it full again. Theldry set an earthen jug
on the empty chair beside him and returned to her seat across the fire. She
put thread to needle but did no more than pick at her mending. Tom drank
down another mug of sweet cider and filled it again, no less thirsty than
before. He pulled on his other boot with a grimace.

The bell tolled out across the city, a flat clang free of all music. It decayed
to silence, then it sounded once again. Jumble let out a soft *woof* and turned
over in his sleep by the hearth.

"Streets look clear enough." Clarance ducked back into the house. "Most
of your decent folk are in bed by now."

"Then it's time we three rogues were on our way." Huddy Fuller drained
his mug. He reached down to grab an object that lay beside his chair and
tossed it over to Tom. "Catch!" Tom caught the long, sheathed dagger in
both hands.

"I don't see why you're doing this now." Theldry stirred at the embers
with a poker. "You'd have an easier time in daylight."

"Oh, worry not for us, my sweet." Huddy placed a kiss on his wife's
bound hair. "Me and Clarance, we're old hands at this sort of thing and we'll

be sure to look after your dear boy here." He slapped Tom's shoulder on his way to the door.

"If I wait too long, I'll lose the trail." Tom braced himself on his chair and pushed himself to his swollen, aching feet.

Theldry let the poker drop with a clank against the irons. She looked up at Tom. He felt another urge to lay all before her.

He turned away. "I'm just worried that the thief will go to ground, that's all." He buckled the dagger at his waist. "It might be harder to prove a theft if I can't find him."

Theldry sighed. "Just you be careful. All of you. And don't worry for your dog, Tom. I'll look after him."

Clarance opened the door and leaned out. He crooked back a finger and stepped into the dark.

Tom followed at a stumble up to the gate of the croft. He let out a breath and leaned against the low stone wall.

"Now, you're sure you're up for this, Tom?" Huddy Fuller whispered.

Tom reached down to shift his boot. He nodded his head, then raised it. A sleeting fall of snow met his face. The bell rang a third time.

Clarance leaned out and looked both ways. He swung the gate wide.

"I don't understand." Tom fell into step down the muddy street. "Why are we sneaking around?"

Huddy Fuller shrugged. "By the law, we're all supposed to be at home with our fires turfed after night bell. But there's those that don't care for law."

"And there are those that don't have homes," said Clarance. "Besides, you'll find the very top of the town out after curfew if you know where to look, every nob and every merchant's son slumming about the place. That's why the fines never get too high. Curfew's one of them after-the-fact laws, if you follow."

Huddy Fuller set the pace with a springing stride that Tom found it agony to match. Clarance's long hair swung at his neck as he cast careful glances all around him. Tom came to the conclusion, after some time in deliberation on the matter, that the blister on the back of his right foot hurt the worst of all. His knees wobbled, threatening to give beneath him if he placed a step wrong and stumbled in the rutted mud. He was so footsore and so unutterably weary that he almost forgot the jangling fear that lay beneath. Smoke and supper smells rose and mingled from house after house.

In all directions lay the stamp of man upon the earth. They spoke and ate and slept everywhere, all around him as far as he could see; their hearths, their children, their lives laid across one another, all a babble. A distant voice raised up in a shout that might have been a whoop and might have been a scream.

"Thought we'd have a look around at the inns and taverns first," said Clarance. "If he's a stranger here, I doubt he could stable a horse anywhere else."

"And what better way to introduce Tom here to our fair city?" Huddy Fuller shot a wink behind him. "Every alehouse in town—haven't done this sort of thing in ages. What do you say, then, cousin? The Arms, then the Stars, then down to the Wooly?"

"The Stars first, I think." Clarance turned them down a street Tom thought he knew from their entry into the city that evening. "A man who tosses a penny for the toll and doesn't stop for change sounds like one of your wealthy sorts."

Clarance led them on a twisting course through the lanes and streets. The crofts shrank to walled gardens and the lanes gave way to alleys. The roofs above loomed black, the sky between them iron gray. Tom found himself walking hunched, watching the hard-stamped earth at his feet.

Huddy Fuller dropped back a few paces to speak soft at Tom's elbow. "Now, you be sure to keep close to us tonight. There's always your cutpurses about, your beggars who don't mind asking harder questions after dark, if you follow. Don't run off on your own, no matter how pretty she looks, and keep your wits about you. If you see—"

Tom tapped his shoulder and pointed ahead. Four men swung around a corner walking close abreast. They all wore cloaks of a similar cut. Steel glinted at their hips. They approached, stretching out single file to pass Tom's party in the narrow lane.

Clarance put a hand to the axe in his belt. "Evening."

One of the men nodded back as they passed, with the sort of nod that took in a look at them from bottom to top. They returned to their tight and watchful formation and strode on down the street.

Huddy Fuller glanced behind him. "Never seen them around before."

"Nor have I." Clarance watched the men slide into the dark behind them. "Been a lot of that lately—strangers out after the bell, going about in bunches. I think that's why Captain's set us so watchful. We've pulled in a few and fined 'em, but they just paid up and walked."

Huddy Fuller let out a low hoot. "I tell you, I've seen a bit of rough and tumble in my day, but the look on those lads fairly froze me sober. Say there, Tom—you ever been in a fight?"

Tom gave him no answer. They turned south on a rising course. The lanes widened, the mud dried as they rose and then, after one last corner, they trod on cobblestones.

"Aha, here we are," said Huddy Fuller. "Castle Street. See up ahead?"

"I didn't know there was a castle here." Tom peered up at the shadowed parapets looming at the end of the street, then turned to look out over the city, a wide darkness bounded by a few orange dots that marked the watchfires on the walls. They had come up from the twining lanes, up from the low reek of the city, but his hopes had not risen with them. Somewhere in his view John Marshal lay under torture. Somewhere, in all the maze below and around him, the sharp-toothed man who had wounded the strange boy back in the Twintree's orchard and nearly killed him and his friends at the crossroads near Northend had skulked into the city on John's own horse. He had to try to figure out what was happening, and soon.

"Looks grand from up here, don't it?" Huddy Fuller turned an approving smile across his home. "I tell you, there's no better spot in this world to make your living."

A breath of wind raised the hackles on Tom's neck. The sensation of exposure raced his heart; he felt small and foolish, helpless prey caught out on the high broad street. He looked around, down—up. He saw nothing but grand houses set back behind high stone walls, heard nothing but the lowing of cattle somewhere down in the city below.

"Nothing to worry about now." Clarance stepped out into the open. "So long as we're known men and we've coin to buy ale at the Stars, no one cares about curfew up here."

Tom turned to follow. The cobblestones struck like hammers at his feet. A cat alighted on the stone wall of the manor across the road. It flashed yellow eyes at them, then followed, matching their pace along the top of the wall.

"Ah, you know, I do like coming up to Castle Quarter, just to look around." Huddy Fuller sniffed in. "All these grand houses, this fine high air. Something to aim for."

Clarance snorted.

Matthew Jobin

"Just let me dream awhile, hey?" Huddy Fuller adjusted his cowl, throwing the long, trailing end across his shoulder. "Fulling's a good trade, cousin. You never know, never know."

Tom tore his gaze from the cat to stare at the manor behind it. A grand house stood outlined against the clouded sky before him, three stories of solid stone, carved and corbeled, shut fast and dark. He could not see the ground floor behind the stone wall that ran the grounds. The gate looked as strong as any in a castle, made of hard wood bound in iron.

"That's a nice one, hey?" Huddy Fuller put his hands to his sides. "Bet there's nothing like that up in Elverain."

Tom could not share Huddy Fuller's admiration. "Whose is it?"

"Oh, one of your fancy types, I expect." Huddy Fuller swept a dreamily acquisitive look across the front of the manor. "Wine merchant or silversmith, or maybe one of your big men from the castle—seneschal, chamberlain, watch captain. Why sleep in a drafty old castle when there's good lodging right out in front?"

The cat hopped onto the wall of manor and followed along to the gate. It stopped there and turned. Its eyes flicked yellow.

"You two coming?"

Tom looked back. Clarance beckoned from beside a tall building of timber and stone, the only one that fronted right onto the street. A sign hung from its second story, seven stars, gold on a black field. Murmurs escaped the shuttered windows, laughter and glints of light.

Huddy Fuller turned to join his cousin. "Here's the stables, Tom. Let's have us a look."

Tom ducked first through the door to the stables. He let his eyes take in the dark, then crept along the stalls. He passed a short cob pony, then a dappled palfrey, then a pair of draft horses. He reached the end, turned and slipped back past the others. "None of these are mine."

"Ah, well, there's plenty more places to look." Huddy Fuller hitched his belt. "But I tell you, Tom—you look half done in. What say we go in for a sit, and an ale or two? It'll pick you up for the night."

Clarance made a wry face at Huddy, then turned back to Tom. "So this man you're following, the one that stole your horse. Was he a friend of yours?"

"No." Tom stepped out onto the street—then staggered back in a clutch of fear. He only just restrained himself from bursting forth with words of recognition.

"Watch what you're about, you stupid churl!" The young man just emerging from the manor house across the street had nearly tripped over Huddy in the poor light.

Huddy Fuller turned at the step of the inn. "Oh, didn't see you there. Evening to you—didn't mean any trouble."

Tom could not breathe. A single terrified thought raced around and around in his mind. If Edmund could call a torrent of fire during the days of Yule, if the crazed brother and sister could wreak such deadly havoc with their spells, then what could Vithric do?

"It is no trouble of mine that the three of you carry on so loudly you cannot hear another man coming up right beside you." Vithric composed himself a few paces back from Tom, brushing down the sleeves of his fine shirt. He looked no more than twenty-five years old, younger than Tom had last seen him and certainly much younger than the sixty or more years that should have laid on him. He stood straight of back, middle-sized and of middle height, his strong jaw kept smooth of all hint of stubble. "I suggest you save your prating for the inside of an alehouse, perhaps somewhere down among men of your own station, where you might drown it among the babble of your fellows and leave your betters in peace. Good evening to you." He flicked a searching glance at Tom, looking as though he was trying to remember something, then shouldered past Huddy Fuller and into the inn.

"I think that answers the question of who owns the fancy house across the way, there." Huddy Fuller turned to Clarance. "You know him?"

"He's new in town," said Clarance. "Moved here just this year. I'd heard he'd bought a place up in Castle Quarter—didn't know which one—but it's said the man who sold it to him went off south wearing fine silks, with two dozen trained men-at-arms to guard his wagon full of gold."

"Well, I'm not letting some cock-snooted nob keep me from an honest ale." Huddy Fuller turned to scowl at the inn. "My coin's as good as any man's!"

Clarance shook his head. "Listen, cousin, we're never going to find Tom's horse if—"

"Let's go in." Tom did not know where he found the courage. He put his hand to the door and stepped inside.

High ceilings graced the wide tavern room above a maze of booths, each enclosing a trestle table and a huddled group of revelers. The walls sloped down in curves, smoothed with plaster that took the warmth of the fire and held it in the room, leaving the bite of winter forgotten outside. The whole of the walls and ceiling had been painted in rich russet tones. Talk ran in swells through the room—all men save for the very pretty girls who brought the ale.

"A good evening to you." A girl met them at the door. She wore her dress tight at her middle and wide open at the top. She folded her tray under her arm and looked Huddy, Clarance and Tom up and down. "Are you new to our fair city?"

"He is." Clarance pointed at Tom. "We're locals. Anywhere to sit?"

The girl wore a painted smile. "Ale's a penny, wine a penny and three—unless you're members."

"We're not," said Huddy Fuller. "We can afford it, though, don't you worry. Let's have us a table."

"This way, then." The girl led them over to the darkest corner. Huddy Fuller slid in next to Tom, while Clarance took the other side alone. Tom glanced around the room and found Vithric fixing a glare on him from a large booth across the fire.

Did he know? Tom stared down at the tabletop. Did Vithric remember him from the seven-pointed star in the chamber of the Nethergrim? If he did, then what could possibly save Tom from his wrath—and why wasn't he casting a spell at him right then and there?

"We cook at all hours," said the girl. "Something for your hunger?"

"I do feel hungry, now that you mention," said Huddy Fuller. "How's about some lamb? Hey, Tom? It's on me."

A man at Vithric's table reached across to fill his goblet. Vithric turned a thin smile to his companions and raised his vessel in a toast.

Clarance clicked down a coin. "And ale for the table—oh, but just sweet cider for the boy, here."

"Lamb, ale and cider, with the fixings, then." The girl bit the coin, then stuffed it into her apron. "Back in a moment."

"Oh, have a look at her." Huddy Fuller watched the girl cross back through the room. "Have a look. You're not married, are you, Tom?"

"No." Tom kept Vithric in the corner of his view, watching him dart glance after searching glance his way across the fire.

"Ah, free you are, free as the air," said Huddy Fuller. "Don't let those days run by."

Tom hunched down in an agony of doubt. He wished more than anything for Edmund's bright thought, Katherine's quick and confident insight, but he was Tom and he was alone.

"This—I tell you, Tom—this is where things get decided in this town." Huddy Fuller jerked his thumb at the table across. "That young nob over there, the one with the sharp tongue, he's sitting down with the seneschal, the head of the weaver's guild—and I think that's the provost. Everyone who counts; I tell you I'd come in here all the time if I could afford it."

The seneschal laughed, loud and drunk. He wore a cloak trimmed in sable thrown back over rounded shoulders. His white hair bore curls arranged to hide as much of his bald pate as they could. He reached out to clutch Vithric's sleeve, his face puffed red in merriment.

"So he's powerful?" Tom tried to keep himself from sounding too desperately interested.

"That young newcomer?" Clarance rubbed his good ear. "Not half. So far as I've heard he's already got his hooks into just about everyone."

Huddy Fuller shrugged. "Don't worry about him, Tom. He's not the one who stole that horse of yours. Ah, thank you, my lovely. Here's for you." He gave the girl a farthing tip as she set down their fare, then he pushed a mug across to Tom and another over to Clarance.

"Good health." Huddy Fuller hoisted his mug, as did Clarance. Tom glanced up, then raised his. Huddy Fuller knocked them both and took a long pull of ale.

"I'll tell you something about that house across the street." Clarance cast a cautious look over at Vithric, then leaned close. "Captain's had a few of us go by the manor grounds lately. He's had some folk come in to say they thought they heard screams from the place, late at night, just in the last week or so."

Tom clenched his hands under the table.

"Hunh." Huddy Fuller slurped another drink. "Probably just knocking a slave around. Them nobs—I tell you." He shook his head.

Vithric flicked another glance across the room. He stood and made a brief apology to his table, then strode from the inn.

Tom glanced at each of his companions. He barely knew them. Huddy Fuller had children. No—alone. It must be done alone. It was not a difficult thing to let weariness draw him down.

Clarance looked over. "You all right, there, Tom?"

"I'm very tired." Tom faked a yawn. "I think we should look for my horse tomorrow."

Chapter 18

T he tears came, unbidden and unwanted, while Katherine hitched up the bridle and set the saddle on Indigo's broad back. She wanted to believe that she was weeping only for the doomed little boy in the cage, but she knew herself too well.

"What are you crying for?" Edmund stepped out of one of the stalls down the passage, tugging at a lead to signal that the horse behind him should follow. "So Harry's getting married off to some noble girl. Did you really think that was never going to happen?"

Katherine composed herself and led Indigo forth from his stall. "I'm not crying about that and you know it." She kept her face in shadow to aid her lie. "Are you sure you can't do anything for the prince?"

Edmund stole a glimpse outside at the gathered gang of nobles lit by torches near the gates. He turned a secretive smile on Katherine, but a gruff shout from outside broke across his reply.

"You in there—Lord Harold's folk!" One of Wolland's men-at-arms leaned in through the doorway. "Tack your horses and get out here! The lords ride, and you ride with them, if you know what's good for you!"

Katherine followed Edmund out into the moonless courtyard. Harry sat astride a borrowed palfrey, slumped low in the saddle beside his mother. Wulfric mounted his behemoth charger at the front of the party, ahead of Lord Balamar, the Duke of Westry and the grand *Mrekos* of Ausca, who was still humming the tune of a song sung at dinner to the irritation of all present.

"Edmund." Katherine walked Indigo over to the nobles as slowly as she could. "It's Yule. You said magic is powerful right now. Please—think of something."

Edmund merely shrugged in reply, with a look of suppressed mirth on his face that made Katherine want to slap him.

"You're cruel, sometimes." Katherine pulled away from Edmund. "You really are."

Indigo turned his head, tugging back at the reins in Katherine's hand. He flattened his ears and let out a snort at Edmund, or more likely at what Edmund led behind him.

"None of that right now." Katherine jerked Indigo's head back around with much more force than she usually used. "I don't care if you don't like Edmund's horse—he's just a packhorse, anyway."

Indigo turned around, but raised his head and gave Katherine a haughty look that could say only one thing—*do you really think I turn or walk anywhere without wanting to do it?*

"Please." Katherine touched Indigo's face in supplication. "Please, let's just go from here." The pain of helplessness burned her from within, a draft that poisoned her as she drank, but she could not stop drinking.

"Katherine Marshal. Edmund Bale." Lord Wolland stopped them before they could join the departing nobles. "I shall soon be earl of all the north and overlord to your beloved Harold there. I thus suggest that you flee while you can, as far south as you can get, for the reach of my law will soon be very long indeed."

Katherine weighed the value of striking Wolland down then and there against the sure death that would follow from the ring of crossbowmen on the walls. "He's just a little boy, my lord. Please, I beg you. Don't kill him, just hide him away somewhere and say that you did."

"Oh, my dear girl." Wolland mounted the fine riding horse his servants had led out for him. "You are so very weak in every place where you are not strong, so soft everywhere that you are not hard. Pray do run far from here; I'd rather not hang you. It pleases me much more to think of you living out some little life far off south. Perhaps you will tell your children of the hero you once hoped to be, while you cook their supper in the hovel you keep for them."

Katherine let the barbs sink in—Wolland overlord, Harry his kin and underling, the little prince dead. She hoped at least that they would kill the boy quickly.

Edmund bowed low. "My lord. I thank you for your fair warning and for your gracious hospitality." He kept what seemed a carefree calm, but Katherine noticed beads of sweat slicking his bangs to his forehead.

Lord Wolland cast a smirk at Edmund, then along the lead rope Edmund trailed behind him. "Horse." Wolland blinked and stared, then turned back to Edmund. "Yes, horse. You should give up studying magic, my boy, and become a horse groom!"

"Thank you also for your wise advice." Edmund shook the rope lead. "I will become a horse groom and lead packhorses, just like this one."

Lord Wolland laughed and walked away. "I wish you good fortune at it!" He strode back toward his keep. He paused, looking at Edmund, then at what Edmund led. "Horse. Ha!"

A castle guard came by with a heavy pack. "So you're the horse groom, are you? Where can I stow this?"

Edmund hesitated, then pointed behind him. "On the packhorse I'm leading."

The guard turned to look at what Edmund led. "Horse." He walked along the rope, then shifted his pack off his back. "Yes, right. I'll just set this on the packhorse, here."

Katherine got astride Indigo and held out a hand to pull Edmund up into the saddle behind her. "We failed, Edmund." She got Indigo moving behind the pack of nobles and guards on their way out of the castle. "I hardly even understand what it was at which we failed, but I know that we failed."

"Yes, right, horrible. We failed." Edmund gave a tug on the lead in his hand. He cast a look around behind him. "Come on, then, you. Walk."

Harry spurred his horse along with the rest of the nobles. He cast a look behind him at Katherine.

"Turn forward in the saddle, son." Lady Isabeau's voice snapped out of the dark. "Don't stare at the servants. It gives them ideas."

Edmund snorted. "Look at him mooning. Like getting married to the wrong girl is the only thing that matters in the world."

Katherine rounded on Edmund. "Harry's doing this from duty! He's doing this for us! If Balamar becomes king, and Wolland earl of the north, then his only chance is to do as he is told and marry into Wolland's family."

Edmund usually flinched when Katherine got angry at him, but just then he seemed as calm as the moon. "So you mean that if the prince had been saved, Harry would be free again?"

"Yes." Katherine put her head in her hands, even though by doing so she jerked the reins and annoyed Indigo even more. "But there's nothing we can do. Dozens of guards, that cage . . . oh, it was hopeless from the start."

Edmund turned around, seeming to speak to no one in particular. "I hope you appreciate what I'm doing." At Katherine's quizzical look, he merely smiled and fell silent until they had ridden through and out the gates of Castle Dorseford.

"All right, I think we're safe enough." Edmund leaned very near to Katherine to speak in her ear. "Look at the packhorse I'm leading. Don't be obvious about it."

Katherine waited until they had ridden through the gates before she cast a seemingly casual glance behind her. "Just a broken-down, swaybacked old rouncy. Just like Wolland to send along a horse who should be retired out to pasture."

Edmund's eyes glittered in the moonlight. "So you think it's a horse, then?"

Katherine turned to regard him. "What else would it be?"

Edmund looked all about him, then dropped his voice still lower. "You wouldn't, I suppose, say that it was a boy holding up a sign that showed a drawing of a horse with the word *horse* written under it?"

Katherine turned again. She peered—the world shifted. Her eyes widened. She looked about, as though staring off into the starry night, then flicked one more look back, skimming her gaze across the pretend packhorse she led as though he were the least interesting thing in the world.

"It didn't need to be a very good drawing." Edmund seemed terribly pleased with himself—but then, he had every reason to be pleased.

Katherine wanted to poke Edmund hard in the ribs and hug him, both at the same time. She settled for a wry look. "You could have told me earlier."

Edmund stroked his hairless chin—Katherine had not noticed the slight cleft it was getting. "I wanted to make sure you didn't give us away by acting too happy."

"Then . . ." Katherine shook herself. "Then what happens when Wolland's men go back into the castle and find the cage empty?"

"They won't find it empty, not for a while," said Edmund. "When the spell wears off, I'm sure there will be at least a meal or two heaped on top of a parchment sign that reads *boy*. I'm afraid the drawing on that one is even worse, but it will do well enough for the servants who can't read."

The guards at the barbican moved in toward the entrance "They're all through!" The guardsman called up to the gatehouse. He turned a hard look on that which Edmund led by his rope.

Katherine held her breath. The young prince gripped tight to his lead, while with his other hand he waggled his parchment sign in the guard's face. The pack he had been given sagged across his narrow shoulders.

"Horse." The guard said it as though repeating the word. His sour expression returned. "Ugh. Ugliest horse I've ever seen." He walked straight past the little prince and stepped inside under the lowering gates.

Katherine shuddered with silent laughter. "Now what?"

Edmund nodded to the young prince. "We've got some ideas." He gauged the distance between the noble party and the darkened streets of Dorseford. "First let's hope the spell keeps up until we're through the town and clear."

Katherine slowed Indigo to a pace more comfortable for a boy with a heavy pack on his shoulders. She waited until the walls of the town had receded from view and the night pressed in hungrily around every torch carried by the guards. She called out ahead. "This packhorse has gone lame, my lords." She nudged Indigo to a halt. The prince stopped right behind, looking rather weary from his load.

"If it's lame, bring up its supplies and let it go." Wolland turned in his saddle. "Stay on your own out here at night and you're asking for trouble."

"We'll be but a moment, my lord." Katherine dismounted.

Wolland laughed and rode on with his party. "It's all the same to me." Harry cast a longer, far more significant look behind him at Katherine before the gloom swallowed him.

"Turn around, turn around." Edmund pulled the prince up into the saddle once the last of the noble party disappeared into the dark. "Can Indigo carry all three of us for a few miles?"

Katherine twitched the reins to point them back in the direction from which they had come. "Yes, but where are we going?"

The prince perched himself on Indigo's withers and took a grip on Edmund's shirt. "Lum's Graves." He rubbed the gem in his forehead, as though it itched at him and he could not relieve it. "We must go there at once."

Katherine sized up the boy. "Last time we met, you could hardly babble out two words of sense together."

"It's all rather complicated," said Edmund. "Trust me, Katherine. Trust us both. We have very little time."

Katherine shook her head. "I am not riding wherever I'm told to go without being given a reason, Edmund, even if a prince wants me to do it. He's not my overlord, and I don't need to do what he says."

"I'm not a prince," said the boy.

Katherine blinked. "You're not?"

"Of course I'm not," said the boy. "I am the eldest child of King Bregisel, who is dead. I am not a prince, Katherine Marshal. I am your king."

Chapter 19

Snores rolled down from the chamber above. The chill of night hung in the room, a damp not far from freezing on the wattle of the walls. Tom lay on his side, heaped under blankets on the floor. The fire slept beside him.

He should go, came a thought, go now and have done with it. He should wait, came another, wait just a while longer to make sure the city slept its deepest. He looked around him, trying to fix on some object that could occupy his attention. Closed shutters and turfed fire gave him next to no light; he could not tell whether he was looking at the shadow of Theldry's cupboard or the memory of its shape. He reached up to touch the edge of the folded table and found that he had guessed wrong by more than the length of a hand.

Another wave of weariness rose to drown him. He pinched at the inside of his arm, felt the bite of pain and came awake. He rolled onto his back.

The wall of the shadowed manor stood across his thought. Vithric's sharp and mirthless face glowered down at him. He had no plan, nothing but a desperate lunge into the dark. He could lie here and wait for another plan to come. That would be no more than sense. No one could say that he did wrong by it.

The rhythm of the sleepers changed. Tom wrapped himself under his covers but kept an eye half open. Someone padded down the steps, then stopped at the last from the bottom. The snores continued above. The

Matthew Jobin

shadow stepped off the stairs and crept around the other side of the fire. Tom gauged its height—it was Emmie.

The cupboard door drew back with a squeak. Tom listened to the sound of Emmie fumbling through the shelves. She dropped something on the floor and froze. From above them came a snore, then a mumble. Emmie picked up what she had dropped and put it back, then rummaged on with greater care.

Tom came back to his thoughts and found them lying on top of one another, bound into a burden that had ridden him all the way from Elverain. He did not know how he had gotten out from under them. He looked upon his hesitation, there in that kind house, and knew it for envy at his hosts and the comforts of their lives. He looked upon the muddy swirl of his plans and knew there was but one plan; do and risk, or do not and grieve. He looked upon his caution and knew it for fear.

Very well. Tom shut his eyes. Tell me, fear, what is it that I should do?

Stay here. Hide. This is too big for you—don't throw your life away. There is nothing more you can do. No one will blame you.

Let John Marshal die?

Let him die.

Tom nearly laughed aloud. He held out his hand over the embers. Scant warmth remained, just enough to kindle in the morning.

Emmie shut the cupboard. She crept back past Tom and up the stairs, chewing on what she had found. Tom sat up; cold rushed in under his tunic. He waited for Emmie to crawl back into bed, waited for her breath to join with her family's in slumber. They murmured and sighed all together, all safe and all at peace. Tom reached for his dagger and stole from the house.

Ice filled every wagon rut on the street. The sky had split—clouds broke apart beneath the waning moon. Tom crept back through the wind of lanes and alleys, keeping to the doorways with a hand on the hilt of his dagger. He took a few wrong turns on his way up to Castle Quarter, but traced back his steps with care when he did and soon found himself walking on cobblestones again.

Tom found the Seven Stars still awake, still leaking light and noise into the night. He slipped into the open, narrow space beside the stable—it kept him out of view of passersby and gave him a vantage point from which he could spy on Vithric's new home. He turned to look across at the dark hulk of the manor. The wall ran well above his height and looked to be sheer along its length. He had hoped to use the beech tree that stood on the corner, but a closer look showed its branches pruned well back of the wall—no help for getting over, but there was always the back. He stepped out to cross the road.

The door of the inn kicked open. "*—and then the Tinker's Daughter, her eyes a' bright and green, she said to me, oh, come and see my—*"

Tom flew back into cover just as two men lurched from the inn. One held an arm around the other, half bracing him, half dragging him out onto the street.

Tom leaned back into the shadows and waited for them to wander away home. The singing man looked to be in terrible shape—his companion had to keep him from toppling over with every step. Tom watched them weave out onto the middle of the road, then lurch across. He blinked in surprise, then crept to the corner of the inn. Their direction was no drunkard's stumble—they were headed for the manor. Tom took a breath, then took a leap. He stole across the street at an angle to their course and skulked up to the wall a few yards from the manor gate. He hunched down with nothing but shadow to hide him.

"*—come and see my* . . . what's the next bit?" The singing man slumped against the wall.

The other man thumped loud on the gate. "It's us. Hoy, it's us! Let us in!"

Tom peered closely at the men, ready to spring up and bolt if one should chance to glance over and notice him. He had seen them both before. They and two others had shouldered past him in the alley earlier that evening on his way up through the city with Clarance and Huddy Fuller. The singing man sported a mustache of grand proportions. His companion stood much the shorter, but bull square and thick of neck. Ale had dulled the hard edges of their looks, but Tom liked them none the better for it. The singing man bore a sword in his belt; the short man a thick, flanged mace.

"Open up!" The short man leaned his companion against the wall and put his fist to the door. "It's Roger, blast it all!"

Tom took a creeping step, coming up to weapon's reach at Roger's side. He could smell the ale on them both, see the sheen of sweat on Roger's face despite the chill. Footsteps approached from the manor—two legs, then four. Claws clicked on stone, then stopped. A throaty growl rose from just behind the wall. Tom cursed in silence.

Bolts slid back in the gate. The singing man leaned through. "*Are you the Tinker's Daughter, 'cause I hear she's got—*"

"Shut it!" a woman spoke. "Have you both gone mad? The boss'll have your heads!"

"What, is he still up?" Roger reached over to haul his companion to his feet. The singing man tried to stand, then lurched and fell headfirst through the gap. Growls turned to barks that struck off the walls all around the quarter.

"Of course he's up! Mugger, quiet!" The woman turned in the gap of the gate. "Quiet, Mugger! Stop! It's just Hugh and Roger."

Tom clenched his fingers into the stone of the wall, his hopes fading. He tensed himself to spring away.

"Here then, help me pick him up." Roger bent down, so close Tom could reach out to touch him. He thought of the dagger at his belt. Would Katherine—

"Mugger!" The woman let Hugh drop again. "Mugger, get back here!" The barks increased in volume but moved away at speed.

"Oh, now what's he on about?" Roger stood, then stepped inside and out of view.

Tom sucked in a breath. He slid along to the edge of the wall and shot a glance around the corner. Hugh lay pitched over on his face, his long mustache folded up across his nose.

"What is he after?" The woman stood just off the path that led from the gate up to the manor. "Should I get the others?" The door to the manor stood ajar behind her. Tom was through and creeping across the grounds before he knew that he had made up his mind.

"Just . . . just give me a moment, will you? Shut your carping." Roger stumbled off in the direction of the barks. "Probably just a—you know, one of them weasels." He disappeared into what looked to be a row of orchard trees.

"A weasel?" The woman put her hands to her hips. "Up here?" She looked over at the open gate, then at the house. Tom kept low and sidled around behind her back, creeping between the withered and harvested rows of a garden. He had no cover at all, nothing to trust but luck.

Mugger's barks turned muffled—he had his teeth around something and worried at it. The gurgling sound of his growls echoed short between the walls and the manor.

"Let it go!" Roger's voice came between what sounded like slaps. "Let it—fool dog, drop it!"

"Roger, the gate," the woman hissed. "If the boss comes out—"

"Look, just drag him in, will you? Mugger, drop! Drop it!"

The woman rushed over to grab Hugh's arms. Tom slipped past her, then padded up the steps and shouldered through the door of the manor house.

He had not known what to expect inside. He was so afraid that someone—perhaps Vithric—stood just on the other side of the door that all his thoughts spun in relief when he found no one there, then in awed confusion at what he found instead. His last footstep, quiet as it was, echoed off the painted plaster of a grand chamber the size of Lord Tristan's hall in Harthingdale. It ran up past two sets of wide windows, each of them fitted with what looked to be real glass behind the shutters. Shapes threw shadow over shadow, all of the strangest aspect—forms, bodies, overlarge faces cast in stone. A grand staircase ran from the center of the room to a running balcony around the second story. Tom stepped farther inside, feeling terribly small and at a loss for where to go next.

"You ask me, you should just leave him out there." The woman trod up the steps outside. Tom darted behind a statue. He found a doorway behind it, obscured by a linen curtain.

"No one asked you." Roger hauled Hugh through the door. The woman shut it behind them.

Tom ducked under the curtained doorway behind him. He found himself in a buttery and hunched in between a pair of kegs. He tracked the progress of the folk in the grand room by the sound of Hugh's heels dragging on the floor.

Roger grunted with the effort of pulling his companion along. "Where's the boss?"

"Where do you think?" said the woman. "I'm going to bed." Her course diverged—she strode up the stairs and threw open a door above. Roger staggered on toward the back of the house.

Tom let himself draw slow, full breaths. The smell of wine-must tickled at his nose. He felt the itch of belated danger, then a swell of elation. He was inside. He heard Roger rustling and bumping around—Tom had come to know him by his footfalls. Seconds passed, then Roger stepped back out alone and stomped up the stairs. Tom let himself rest for a few moments, let the silence fall thick on the house around him.

In that silence came a sound that tore his heart.

Matthew Jobin

Someone gave a thin, hoarse shout, a cry of simple pain, muffled and distant in the recesses of the house. It sounded worse than any scream could sound, for it lacked the tiny shred of hope that feeds terror. Tom knew the voice well.

He got to his feet. The dim trails of the cry gave him no clue where to look first, so he guessed at the doorway that led beyond the buttery. He found himself in a kitchen, the largest and finest he had ever seen, with more pots and crockery stacked at its walls than the whole of his home village could put together. There seemed only one way out, back toward the center of the house, but as he reached another doorway leading to the hall he found a thick door opposite, and just then another scream shook his bones.

Tom put his ear to the door. The scream had come through its wood—he could barely make out another voice, one raised in command. He drew the door back by fingers, waiting whole breaths between each nudge. He did all in silence and found stairs leading down into a pitch gloom beyond.

"You will tell me what you know!" The commanding voice grew clear. "You will tell me all you know! Where is he? Answer me!"

Tom eased the door open, fighting the urge to rush down and stop the horror he heard below. He felt his way step by step down the stairs with his back to the wall.

"I don't remember! Please, please! I don't remember!" The voice was half a moan, interrupted by hiccups. All control had left it, all reserve; it sounded like a man performing a perfect imitation of a wailing child.

"You lie!" Another scream rose across the second voice. "Where is he? Where is the boy?"

"I don't remember! I can't remember! Please—please! I swear, I swear I would tell you. I would tell you. I would tell you what you wanted. I don't care anymore. I don't care."

Tom reached the bottom of the stairs. He found himself in a room whose size he could guess by the reverberations of the next scream. He stood somewhere small—three arm's lengths, no more—with a ceiling that brushed against his hair. Both voices came from farther below. Tom dropped to his knees and swept out his hands before him. He felt past a collection of dusty furniture, caught a splinter from a stack of firewood, then found a hole in the corner of the floor. The edges felt rough and uneven. The smell of old earth rose through the opening.

"Look at me, curse you!" Vithric's voice drew out in long, chambered echoes. "Where is the boy?"

Tom rocked back on his knees. He felt at his face. He had not known he was weeping.

"Please stop. Please. I will tell you anything I can remember. Anything. The boy spoke numbers, numbers, but I don't know what they're for. Four, one, two, three, six, five. Does that help, does that—"

"Silence! Where is the boy, the reason that you fled down the Longsettle road two nights ago? Where did you take him?"

"I don't remember. Please—"

Tom slipped a foot down through the hole and pressed it to the top step of a ladder. He descended into a long shaft within the earth.

"PLEASE STOP PLEASE STOP I DON'T KNOW STOP STOP STOP . . ." The words trailed to babble.

Tom put his foot to earth. He stood in a tunnel of faced stone that ran out of view before and behind him. The light of a torch flickered through a doorway in the wall just ahead. Other doorways stood staggered along—one next to Tom, another a few feet beyond and opposite. Tom backed against the tunnel wall in the lee of the light.

"You will tell me, and perhaps then I will allow you to die," Vithric said from the lit room ahead.

Tom stepped foot over foot, sideways down the tunnel wall. He drew his dagger.

There came a shuffling, then a clank. The glow moved inside the room. "This does not end until you tell me what you know."

Tom lost his nerve. He leaped across the tunnel and through a darkened doorway.

"Please." The word drew out into a wail. "Please, I don't—"

"Silence." Footsteps scuffed out into the tunnel. Tom kept his back to the wall of the room he had entered, crouched low and tried to think about nothing but breathing slow and quiet through his nose. He kept his eyes wide and saw the glow change in aspect as it moved past his doorway.

Tom risked a glance out and watched the torchlight turning a few yards away. He caught a glimpse of Vithric's face before he passed into the next room along the tunnel. Tom waited—watching, listening, not daring to move. The wails turned to moans, then to sobs.

Matthew Jobin

The sobs sank away. He strained for any hint of Vithric's movements. He risked a roll forward onto his haunches, then felt his way to the stacks before him. He put his hand on a bundle of sticks, then felt their smoothness and ran his fingers over the steel points at the end. He searched farther on and found a pile of armor, a row of shields, then a dozen swords stood up in a barrel.

Tom felt the gripping urge to slink away and run for his life. He slid up the wall and stepped into the tunnel before the feeling could set in him and change his course. He kept his eyes fixed on the glow from the next doorway along, expecting Vithric to step out at any moment and find him skulking about with nothing but a dagger to protect him.

Vithric did not come out. Tom reached the door whence the screams had come and found it barred on his side. He pressed his ear to it but heard nothing from within. Quickly, before a thousand mounting fears could stop him, he pulled up the bar and set it on the floor of the tunnel. He kept his fingers pushed against it, letting go with slow care to make sure it did not rattle away down the tunnel slope. The door gave and swung without a squeak.

A moan rose from the table within. "Please, no more. Please—"

Tom darted forward, flailing with his hand until he found the face. He clamped his hand on the mouth.

"It's me." He leaned down to breathe it. "It's Tom."

John Marshal bit him hard.

Tom winced and drew back his hand. John Marshal lay splayed on a rack, his hands and feet bound to either end, lit only by the embers in an iron brazier near the door.

"It's Tom." He whispered in John's ear. "I am here to get you out."

"No, no." John shook his head—all he could move. "No."

Tom drew his dagger and hacked through the bonds at John's feet. He did the same for each hand. He reached down and grabbed John's arms. "Can you stand?"

John stared at the ceiling. His eyes bulged glassy. He smelled of filth.

"You must stand up." Tom bent down and tried to put his arms around John's shoulders. "Stand."

"I can't remember. I can't remember. Please," John said over and over.

"I'm not Vithric." Tom bent and hauled John halfway to sitting. John's dead weight was too much. He sank back again.

Tom gripped John by the jaws and stared down into his eyes. "Your daughter needs you. Katherine needs you. We must get out of here and find her."

John seemed to see Tom for the first time. "Katherine."

"Katherine. Katherine needs you." Tom bent down again. His back ached from the strain, but this time John tried with him. He got him sitting, then threaded an arm under his shoulder.

"Katherine." John seemed to come awake. "Where?"

"Sssh. We must get out first." Tom braced his feet. "With me."

He heaved with all his might, but John could not seem to work his legs. They slumped together on the floor. John moaned.

Tom's heart thundered. "Quiet. Please, you must try." He put all he could into an overhand pull and managed to get John up and leaning on him. John slumped on his ankles, the whole of his limp weight hanging on Tom's shoulder. They took a step, then two ragged breaths, then another agonizing step to the threshold and through.

Chapter 20

The Day of the Hearth, The Third Day of Yule

Katherine hopped from Indigo's back. "This is Clover." She reached up to touch the face of the mare who was hitched to a tree by the roadside. She turned to look back at Edmund. "One of the horses that went missing from my papa's farm."

Poor Clover looked to have been ridden hard. She had eaten all the scatter of oats tossed before her that she could reach, but many of them were out of the range of her haltered muzzle. She had paced many a circle around the tree where she had been tied, yanking the knots that bound her so taut that nothing but a knife could set her free.

"Those two wizards." Edmund peered down the darkened road, first onward and then back the way they had come. "The ones who brought that creature forth in the Dorwood—and then said they were going to your father to borrow some horses."

Katherine felt a sudden churn. Her papa's face returned to her, bitter and haggard, his words more cutting than she had ever known them to be.

"We're here." The boy king rubbed absently at the gem in his forehead. "Yes, here. Soon."

Katherine pushed her papa's face aside. "And where is here?"

Edmund slithered out of the saddle and heavily down to the earth. "Lum's Graves."

"I've heard of those," said Katherine. "A bunch of old tombs, aren't they?"

Edmund nodded. "Very old tombs, older than the kingdom itself—and the place those sister and brother wizards said they were going next, remember?"

Katherine helped the boy down from Indigo's back, just off the road before the first hovels of a night-cloaked village. "Where now, then?"

The boy king strode off into the dead dark as though he knew exactly where, disappearing through a hedge into the gloom in but a few steps.

Katherine brought Indigo to the verge. "Should we follow him?"

Edmund picked himself up, dusted the snow from his breeches and slung the metal disk in its satchel on his back. "He's our king." He hopped over the roadside ditch and shouldered into the hedge beyond.

Katherine swept the remaining oats within range of Clover. "Back soon. I promise." She patted Clover's snout, then led Indigo off the road, trampling through the bushes behind Edmund.

Beyond the hedge, above the fields south of the village, rose a long, low mound touched but gently by the light of the stars. It cut across long strips of barren field, its crown of trees marking it out above the surrounding land as much as did its modest height. For the briefest instant, Katherine thought she caught sight of stealthy movement around the mound's far side, but a longer look showed her nothing and made her wonder whether she had started jumping at shadows.

The boy quickened his pace just as Katherine caught up to him. "He's already started. The path splits—he's alive and he's dead. Hurry."

Katherine had no trouble keeping pace with the boy since one of her strides counted for nearly two of his. "Who has started what? Edmund, you never explained a single thing on our way here, you just fiddled with that silly disk the whole time."

The boy touched the gem on his forehead as though it hurt him. "Girl, go around to the west." He waved to the place where one end of the mound sloped down to meet a hedgerow. "Keep your sword out. Come in at any sound of trouble, as quickly as you can."

"What? I'm not taking orders from—" Katherine checked herself and raised her sword in salute. "I beg pardon, Your Grace. As you will."

Matthew Jobin

Edmund drew his own sword, then seemed to think better of it and sheathed it again. He gave Katherine one encouraging nod of his head, then followed the boy king due south toward the center of the distant mound.

Katherine hopped back up astride Indigo. She stroked his mane. "You're the only boy who always makes sense."

Indigo let out a snort, tossed his head and followed the nudge of Katherine's legs around to the west of the great burial mound. Katherine got her papa's shield strapped to her arm, then drew Lord Tristan's sword. She had ridden to the far edge of the field by the time she heard another voice from high among the trees:

"You are summoned and bound by covenant. On pain of the crumbling rust, you are bound to my will. Attend me."

Katherine had heard the voice before. It was one of the wizards she had heard outside the hut in the Dorwood, the one called Roki, who had helped guide the strange creature she had heard there out of the forest. Roki had said that he was going east while his friend Seb would go south—it seemed that Katherine had found Roki's intended destination.

"Attend me! You are summoned and bound by covenant." Roki followed his attempted spell with a muttered curse. "Would have thought this one would be easier."

Katherine found a deer track leading up into the trees on the mound. She steered Indigo along the slope, holding up her shield to knock ice-laden branches from her path. There was no way to do it quietly, so she contented herself with the hope that Roki would be like Edmund often was, sunk so deep in the trance of his magic that he would not spare a thought for anything he saw or heard. She cast searching looks along the broad northern rise of the mound, but caught no sign of Edmund or the boy.

"King's command or not, this makes for bad tactics." Katherine slowed Indigo to a careful walk. Any other horse, surrounded by reaching branches in the dark and approaching a chanting wizard, might have shied back or at least made a nervous whinny, but Indigo knew what Katherine wanted of him. He moved his muscled bulk with as much care as he could, breathing low and quiet while he waited for his rider to give the next command.

"All right, I'll try it the way Seb would do it." Roki took in a long breath. "What is the boon and bane of men? Come you forth, protector and destroyer."

The rumble that followed knocked Katherine back in the saddle. She dug her heels down in the stirrups, doing her best to move with Indigo's lunging steps as he tried to find his footing on suddenly shifting ground. Up ahead, on the long brow of the summit, an unearthly, metallic grinding contested with the crunch of tearing stone for the most horrific sounds Katherine had ever heard. Doors swung wide from the earth atop the mound, then a light sprang up as bright as the sun, blinding Katherine and making Indigo stumble almost to the ground.

"Come you forth, heart of the home and ruiner of the house." Roki's voice rose with the intensity of the light. "Come forth! I place my yoke upon you."

Katherine got control of Indigo, thanking him in silence for being the bravest horse she had ever known. He even approached the summit at her silent urging, head down and striding with steady purpose, ready at an instant's notice to spring to a charge.

"There we go." Roki moved in the shadow of the flame before him. "Now—um, sit. Stay. There's a—"

"Why, good evening, Roki." A sweet, soft, thoroughly feminine voice floated across from the trees opposite. "What a happy chance, to meet you all the way out here."

Roki whirled around, words of power at his lips. The girl from the crossroads met them with her own, somehow louder than Roki's, without raising her voice. A pall of steam formed among the coalescing shapes that made war upon each other. Indigo broke and shied, for brave as he was, he could not fathom what he saw or smelled in the clearing ahead. By the time Katherine got control again, it was over.

The sharp-toothed brother stood in starlight over Roki, who was desperately trying to crawl away beneath him. "We were tasked with finding and killing the last heir of the Hound." He put a boot on Roki's back to stop his feeble attempt at escape. "Wasn't your job to kill off the last few wizards who would not join us? I can't see how you could accomplish that all the way out here."

Roki collapsed. "Couldn't do it."

"Dearest Roki, don't you want the new age to dawn?" The sister's voice was a giggling imitation of soothing pity. "Don't you want us to be free at last of the chains placed upon us by the needs and cares of lesser folk? Everything past the end of this Yule can be ours to do with just as we like.

How silly of you to toss that aside, merely to die on a cold lump of ground like this."

Roki coughed. "Please. Let me go."

The brother pressed his foot hard into Roki's back. "Mother's grace, Roki, are you the reason we couldn't find the Beast of Life up in the Dorwood? Did you hide that great lumbering thing somewhere?"

"Please." Roki gasped and wheedled. "Mercy!"

"Oh, Roki." The brother laughed. "You saw what old Warbur Drake did to my sister, to me and Ellí, out there on the moors. I remember—you were there. You watched."

Roki let out a wheeze. "Wanted to stop it. Would have."

"But you didn't," said the brother. "And now you ask for mercy, something that you know I no longer have."

There rose a piercing scream from the clearing, then another—cut short.

Katherine got Indigo wheeled around at last. She raised her shield, heart in her mouth. She made a silent wish for Edmund's aid, then spurred Indigo to a charge. She did not know what she would do with Roki, if she got the chance, but knew what she needed to do with the other two.

The sister noticed first, wheeling with a screech that seemed to tell the truth under the purring tones of her voice. She spoke words that crackled and pulled lightning in across the sky. Katherine felt the buzz, the burn, and then saw white. Indigo let out a bellow and stumbled, throwing Katherine forward from the saddle.

The world spun—ground, flame, stars, the sword Katherine had let fall from her grip. She had time and thought enough to land shoulder to the ground, but landed hard, the force of it knocking her breath from her body. By the time she had her wits, it was too late. The sister stood over her, one elegant boot atop her upturned shield.

"Now, who might you be?" The sister drew a thin dagger from her sleeve. "No, no, never mind. I'll ask your corpse. Less chitchat, that way." She leaned in, blade gleaming—

—and was suddenly pulled, squealing, high into the air.

"No one hurts her." Edmund's voice seemed to drum the ground. He held his hand high, his fingers curled, his eyes twin pools of heartless winter ice. "No one *ever* hurts her!" He clenched his hand tight. The sister's screams suddenly ended among the crunch of bone.

Katherine caught her breath, surprised to be alive. She hauled her shield across her chest. The sound of Indigo's whinnies roused her to wakeful fear. She looked up, just in time to see the crushed, ruined corpse of the sister thud to the ground beside her.

"Edmund!" Katherine rolled aside, leaping to a crouch with her shield up in the direction where she had last marked her other enemy. "Edmund, the other one, the brother, where—"

Her vision cleared. She stood up.

The brother lay on his back, eyes glassy in the light of the flame across the tomb, his chest caved in by two round indentations. His last breath came out like a sigh.

Indigo let out a snort. He cocked his tail, then walked away, leaving bloody hoofprints in the snow.

Edmund sank to his knees. His eyes met Katherine's. He looked away.

"This other one is also dead." The boy king stopped over Roki's sprawled form. "This is not the ending I had hoped for. We were too slow."

Horror shot through Katherine in waves. "Well, if you had told me why we were hurrying, I might have known what to do!"

The boy king shook his gem-studded, unevenly featured head. "I did not yet know why we were hurrying. I only saw the path splitting, and this one here both alive and dead."

Katherine found Lord Tristan's sword and sheathed it. The sister lay there before her, half delicately pretty and half a crushed and gory ruin. A noise drew Katherine's attention and her gaze. She spun and recoiled from the thing that had crawled up from Lum's Graves to loom before her, standing as tall at the shoulder as she sat in the saddle.

"Its heart," she said, as Indigo backed away beneath her. "How can such a thing be alive?"

The creature that stood before her was a dog, though it seemed wrong to use the same word for such a beast as well as for Jumble. The flesh of its chest looked like it had burned away, exposing charred and blackened ribs— and its heart, which burned white-hot, blazing and blazing without ever seeming to consume itself. The creature stood over the mouth of an opened tomb. It let out a mournful howl—the sound of it like the roar and whistle of a bonfire.

Katherine kept her shield raised and her sword at the ready. "Edmund." She walked Indigo back a pace. "Edmund, what are we supposed to do?"

Edmund stood pale over the body of the sister. He trembled, one hand over his face. Through her own revulsion, Katherine felt an unexpected twinge of relief at the sight of his remorse, but she had no time to humor it.

"Edmund!" Katherine snapped him from his trance. "What is this thing? Do we fight it?"

"I don't know." Edmund turned to the huge, ever-burning creature before him, then to the boy king. "Your Grace?"

The boy king shook his head. "I'm afraid I can't see that far."

"This one called Roki, he helped call forth that other creature, then he borrowed a horse from Papa," said Katherine. "He came here, and these other two ambushed him—the same two who have been trying so hard to kill you, Your Grace. What side does that place him on?"

The burning dog crouched low, as though making ready to spring. It turned its gaze—eyes that glowed red as embers—on Katherine and Indigo. A growl erupted from its throat, one that sounded at the same time like the roar of coals blown by the bellows of a blacksmith.

"Say the word, Edmund." Katherine grabbed for her sword. "Say the word and I'll do what I can against it."

Edmund looked down again at the dead brother and sister, then at Roki. "No. Let it go."

Katherine backed away from the entrance to the tomb. The burning dog strode forth, its every step melting snow. It lowered its head to Edmund, sniffed the ground, then turned and dashed off the grave mound, breaking into a gallop that not even Indigo could hope to match.

Katherine watched the creature diminish into the west until it looked no larger than a candle flame. "Was that what was supposed to happen?"

"I don't know." Edmund held his head.

The boy king stepped over the bodies of the three dead wizards and to the edge of the tomb. "Strange. I know this place. I've been here before, but I can't remember when."

Edmund sat down. He laid his head on crossed arms. "Should we bury them?"

Katherine came to his side. "Edmund, you saved my life." She reached down a hand. "Would you have it any other way?"

That seemed to shake Edmund from his trance. He grabbed the metal disk and slung it over his shoulder, then accepted Katherine's help onto Indigo's back. "Your Grace, by your leave." He held out his own hand in turn. The boy king took Edmund's hand and clambered onto Indigo's back. Katherine looked out across the three bodies strewn across the summit. She set her heels, urging Indigo on and away.

Chapter 21

T om could barely hold John Marshal up. He turned from the light, away Vithric's underground chambers, following the passage down into the earth. John seemed to know not to cry out, but with every few shambling strides he sank, gripping Tom at the join of shoulder and neck, each finger pressed to the bone.

The tunnel narrowed in, forcing Tom to bend, making the limp weight on his shoulder all the harder to bear. He risked a glance back, but could not discern any sense of direction—the glow from the chamber had faded to nothing.

"Wait." He spoke a puff of breath, no more, but stopped moving. "Rest. Rest a moment." He leaned to the wall—then away, brushing filth from his hair with his free hand.

"Where is Katherine?" John Marshal raised his head and gave throat to his voice. "Where is my daughter?"

"Please, Master Marshal. Please be quiet."

Echoes died, then John sagged lower. "A dream. I am dreaming."

"Onward." Tom tugged John moving again. A strange feeling woke in him, the same sort of hushed, tingled feeling he had gotten in the Dorwood, but instead of teeming springtime warmth, this feeling came cool, dry and solid. He suddenly knew what it might feel like to stay silent and not move for a thousand years.

"There are carvings on the wall." He reached out his free hand to trace them, then walked on. "I've seen this in places like this before, under the—"

John's grip hardened on Tom's neck. "No! Wait."

Tom stopped. He scuffed his foot and listened to the sound of its return as though from miles away. He pushed his toes forward to feel out the edge before him.

"Chasm." John's breath seemed able only to get out his words one at a time. "Ahead. Deep."

Tom clapped his hands, just once. "Nothing." He listened to the echo. "A long nothing."

"Hurry." John slipped and slid—for a frightened instant Tom thought he was about to tumble them both down into the chasm before them. "Must hurry."

"Wait here." Tom lowered John down against the entrance, then crept up to the edge of the chasm. Wind rushed through his hair from below, far below.

John made no sound save for his labored breathing. Tom crept sideways, tracing his fingers along the edge of the chasm before him, listening all the while for any sound of the pursuit whose coming would doom both him and John. His hand struck stone projecting out over the chasm. His fingers slid along an expanse that sloped gently upward. "Master Marshal, here. A bridge." He turned back to find that John had managed to crawl his way. Breath by breath, on hands and knees, carefully testing each length of stone before him, he led John across the split in the earth.

"On." John heaved himself up with a gasp of effort. "Onward before Vithric finds us."

Tom lent John his arm. "I don't understand why he hasn't found us already." He helped John across to the other side, then stood and unbent his back, for the ceiling rose high above. "I've seen spells in the last few days that I could never dream were possible. Vithric's the greatest wizard of all time. Why isn't he casting spells?"

"Whole city . . . is a spell that . . . stops other spells." John had to pause between ragged breaths. "Been that way for years . . . it's why wizards hate the place."

Tom did not know quite how such a spell would work—but then, he did not understand that sort of magic at all. All he knew was that Vithric was somehow limited in his power, and that gave him some hope again. He began to wish that he had tried his dagger, back when he had been within striking distance of Vithric, then hated himself for the thought.

Matthew Jobin

He lowered John to rest on the floor. "I'll find a way out." In the darkness, he traced his fingers up worked stone and found an opening almost at once, no more than an arm's length along. "Here. No . . . too short." He traced his fingers along the low, rough ceiling—waist high, and too narrow to turn around. "I couldn't pull you through here."

John answered with a moan that seemed to fall down and disappear into the crack in the earth. Tom turned back to the wall before him and felt frantically along it.

"Here—no, it's blocked." Tom fumbled ahead into an open space. He groped and touched jagged stone, then rubble.

John struggled and fought to crawl up behind Tom. He collapsed, moaning again.

Tom traced his hand along the facets of the wall and past the carving of a face. He recoiled from the teeth. "Nothing here—wait, another short one." He turned back, trying to fix the locations of the entrances in his mind. "Two in one wall, then a blank one. They're off the centers."

"All these tunnels . . . streets above . . . symbol in some old language," said John through ribs Tom knew had been cracked. "He's trying to find . . . secret place."

Tom felt farther along the far end of the chamber. "Master Marshal, what does this have to do with that boy from the inn?"

John wheezed. "I don't know."

"Master Marshal, it's just me. It's Tom. I'm not trying to trick you." Tom waited for John to explain. Something boomed—it could have come from any direction. He turned back to his search.

"Here . . . here!" Tom felt out a tunnel mouth of similar size to the one through which they had entered and more or less directly across the chamber. "Moving air. Faint—there's life ahead." For the briefest instant he caught a scent. . . he could not name it, but it was not far away.

John answered with a moan, then a scuffle as he tried to get onto his hands and knees, only to collapse to the floor again.

Tom moved back to John. "Here. It's me. Take hold."

A hand flailed out. "Tom?"

Tom gripped it. "Master Marshal. Yes, it's me."

"Not a dream."

"No." Tom picked him up.

"Katherine."

"We must go to find her."

"I will try." John sagged, walking on his ankles, but it bore some of the weight. Tom squared his shoulders and pulled him through the entrance. Not twenty paces farther on, Tom knocked his broken toenail on an unseen step.

"Ssss!" Tom hopped about in pain for a moment, then slipped from under John and crept onward, up a few stairs barely wider than his shoulders. He touched rotted hardwood before him, then felt it give way and fall outward. He seized and caught it with his fingers before it could clatter to the floor beyond. With the greatest care he brought the piece of old planking up standing again, then shifted it inch by inch to one side.

A new voice spoke, from ahead. "It's opening!"

Tom froze. The voice was high of pitch—a child, whispering from an arm's length past his head.

"Quiet!" A second voice, lower than the first but no older. Tom strained to listen—more breathing, four or more in a tight space.

"You, there." The second voice came again—a boy. "Password."

"Just me." Tom slithered out. "It's just me. I—"

He crouched in a tiny, filthy room, less than ten feet on a side and so short that he could not sit up straight in it. Around him, pressed in so close that he could hardly help putting his hand on one or the other, lay children piled in together on heaps of old sacking. He could not read their faces in the dark, but they were all turned his way, all awake and all afraid.

"Master's asleep." A girl—the first voice—clutched a smaller boy in tight at Tom's elbow. She might have been nine or so—the boy could not have been more than three. "Are you from the—"

"Shut it!" The older boy crowded her back. He put up his face to Tom's. "Password."

Tom felt something worse than the fright of the moment. The ceiling seemed to press him down. Words did not come. Behind him, on the stairs, John Marshal let out a groan. The older boy turned to flee, crawling and shoving past the other children.

"No!" Tom flailed out, grabbed the boy and pinned him. He kept his voice to a hiss. "You must listen—listen, they're going to—"

The boy raked his face, kneed him in the groin and wriggled out. "Master!" He raised his voice to a shout. He stood at the edge of the room and hopped up more stairs just out of view. "Master, help!"

Tom writhed and clutched down, sprawling across some of the children. The urge to be sick took him.

"You fool!" John dragged himself through the entrance. He seemed to find strength in his anger, for he shoved Tom aside and crawled out on his elbows.

The other children pressed to the corners, whimpering as one. "Don't kill us." The older girl grabbed a toddler from under Tom. "Please don't kill us, we're worth money. Master will be angry."

Tom rolled over, grunting, his teeth clenched hard to fight the vomit down. He reached out a trembling hand. "I'll get you out."

The girl drew back. "Go away."

"They'll kill you if you stay here." Tom looked around at the children. "Please, come with me."

"What in thunder?" an alarmed voice resounded from above. "Hey—!" There followed a toppling crash.

"I will come back. I swear I will come back." Tom crept from the room. There were only three dirt steps; John Marshal's bare and bloodied feet hung out over the last.

"Here. Here, let me help." Tom pushed past and threaded an arm under John's. They staggered up together. The chair in front of them had been knocked on its side, and so had the table just beyond. A young man lay in one corner, groaning and clutching at his head. Clouded moonlight shone through a doorway—the flimsy door hung twisted over on its one leather hinge. The place smelled of old, bad food.

"Now who might you be?"

The voice turned Tom's guts to water. Someone stepped in from the next room, a man of fifty but soft in feature, with a beard trimmed neat and waxed to a tip. He spoke in smooth, curling rounds, sounding calm even in anger.

Tom stared at him. He willed his legs to move. Why could he not move?

"You'll just put your friend down, now." The man came closer. He raised a hand—that smell, Tom knew the smell of the wax in his beard. "Then you'll tell me why—"

John Marshal spun and struck the man, sprawling him back into the dark. "Run." He slumped and nearly dragged Tom to the floor. "Tom, go!"

"I will not leave without you, Master Marshal." Tom heaved John up again and plunged through the doorway. They tripped and staggered through a soggy, weed-roughened yard, banging past a pen and startling one very sickly old pig.

"Outside, outside!" the neat-bearded man called out low. "Catch them, bring them down!"

Tom darted looks at the odd-angled buildings all around them. "There." John shoved him left, toward a low wall.

Tom fumbled over and found the catch of a gate—no point, the gate fell over at a touch.

Someone tripped over the door of the house. "Grope Street. Grope Street—go, curse you! Out the back!"

Tom could see nothing to help him figure out the way back to Huddy's house. He guessed left because left sloped upward. The street smelled like an upturned chamber pot. With every shambling pace John let out a grunt, but he kept it up—nothing quite like a run, but something better than a walk.

"Can you go faster?" Tom tried to strain out an extra few inches on each stride. "They're getting closer."

"No," John grunted. "Tom. Run. Let go."

"No, Master Marshal. No!" Tom seized him tight. "There's a street just up ahead. We can try to—"

"That's far enough." The gruff-voiced man rushed out into the cross street ahead—one of the men who had passed Tom in the alley with Clarance and Huddy Fuller earlier that evening. His bald forehead shone with sweat. He held a long knife in his hand. "You'll get nowhere, so just stop where you are."

Tom looked back. He swiveled left and right, seeing nothing but crooked doorways and tight-pressed walls.

The gruff-voiced man stepped in. "That's right, nowhere to go." His lip curled—he raised his knife—then Tom felt John slip off his shoulder. Tom recoiled, reaching down in a desperate lunge to pull John out of the way of the thrust of the knife. But John was not falling—instead, he leaped forward, his elbow knocking Tom back from the flurried scuffle before him. When Tom regained his feet and his vision stopped spinning, he found the gruff-voiced man standing over John's collapsed form—staring at the knife in his gut.

"What . . ." The gruff-voiced man tried to tug it from his belly, then fell backward.

John raised an arm. "Help, Tom. Hurry. Got to run."

"Murder." Someone leaned out a window, hauled in a breath and screamed: "There's murder! Help! Murder in the street!"

Tom shouldered John up to standing. He shot a look back. Shadows poured from every hovel. His legs screamed from the strain, but he got John moving at a dragging lope up out of the foul lowland district where they had emerged.

"Murder!" The cry rose in multitudes, growing in volume and in terror. "Grope Street, murder! There's men in the street—an attack!"

"Sound the bell!" A man jumped half naked from a house with a spear in his hand. He dragged a watchman's tabard behind him. "To arms! To arms!"

"Where, Tom?" John had to gasp between each word. "Where are we going?"

Tom came to know that he had a place in mind. He turned all about, looking for a landmark.

"We're—in Tumble Bridge," said John. "Market Street's—there, the river's there."

"Then it's this way." Tom dove left, then right, out onto a wider lane. The city bell rang loud, calling the folk forth from their homes. A rising swell of men rushed up and down the muddy streets, only a few of them armed, and even fewer of them looking like they knew what to do.

"Got to get . . . inside somewhere." John slowed, then sped up again. "Vithric has . . . many men in his pay."

"I know." Tom looked back and forth—Market Street, then left—no, right.

"Hey. Hey, you! What's your quarter?" An armed man passed close, then stopped. "Where do you live?"

John Marshal raised his face. "Murder. Grope Street, Tumble Bridge. They nearly got me!"

The man squinted at them, then carried on. "Attack! Murder, down at Tumble Bridge!"

"Here, this way." Tom felt a swell of hope as they passed the tavern where folk had called Clarance in for an ale. "Down the alley."

"Huddy Fuller?" An elderly man called out from the corner as Tom placed his hand on the gate in front of Huddy's house. "What are you at, there's an alarm going on!"

"I'm not Huddy Fuller, just a, er, cousin from down by Dunston." Tom threw his reply over his shoulder. "Got Clarance here, he's drunk."

"Oh, that figures, hey?" The old man passed on. "Guards—never no use when you need 'em."

Tom shoved the gate wide and staggered through. He could not believe he had come this far—he could hardly feel his legs. John's strength failed him again—he sagged across Tom's back, uttering a soft cry with every step, but just a few more, a few more. They passed the cart, then the chicken coop. Tom shouldered the side door open, but before he could say a word he found himself being thrown to the floor.

He felt steel at his throat. "It's me." He had nothing left—he croaked it.

Theldry drew the knife away.

"Mama." Emmie whispered from the stairs. "Mama, who is it?"

"I'm sorry," said Tom. "Sorry. Nowhere else to go."

"Murder! Attack!" The cries moved away down the street. "Get out the guard!"

John moaned. He lay helpless by the turfed fire, sprawled with his back across Tom's bedding and one foot out the door. Theldry flicked a glance at him, then back at Tom.

"He's why I came here," said Tom.

Theldry rolled John over into the bedding. "Upstairs, Emmie. Watch your brother." She shut the door, then turned a look on Tom that made him feel safe and deep in trouble all at once. "You are going to tell me everything, and you are going to start right now."

Chapter 22

Not the merest breath of wind came to howl at the door of the abandoned shepherd's hut. No sound of pursuit crossed the junction of the roads nearby, be they wizards in Vithric's service or men-at-arms in the employ of Lord Wolland. There was nothing to prick the nerves, nothing to excite the senses, nothing to draw Edmund's mind away from what had happened and what he had done.

"You did what was needed." Katherine sat near to him. "Edmund, you had no choice."

Edmund had wanted such simple things, and so recently. That summer, before the coming of the Nethergrim, all he had wanted was Katherine's favor and interest. All he had wanted, all he had hoped for, was for her to notice him, think of him, hold his hand and maybe, just maybe, one day stoop to kiss him. He had wanted to study magic, to become something his father could not control or understand, and to make Katherine's eyes turn his way. A single autumn—a few short, spare months—had been enough to make such dreams seem like the idle fancies of a child. He hardly knew that other Edmund anymore—that one from last summer—powerless, just turned fourteen and in the grip of silly love. He had killed. He and Katherine had made war together. They had saved and lost. They were swords honed keen and taking nicks along their lengths, whittling their cores away with every stroke. No happy home could be made by such implements. They were weapons made for strife and hardship, to be broken in the fray and hung up as trophies on the wall when peace came again.

Katherine gained her feet. "We can't stay here long." She peered out through the flap of fabric that blocked the only window. "It will be dawn soon. We must decide where to go next."

Edmund took out the metal disk from his satchel and forced himself to think. He stared at the innermost symbols: *Horse–Ocean, Land–Blade, Crow–Road*. Thoughts chased themselves around and around in his mind, but it was better than what he saw in the eye of his mind when he was not thinking them.

"That horrible calendar-thing again." Katherine reached out to soothe Indigo, though he seemed to want nothing just then save for more oats. "Edmund, how can time just *end*? It doesn't make any sense!"

"I think this calendar is a warning, made long ago but meant for the people of our own time." Edmund glanced up at Katherine. "At the end of this year, a cycle of the world will close and the Nethergrim will rise as the new sun. For all I know, everything that has happened with the Nethergrim this year—and maybe as far back as your father and Tristan's campaign in the mountains—might have been preparation for this, her appointed time, her chance to make an end to our world."

Katherine turned to the boy king, who lay on the only cot in the place, next to the fire that none of them had dared to light. "Can that be true?"

The king nodded.

"You knew," said Katherine. "Your Grace, you knew what was about to happen, back there at Lum's Graves."

The boy king rubbed the gem in his forehead with a wince. "It's not nearly so simple as that. You cannot understand what it is like."

Edmund looked up from the rings and symbols at his fingertips. "You don't see everything, though, do you?"

"No." The boy king relaxed his uneven face. "I'd be in a lot less trouble if I did."

"Please." Katherine spoke more in demand than in supplication. "One of you, explain."

Edmund turned the rings of the disk. "What folk call magic is divided into three paths. I study the path of *Dhrakal*, the balance of forces in the world, Order against Chaos, Fire against Water and so on. Tom's friend Thulina Drake is the Revered Elder of the *Ahidhan*, who say they have learned a secret wisdom that lets them ask the world for favors that cost nothing. The third path of magic, the one to which His Grace, the king, belongs, is called *Eredh*. They study fate and chance, time and change."

The boy king sat up on his cot. "I'm just an apprentice, a seer of the fourth order. All I get are flashes, sometimes, through here." He tapped the gem. "They're hard to control, but when I get them I see things about to happen like seeing a split in the road ahead. I can see what happens for some way down either path and try to guess which one is best to take. I'm sorry that I didn't tell you what I saw back at Lum's Graves, but you see, telling others where the path splits changes where they go."

Katherine got up to feed the horses some of the oats she kept in her saddlebags. She did not need to go out into the cold to do it, for Indigo and Clover had been brought inside to stand in the sheep pen that took up the far end of the hut. "Can you see where to go next?" She emptied out the remaining contents of a saddlebag in front of the horses. "Can you at least tell me where my papa has gone?"

"I'm sorry," said the king. "I can't do either of those things."

Katherine punched the post that braced the flimsy roof of the hut. The impact startled Edmund—so did the helpless anguish on Katherine's face.

Edmund turned back to the symbols before him. "Your Grace, you spoke some words when you were in the cage in the castle—two lists, one of places, one of things."

"Did I?" The boy king scratched his head. "I don't remember them— apprentices of the *Eredh* don't always remember what they see, I'm afraid."

"I remember them," said Edmund. "The Dorwood, the Hundredthorn, Lum's Graves, the Harrowell, sky above and pit below. Then plow, spear, hearth, ship, wind, tower." He stared down at the disk—six symbols . . .

Aha!

Edmund gave the rings of the disk a spin, just for the fun of it. They made a squealing noise before coming to a halt with three of the inner symbols joined at the center. "Katherine, come here and have a look at the disk again. I said before that this side of it works like a calendar, twelve months of thirty days apiece. Then, when I turn it past the last day of the last month, these Dhanic symbols start moving inward, see? This one first, *Land–Blade*, then across from it *Snake–Battle*, then over here *Heart–Home*, then *Horse–Ocean*, and so on."

"I don't know why you always expect me to work this stuff out with you." Katherine ducked under a crossbeam and sat down heavily across from Edmund. "I'm not even much good at reading and writing."

"You still can think just fine," said Edmund. "I need someone to tell me if I've gone astray. Now, what are the names of the five days of Yule?"

"The Day of the Plow." Katherine counted on her fingers. "The Day of the Sword, then the Day of the Hearth, which is today. Then the Day of the Ship and last the Day of the Wind."

"Have you ever wondered why they are called that?" said Edmund.

Katherine smiled a little. "Honestly? No."

Edmund pointed. "Look again at the symbols. That one there, *Horse–Ocean*. It's a fairly simple one. Horse, ocean."

"I don't . . ." Katherine's dark eyes lit up. "Wait. A horse of the ocean—a ship!"

"Yes, exactly." Edmund turned the wheel so that the first symbol moved in toward the center of the disk. "How about this one here? What is a blade of the land? What cuts the land?"

"What cuts the land?" Katherine bit her lip in thought, but for only an instant. "A plow!"

"And the first symbol to move is the plow, the first day of Yule." Edmund spun the rings farther on, drawing each symbol inward in turn. "Next is the snake of battle, that which stings in war—the sword, see it moving inward? That's yesterday and straight across from the first one. Then today we have the heart of the home, the hearth, the fireplace where the family gathers, and then the horse of the ocean—the ship. See how those two are also across from one another? That's four, one moving in from each direction, and then last, these two, turning at the very center of the disk— *Crow–Road* and *Man–Mountain*."

"What were the names of those places again?" Katherine looped her finger in her hair, looking deep in thought. "The Dorwood, the Hundredthorn, Lum's Graves, then the Harrowell. That's in Quentara—the Harrowell's just south of Bale, where you were born, isn't it?"

"The next day," said Edmund. "The next place."

Katherine examined the disk on the dirt floor between them. "There are six symbols here, yet only five days of Yule."

Edmund smiled. "That's why this took me so long to work out. Every month is thirty days, twelve months to a year, but then there are five days of

Matthew Jobin

Yule, the days that do not fit into any month. It's all nearly perfect, but not quite. That made me think—what if it even less perfect than we knew? What if there are longer cycles, wobbles of time we don't know about because we have not lived long enough for a cycle to complete? What if, sometimes, there are *six* days of Yule?"

"A sixth day of Yule?" Katherine shook her head. "That's silly. There are never six days, only five."

"Not this year," said Edmund.

Katherine folded her arms, as though it had gotten colder in the hut though the chill of night had passed its worst. "But that's . . . the year is the year, it's steady, a circle. Always the same. It can't ever change, it can't, because . . ."

"Because that means the world teeters and spins." The boy king looked far too grave of countenance to be so young. "That means that there is nothing sure and certain. That means that someday the sun might go down and not come up again."

Katherine hugged herself. "Yes."

"Your Grace." Edmund was not sure how much reverence to use before the strange and solemn boy stretched out on the cot beside him. "Perhaps it is time for you to tell us how you got this thing."

"I thought you'd already guessed," said the boy king. "I stole it."

Edmund had indeed guessed just that. "Why?"

"The disk in your hands has a name in Old Paelic—the Darknot." The boy king rose from his cot, bending slats worn weak by long neglect, and turned to Katherine. "My teacher, the Lord Exalted Seer of our kingdom, once told me that it was the reason why I was trapped there in Eredhros, the reason why I had been hidden away in a lightless tomb all my life instead of being acclaimed as heir to the kingdom. He also told me what Edmund figured out on his own—that the cycle of years inscribed on the Darknot come to an end this very Yule."

He reached up to touch his gem, wincing again.

Edmund watched his face. "Does it hurt?"

The boy king took his hand away. "Always." He turned to Katherine. "I came to your father to beg shelter because he helped my father to gain the throne in the old wars, doing secret things along with Tristan and Vithric."

Katherine sucked in a breath. She reached into her belt and drew forth the strangely marked coin.

"I met John Marshal once," said the boy king. "A year before I was sent to Eredhros. He was kind to me. I hoped . . . I did not really know what to hope. I just wanted to see the sun again."

Katherine shifted her saddlebags so that Indigo could eat his fill. "Those wizards, that nasty brother and sister, they were trying to kill you."

The boy king nodded. "Back at the inn, I think I remember that you asked me about my friends." He looked terribly small and weak. "I couldn't answer because I have never had any."

Katherine turned away, then in a single swift action, drew Lord Tristan's sword from its scabbard. The boy king let out a surprised whimper—even Edmund flinched.

"Your Grace." Katherine lay the sword on the ground before the cot, at the feet of the boy. "This sword is in your service, if that be your will."

The boy stared back at her, lips half open, gem glittering. Edmund thought he caught the glimmer of returning hope in his unevenly set eyes.

"You are the elder child of His Grace, King Bregisel, who is dead." Katherine knelt down beside the bed—knelt like the knights in the carvings on old tombs Edmund had seen, down on one knee with her hands opened out. "All that I know, all that I have believed in my life, tells me that you are thus my true and rightful king. I am but the daughter of the marshal of the stables, but what skill and strength I possess is in your service, if you will have it."

Edmund felt the hairs prick up along his neck. He could not see the future as the boy king could, but like anyone, he knew an important moment when it arrived.

The boy king leaned forward. "I still remember the words from watching my father do this when I was little." He placed Katherine's larger hands in between his small ones. "Do you swear fealty to me?"

Katherine bowed her head. "My king, so I do."

The boy king, though but a child and rather small for his age, seemed to grow in the office of his words. "You place none other before me?"

Katherine answered without hesitation. "My lord king, this I swear, to do always that which aids you and to do nothing that harms you, to do my utmost in your defense and to place no other above you in my heart."

Nothing seemed left of the poisoned, babbling boy Edmund had watched struggling for life in his parents' inn. "Katherine Marshal, look upon me."

Katherine raised her head. The boy king drew back his hand and smacked her across the cheek, so hard that the sound of it made Indigo snort and throw back his ears.

The boy king sat up straight and tall. "Do not forget your oath, not from this day until the day of your death."

"My lord king." Katherine bowed again, her hair spilling wild to the floor. "I will not forget."

The boy king picked up the sword, though it took some effort for him to hold it steady. He placed it flat across Katherine's outstretched palms. "Then I shall cherish you as vassal and never fail to reward your good service. Thus are we bound."

Katherine took back her sword and placed it in its sheath. Edmund felt a longing to do as Katherine had done, to kneel down and swear faith and by so swearing commit himself to a course through the world. His sense of reason intervened. He looked down at the disk once again. *Courage–Upward.* "I must reach the Harrowell by tonight at midnight. Roki's dead—for all I know that was his next destination. I'll have to work out what he was going to do when he got there and do it myself."

Katherine put her hand to her reddened cheek. "What about my papa?" She held out the marked coin. "I'm not asking just because I . . . what I mean is, Your Grace, I think I've met your teacher before, the Lord Exalted Seer. He gave me this coin to give to Papa. Do you know what it means?"

The boy king touched his gem again. "I'm afraid I don't—but if we can find your father, I hope he will."

Edmund set his tooled leather satchel on his lap and pulled out a book. "There's something I can try. I would never dare at any other time, but this Yule magic seems to just work."

The boy king leaned over Edmund's shoulder, seeming entranced by the turning pages of *The Sworn Book of Gunthacram.* "You mean a spell? How do those work, anyway—can you simply read them out?"

"Every spell in *Dhrakal* is unique," said Edmund. "Spells get written down like notes in music. You can read the notes if you learn how, but each time you play the song, it will be different. You can only do it well if you change it to fit the moment and put your inspiration into it. All that's a long way of saying that it's easier to understand spells once you know the laws of magic."

"Magic has laws?" said Katherine. "Like the laws handed down by kings?"

"No, real laws—laws that explain how the world works," said Edmund. "One is the Law of Balance, which states that everything you change must be paid for. Then there is the Law of Rot, which says that spells cannot be used over and over without new inspiration, or else they will wear a groove into the world and stop working. Then there is the Law of Irony, and the Law of—I'm lecturing you, aren't I?"

Katherine smiled. "You are."

"Well, one of the laws is the Law of Tangling," said Edmund. "According to this law, nothing that was ever together is ever really apart again. It's the closest we wizards of *Dhrakal* ever get to talking about time. What it really means is that time and space are not truly real, that everything is folded up together, everything is connected and—well, *involved* in everything else."

Katherine glanced at the king, whose face gone completely blank. "I'm not sure I got any of that. Did you?"

The boy king shook his head. "I did not get much book learning in Eredhros. No light to read by."

Edmund stretched out a hand. "Katherine, do you have something of your father's with you?"

Katherine pulled her father's shield off her back. "Papa's had this since he was my age."

"Good." Edmund shoved the Darknot aside and placed the shield handle upward in between him and Katherine. "Give me your hands. Clear your mind. Think about your father."

Katherine shut her eyes. Pain and sorrow crossed her face. "It's not so easy to do that right now. I still don't know why he was so angry with me."

"Just hold to him—all of him, good and bad." Edmund found the Signs of Joining and of Life at his instant beck and call. "WHOSE HANDS FIRST GRIPPED THIS HANDLE? WHOSE FINGERS LEFT THESE TRACES?" Even though the spell invoked one of the Seven Pillars of Dhrakal—*Boladham*, the Pillar of Distance—and should have been well above his novice level of skill, he felt his senses immediately come unstuck from his body, roaming at a dizzying speed over snow-choked field and forest outside.

An image swam up to Edmund. "North." He shivered. "He's to the north."

"No, Edmund—south." Katherine's voice came out clear as a bell. "Papa's in the city, in Rushmeet. How strange—I can *feel* him there."

Edmund's senses stretched from horizon to horizon. "No, Katherine. North."

"No, south, Edmund." Katherine hissed. "Oh—oh no. Is he in pain?"

Edmund winced. "He is." He grabbed for his belly. "Oh, Father." He opened his eyes to find Katherine clutching at her father's shield, but regarding him with a contemplative expression.

"Edmund," she said. "Who owned that satchel you've got before you did?"

Edmund had forgotten that he was holding the tooled leather satchel on his lap. "This used to be my father's. It was a gift from Grandmother, long ago, back when he was not much older than I am now."

"Edmund, you're not seeing my father," said Katherine. "I think you're seeing yours."

Chapter 23

"**S**o how do I look?" Huddy Fuller ducked under the beam from the stairs and stood with arms akimbo. He wore a trimmed and worsted tunic under a bright mantled cowl and the pointiest shoes Tom had ever seen.

"You could go before the king himself, my love." Theldry set her bowl of porridge on the seat of her chair and stood to brush her husband down. She swept her hands across his back, then arranged his mantle so it sat squarely on his shoulders.

Huddy Fuller turned around to let Theldry adjust his belt. He glanced behind him. "All set, Tom?"

Tom felt through his blankets by the fire, but all he touched was Jumble. "I can't find my tunic."

Theldry turned to call out the door. "Emmie! Bring Tom's tunic in."

"It's not dry yet."

"Bring it anyway, we've no time." Theldry took her bowl and spooned up some porridge on her way back to the kitchen. "Tom, there's some on the table for you."

Tom nudged Jumble off him, tried to sit up, then rolled back on his side. He felt even worse than he had when he had dropped asleep the night before—weak and shaky, his knees and hips sore to the bone. He cast a glance through the sliver of unshuttered window and gauged the rising sun. He had never slept so late in his life.

"You're sure it's him?" He reached for the table and nearly turned it over in dragging himself to his feet.

"Sure as I can be about a man I've never met." Huddy Fuller caught him by the arm and lowered him into a chair. "They say he went straight up to the seneschal, but he's coming down to guildhall for noon—don't know what for. Did you know he'd gone blind?"

"Mama! Mama, look!" The child, John, raised a ladle and a pot. Tom winced, but the racket never started. He opened his eyes to see Theldry plucking the ladle out of her son's hand and placing it on top of the cupboard. She returned to folding parcels of bread and eggs in squares of thin cloth.

Emmie dumped the tunic over Tom on her way up the stairs. Tom swam through the damp fabric until he found the collar. "I haven't had a chance to thank you for taking us in." He pushed his head through. "Master Marshal has money. I promise you he'll pay for all of this."

"Never you mind it, never you mind." Huddy stooped to turn ashes over the coals. "When your wife says trust a man, you listen. You'll understand one day."

"Don't you push all this on me, Huddy Fuller." Theldry set a plate of eggs on the table, then sat with her son on her knee. "Here, Tom. You must be starved."

Tom picked up a wooden spoon. His stomach ruled him for a while. Theldry doled out the scraps for Jumble, who set to them as though he had not eaten in a month.

"Who's Katherine?"

Tom turned around. "His daughter. What's he saying?"

Emmie leaped off the second stair from the bottom, her hair a-bounce in a bright red ribbon. "Just her name, and being sorry, then a bunch of numbers over and over." She reached for her breakfast. "Has he gone mad?"

"No."

Emmie jammed in her spoon. She spoke, sticky with porridge. "Why were they torturing him?"

"Less you know about it, the better." Huddy Fuller wagged a finger. "Now, you remember, not a word about him, not to anyone, until we've worked out what's what."

Theldry set the child John down in Tom's blankets. "Are you going to talk to Clarance?"

"When I can find him." Huddy pulled his cloak off the peg. "Guards are all running about like headless chickens this morning."

Tom slid on one boot, then the other. He gasped. He had forgotten the broken nail. "Can I help with anything?"

Huddy Fuller let the door hang open behind him. "You can help us bring the cloth down to market on the way, how's that?"

Emmie picked up a yoke from which hung a pair of buckets. She took her lunch, then a kiss from her mother, and stepped outside.

Tom followed, then stopped at the door. He turned back to Theldry. "I'm sorry I brought all this on you."

"Instead of that, you can just say thank you." Theldry turned from the cupboard to smile upon Tom. Tom saw her face in full light for the first time since they met. Sunshine made her a girl again; something squeezed in him, an ache he could neither name nor place.

Theldry's smile held and froze. She turned away and bent to the wash pail. "I'll keep good care of your master Marshal till you're back. Don't you worry."

Tom stepped outside, past the low gate behind the Fullers' house—then leaped back before a passing drove of oxen could trample him down.

"Just over here, Tom." Huddy Fuller dragged the rented cart out from the croft. "Bear a hand."

Tom took hold. "Where are we going?"

"Down to market, then we're off to see if we can get you into guildhall to meet Lord Tristan."

"Does that cost money?"

Huddy laughed and started pushing. "Just the price of hot air. Don't worry for it, guild's got me in hand, got a few friends and a few favors to pull in."

Tom dropped his lunch on the load of broadcloth and helped Huddy pull the cart into the street. Emmie fell in step with the yoke over her shoulders. The sun had risen yet weaker than it had the day before. No one but Tom seemed to notice that it was lower in the sky at that time of day than it had ever been on any day in any year he had known.

"Now, there you can see the castle." Huddy Fuller nodded to his left. "And over by—" A peal of bells and a burst of oinks drowned the rest of his words. A man drove his pigs around Tom's feet—they snuffled the ground, picking over stray bits of food and refuse. A man stretched his hands to beg

Matthew Jobin

for bread, another tried to sell him a goat, a third leaned in to whisper the whereabouts of a game of dice, fair dice, all the worthies of the town were sure to attend. Tom found himself hunching down before the cart, his heart thumping loud.

"Is this the main street?" he muttered, overwhelmed by the crush of townsfolk all around him.

Huddy wagged a pudgy finger at the man selling the goat. "You mind yourself selling that goat on this road—butcher's guild will be around your neck if the shepherds don't have you first. Look, I don't care where you got it, this town has laws and I've got every right—" He gave up on his lecture and turned to Tom. "What was that?"

"Are we on the main street?"

"Oh, no, just turning onto Market now. Here we are." They trundled into a scene that made Tom want to let go of the cart and run. A road stretched out broad left and right, running up toward the castle one way and in the other to a square capped by what looked like a grand stone hall. Tall houses jammed shoulders all along the route, many of them seeming to be holding one another up. Each and every one had a shop at the ground floor, each a sign, a spread of goods on shelves out front and someone crying the prices. Between the houses, laid out in a wild maze, stood row upon row of wooden stalls, none quite the same height or construction as any other, each decked with all the color its owner could afford. A smith banged his anvil; a pack of dirty children squealed after a stray dog.

"I'd say watch your purse if you had one." Huddy Fuller led them in among the swirl. "The Yuletide market's the worst of the year for pickpockets. Less travelers, but the local urchins are getting powerful cold and desperate this time of year."

Smells assaulted Tom all at a charge—meat, baking bread, dung in the gutters. He bent down over the broadcloth in the cart before him and tried to breathe nothing else.

"Knifed right in the gut." A man ate standing before the first stall in the lane—a dyer, by the stains on his fingers. He spoke to the young woman across the counter, waving his meat pie around and then stabbing himself in the chest with it. "Right there in the street and—morning, Huddy. Who's this?"

Huddy nodded to Tom. "Cousin, from out by Dunston."

"Hunh." The dyer held a look on Tom, then dug a finger in his teeth. "You hear of it? They've shut the city gates!"

Huddy turned. "Why, because of the murder?"

"No, 'cause of all the folk camped outside the walls," said the dyer. "Some sort of trouble up in Harthingdale."

"I'll catch up with you at guildhall, Ned." Huddy Fuller started his cart moving again. "Got to set up for market." Tom felt the man watching him all the way to the turn.

"Hoy there and harken! Harken to my news!" A young man in the colors of the city tooted a horn from horseback. "The seneschal of the castle commands that the gates be kept shut this day and all days until the present troubles pass." He held a grim pause, looking about him at the crowd around the cross of the lanes. "No one may open the gates or let anyone within the walls by any means until the ban is lifted, on pain of—"

"Hark you now to this news!" Another man raised his voice. He was much more shabbily dressed than the first, but also much the louder. "Pell Fleshacker offers a fine price on salt pork, very fine pork salted deep and well, for just two pennies to the hock!"

The first crier sounded his horn and tried again. "I announce the official news of the city! By order of the seneschal, the gates of the city will remain closed until—"

"Here, now. Just here." Huddy Fuller dragged the handcart in behind an empty stall. "Oh, now what's this? Hoy—hoy, Arno! Arno Wheeler, curse you! Who's moved our stakes?"

Emmie grabbed a roll of bunting and dragged it into the narrow space. Huddy Fuller started loading broadcloth onto the shelf, all the while shouting left and right at the folk in the neighboring stalls, one a wheelwright from the look of his stock, the other a tanner by the smell. Tom tried to find something useful to do, but Huddy and Emmie moved bolts and decorations into the cramped stall with such practiced speed that he could do nothing but get in their way. The folk of the town shoved and jostled past. None who spared Tom a glance looked on him with anything but cold suspicion. He crouched beside the cart, then put his hands over his ears. Jumble curled up at his side, casting nervous glances at the packs of strays patrolling the edges of the market.

Tom felt a tap on his arm. "Are you all right?"

He looked up. Emmie leaned out from the dirty curtains at the back of the stall.

Tom tried to pull himself upright. "I'm from a quiet place. Most of my life I wouldn't see ten people in a day. This . . . there's just too much—"

"I guess I'm used to it." Emmie sat down at his side and smoothed out her skirts. "Where are you from?"

"Moorvale." Tom shook his head. "Though—it's strange to think, but I was likely born right here in town somewhere."

"You were? Where?"

"I don't know," said Tom. "My old master bought me in an alleyway. He told me that my mother left me out on the step of an inn when I was a baby."

Emmie stared at Tom for long enough that he began to wonder if he had said something wrong. She stood, then backed up and stared longer still. "How old are you?"

"Emmie—Emmie, there you are, why aren't you up at the counter?" Huddy Fuller appeared around the side of the stall. "Just saw master embroiderer go right on by, right on by with a full purse! On with you!"

"Sorry, Papa." Emmie pulled back the curtain, still watching Tom, her young forehead wrinkled high.

"Now, you mind, I want to count cloth or coin when I get back." Huddy Fuller reached down a hand for Tom while shaking a finger at his daughter with the other. "And don't you go anywhere—if you've got to run off for a moment, you get the widow Tanner to watch the stall—no one else, d'you hear?"

"Yes, Papa."

"And no talking to boys. You're too young."

Emmie pulled a face.

Her father tapped her cheek. "That's my girl! Off we go, Tom. This way, this way."

Tom followed Huddy Fuller out between the lanes with Jumble at his heel. The closer he got to the great stone guildhall at the end, the clearer it seemed that folk were not simply moving to and fro about their business. They were instead shoving themselves into an ever-narrowing crush toward the hall's grand gates.

"Hoy there, Huddy." Ned the dyer elbowed close. "Lord Tristan's already inside."

Huddy Fuller craned, then hopped to get a better view ahead. "Well, what's he doing?"

"Begging, from the sounds of it." Ned let out an unkind laugh. "It's his own folk swarming outside the city gates. Must be hard living, off in that valley of his."

"What?" Huddy hopped up and down to get a better look. "What sort of—hoy, Tom, no need to grab on so hard!"

Tom felt sweat on his face. He wanted to run and knew he could not. No matter where he turned, strange folk pushed in, breathing and speaking and stepping at his heel.

"Come on, then, Ned, let's do this proper." Huddy Fuller set a shoulder against the dyer's and they drove a wedge through the crowd. Tom grabbed Jumble by the scruff and held on to Huddy's belt, bent nearly double.

"Who's this?" the familiar refrain rang out, this time from a man holding a spear across the doors.

"Cousin, from Dunston." Huddy Fuller made to go past. "You know me, Bugwald, and you know Ned. We're guild men."

Bugwald brought his spear across the doorway. "You picked the wrong time to bring in a cousin, Huddy Fuller. Watch captain's asked us to look out for strangers."

"I said he was a cousin. What's my word good for? Hey?"

A babble rose from within, the echoes of shouting voices. Ned Dyer craned over the shaft of the spear. "What's he talking about in there?"

"Justice, brotherhood, the common duty of all men." Bugwald snorted. "Asking for aid and shelter for his people—something about foul beasts up in the mountains. You ask me, that's why you don't go trying to live in the mountains. You ask me, they all got what they deserved and it's no use running to us now. I hear that's what the seneschal told him, so he's come to beg the guild men to make his case for him again."

Tom looked about him, his skin prickling. "We must reach Lord Tristan." He whispered in Huddy's ear. "We must tell him about Master Marshal." Jumble cocked his ears, then flattened them and let out a growl.

Huddy Fuller's gestures were like those of other folk—hands open to beg, closed to threaten—but they were made on a grander scale. "Bug—come now, Bug, you know me! Come now!" Huddy tried to wheedle, then bully passage. "Look, the fullers' guild's got say in this town—"

"Not more say than the watch." Bugwald stood his ground. "You can go." He pointed to Tom. "Not him—and no dogs, anyway."

Tom grabbed Huddy's sleeve. "Just find him. Try to get his ear, tell him Tom from Moorvale is outside. Please."

Huddy nodded. "All right, then. I'll try it." He stepped forward alone, and Bugwald let him in under the spear.

Tom put his back to the pillar by the door, able to do no more than hold his ground against the crush of folk seeking entry. He slid down to sitting, then curled up his knees. Bugwald seemed to pick who got through by a variety of means: odd signs made with hands held close to the vest; pleas to friendship or a family connection; and more than a few palms of coin.

Jumble growled again, then took up barking, then dropped to a whine. His tail fell. A hard shiver seized at Tom. He looked up.

"I know you now." Vithric gained the first step of the hall, stepping forth from the crowd of folk pushing in toward the guildhall doors. "You nearly died at my hand beneath the mountain of the Nethergrim. More fool me not to have killed you when first I saw you in the street, but I have a weakness in my memory when it comes to faces."

Tom stood up against the pillar. He looked aside—Bugwald seemed caught up in arguing passage for an old widow, his broad hints for a bribe falling on truly deaf ears.

"I could kill you." Vithric came nearer. "With but a wave of my hand and a word I could rip you to tatters."

Tom's fear found its limit. "You would only say that if you really couldn't." He saw the shaft hit home—Vithric's eyes widened in surprised rage. "You're powerless here."

"Where is John Marshal?" Vithric reached the step just below Tom. "Where are you hiding him?"

Tom squared his shoulders against the stone. He brought his arms out before him and held them at the level of Vithric's neck. They stood near enough to embrace.

"When I find where you are keeping him, I will have the place burned down with everyone in it." Vithric curled his lip. "Have you ever watched someone die burning?" Downy stubble covered his chin. His eyes were shot red.

"You're failing the one you serve." Tom glanced up at the sky. "What will you do when she finds out?"

Vithric twitched his fingers. His voice rose and snapped. "Tell me where he is!" He leaned closer. He was shorter than Tom, but thicker of muscle. At twenty-five years of age or so, he looked like a young man in good health, easily Tom's match for strength. His chest met Tom's outstretched arms—his hands moved upward . . .

"Are you bothering my friend?"

Tom had never felt such relief in his life. Katherine stood in the doorway beside him—sleepless and bleary, road mud up her breeches to her hips—and Lord Tristan's sword-of-war at her side.

Vithric's mouth twitched.

"Whoever you are, you back away from him, before—" Recognition flared across Katherine's face. "You!"

Vithric retreated a step. "Do you think I am alone in this crowd, girl? If I raise my left hand, my men will shoot you down."

Katherine did not flinch in the slightest. She gripped the hilt of her sword. "Can you raise your hand quicker than I can raise mine?"

Vithric's face curled into a sneer that betrayed his fright. He stepped back farther, one hand held at the level of his belt. Katherine followed his retreat, with the set, expressionless look she got when her next move was with a blade.

Tom advanced with his friend. "Katherine, hear me. If you kill him here, you will be taken for a murderer and hanged for it."

Katherine never took her eyes—nearly black with focused rage—from Vithric's face. "Maybe the world will be better for that, all the same."

Hands—both Vithric's and Katherine's—fluttered. Jumble snarled and paced down the steps. If Tom had not reached down to seize him, the fight might have broken out whether either Vithric or Katherine wanted it or not.

"Tom." A heavy, battle-scarred hand gripped at the stone frame of the doorway. "Are you here, Tom? Did Katherine find you?"

Bugwald looked behind him, then drew up his spear and bowed low.

Tom turned around. "I am here, my lord."

"Tristan." Vithric's smile was a delicate knife. "My, my, how terribly old you look."

Lord Tristan of Harthingdale might indeed have been old, but it was not the sinew of his limbs that had betrayed him in his declining years. "Who speaks? Who else is here?" His milky, sightless eyes darted left and right, searching for what they could not find. "I know that voice." He lurched forward, one hand out to feel for a post. The sun shot bright off his long, thick white hair. He curled in the fingers of his free hand. Had he known Vithric's exact location, Tom had no doubt that Tristan's fist would have dealt his former friend a thundering, perhaps deadly blow.

"Hold, my lord." Katherine intervened. She pulled her shield off her back and stepped out to protect Tristan, darting her eyes left and right among the crowd and the building around for Vithric's supposed followers. She found none, but her action gave Vithric the chance to slip away into the crowd.

"There he is!" the folk of Rushmeet spoke as one. "There he is—hail, Lord Tristan! Hail to you, the slayer of the Nethergrim!"

"And hail to you, one and all!" Tristan waved out to the crowd. "I wish that I was here only to celebrate a Yule with you and a turn of the new year, but I fear that what brings me before you is something far more grim. Hear me now, folk of Rushmeet, harken to what your own seneschal refuses to heed. All the north is under assault, beset on every side by foul creatures not seen in many years. If we do not band together as one and do what is needed to turn them back, this will be the last Yuletide that any of us ever see."

Chapter 24

E dmund dismounted, getting first one boot in the ashes, then the other. Before him rose the pale and sickly sun, while behind him, over the hazed far peaks of the Girth, another light broke sharp and hard upon the world.

Everything you make, everything you dream, everything you cherish comes to dust. The Nethergrim was a hole in the sky that cast its mockery of light eastward from the horizon, giving everything a double shadow. **Perhaps now you begin to understand.**

Edmund looked up, past the smoldering, burned-out ruin of his parents' inn and tavern—his home. "The sun, the real sun, it's weak." He could not remember ever in his life being able to stare straight at the unclouded sun, but now he could do so without difficulty. It bore spots on its surface, a spreading, darkening rot, and seemed to roil and reel from the onslaught of the other light. "It's dying."

This is not your world, Edmund Bale. The Nethergrim's Voice had never been louder in Edmund's mind, seeming to blast across the sky with a ringing of bells and a chorus of squeals, a thousand voices all in chant together with the thudding might of all things that cannot be changed. **It never was.**

Edmund let go of the reins of his horse. He sank to his knees. Something collapsed, somewhere in the village nearby, timber and thatching falling inward with a crash made all the worse by the following silence.

Time is my sword. The Nethergrim rose full over the mountains. The second, eastward-lying shadows cast by the Nethergrim seemed to waver and leap, echoing her words, dancing in worship and praise. **Men perish, houses crumble, kingdoms fail and fall—yet here am I.**

Edmund felt the empty chill of the air—still and yet frigid, draining away the warmth of his body into the outer world. He looked down at his second shadow, the one cast from the west. It looked like it was kneeling down in homage, just as Katherine had done before the king inside the hut. He shut his fists. "I will stop you. I will find a way."

I have told you before, Edmund, more than once. If you carry on against me, I will be your death. So it has been foretold in the ages before you were born.

Edmund looked about him at the soot upon the snow, the forest of charred timbers that were all that remained of the village of Moorvale—and then, drawing his arms over his head, he curled down into the blackened earth. He felt sick, small, hopeless—but then a thought struck him. He raised his head again. "You said that if I carried on against you, I would die, but you did not say that I would fail."

The chill of the Nethergrim's light seemed also to burn. **Oh, my foolish child. Do you yet not know what death is? Cleave to me, Edmund, kneel to me, and you will survive what is to come.**

Edmund looked around at his broken, ruined home, then straight at the Nethergrim, straight at the second, spectral sun. "That's it, isn't it?" He felt an awful tingle up his whole body. "That's what you've been telling me all this time. If I try to stop you, I will die—but I will still stop you. If I give everything I can give, I can win. I can defeat you, I alone, and you have always known it."

Silence fell in Edmund's thoughts. The Nethergrim gave no answer.

"You just made a big mistake," said Edmund. "You thought you could scare me away from what I was always meant to do by telling me that I would die if I did it. Did you really think I would let you win, let you take everyone I loved in exchange for my own life? You don't understand me at all."

The Nethergrim hung mute in the sky. Her silence changed Edmund's suspicion to a thrilling certainty.

Edmund got back onto his feet. "You have always known that I am meant to be the one who defeats you." He advanced toward the west, as though he might pluck the Nethergrim from the sky and throw her writhing to the ground. "So hear me now. Whatever is costs me, whatever it takes, I will stop you, and all you have feared over these long ages will come to pass. Do you hear me? I will put an end to you!"

"Edmund, why are you yelling at the sky?"

Edmund looked down. Across the soot-caked, snowy village green, past the torched and ruined husks of his neighbors' houses, stood Geoffrey, at the edge of the trees on Wishing Hill, one hand on the reins of Edmund's horse and the other on the undersized bow that had once been Edmund's own.

"Geoffrey." Edmund stood. He walked, then he ran. When he reached the trees, he came very near to throwing his arms around his brother—but even if he had wanted to do so, he could not, for Geoffrey turned around at once and plunged back under the branches.

"I hope that whatever you've been doing since yesterday has been very, very important." Geoffrey led Edmund up the path that wound around Wishing Hill, one that Edmund had taken many times with Tom and Katherine. "We could have used your help."

Edmund's words gushed forth in a babble, remorse and relief tumbling over one another. "All the way up the road, the whole way here, I looked for you. I searched for you." He followed Geoffrey up the hill to the crumbled old keep at the summit, the place where he had crept out at night to play with his friends on many summer nights before the coming of the Nethergrim. He glanced up at his neighbors standing grim and weary on the battlements, longbows in hand, then followed his brother in through the tumbled-down wreck of the gates. "Folk are fleeing, running south down the Kingsway. I reached Longsettle this morning, and they said that no one north of Thrawnthrup's been seen since the day before yesterday . . . I was afraid that . . . Geoffrey, slow down, please tell me, is Mum, is—"

Edmund stopped just inside, then took a step back. "Father."

"Son." Harman Bale sat against the tall, dark Wishing Stone that stood in the center of the courtyard, a single weathered monument far older even than the ancient walls of the ruined keep that surrounded it. He tried to get up, then fell back against the stone, one hand on his belly.

"Father!" Edmund rushed forward in fear. "Father, I'm sorry, is it—are you—"

Harman Bale cracked a wry smile. "It's nothing so bad, son. Just strained my old wound hauling some firewood."

Edmund knelt in the thin dusting of snow. "Father, forgive me."

"Nothing to forgive, son." Harman Bale reached out with his good hand. "Glad you're back."

Edmund hung his head, then raised it and looked at his brother. "Mum?"

"She's up on the walls feeding the archers." Geoffrey led Edmund farther on, past rows of their neighbors camped out in blankets along the hall. "The mountains, the moors—it seemed like they came from all sides. Bolgugs, then thornbeasts, then other things I can't name. I think the fire started last night, when Baldwin's house collapsed onto his hearth. The wind took the flames from house to house, and all we could do was watch everything burn from up here."

Edmund wanted to sink into the ground. "Our home." He wanted to beg forgiveness from his whole village, even though everyone he passed looked up at him in happy surprise. "The houses, the village. Oh, Geoffrey, I'm sorry."

Geoffrey shouldered his bow. "It's not as bad as it looks."

Edmund followed his brother back toward the entrance, stepping over the salvaged possessions of his neighbors. "It's not?"

Geoffrey picked up two apples from a basket and handed one to Edmund. "No one's died. We've been under siege for two nights and a day and haven't lost a single one of us." He nodded at a wizened, huddled figure sitting alone in the shadow of the walls. "Not even Athelstan."

Edmund felt just as confused as he did relieved. "That's wonderful. It's almost—unbelievable. Bolgugs, you say? Lots of them?"

"We had some help." Geoffrey led Edmund back through the courtyard, out through the gates and around the side of the keep.

"Help? What sort of—" Edmund dropped his apple. He leaned back to stare—up.

"Quite something, isn't she?" Geoffrey's closed look revealed itself at last as suppressed mirth. "We'd all be dead if it wasn't for her."

Edmund shook himself free of his amazement. "Her?"

"Take a look at the belly."

Edmund stepped forward with the greatest caution and care, for his whole body was not as big around as just one of the legs of the creature that stood before him. He gazed along the immense expanse of fur. "She's pregnant."

"Very pregnant," said Geoffrey. "No one has a clue how long a beast like that takes to give birth. All we know is that if she was just a cow we'd have her down in a birthing stall right now—not that there's a stall that big in all the world."

Martin Upfield set down his militia spear and seized Edmund in a bear hug, after which Nicky Bird slapped his side, then drew an arm across both his shoulders. "There's our lad. There he is! Now we'll be all right!"

The creature—so tall and broad that one of the archers on the walls could easily have leaped onto her back without a fall, lowered her head and set to her meal. That forced everyone to step a few yards back, for the beast's great horns were as long as swords-of-war, as sharp as lance points and thick as the trunks of young oaks.

"I'll tell you this, I've had to clean a good amount of bolgug off those since yesterday." Hugh Jocelyn stepped right up beside the creature's head, ducking under a tuft of fur that hung like moss from a river willow to stroke her enormous, wattled chin. "That's my girl. I'll tell you this else, Edmund—it's a hard thing, losing your home, but I'll wager it isn't half so hard as dying."

Edmund took another step toward the colossal beast before him. At five paces' distance, he felt the heat of her body. At two paces, the smell of her musk made him choke.

"It's all right, go on and pet her," said Geoffrey. "She likes it."

Edmund reached out a tentative hand. He felt the enormous, swollen belly. The kick of the baby from inside made his hand jump back so hard that he almost smacked himself in the face.

He turned to his brother. "Of course." He reached into his sack and set the Darknot in the snow at his feet. He traced the symbols on the inner two rings of disk, the ones that matched both the days of Yule and the Signs of the magical Wheel of Substance. "Life. The Sign of Life."

Hugh Jocelyn took up a pitchfork and shoveled in enough feed for five cows. "She thundered into the village just after you left with Lord Harry for the city. She made an awful mess—knocked over barns, trampled fences and suchlike. We were just trying to figure out how to bring her down when the bolgugs showed up. I bet those bolgugs thought—that is, if things like that can really think—that they'd be coming in to gut and guzzle down some soft-bellied villagers. Well, they had themselves something of a surprise. Sure, old Bossy here might have tumbled down a few more houses and started a fire that burned everything from Gilbert's place to the bridge, but when the dust settled here we all were, alive and hale."

Edmund kept one finger on the symbol for the first day of Yule—*Sword-Land*, the plow, the symbol of Life, rebirth, abundance and food. He glanced at Nicky and Martin, then at Hugh. "Bossy?"

"Aye, Bossy." Hugh Jocelyn removed his cap to rub his shiny head, then replaced it. "After my pig who died, you remember? Reminds me of her."

Martin wheeled in a fresh barrow of feed. "Houses we can build again." He took his turn with the pitchfork. "I'll raise the beams of a hundred houses if we can find a way to make it through all this in one piece."

"The fields are still there for plowing come spring." Hugh opened his calloused, wrinkled, work-scarred hands. "Moorvale's still here." Edmund thought at first that he was gesturing to the land around them—but no, he meant his hands.

Edmund traced a finger across the disk. Life from the eternal springtime of the Dorwood, from the north, then Metal from the south, from the creature melded from the swords that hung from the Hundredthorn. Last night he had seen the creature of Fire at Lum's Graves—he only wished he had thought to yoke it to his will. He would have to find it—but a dog with an exposed heart that was perpetually on fire should not be all that hard to track down. He spun the rings, watching each of the symbols move in toward the central point.

He looked up at Geoffrey, who had come to stand near. "I'm starting to understand." He slid the Darknot back into his satchel. "Whether the Nethergrim likes it or not, I'm starting to—"

Arms seized him. He lost his breath. "Mum!"

Sarra Bale hugged Edmund close, then stepped back and gave him a fierce smack on the cheek—then her face crumpled in and she seized him again.

Edmund felt her fright, saw in her the clearest expression of the terror held only just in check among his neighbors. "I'm sorry, Mum." He let her hold him as tightly as she wanted. "I'm here. I'm here now."

Sarra kissed Edmund's forehead. "You're a good boy, Edmund. You always were."

Edmund wondered whether that was really true. No matter—he would make it true. "Everyone, listen." He stepped into the doorway of the manor, so that folk inside and out could hear him speaking. "We must move from here. Things are going to get worse. I will protect you and lead you to safety." He did not pause to ask whether they would follow him, whether the men and women of Moorvale would heed the commands of a fourteen-year-old boy. No one argued, no one so much as raised a word of scorn or protest. Instead, they simply got up and started packing, as though they had been waiting for him all along.

Edmund turned to Hugh. "Bossy seems attached to you. If we move down the road, will she follow?"

He tossed out a load of parsnip tops and leaves of bitter vetch before the beast. "Aye—aye, she will. We'll want some carts for feeding her as we go."

"I can help with that." Gilbert Wainwright passed by with his wife, Mercy, and their baby. "My work shed collapsed but it never caught fire. We'll bring out every cart and wagon I can fix and make roadworthy."

Edmund slung his satchel. "We'll go at as quick a pace as we can manage." He hoped it would be fast enough. "Listen, everyone—bring only what you need to keep yourselves alive. Water, food, clothing—weapons, if you have them. Nothing else."

Geoffrey tapped Edmund's shoulder. "Watch this." He strode over to the great beast of Life, reaching out for the fur of her belly and grabbing it in clumps. He hauled himself hand over hand until he clambered up onto her back and stood three times the height of a horse.

"It's like a moving archery tower." Geoffrey sat cross-legged, his bow across his lap, amidst fur as thick as crabgrass. "I can see trouble coming for a mile from up here."

Edmund waved to him. "Good! Take Miles and Emma up there with you—she can shoot fairly well."

"I'm a better shot than you!" Emma Russet stuck out her tongue on her way up to the belly of the creature. Geoffrey reached down to help her scramble up.

Hugh gave a whistle. "Come, Bossy. Come!" Bossy thundered the earth with every step. Her heavy belly swung back and forth—Edmund thought he saw the outline of her baby shifting in the womb and pressing out, a leg and a hoof of a beast already as large as a full-grown bull.

"Here, Father." Edmund led Clover in through an assembling congregation of villagers, draft horses and donkeys in the village square. "She's not too tired to go at a walk."

Harman hesitated, then took the reins. "Thank you, son." He winced as he tried to mount, grabbing at his old wound. He got up on the second try with Edmund's help.

"Half of what happened between us was me." Harman got his feet in the stirrups, sitting in the saddle in a way Edmund knew was clumsy and peasant-like and at the same time knew was just the way he rode himself. "I had no call to—well, you know."

Edmund drew down the stirrups to better match his father's height. "We're alike, Father. I'm your son, and no one else's."

"Pig-headed, aren't we?" Harman smiled. "Let's try to make things easier on your mother, though. She deserves better from us."

Edmund got his mother up on Bluebell, who he found to his surprise had not only survived the assault south of the castle but had made it home on his own. He led his parents to the front of the growing swell of folk in the square, then stepped back into Bossy's enormous shadow.

"How much food will we need?" Horsa Blackcalf struggled to get a sack up onto his back. "We only need to get to Northend and the castle, don't we?"

Edmund shook his head. "Northend's been sacked." He kept speaking right over the round of gasps and frightened chatter his words evoked from all who had heard them. "I passed it on the way here. The gates have been knocked down and the place ransacked top to bottom."

"How?" Martin emerged with his longbow, arrows, a cudgel and enough provisions slung over his broad back for two men at the least. "Who could do that to a castle?"

"Wizards." Edmund considered—and not for the first time that day—whether he truly felt sorry for killing the sister, after all. He glanced up at Geoffrey. "They're looking for that boy we brought into the inn—they'll knock down every building and kill everyone in Elverain to find him."

"Then where?" Geoffrey blanched. "Where can we go?"

Edmund strode to the front of the crowd. "Rushmeet." He raised his hand, pointed south and started walking.

Chapter 25

T hey both spoke at once, Katherine's voice mingling with Tom's.
"Papa." Katherine crossed over to the doorway, searching for
something in her father's face that she could not find. Jumble
snuffled up to her; she pushed his nose away without looking.

Tom's voice carried neither Katherine's fear nor her certainty. He tripped
over the word he spoke, taking three tries to say it. "Mama?"

"By the cloven crown!" Huddy Fuller stood in the doorway of Tristan's
meager lodgings in the room above an undercroft tavern, bearing John
Marshal on one shoulder and his young son in his other arm. He looked
upon Tom as though he had met him only once, long ago, and was
struggling to remember his name. "How did I not see it before?"

The word Tom had spoken came back again in Katherine's ear, jolting her
and whirling her around. "What? Tom, what did you say?"

Emmie took Theldry by the hand, bringing her full into the light, though
it seemed at first as though Theldry wanted to resist and stay hidden.
"Tom—look at her."

The shock of understanding seemed to stand Tom taller and then knock
him down again. Red rims encircled Theldry's eyes. Her lips quivered, then
pressed together in a smile that carried nothing in it but remorse. "Tom, do
you have a birthmark on your back, a small one, just a little brown dot
between the blades of your shoulders?"

Katherine felt a fall in the pit of her stomach. She had seen Tom's naked
back, on days when his vicious old master had rented out his labor to her

Matthew Jobin

papa and he had stripped off his shirt while pitching hay. She knew exactly the mark Theldry meant. She turned from Tom to Theldry and back; green eyes to green eyes, long jaws, rounded foreheads, thick dark hair not quite straight. The merest suggestion made it as clear as summer sky—mother and son.

John Marshal let go of Huddy and fumbled over to Katherine's side, catching her arm when he lost his balance. He gave her a weary but welcoming smile. "My dear child, I am glad to see you."

Katherine could find nowhere to stand in the shifting world. "You are?" She felt the wet touch of Jumble's nose again. This time she petted him, just to give herself something to trust.

Tom snapped from his trance, turned around and raised his shirt. At the sight of the mass of whipping scars crisscrossing his back, surrounding the tiny birthmark in the hollow of his shoulders without quite erasing it, Theldry's legs gave way. Emmie was there to hold her up.

"Old friend!" Lord Tristan rose at John's murmured greeting, as though he meant to find John a good seat with his milky, sightless eyes. "Welcome to you—but why do I hear weeping? Who else is here?"

John took Tristan's offer of help and used it to guide them both down to rest in the only two chairs in the room. "Tom has found his mother. He chanced upon her here in the city, and the woman's daughter noted the resemblance."

Tristan's face, at least, could show happiness without complication. "What a wonder! Make no mistake about it, John, this is the merciful working of destiny."

Theldry bent double over her daughter's arms, as though she meant to abase herself at Tom's feet. "Forgive me." Her voice came out choked, in gasps so desperate that her words could hardly be understood. "Oh, Tom, forgive me. I was only fourteen."

Katherine could not help but wonder what she would have done in Tom's shoes. Tom had been abandoned as a baby, purchased on the step of an inn and bound into a life of endless, thankless labor. His master had often said that he would likely die at the plow, whipped and driven into an early grave. Had it been Katherine and not Tom, what would she say to the woman who had left her to such a fate? No matter; it was Tom, who would do just as Tom always did.

"Mama." Tom simply said the word. He took Theldry from Emmie's arms and said it again. It rang with more power than the chant of any spell. "Mama."

Night had come in cold despite the generous fire in the hearth. Two of the floorboards squeaked, one by Katherine's feet and another beneath her father's chair. Tom helped Theldry down onto the bench by the wall. Jumble hopped up to join them, stretching himself across both of their laps.

"Well." Huddy slapped his leg. "Well, now, Tom, I'd no idea what I was in for when I let you load my cart! My reverence to you again, my lord Tristan of Harthingdale—never thought I'd say those words once, let alone twice! Well met again, Katherine Marshal—and who's this young lad in the corner?"

"That is your true and rightful king," said Tristan.

The look on Huddy's face was worth a good laugh, even then.

The boy king got to his feet. "Please don't be afraid." He kept his hood low to hide the gem in his forehead. "It's good to meet you."

Huddy dropped into a townsman's bow, rough and quick but honest. "Your Grace. This here is my son." He held his younger child forth. "Name's John, like John Marshal there, but no relation—unless there are more surprises coming tonight. Won't you kiss him?"

The boy king knit his brows. "What?"

Lord Tristan turned in his chair. "You should kiss the boy's forehead, Your Grace. The kiss of a king is thought a great blessing."

"Oh. Very well, then." The boy king leaned forward to plant a kiss on the forehead of the child John, who giggled and swatted at his nose.

"Now, now, my son." Huddy took his son back out of reach. "We don't do that. Remember what I said about never hitting girls? The same goes for kings."

Lord Tristan swept out his heavy hand toward the sideboard—or near it, since he could not see precisely where it was. "With a glad heart do I welcome you, friends and kin of those dear to me. I beg you to share in what meat and drink I have here. Refresh yourselves as much as you need, then come and let us sit all together. We have tales to melt and meld, then plans to hammer hard. Master Fuller, you do indeed have more surprises in store tonight, for you have stepped into a council of war."

Huddy Fuller wrung Tom's hand. "Stepson it is, then. Pleased to know you, more than ever." He guided Emmie away from them. "Now then, my

Matthew Jobin

lord, I must ask—this council of war won't have things said at it unfit for a young girl's ears, will it?"

"Father!" Emmie crossed her arms. "If Katherine can hear things, why can't I? She's only two years older than me!"

Katherine knew the answer to that. She felt a sudden wish to trade places with Emmie, to be the one whose father could protect her from the hard truths, to be the one who had never raised a sword in war.

Lord Tristan put his hands on his knees. "We will speak of nothing untoward without need, Master Fuller—but I must warn you that we have come to a somewhat desperate pass. If what Katherine and Tom have told me is true, then we here have much to do to save the folk in your fair city and the world beyond."

Huddy leaned against one of the posts that held up low-slung ceiling. "I've no doubt of that, after a day like we've just had. There's bad trouble brewing. We had a deal of work bringing John Marshal here with no one noticing."

"We took the tunnels." Emmie moved over to the sideboard to arrange plates of food. "Mama knows the way."

Katherine shot a glance at Theldry, who made no sign that she was listening. She sat with Tom, her hands clasped with his as though there were no one else in the world.

Huddy bowed to the boy king again. "Begging your pardon, Your Grace, but you're not the first king I've heard proclaimed today. There was a grand announcement, you see, a parade of all the guilds, nobs done up in their fur and silk, trumpets and all such—you must have heard it even out this way. They're to crown Lord Balamar tomorrow, after they marry him to Princess Merofled."

The boy king hauled on the frame of the bed, dragging it along the wall until it could serve to close a makeshift circle for his council. "My sister's here? Did you see her? How did she look?"

Huddy hurried over to do the labor that a king should not. "Done up like a little girl playing grown woman. Trying not to tremble too much."

The king took his seat cross-legged on the bed, seeming a boy like any other since his hanging hood still masked his gem. "We used to play-fight in the halls of the Spire. We jousted with sacks of feathers, riding on the shoulders of our nannies. I called her Mer-Mer and she called me Bert-face.

She gave me her favorite doll when they sent me to Eredhros, but my father took it away before they sealed me in."

"Fifty married off to ten." Huddy Fuller took his turn ruffling Jumble's fur. "I'd never let my daughter go to a man older than me, not for all the kingdom, I would not. Them nobs, I tell you—er, present company excepted, of course."

Tristan took some time swiveling his feet to the floor, slowed both by his blindness and by age, though when he gained his feet, he still stood tall and broad of shoulder beyond equal. "Young princess Merofled was gracious to me, when I went to plead refuge for my people in the citadel this morning." He moved by feel to the sideboard—when he got there he found Emmie placing a ready cup into his hands. "She played the role of queen as though the crown already sat on her head, interceding with the king to show mercy for my people. Should she marry Balamar, she will rejoin the sundered lines of the families that fought for the throne in the days of my youth."

"But it's treason!" Katherine nearly shouted it, then lowered her voice. "Saving your pardon, my lord, but it's treason, isn't it?"

"Not if I'm dead." The wry turn of the boy king's face accented its lopsided cast. "Then it's just murder."

Huddy took the meat his daughter handed him, then found himself fighting for it with Jumble. "And while they're raising up a new king by marrying him off to a slip of a girl, dozens of Lord Tristan's folk are sitting camped outside the city bounds, waiting for more awful whatsits to come out of the wild and crush them against the walls."

Emmie served out food to everyone, save for Tom and Theldry, who did not seem to want it. "I don't understand, though. Why won't the city watch open the gates?"

"They're afraid," said Katherine. "If an attack should come while the gates stand open, the city might be stormed."

Huddy spoke with his mouth full. "And while those poor blighters sit outside the walls, no one inside has to worry about how much food they'll have to share." He seemed to notice the irony of eating while he said such words—he hesitated, shrugged, then took another bite. "I am sorry, my daughter, that you have to hear such a thing said about your own neighbors, but it's the truth."

Tristan moved to face the window, as though he could somehow peer through its closed shutters. "Balamar thinks as any greedy man thinks—that this problem is a complication to his desires and so must be rated as less serious than it truly is. He hopes it is no more than a small outbreak of trouble in the most far-flung of the baronies he hopes to rule. The crown of the whole kingdom lies within his grasp, lands far more broad and rich than our tiny northern homelands. He told me as much at the citadel—that I could await his pleasure once he sits upon the throne and ask him then for his aid."

Katherine turned to the boy. "But if we set the crown on your head, Your Grace, the gates would open at a wave of your hand."

"And I would do it," said the boy. "I don't know what sort of king I would make, but I know I would not leave any of my people outside the walls of my own city with monsters closing in."

"But if you show your face to claim the crown, you're as good as dead," said Huddy. "What a pickle."

Katherine found herself up and pacing the room with Tristan. "Maybe we should try again with all the people, my lord. Go down to market tomorrow and tell everyone what is happening. They might open the gates themselves."

"I have considered it," said Tristan. "I worry, though, that their fear might win out over their valor. This much I know—it is a hard thing to ask folk to risk for others without the promise of gain for themselves. It can be done, but it must be done with care."

Huddy pulled at his chin-hugging beard. "So then, task number one is to get the rightful king onto the throne past the daggers of his enemies, so that he might throw wide the gates and bring in your folk outside—and without leaving us all in danger of being overrun by creatures not seen since the days before you slew the Nethergrim."

"That's about the size of it," said Katherine. "Except that the Nethergrim isn't really dead."

Huddy blew out a whistle. "Well, then."

Katherine felt no hunger, so gave her meat to Jumble. "I've got some ideas about how we might protect the city while we bring the folk inside, if only we could get the gates to open. I'm sure my papa has some of his own."

John Marshal nodded. "A feint and draw, child?" He seemed to come alive, shrugging off the worst of his injury at the promise of fresh action. "You're thinking of that old story, one of your favorites—Rufus of Starlingham up on Brunan Hill."

"That's just what I was thinking, Papa." Katherine returned his smile. "And if we can string some rafts across the river just upstream—"

"—a cavalry encirclement." John tapped his chin. "Yes, child, very good—when it's light, we'll want to survey the ground."

Huddy laughed. "Do you folk do this sort of thing all the time, then?"

"More or less," said Katherine.

"It is known by too few that John here was our master of tactics, back in the days when we rode together in the Ten." Tristan beamed at Katherine as though he were her other father, as proud of her as John was. "The apple has fallen near the tree."

Katherine took a seat on the wooden chest at the foot of the bed, perching on the corner nearest her father's chair. "Are you feeling well, Papa? You're not too badly hurt?"

"Tom had to set my arm back in the socket." John rolled his sword arm back and forth. "He did a fine job of it—I can hardly feel a click."

"That's good." Katherine did not know who owed an apology to whom. All she knew was that the last time she had seen her father, he had never been so angry with her in his life. She had prepared for a storm, either to roil on or to break—but not for clear skies from the start. "Then—you're not still angry with me?"

John searched her face. "When was I angry with you? Why would I be?"

"I don't know," said Katherine. "I've never seen you that way before. It was only two days ago."

"Two days." John stared at the window. "No. I do not recall it."

"Do you remember me, Master Marshal?" said the boy king. "Do you remember why you were taking me south?"

John scratched his head. "I was in Moorvale; it was the eve of Yule. I found you lost and injured in the orchard, Your Grace—and the next I knew I was on the rack with Vithric leering over me."

Katherine felt sick. "What did Vithric do to you?"

John shrugged. "He tortured me."

"With magic?"

"No," said John. "Vithric can't use magic in this city. No one can."

"So that's why I feel so good here." The boy king leaned back against the plaster wall. "They're gone—the flashes, the other sight—all gone. No more falling in and out of myself, no more seeing things before they happen, no more pain."

Matthew Jobin

"Vithric always hated Rushmeet," said Tristan. "He once told me that someone had worked a spell here long ago, one that made all other sorts of magic impossible inside the city walls. I seem to recall him saying that he thought the city *was* the spell, somehow, though I was never quite sure what that could mean."

"I'll bet Edmund would understand." The force with which Katherine felt her next words surprised her: "I wish he was here."

"So do we all," said Tristan. "But consider—Vithric remains within the city bounds, though he is deprived of much of his power. We must ask ourselves why."

"He's searching for something under the streets," said John. "He loves nothing more than the power his magic gives him, yet he remains here within these walls where his power is nullified. That must mean that what he wants to find is important to him."

"And what Vithric wants, we must prevent," said Tristan.

Huddy snapped his fingers. "Task number two, then."

Tristan returned to his chair with Katherine's help. "I was the closest thing Vithric ever had to a friend, before he turned down that dark road on which he now treads. This I tell you—Vithric never did anything without a deeper purpose, and never took a risk without a plan."

"But how can we prevent something if we don't know what it is?" said Katherine. "And if he's searching for something under the city, how can we hope to find it first?"

"I will take you."

Katherine turned to find Theldry on her feet next to Tom, no longer holding hands but still standing close to one another. She felt a burst of happiness at the sight of them together, no matter the enclosing dark.

"I've been through every tunnel and sewer under Rushmeet, many times," said Theldry. "There are places I can show you I doubt anyone could find without having years to search for them."

"Why do you know the tunnels so well?" said Katherine.

Theldry knit her hands in her apron. "I was myself what Tom once was."

John dragged himself up, then leaned against the post that buttressed one wall. "No, child, don't help me." He waved Katherine away. "I'm not as badly off as I look. Let us make our plans and move to act on them. I cannot imagine Vithric sitting idle and waiting for us to find a way to thwart him."

A knock at the door ran across the end of his words. There was a pause, long enough for the log to split and collapse on the fire, then the knock came again.

Katherine reached for her sword and said, "Who goes there?" The boy king leaped up, got his foot caught in the blanket and spilled down onto the floor.

"John." Tristan felt out with one hand. "John, take this." He held a sword.

"Thank you." John took hold of the offered sword, slid beside the uneven frame of the door and stood ready. Katherine took up a position on the opposite side. Footsteps approached, a clop of boots on the hard boards of the stairs.

A knock sounded. "Open up."

Tristan let his voice boom. "Who dares disturb the slumber of a lord of the realm?"

"Open, I say!" The voice behind the door kept low. "Open for the city watch!"

Tom waved Katherine's sword down. "It's all right, I know him!" He opened the door.

Clarance slipped into the room. "My lord." He removed his leather cap and bowed to Tristan, then the boy, then brushed back his long hair and put it on again. "I'll have to ask you all to get up, right now, and come with me. You are not safe here."

Chapter 26

E dmund did not know the name of the stretch of country that led south from Harry's castle. He had only traveled through it once before, when he and his family had moved to Moorvale back when he was ten. Had he known more of the place, had he been able to guess at likely spots for ambush or roadblock, he might have been able to make some use of his vantage above the moonless fields. As it was, he could only peer about him, anxious and watchful, until the winds of winter stung his weary eyes.

"More posset?" Emma Russet seemed to be enjoying herself, or at least trying to draw their thoughts away from the strangeness and horror of the last few days. She held out a cup to Geoffrey and another to Edmund. "It's cold, but I don't think I should light a fire up here."

Miles Twintree ruffled the musky tufts of fur that stuck up between his crossed legs. "I don't think Bossy would like that." The beast of Life had a back so broad that Miles could sit across from Emma without either of them being in danger of falling over the side. The undulations of the enormous spine beneath them came at regular intervals, cushioned by a hide too thick for swords. The heat rising from the beast made the trip through the winter night far more bearable that it would otherwise have been, but that only made Edmund worry more for the folk on the road below.

Edmund grabbed some of Bossy's fur so that he could brace himself and lean down to call to the swarm of people ranged out behind the great beast of Life. "Is everyone well down there? Not too cold?"

Martin Upfield stepped into the glow of a torch on the road below. "Some folk want to stop and camp for the night." He cupped his hands to call upward without shouting. "We've got old and sick with us, babies, too—every wagon's loaded to the axles."

"I'm sorry, Martin. We can't stop." Edmund wished he knew the crossroad-twisting spell—but then again, he had no idea what distant land he might dump them all in if he tried such magic. "When we reach Rushmeet, we'll have safe shelter, and then everyone can rest. Keep up your guard all around until then."

Martin dropped out of the light. "We're archers, Edmund. You know that's what Lord Aelfric trained us for. It's not much use in the dark."

"Please just do your best." Edmund felt another wave of worry and another squeeze of guilt. "Everyone able and willing to fight should be given a weapon, even if it's just a stick, and posted to the flanks. Tell them that if they see or hear trouble they should shout a warning first, so that help will come quickly."

"That help will mostly be from Bossy or from you, Edmund." Geoffrey kept his horn-handled bow on his crossed legs. "Even from up here, I doubt I could hit much. It's the middle of Yule—there's not even a moon."

Edmund peered out again. "Where are Mum and Father?"

Geoffrey pointed. "Down there, somewhere behind the back left leg. I've been calling down to them from time to time. They're luckier than most—they've got horses." He shot Edmund an accusing look. "It's no use fretting about them now, you know."

"Shut it." Edmund reached into his satchel. "You've got no idea what's going on or why I left."

"Then why don't you tell me?" Geoffrey puckered his freckles. "Is it secret wizard stuff again—no stupid peasants allowed?"

"Please don't fight." Emma crossed her arms and leaned away. "You two always fight."

Edmund squashed down enough fur to lay out the Darknot before him. "Geoffrey, keep one hand on this so it stays steady." He drew out his cracked hunk of crystal. "Emma, Miles, take turns watching."

Miles turned to face backward off the long rump of the beast. "Are we allowed to listen?"

Matthew Jobin

"Of course." Edmund began to wonder whether folk had started to fear him. "You can even ask me to explain something again if it doesn't make sense. All right?"

"All right." Miles seemed to relax. He tossed a smile over his back. "I bet you never thought you'd ride on top of a beast like this."

Edmund had to spread out the fur with his elbows to give himself enough space. "Never. I'd read about the *orox*, but I didn't even know whether there were any of them left in the world." He prepared his spell, the one named Trap The Stars in *The Fume or the Flicker*, weighing out just the right cost for what he wanted. He raised one hand and turned his mind to the eternal all-color of Light. He did not give himself time to fear that he would fail. "LET THE LIGHT OF THE STARS DESCEND." The crystal sprang to a glow, cupped by his hand to direct its light downward to the disk, while above, one of the stars dimmed its light.

"This is a calendar, a thing folk once used to count the days and years." Edmund started with the side of the disk that bore the rings of symbols. "These are old Dhanic glyphs, like the ones we saw in the mountains around the lair of the Nethergrim."

"Ugh." Geoffrey scowled down at the symbols Edmund rotated on the disk beneath him. "I hate those stupid things."

Edmund let that pass. His brother had good reasons for his hatred. "Now, see those symbols moving inward once I get past the last day of Deadmoon? Those are the five days of Yule: The Day of the Plow, the Day of the Sword, Hearth, Ship and Wind—but look. There's a sixth symbol, a sixth day."

Geoffrey's curiosity seemed to overcome his revulsion. "Six days of Yule." He touched the moving symbols as they joined in the middle of the disk. "I can believe that—the days have been so strange this year, and the stars are changing, like they are slipping and falling across the sky."

Edmund spread out his hand across the Darknot, moving the weak but steady light of his crystal. "Each symbol here is a day, but it is also a direction and a realm bound to one of the Signs on the Wheel of Substance." He let the light fall on the central six symbols, the ones that tracked the days of Yule. "We are sitting on the back of the beast of Life, who came into our world on the Day of the Plow—and plows are the way a farmer draws life out of the soil. Life sits across from Metal—Harry told me he saw a creature being formed out of the swords that hung from a great tree, somewhere far away when he was stuck in those twisted crossroads."

"That's the Hundredthorn!" Miles spun around—then seemed to remember his duty, for he turned back to watch the rear quarter while still speaking. "Everyone knows that the men of the Hundreds bury their chiefs on an island with only one big tree and hang their swords in the branches."

Edmund nodded. "That's the second day—yesterday, the Day of the Sword, the day of Metal." He pointed at the first two moving symbols on the disk. "Then last night, just after midnight, I found a beast of Fire at Lum's Graves, to the east. That made me understand not only the pattern, but where these symbols must all converge. We're north of Rushmeet, the Hundredthorn is south of it and Lum's Graves is to the east. See?" He turned the rings.

"A beast of fire?" Miles forgot his job again. He leaned over the disk, the glow of the crystal picking out the fascination on his mousy little face. "What was that like?"

Edmund did not want to say more about his encounter at the graves just yet. He stopped turning the symbols—each one of them was another day, one day closer to the end. Three days, just three days left. "That's why I want to move so quickly." He reversed the rings, backing up the symbols. "As soon as we reach Rushmeet, I'm getting on the fastest horse I can find and heading west for the Harrowell. I've got to reach it before the Day of the Ship, the day of Water."

Geoffrey stuck out his chin as though offering a fight. "I'm coming with you."

Edmund gave him no fight at all. "As soon as we know Mum and Father and all the folk are safe, we're off—together."

Emma leaned over Edmund's shoulder. "Then what's next? North, south, east, west—then what?"

Edmund glanced at the sky, then the ground. "Up and down. Air and Earth." He managed to cover his own ignorance with what he hoped was a convincing smile. "Let's tackle the days as they come, though."

"But how do we know it's this year for certain?" said Geoffrey. "How do we know this is the Yule with six days, when the sixth day hasn't happened yet?"

Edmund flipped the disk over. "Look at the stars. They're in a pattern no one's ever seen before. Now look up."

Matthew Jobin

Geoffrey scanned the horizon. "I can see it." His breath steamed out. "Over there, in the west—the constellation of the Archer is turning into this new shape."

"Then what about the rest?" Miles touched the other face of the disk. "Why two suns?"

Edmund kept his silence. There was no reason to scare Geoffrey and his friends beyond need.

"Fire, Edmund!" Emma pulled on Edmund's sleeve. "Fire up ahead, there, on the road!"

Edmund stood up on Bossy's back, though the working of the great shoulder blades nearly knocked him tumbling to the ground far below. Geoffrey grasped him by the belt to hold him steady, giving him a chance to look ahead. The wind blew hard, forcing him to squint, but the fire ahead was much larger than a torch, moving slowly out from a field to block the road.

"What is that?" Emma shrank back against Edmund's legs. "Mother's grace, it's on fire—from inside!"

Edmund could hardly believe his luck. "Hugh!" he called down. "Hugh, stop us! Stop Bossy! I've got to get down there!"

His shouts were drowned in a rising chorus of alarm as the vanguard of the refugees marched past the next bend in the road. "What's that? Look! A monster, a beast of fire!"

"Grab your bows, boys!" Martin Upfield raced to the front of the line. "We'll have no trouble seeing that thing in the dark. Nock arrows—bring it down!"

"Hold!" Edmund crawled onto the beast of Life's neck, holding himself up by clinging to its five-foot-long ruff of rope-thick fur. He raised his voice until it broke into a screech. "Martin, hear me! Hold your fire! No one shoot!"

Martin heard just in time. "Hold!" When he raised his voice to boom, folk listened. "Wait for Edmund. Hold, I say!"

Edmund clung to the lowering head of the beast of Life, clambering hand over hand by grasping at the ruff. He passed the beast's huge eye, which swiveled to regard him with a glassy bovine calm. He felt as much as smelled the fetid exhaust of its breath as he dropped to the ground. Nicky Bird helped him up and brought him forward through the men.

"Why not shoot?" Some of the Northend men had a harder time understanding why they should obey the commands of a fourteen-year-old boy. "Look at that thing, it's horrible! We've got to kill it!"

"It's the Nethergrim!" Someone took her panic right where panic always went—to guess the very worst. "The Nethergrim takes many forms, all the stories say. This one is the nightmare hound!"

Edmund rushed forward. "No one shoot." He tapped Martin's side as he passed. "Make sure. Tackle them down if you must."

"Aye." Martin turned and rolled up his sleeves. "You heard him—arrows off the string! That means you!" He advanced on a man who had an arrow nocked, startling him into dropping it.

Edmund sped to a run, crunching through crusts of ice to the frigid water in the ruts of the road. The horse of Metal was visible only because the dog of Fire stood near to it, burnishing one side of it in a ruddy glow from the burning heart within its open ribs.

"*Ränu rakün, tonitta?*" a voice cried out over the wind from ahead, questioning and wary. "*Räni Seb.*"

"I don't speak Vhakkat, but please believe me, I am one of you!" Edmund drew the Darknot from his satchel and advanced with it held before him. "I'm on your side!" He hoped with all he had that he was right.

The voice barked out a command. "*Hetra.*" The dog of Fire lowered down onto its haunches. The rider dismounted from the horse of Metal and approached, his hands held out open.

"I bear no weapons either." Edmund wished he had thought to drop the sword from his belt. "Not in my hands, anyway—but I'm with you. We're working to the same end. I've got the beast of Life with me."

The young man stepped close enough for Edmund to perceive his features—small and dark, black of hair and eye, wrapped in furs too large for his body. "But how come you to know of us? Where is Roki?"

Matthew Jobin

Chapter 27

C larance had a guardsman's tabard for Tom and another for John Marshal. "Here, put these on. If it comes to it, we'll say we're Lord Tristan's escort and hope for the best."

Tom slipped his neck through the hole. He bent down to ruffle Jumble's neck and pointed to the boy king. "Watch him. Guard him."

Jumble let out a woof. He paced over to the king, hopped up on two paws and licked his face.

"What danger stalks us?" Lord Tristan let himself be led by Clarance through the doorway and out onto the nighttime street. "What have you heard?"

"There are men coming this way, my lord—Balamar's and some of the men from the watch, all together in a gang." Clarance peered around the corner of the bakery next door. "It's no great leap of thinking, if you're searching for John Marshal, to look in at his old friend Tristan's lodgings. They've got torches and oil—they'll burn this place down if they find us inside."

John belted his tabard and sheathed his borrowed sword. "Below, then." He turned to Theldry. "Lead us—and thank you."

Tristan had taken lodgings at an inn much more modest than the Seven Stars, set down by the market at the place where it turned onto another street—Tom could not remember the name, there were far too many. Nothing remained of the stalls from the market, every shop shuttered, nothing left but hard wind and rats in the alleys.

"Here, Tom—I stole these from the armory." Clarance held out a canvas bundle from which projected the hilts of several swords. "Take one."

Tom knew better than to protest that he was no good with a sword. "Thank you." He drew a long, slender blade from the bundle.

"My lord." Katherine unsheathed the great sword-of-war at her belt and tried to put it in Tristan's hands. "I can take a different sword—this is yours."

"My dear girl." Tristan waved the sword away. "What would I do with it?"

The boy king sidled up to Clarance. "May I please have one?"

Clarance chuckled low. "If I come through this alive, I'll have a tale to last me my whole life long." He pulled out a short blade. "The king once asked me please."

"It's this way." Theldry rounded the corner of the alley ahead. "Come, hurry."

John Marshal moved with Clarance to take a position just behind Theldry's quick-flitting form. "How far to the entrance underground?"

"Not far." Theldry led them on, keeping to the side of the street, skulking in the shadows with a practiced ease that belied her modest and motherly dress. "The sooner we're under the city, the better."

"Just a few streets to cross, then we'll be out of view." Clarance followed close behind, his axe drawn and held in a fighting grip. "Though I'll be hanged, Theldry, if I know where you're trying to go once we get underground."

"You're too young to remember," said Theldry. "Follow."

Tom padded along next to Clarance on streets bounding what looked like tiny orchards, places that did not seem quite so ugly as the rest of the city. One corner on and the orchards may as well have been a hundred miles away. The street dropped steeply down, and over everything beyond it hung a smell of fish.

Tom stole a glance at Clarance, then another. Clarance stood just above Edmund's height. He walked with less noise than most folk—it was the deliberate way he put one foot in front of the other. At a thin-angled cross street he stopped, turning his head and exposing his missing ear, a mass of scarred up and badly healed flesh around the hole. Starlight shifted across his face—and Tom knew.

"You're not Huddy Fuller's cousin," he said.

"Hm?" Clarance turned. "No, I'm Theldry's little brother. We'll say cousin when we mean brother-in-law or the like. Don't you folk do that? It's shorter."

"Your ear."

Clarance pushed his long hair forward to cover it. "Got caught stealing. They were going to take my hand instead, but Theldry—they settled for an ear."

"They cut it off?"

"Nailed it to a cart, then set the cart rolling down a hill," said Clarance. "That hill we just came down, in fact."

Tom darted a glance about him at his motley, skulking party. John stayed near to Tristan. Katherine guarded Emmie and Huddy, who carried his young son in his arms. Jumble kept close watch over the king. Each of John, Katherine and Jumble met his gaze, their silent reponses the same—all well, so far.

Two cats got into a fight somewhere nearby—a wail rising and dragging Tom's hackles up with it, then the puffs of attack and a clatter, the victory chase. Tom turned back to Clarance. "You and my mother were slaves, just like me."

"More or less." Clarance watched Theldry pick her way through the maze of streets ahead. "We were orphans—parents dead, kin all gone, nowhere to go. We fell in with a rough crowd down in Tumble Bridge, and before we knew it we were sneaking through the tunnels, popping up to pick pockets on market day or burgle houses or . . . things I can't speak about, even now."

Theldry poked her head from between two houses, taking a careful look about before crooking in her finger. Tom took the long way around a pile of dumped, snow-topped refuse—and at once came to regret it.

The cry came from down a side street. "Hoy—guardsman! Up ahead, there!"

Clarance leaped out next to Tom. He stepped quickly in the direction of the hail while hissing under his breath. "Theldry, hide them!"

Tom glanced behind to find John pulling Tristan out of view down a side lane, with everyone else following as quickly as they could go. Tom made to leap into hiding himself, but Clarance grabbed him by the flapping back of his tabard and held him in place.

"You're spotted, Tom. Don't run." Clarance waved a hand to the approaching figure while leading Tom away at a walk. "Evening, Caed. No time to chat. Got to keep moving—on a job."

"No, no. Hold up there a moment." The shadow broke into a jog. The bright design of the man's tabard became visible before his face did. "You'll want to hear this."

"Listen—Caed, listen, I really should—"

"Hold up, curse it all! I've been looking for you two." The watchman caught up to them. He stared at Tom, bright red brows raised in suspicion. "Oh—thought you were Stick Barker. Clarance, who's this?"

"New man, hopes to get on with us." Clarance scratched his neck, looking off. "Just thought I'd show him the walks."

"Tonight?"

"We could use some extra boys about now, don't you think?"

The red-haired watchman shook his head. "Clarance—I wouldn't push things, all right? You're young yet, and don't think most folk have forgotten what—well, that you were—"

Clarance shot Caed a hard look. "That I was a gutter brat bound to be hanged before I saw twenty winters, just for trying to find enough food to hold off starving for another day? Odd, that—I haven't forgotten, either."

The other watchman did not look a hard sort. "I just mean that it's better for you to stay inside the lines, Clarance, more than for most, and especially just now."

"What lines?" Clarance crossed his arms. "Come on, then, Caed. What's your news?"

Caed glanced at Tom sidelong, creased his forehead again, then shrugged. "Captain pulled a dagger on the seneschal. Saw it myself! Called the man a traitor to the crown for accepting Lord Balamar's claim to the throne as legitimate, told him to start running before he finds a way to put him in a noose. Think the seneschal's gone up to bang on Lord Balamar's door. Captain's put out the word to pull in every loyal man, bring them all together. I tell you this—something's getting sorted in this town tonight."

"I see." Clarance slid a half step nearer to Caed. "Aren't you friends with the seneschal?"

Caed seemed to back up without knowing it. "Well, not as you'd call close, not close friends. You know me, Clarance. Come now—I only looked for you 'cause Bennet put your name in the captain's ear."

Clarance ran his fingers over the head of the axe in his belt. "Bennet hates me."

"No, he doesn't!" Caed made a vehement shake of his head. "That's just his way, is all. He's like that with everyone."

Clarance rubbed his chin, then scratched his neck. "Where's he gathering us, then? The guildhall?"

"Up at the citadel," said Caed. "When you go, tell them at the gates you left your helmet in the armory. Captain's staring holes in everyone tonight—think he figures some of us are on the other side of—whatever this is all about. So, the word's going out—just the men he trusts—and we get to the bottom of it tonight."

Clarance nodded. "All right. I'll just see this boy home, and be right up."

Caed darted glances up and down the street. "Don't be long. I tell you this else—I'd guess the men who come with him tonight will be his men from here on, and be paid like it." He slapped Clarance's shoulder as he passed by. "See you there."

Clarance turned to watch the man go, around the corner and up the steep hill. "What do you make of that, Tom?"

"It seemed to me that what he said could be a trap," said Tom. "He could be on the other side, and just trying to get the captain's loyal men all in one place, at night."

Clarance smiled. "You're a quick one, aren't you?"

Tom could not remember anyone saying the like to him in all his life. "I think I'm learning."

Clarance beckoned the others from hiding. Theldry took the lead again, winding them with slow care through what felt like every back alley in the city until she emerged on a lane that seemed strangely wide to be so short. It ended at the river not three houses on, at a gap in the city walls, between which stood a pair of great posts of weathered stone that struck Tom at once as familiar, though he could not say from where.

"That's Tumble Bridge." Clarance turned aside to an alley that ran right along the wall.

Tom stepped near to the edge. Someone had made a rubbish dump beside a dock that stank the way that only fish guts could stink, even in the frigid Yuletide air.

Katherine held her nose and leaned out to peer over the frozen Tamber. "It looks just like the bridge up in Moorvale."

"Save that your bridge actually goes across the river, so I'm told." Clarance spared a look across the water. "This one's been broken since no one knows when. See there? Right past the first piling, hardly anything left of it."

Tom turned back and forth, his memory prickling. He had been here before, he could feel it in his bones, but when?

Clarance rubbed his chin. "Father's thunder, Tom, I think you actually remember!"

"Remember what?" Tom stopped behind Katherine, who had halted next to Theldry by the corner of a tavern—a leaning, leering little hut through whose tiny windows could be seen men slumped at tables lit by rushlights, mugs in hand.

Theldry bent down to touch the step. She stood back and seemed to hug herself. Clarance came to stand near to her—not quite touching, but near.

"This is the place." Clarance swept his foot on the step. "This is where she left you."

Emmie came up alongside Tom. "You know it's going to be different now, don't you? I'm your half sister. You've got kin—Clarance is your uncle. I hope you're ready for it."

Tom would have said that he had never been so ready for anything in his life, but just then no words seemed right to say.

Theldry passed onward, around the side of the tavern, leading Tom past piled offal that stung hard at his nose and the picked-over corpse of a dog that attracted Jumble's snuffling attention. Tom found Katherine walking close at his side, looking worse off than he felt.

"I always thought it was bad, how things started for you, but I never guessed . . ." Katherine bit her lip.

John Marshal followed up beside his daughter. "A mother, Tom." Happiness took years from his face. "You have a mother, here and alive. They say Yule is the time of miracles. I'm starting to believe it."

Tom followed Theldry around the back of the tavern and helped her clear away some of the refuse from a set of rough stone stairs that led down into the utter dark.

"Don't strike a light." Theldry descended, soon becoming no more than a voice. "Hold on to one another. I know the way."

Tom felt Katherine's arm link through his. In his turn, he reached out and grasped Theldry by the strings of her apron. He did not know whether he wanted to laugh or weep, or what either would mean.

"Here I might be of more help." Lord Tristan moved to the lead of the group beside Theldry. "I have gotten used to moving without seeing."

Tom brought the king forward. "This way, Your Grace." He moved to pet Jumble's head. "Good job. Stay near him."

"I explored this place from one end of the city to the other, back when I was . . . kept." Theldry's voice trailed softly through the dark ahead. "I would sometimes sneak down here to be alone, down from the chamber where the master held us at night."

"I don't understand," said Katherine. "If you could get loose down here, why didn't you run away?"

Theldry turned back to her. "Where would I go?" She could not be seen in the gloom of the tunnels, but Tom could guess her expression from the tone of her voice. "I had no family, no home, no one to help me make a living. I had Clarance to look after—he's almost ten years younger than me, just a little boy back then—and it wasn't all that long before I found out I was pregnant."

Tom could feel the question hanging, the one he could not bear to ask. To his relief, it seemed that no one else could bear to ask it, either.

"Huddy's a good sort." Clarance took up the rear guard, whispering over Tom's shoulder. "He's a fat bag of wind, but a good sort, all the same."

"I heard that!"

Clarance laughed. "His parents disowned him when they found out he'd married my sister. We started from nothing, all three of us, but we've made a go of it."

Theldry shuffled leftward. "Here—this way." They moved together, weapons at the ready, through the reeking sewers and twisting, rot-stoned passages under a city whose every sound and smell inspired panic in Tom— yet he could not remember being so happy in his life.

He mouthed the words in silence, again and again: "Mother. Mama. Mama."

Clarance tapped his shoulder. "That's a light. Side passage, over there."

"In here. Hide." Theldry led them into an alcove so quickly that Tom could hardly believe she could not somehow see in the dark. Katherine eased her sword with an oiled hiss from its scabbard.

"Place me where it's darkest." Tristan let John lead him partway into the hiding place, blocking all approach to Huddy, Theldry, their children and the king. "If there is trouble, I will only let anyone pass if they tell me their name."

Katherine unshouldered her shield. The light swelled, weak and low.

Tom heard the rapid approach of more footsteps. A cough sounded, then a murmur that Sibby should shut up, there were monsters down here.

Tom stepped out in front of his group. "Everyone, put your weapons away. Stay here until I bring you out." He folded his long form to sit on the fetid floor, keeping his feet out of the sewer channel. A train of figures half his height approached, ragged and shuffling. The first of them startled; he waited. They did not run.

"I saw you before." The girl who led the little pack of children raised her lantern. "You came up from below in Master's house the other night. You were with that injured man."

"I have him with me, and some others," said Tom. "They are good. Some of them used to be just like you." He hoped that the others would understand and stay hidden for a while longer. One false move and the children would scatter—some of them would likely make it back to warn the slaver.

The smallest of the boys grabbed for the lantern girl's skirts. "Run away. We should run away."

Tom did not try a smile. He knew that the children in front of him had learned not to like it when bigger folk smiled. "My name is Tom. I was born where you live. I was once one of you."

The lantern girl seemed to believe him. "I'm Sibby. Do you live down here?"

"No," said Tom. "I have my mother with me. I want to bring her out, but I don't want you to run."

Sibby looked left and right, the tallest of the four children in her pitiful party. "Is she nice?"

"She is." Tom raised his hand. Theldry came forth from the shadow. The littlest boy stepped back, but Sibby held him firmly by the hand.

"We're not supposed to talk to anyone." The littlest boy tugged, but could not get free. "We'll get in trouble." The other children wavered, dragging back out of the light.

Theldry sat down beside Tom. She looked at the children, then curled onto Tom's shoulder and wept. Tom had not planned it, but it worked—even the littlest boy came forward.

"Why is she crying?" Sibby set down her light in front of Tom. "I had a mother. She's dead. You're lucky."

"I am," said Tom.

A snatch of Clarance's whisper drifted through Tom's hearing: "It's not so easy as that. They're slaves because no one wants them and no one can afford to keep them."

"Master's sent us looking everywhere," said Sibby. "We've got to find a chamber with a painting of a boy on the door. If we don't find it, we'll be in trouble."

"We'll help you find it." Tom did not know what he was going to do with them all. He only knew that he must act, must try to do right as best as he understood it. "Come with us."

The children followed in a clump through the passages. After a while they dispersed among the older folk. Tom found Sibby hovering at his side, while the smallest boy clutched at his breeches. Theldry took two of the others in tow as though they were her own, while Katherine gave her knife to the bigger of the two boys and asked for his help to guard their party.

"Your dress is pretty." Sibby looked from Emmie to Tom. "Are you sister and brother?"

"We are." Tom could not have spoken prouder words. He pointed at the child John, in Huddy's arms. "And that's our little brother, there."

"Oh." Sibby looked around her. "Then, how about that boy? Is he your brother, too?"

"No, that's the king."

"Under this—duck low." Theldry got down on her knees and scraped her way along. "I am sorry for you bigger folk. This was a tight squeeze even when I was a little girl."

"I will do my best," said Lord Tristan. He only barely made it through, into a tunnel set so well out of view that Tom doubted he would have spotted it had he passed by a dozen times. The chamber beyond felt almost as choked as its entrance, for it soon contained the whole of the motley party.

John Marshal gained his feet—weary, but smiling. He nudged Tristan. "Strangest adventure we've ever been on. Could you ever imagine that we'd still be stomping through tunnels as old men, led by my daughter, her orphan friend, some city folk and a gaggle of street urchins?"

"And Jumble." Tom bent down to pat and reassure. Jumble did not like the enclosed spaces through which they had been traveling, that much was clear. He would not abandon Tom, though, nor the king.

"It's here." Theldry stopped before a doorway. "Is it safe to bring more light?"

"As safe as anything can be down here." Clarance struck flint to steel, then set tinder to wick. His lantern was much stronger than Sibby's, casting sharp outlines of the little chamber around him. One look at the far wall was enough to draw a gasp from everyone.

"There!" Sibby raised her light. "A boy painted on a door!"

The image on the door was not in truth painted—instead it was formed from setting tiny colored stones in the shape of a solemn-looking boy of uneven features. One stone in particular gleamed brighter than the rest, the blue one set in the boy's forehead.

The king drew back his hood. "That's my picture. That's me." He turned around.

"Your head!" Sibby recoiled, then reached out in sympathy. "Ugh! Did it hurt?"

"It did," said the boy king. "It still does."

Theldry felt the stone-set door before her. "I used to come down here often, when my master thought I was asleep. I don't think anyone ever found their way this far, but I was never able to get past the door. It was far too heavy for me."

"Then allow me to assist." Tristan stepped forth, felt out along the jamb of the door, then set his back to it. Tom was about to set down his sword and help—but with a scrape and a crunch and one heave of Tristan's mighty arms, it gave way.

Katherine took the lantern from Clarance. "I wonder how long it's been since someone came through here." She ducked in through the doorway ahead. "Oh—Tom, look!"

Tom had to bend almost double to get through. He stood up next to Katherine, in a chamber no larger than the one before, one hardly large enough for the object it contained. "A chariot." He reached forward to feel the railing, then one of the wheels.

Matthew Jobin

It took some maneuvering to get inside. Huddy and Theldry kept their own children back—Tristan did the same for the slave children, leaving Tom, Katherine, John and the boy king to approach the bronze-and-golden chariot that stood on a raised platform, its massive harness coiled in front of it, looking as though it had been left there the day before.

"It's Yule," said Tom. "Remember the ritual back in Moorvale?"

Katherine picked up the harness. "Sized for six." She looked at her father. "Edmund's trying to assemble six creatures. The sun is failing, the Nethergrim rising."

John turned, as though he could somehow see up through the walls of the chamber and the ground under the city. "The wind grant you speed, Edmund Bale. The world is on your shoulders once again."

Tom touched one of the wheels—it rocked, as though it had just been oiled. He looked inside. "Katherine." He stared down at what lay on the floor of the chariot. "Come here."

Katherine joined him—and before Tom could think to stop them—so did John and the boy king. No one gasped this time. There are some sights, some moments in life, for which there is no right reaction.

"That's me." The boy king passed a hand over the skeleton that lay in stately repose on the chariot, a full-grown man with a sword upon his breast and a blue gem in the forehead of his skull. "That's me, too."

Chapter 28

"Edmund, you cannot stay long." Seb followed him out from the trees. He paused to muffle himself in his scarf until Edmund could see nothing but his eyes. "If you are to find the beast of Water, you must soon ride."

Edmund had to try again. He shouldered through the torch-lit folk encamped before the walls of Rushmeet, then cupped his hands over his mouth to shout upward. "We are the folk of Elverain and Harthingdale, northerners like you! Some of us have kin inside your walls. We are your friends and fellow countrymen—please, let us in!"

The guards on the walls could be seen as nothing but the silhouettes of their helmets against the moonless sky. One of them stopped to look down, but none of them answered.

Edmund had no idea how far past the walls his voice might carry at night. "Katherine! Katherine Marshal, can you hear me? It's Edmund!"

The nearest guard leaned out between the battlements, his face almost visible in the torchlight from below. "We don't let any Katherines into the city watch, boy, so save your breath." He called down with a cutting voice. "For the last time, you're not getting in."

"We beg you!" A crowd of dozens, maybe hundreds of folk pressed up to the foot of the walls in a wailing mass. "We beg you, let us in—there's been fire—there are monsters!"

"I've got my orders." The guard leaned on crossed arms. "Can't open the gates—the enemy might come upon us at any moment. Best you all keep running."

Edmund pushed his way to the huge double doors. "Curse it all, open the gates! These people need your protection!"

The guard shook his head. "Got my orders."

"Whose orders?"

The guard hesitated. "None of your business!" He waved a hand at the crowd. "You folk just keep a-running if you know what's good for you! There's no shelter for you here! We've got trouble enough in this city as it is without—"

"Will you be quiet?" Another helmet stuck up beside the first. "We're not supposed to talk to them."

Edmund backed away from the walls, his plans unraveling. He took Seb aside. "You're sure we can't just batter down the gates?" He led him back the way he had come, to the place where the beast of Life stood visible as a shadow nearly as tall as the trees around her. "I'll bet that *orox*'s horns would make short work of them."

"No," said Seb. "The spell on the city prevents not only magic within the walls, but creatures such as these from entering. They would not survive within the city until the spell is gone."

"So, just one more little task for us." Edmund turned to look westward over the silver-gray of winter fields under the stars. "Not only must we assemble all six creatures of the Signs, somehow including one from above the city and one from below it, and then find the chariot they will pull, but we must also break a centuries-old spell so that we can bring them all together."

Seb listened carefully. "Yes. We must do all that." He used a shake of his head that looked like no for yes, but Edmund had learned to read it properly. "We have never known how to do the last part."

"Edmund? Edmund Bale, are you here?" A full-throated voice preceded a large, tall young woman with a crossbow slung on her back and hair bound in a braid that swung to her waist. "Edmund, there you are—do you remember me? I'm Rahilda, from Harthingdale."

"I remember you." Edmund stopped for Rahilda. "Good to meet you again. Do you know where your lord Tristan is? I'd hoped he could step forth before the walls and persuade the guards to let us in."

"He's already trying it," said Rahilda. "We've been here for a whole day—they let my lord Tristan inside to make his case for us, along with your friend Katherine and her little brother."

"Little brother?" Edmund raised his eyebrows—then he understood. He turned to Seb. "The king."

"Ah!" said Seb. "Good. He is with them."

Edmund beckoned to Rahilda. "Will you come with us? Since Lord Tristan's not here, you can speak for Harthingdale." He returned to the trees that served to break the worst of the winter wind—and provided shelter from bowshot in case the guardsmen of Rushmeet got truly angry or received an even worse set of orders than the ones they already had.

"Everyone, heed me. Gather in close." Edmund stepped within the circle of a council stranger than any he had ever guessed he would attend. It had taken some work to convince the folk of the north not to fear the three strange creatures clustered at the edge, especially the dog whose heart beat with pulses of fire through is fleshless rib cage. Geoffrey sat nearest on a cleared spot of dirt next to their father, his horn-handled bow on his lap and two quivers of arrows on his back. Martin Upfield, who had been chosen against his will to speak for the folk of Moorvale and the villages of Elverain, sat with his spear across from Geoffrey. Rahilda took her place, looking quite content to be speaking for Harthingdale. Other folk hovered near in their dozens and hundreds, huddled in misery wherever they could among the fields and hedges surrounding the walled city, their meager fires giving the impression of an encamped army that was dashed at once by the wails of babies and the groans of the old and sick.

"The watchmen of Rushmeet will not open the gates." Edmund felt the weight on him, the pressing fears of almost everyone he knew dragging his shoulders down toward the frosty earth. He spoke over the frightened moans his words evoked from the folk around him. "They tell us that their orders come from the seneshcal, who received them from the king."

"King?" Edmund's father crossed his arms. "What king?"

Edmund shook his head. "I don't know, Father." He stepped into the middle of the clearing, turning this way and that so that he spoke to everyone. "I had hoped to get you all safely within the walls tonight. I still must leave right away, if we are to have a hope of seeing the new year."

"Leave?" Martin's shout was echoed by the many folk listening in, telling Edmund exactly what he had come to mean for all of them. "You can't leave us, not now!"

Edmund felt rather flattered, but tried not to let it show. "I must reach the Harrowell tonight. That's in Quentara—the fastest way there goes through Bale, the town where I was born and where my family got its name when we moved to Moorvale. I lived there until I was ten—I still remember the way. That means I should be the one to do what is needed next."

"Hunh." Edmund's father stroked his stubble. "Well—say hello to your uncle and your grandmother for me, then."

"I will, if they're still there." Edmund regretted the words as soon as he had said them. "Everyone, please gather your folk into this copse of trees around these creatures. They will not harm you—Seb here will make sure of it."

Geoffrey shook his head. "Edmund, even if you got the fastest horse alive and galloped it to death, you would never reach the Harrowell in time."

Edmund pulled Geoffrey out of the circle. "We'll be going much faster than that."

"We?"

"You said you were coming with me, remember?" Edmund turned to Seb, who beckoned the horse of Metal forth from the thickest of the trees. The horse made creaks as it moved, starlight glinting off the intricate designs on its flanks.

Edmund walked out to the road, then handed the chain-link reins to Geoffrey. "Will you stay here with it for a while?"

Geoffrey eyed the metal horse up and down. "What if it decides to run away?"

"It won't. It's a beast of Metal, not Fire. It's not in its nature to run." Edmund stepped out before the walls. He turned to speak to the folk assembled there. "Anyone who seeks protection, go now into the trees. Don't worry about those two creatures—they are on our side."

"What? Who's that?" asked some of the folk from more distant villages, crowding close. "I'm not taking orders from a little boy!"

"Suit yourselves." Edmund drew his sword and thought on the Sign for Earth. He marked out a space to begin. "This part behind me will be the gate. You'll need to guard it."

Even the folk who knew him did not understand. "Gate?" Martin Upfield approached from the gloom. "Gate to what?"

Edmund waved him back. He turned his mind to the Sign of Sundering. He chose his cost and drove his sword into the ground. "I SUNDER TO GATHER. I BREAK APART TO KEEP WHAT I LOVE WITHIN."

The ground beneath him rumbled, then split, opening a trench too wide to leap across and deep enough that its bottom was not visible in the dark. Quickly, before his hold on the magic Signs could weaken, Edmund dragged his sword behind him, tracing a circle all the way around the copse of trees, leaving only a small gap where he had started, just wide enough to let two horses pass side by side.

"There." Edmund would have appreciated the stunned praise of the folk around him had he not known that it was the tilting strangeness of Yule that had made the spell so easy, the very same strangeness that had allowed the Nethergrim into the sky and spurred on the monsters that had driven them all from their homes. "I'm no captain of war, so you'll have to work out how best to defend this yourselves."

"Leave that to us." Martin took up a post at the gap in the ditch, the butt of his spear to the ground. "Everyone inside. Come on, bring your packs. Edmund's made room for all of us."

"Take shelter in the trees, deep in as you can go." Edmund gave his mother no time to clutch at him and worry. He turned her away through the gap in the ditch. "If your torches go out, light them from the chest of the beast of Fire. He won't mind."

Geoffrey waited by the metal horse. He looked Edmund up and down. "You don't even look tired."

"I didn't have to draw that one through the center." Edmund helped his brother up onto the metal horse. "I counterweighted it—found a cost."

"What cost?" said Geoffrey.

Edmund threw up his cloak over his head and drew it around him. "This."

The winds that struck the ditch-ringed trees seemed somehow to come from every side at once. They screamed and howled, forcing the guards on the city walls to hold on to the battlements in surprise and snuffing every open fire in the fields outside.

"Sundering and Earth balance Joining and Air." Edmund had to say it twice, shouting the second time over his shoulder as the metal horse sped to a gallop up the road and away. "Counterweighting—straight across the Wheels."

Geoffrey cupped his hand into Edmund's ear. "How long will it last? I said—*how long will it last?*"

"I don't know." Edmund was not sure he could be heard in reply. "Not long. Don't worry about them." He clucked his tongue and clicked his heels until he brought the metal horse to a gallop—from there it was a matter merely of steering and holding on for dear life.

The horse of Metal strode as any horse would stride, with the important difference that it never varied the pace once it had been set. Walk, trot, canter, gallop—each pace came at Edmund's command, and once asked for it never changed, never slowed from weariness or hunger. Potholes that would have broken the ankle of any flesh-and-blood horse were simply stepped through by the metal beast, the dirt of the road crunching and giving way beneath hooves and pasterns stronger than anything they struck. The only problem Edmund and Geoffrey really had was keeping warm in the howling winter wind, their gloved hands gripped to metal that gave off none of the heat of a real horse. Things got better once they passed from the worst of the ramming cyclone Edmund had called up around the city, but even still, the ride swiftly became an ordeal—hang on, hang on, though fingers froze and teeth chattered, though legs and rumps felt the icy pinch.

Edmund waited until the only wind he felt was made by his own speed before he spoke again. He nodded left and right at the land around him. "Remember this? The Queenstown road, the Ketta stone, the deer parks? Father used to take me out this way on Grandfather's old ale cart before we moved to Moorvale."

Geoffrey leaned in over Edmund's shoulder. "I'm two years younger than you, Father never took me anywhere, and it's pitch-dark."

"There's something I must tell you." Edmund thought that he should feel the pinch of sorrow harder than he did. "It's about Mum and Father."

"What about them?"

"You'll have to look after them soon," said Edmund. "Will you do that?"

Geoffrey held on to Edmund as any brother would, but still Edmund felt him squeeze a little tighter. "Why—what about you?"

Edmund felt some relief to say the words aloud. "In three days' time, I'll be gone forever."

Chapter 29

Sibby turned her lantern back and forth on the floor, so that the light spun in flickering patterns. "What's it like being king?"

The boy king knelt on the stone floor behind the chariot. He touched the gem in his forehead, then the one embedded in the skull of the skeleton that lay in state before him. "I'm afraid all the time. I see death everywhere."

"Oh." Sibby held a hand across the light, making shadow puppets with her fingers. "I always thought it would be fun."

"How can this be?" Katherine could not help but ask the question. "Your Grace, this cannot be you."

The boy king removed his hand from the skull, which rolled over sideways. "It's me."

Sibby smoothed her filthy skirt as she stood. She looked down over the corpse. "You're all grown up. You died old."

"And in peace." Tom held Jumble on his lap, scratching him from ears to rump. "In honor."

"But without a crown." The boy king reached out, hesitated, then grasped the hilt of the sword on the breast of the king. "If this is truly me, then I have as much a right to this as anyone." He drew it forth—the skeleton's hands slid aside and fell into two jumbled piles of bones.

Katherine examined the blade in surprise. "That's the sword I gave to Edmund—the one I found in the armory back in Elverain."

The boy turned the blade over and read, "King Chlodobert had me forged." He smiled.

Sibby swung her lantern over the corpse in the chariot. Her flame kindled reflections in two gems, one set in a living face and one in a dead one. "But how can you be old and dead before you grow up? How can you be both here and there at once?"

"Time." The boy king took the scabbard from the chariot and belted it at his waist. "Sometimes I hate it."

Katherine spied something in Sibby's light. "Look, Your Grace. There, on the rim of the chariot. See those marks?"

The boy king followed Katherine out in front of the wheels. "They look like they're made with a blade. What do they mean?"

"Four, one, two." Katherine counted the marks and the spaces between them. "Three, six, five."

The boy scratched absently at his gem. "What do you suppose that means?"

Katherine turned to look across the chamber, to the place by the entrance where sat the other lantern. "Papa." She crossed over to the island of light, to where John sat with Tristan in low and rapid discussion. "I have something for you, something I was told to give you."

"—all it takes is timing, Tristan. If we can get at least some of the watch on our side, we can screen the retreat with cavalry charge, then—" John looked up. "What is it, child?"

Katherine reached into her belt and drew forth the marked coin. She placed it in her father's hands. She watched him turn it over—saw his shock. "Do you know what it means?"

John looked across the chamber at the boy king, then back at Katherine. "Who gave this to you?"

"An old man, thin of body, with thick white hair and a diamond in his forehead," said Katherine.

Tom joined them. "He saved me from being dragged away by Athelstan. He came just in time."

"You speak of Lord Exalted Seer of the kingdom," said Tristan. "Master of Eredhros and chief among those who tread the narrow path of destiny and time."

Tom turned to regard the boy king. "Then—his teacher?"

"His jailer." John shut his hand over the coin.

"What does it say, Papa?" Katherine would have gotten on her knees and begged him if she thought it would help—but she knew the closed and faraway look on his face, knew it and hated it. "Please, tell me."

John put the coin away. He darted another glance across the chamber at the boy king, but would return neither Tom's nor Katherine's searching gaze.

Light and shuffling movement heralded the approach of others to the secret chamber of the chariot. "That's the lot of 'em." Huddy spoke while groaning his way through the narrow entrance, entirely forgetting the series of pass phrases they had all arranged. "So far as we know, we're bringing in the last of the urchins." Ragged, frightened children spilled into the chamber behind him, recoiled from the light, then spotted Sibby at the back and ran to clump around her.

Theldry brought up the rearguard, shepherding the last of the children into the chamber. "It won't be long before Gwarin starts to suspect that something has gone wrong. Who knows what he will do then."

Tom helped Theldry the rest of the way through. "Mama, who is Gwarin?"

Theldry smiled only with her mouth. "The man who once owned me, the man who thinks he owns all of these little ones." She moved past him and took her young son from her daughter's arms.. "Children, please sit, all together. I'll sit with you. I've brought food—Emmie, hand it around."

Tom leaned out to look down the tunnel, then over at Huddy. "Where's Clarance?"

Huddy shook his head. "We don't know. He wanted to go sniff the air, see what had happened with the city watch. He hasn't come back down yet." He paused, looking about him. "Got some news for you all—you won't like it. Elverain has fallen, blasted by wizards and overrun by the creatures of the Nethergrim. There are hundreds of your people camped outside the walls with the Harthingdale folk, begging to be let in."

Tom sat down with a thump. He seized Jumble and held him close. For a moment, selfish as it seemed, Katherine could think only of her cousin Martin and the horses at the stable he had promised to watch over.

"I am sorry," said Huddy. "Always liked Elverain. Fine folk, lovely place."

Katherine returned to the king. If not for the gem in his forehead and the scars that surrounded it, she would have had trouble picking him out from

Matthew Jobin

among the crowd of urchins clustered behind the chariot. "Your Grace, we'll want to decide what next to do."

The king reached out to restore the skull, turning it to stare back upward. "I am trying to tell myself something with all of this." He looked out over the skeleton, its rotted raiment, the marks on the rim of the chariot. "A circle narrows in, a doom comes for me, but I don't know in what form it comes."

Katherine knelt beside him. "I swore to protect you. I gave an oath to keep you safe."

The boy king turned to her, with a look that reminded her very much of the only other person she had ever seen with a gem between his eyes. "Have you ever lost someone dear to you? Someone that you loved?"

"My mother," said Katherine. "She died when I was seven."

"Is she safe now?"

Katherine felt the punch of it hard enough that anger was her first reaction, but the look on the face of the king reminded her both of who he was and what she had pledged to him. "Come with me, Your Grace. We must choose our way ahead." She led him back across the chamber, only to find that the urgent whispers passing between Tristan and her father had begun to carry an undertone of bitter contention.

"You cannot do this." John had recovered somewhat from his ordeal at Vithric's hands, but the lantern light revealed to Katherine how haggard he still looked, how wild of eye, how old. "Tristan, for once in your life, see the world for what it truly is!"

"He is our true and rightful king," said Tristan. "Do you deny it?"

John scoffed—the sound of it near to a hiss in the cramped spaces of the chamber and the tunnels beyond. "You've read your history, Tristan. You know that it's never so simple as dropping a crown on the head of the eldest child."

"Papa?" Katherine sat with them. "What's wrong—have you changed your mind?"

"I simply ask you all to think on what you do," said John. "I have no love for Balamar, but joining his line to Merofled's will bring peace to the kingdom."

Katherine made a face. "So, Papa, you're happy to see a man your age married off to a little girl?"

John Marshal seemed unwilling to come fully into the light of the lantern. "What I want is to avoid another pointless war for the throne, one where folk die for no reason but to satisfy someone else's urge to power. I have had enough of that to last a lifetime."

Lord Tristan's snowy brows drew together. "John, my people sit in fear outside the walls of this city, along with the neighbors you've lived among these thirty years." His voice had a way of demanding silence without raising in volume. "My duty is to see them all safe. Balamar will keep the gates shut—our young king here will command them to open. My choice is clear."

John's reaction seemed to be a sulk. "You always think the choice is clear. It's always been up to me to arrange things so that you can keep thinking it."

"It is rather late in our days together to tell me that I've always been a fool." Lord Tristan shook his head. "What's come over you? One moment, you're telling me your rescue plans, then the next, you're telling me that there is no cause to make them."

"I don't mean—" John fumbled for words. "We should save the people, but there's no call to risk the king by setting him up on the throne. It invites trouble we don't need."

"Papa, it's the best and straightest way," said Katherine.

"We cannot risk him," said John. "We must protect him."

The king took his place next to Tom, so that he could take his turn petting Jumble. "Master Marshal—it seems to me that my life is my own to risk."

John clenched a fist, then opened it. He did not seem to have a response.

Tristan put his chin on his heavy hand. "Call me a fool if you like, John, but to my mind our young king has but two roads before him. One leads to the throne and the other to the grave. With that gem in his forehead, he's not an easy one to hide, and you may lay any money you like that Balamar will hunt him down and put him to the sword should he take power."

The boy king glanced across the chamber at his torch-lit, skeletal corpse. He nodded to Sibby. "If I'm king, you won't be hungry anymore."

Sibby looked up from her game with the lantern light. "I won't?"

"You won't be a slave anymore, either." The boy king turned back to Tristan and the others. "If we can get the crown on my head, I will command the gates of the city to open. Will you be able to ensure that the folk outside make it through in safety?"

"These times are all risk and no certainty," said Katherine. "But I promise you I will do all that I can in their defense."

Matthew Jobin

John pounded one hand in the other. "You are all blind to the consequences of what you do! If we challenge Balamar openly tomorrow, do you know how he will react? I doubt very much that he will meekly step aside. The city watch has gone to war with itself—we do not yet know the result of it. We might set the king upon the throne just to make him an archery target!"

Tristan's wrath grew like a slow-building storm. "If we do not open the gates, John, my people and the people of Elverain will perish at the hands of the creatures of the Nethergrim!"

"And if we do open them, the whole city might fall!" John did not seem cowed in the least by Tristan's anger. "Are we truly back where we were as youths, Tristan? Must I tell you once again that you cannot do right by everyone at the same time?"

Katherine pointed at the king. "He is the elder child of King Bregisel. He has the rightful claim!"

"Oh, nonsense." said John. "You know as well as I do that he's the son of a usurper."

The king showed no sign of anger at this charge. "Master Marshal, if you did not want me to claim the throne, why were you bringing me to Rushmeet?"

After a long pause, John's shoulders seemed to slump. "Very well, then. Do as you will." He pulled out the coin from his pocket, flipped it over, darted a glance at the boy king, then got up and strode away. Jumble left Tom's side, following John to a place apart from everyone.

"Your Grace?" Lord Tristan spoke into the following silence. "Command us."

The boy king turned away. At first, Katherine thought he was watching her papa, but no, he was still looking at the chariot and the corpse he said was his own. "We will do our best to save everyone." He turned to Katherine. "Do you have a plan?"

Katherine felt just a little insulted. "Of course I do."

Chapter 30

The Day of the Ship, The Fourth Day of Yule

Edmund took the ancient drover's road west through the foothills. The stars above him seemed to swim and drift even as he watched them, aligning in unfamiliar shapes and by their inconstancy painting ever darker the void that lay between them. Snow left no bare spot of ground in the shadow of the Girth; the stars alone could light all the world in its reflection. The view past the turn struck Edmund strange: There the boats stood at harbor upon the rippled Burnwater, off the shore of the town of Bale; hearths rolled smoke; and for the first time in his young life he knew what it was to have old memories jarred awake.

"What you're saying can't be true." Geoffrey had been trying to start a shouting conversation over Edmund's shoulder all the way from Rushmeet, but Edmund had let the wind answer. "You can't be doomed to die! It doesn't work like that, it can't—listen to me, will you?"

"There's no time to argue about it." Edmund's metal steed had lost not a pace over dike or bridge through all Quentara. Edmund had gotten used to shouts of "Did you see that?" and "What was it?" trailing into his ears on the wind. He could only guess that Tristan's folk had fled Harthingdale along the southern route to Rushmeet, for no one here seemed to know that their world teetered around them and made ready to fall, and that two boys galloping past on the back of a horse made entirely from metal was the least of their present concerns.

"You listen to me!" Geoffrey thumped Edmund's back. "You can't go somewhere just to die! It's the stupidest thing I've ever heard!"

"It has to be done by someone," said Edmund. "If not me, then who?"

The metal horse had the whole wet, wide road to itself, a moving statue kicking up snow in a plume, where four hundred cattle often passed in a clump, dogs and drover men all about them barking and goading. It was just as Edmund had seen them when he was but a little child, when he had not yet met Katherine, did not even know where Moorvale was and thought the Nethergrim was a goblin who lived under his bed and lay in wait to nip at his ankles if he got up in the dark. He looked out from on high upon the place where he was born, a place he had not seen since the summer day five years before when his family had packed up a rented wagon and left for Elverain. The Girth rose higher here, their peaks star-white. The river Swift ran like its name down past the logging camps on the north shore. A curlew called its double notes up and up from the water, a sound that called something back in him. It seemed right; one more look, a winding of his life backward from end to beginning.

"Katherine would love it here." He cast a glance over his shoulder. "Promise me you'll show her someday."

"Shut up! Will you stop it?" Geoffrey gripped Edmund as though he wanted to start a wrestling match right there on the back of the horse. "The world can't work that way. We make our own fates!"

"No, Geoffrey." Edmund steered them back onto the Queenstown road, close enough to the town of Bale that he could hope to avoid any of the Nethergrim's creatures he might chance to find on the home stretch. "I understand now. Each of us can make choices, but no one's choices govern everything. The rest—call it fate."

"But it's the future, what's yet to come," said Geoffrey. "We don't know what's going to happen!"

"Sometimes we do," said Edmund. "And when we do, we can't let it change our course. What is right to do is right, no matter what comes of it."

"That can't be true." The motion of the horse could no longer mask it— Geoffrey sobbed. "It just can't."

The old tower on the island in the middle of the Burnwater had lost its dock. Edmund peered across from the turn of the shore—the tower lay all ashatter, spilled down the rockside and half into the water in the place where the dock had once stood. The drover's road met the highway where it turned onto Water Street, and by the time they crossed before the square, he could not help but let his memories sweep him along. He hopped down from the horse's back and led it through the silent market square, past his favorite hiding spot for games of deer-and-huntsman and right up to the steps.

Geoffrey stopped, staring up at the sign. "Home." He wiped his face.

"Grandmother!" Edmund banged on the door. "Grandmother Bale, it's Edmund!"

He did not only wake a light at the old Silver Stag inn and tavern. Dogs barked, then people clattered and clamored in the houses up and down the street. Grandmother Bale was first to her door. She thrust it back in nightcap and shawl, her face far less deeply lined than Edmund had remembered, her hair bundled up under a nightcap, some of it still the same shade as Edmund's own.

"Edmund." Grandmother Bale was not and never had been kindly—Edmund knew that. "Growing up just like him, I see. You'll never be tall, you know."

"I know." Edmund gave his grandmother no chance to ask why he was there. "Get ready to run." He peered past her to find his uncle Aldus sitting up from where he always slept beside the tavern fire, as though five years had not passed by. "Pack up everything you can carry. Sound the alarm, ring the town bell. Geoffrey will be back for you before dawn."

Edmund's grandmother spluttered as only those missing teeth can splutter. "What are you on about? Run from what? Just like your father, you are, barging about without making the slightest sense—head full of fluff, I always said."

"What's he here for?" Uncle Aldus loomed up in the doorway behind Grandmother Bale. "Let me guess, my little brother's even littler inn finally went belly-up, did it? Well, you tell him that he can't just send his sons back here to beg for—"

"The Nethergrim comes." Edmund had no time for such pettiness. No one really did. "Its creatures sweep the land. The only safe place in all the north is within the walls of Rushmeet. You must go, all of you, with everyone in Bale—now, tonight."

Grandmother turned to Uncle Aldus, as though to ask him whether he could believe this twaddle. Folk peered out from their homes along Water

Matthew Jobin

Street, mumbling sleepy curses and threatening to call down the town watch if the inn started taking in guests after dark again.

"You listen to him." Geoffrey stood shoulder to shoulder with Edmund. "You have no idea what my brother's become. You listen."

"Grandmother," said Edmund. "Father's sorry for what he did. He's sorry that he stole from you and Grandfather."

Geoffrey turned to Edmund, his mouth open. "So that's why. That's why we moved to Moorvale. That's why Father—"

"Please, Grandmother," said Edmund. "Please, while you can, find him and forgive him. There's so little time in this world." He turned at once, unwilling to let his grandmother's surprise harden further into disbelieving suspicion. He need not have worried, for Uncle Aldus's torchlight fell upon the horse and showed it to be no creature born of flesh.

Edmund mounted—he noted just then that he was getting better at it— and stretched down a hand for his brother. Geoffrey looked as though he wanted to say something, but could not think of what it was, so he grabbed Edmund's hand and clambered on. They were out of the town and on the westward road by the time the first shouts of alarm began to sound.

The sound of the Harrowell long preceded its sight under a moonless sky with swimming, falling stars. A buzz reached Edmund's ears over the steady gallop of metal hooves, one that rose to a rush and then a roar through a bank of needled trees ahead.

Edmund grabbed the frigid reins. "Slow. Slow, now. Almost there." He relaxed into the saddle, hard metal though it was, and guided his steed through the rising copses to the lip of the Harrowell. He had wondered, all the way along, why the folk around Bale had not yet scattered before an onrush of the Nethergrim's creatures like their neighbors in Harthingdale and Elverain had. At the sight that greeted him from across the gushing falls, he began to understand.

"Why you?" said Geoffrey. "Why does it have to be you?"

"Why not?" Edmund almost wanted to feel what Geoffrey felt, but at the same time felt grateful for the strange calm that had taken him. "Everyone dies, Geoffrey. No one can escape it. How you meet it is all that matters."

Geoffrey hit him on the shoulder blade. "You're only fourteen!"

Edmund got off the metal horse and left it in the scrub trees back of the edge. "Imagine that you are sitting down to eat back at home, at the inn."

"Our home is gone," said Geoffrey. "It burned down, remember?"

"Better still." Edmund cracked through the icy winter weeds. "Remember it, remember the four of us sitting around the best table by the fire, all the guests gone, just you and me, Mum and Father. Imagine we've left two windows open, the one by the kitchen and the one by the front door. It's night. A sparrow flies in from the dark outside. She flits through the room, confused but warm, sheltered but lost—then flies out through the other window, back into the dark. That is life, Geoffrey. Does it matter so very much just how quickly she finds that second window? She finds it and flies out to we know not where. Stop here. It's just ahead."

Geoffrey crouched next to Edmund and peered out over the Harrowell. Both brothers breathed out in fear, though only Geoffrey in surprise. Edmund had seen and faced down bolgugs in twos and threes before. Across the Harrowell they stood in dozens, perhaps hundreds, climbing and clawing over one another on terraces of rock slickened by ice, caring nothing for their danger in the grip of their hungry hate. Quiggans gurgled and slopped through the frigid water downstream of the pool below the falls, trying without success to fight the current and swim up closer to the place where the water fell crashing from above. Shrikes—Edmund had read enough to know them when he saw them—flitted above, their variously jutting pieces never quite seeming to add up to a whole bird. They all pressed in their various ways as though against an invisible wall around the pool. They slavered, they shrieked, but none could seem to enter where the rock enclosed the water.

"Thulina." Vithric seemed to be falling from the cliff across from Edmund, the wind rippling his clothes and flapping the flame of the torch in his hand. He fell, fell and fell, but did not go downward. "You cannot hold out against me forever. No one is coming to help you."

"I am not holding out, Vithric. I am merely here." The answering voice came up from a flat rock in the pool below—a voice Edmund knew. "You are a fool—you always were. I curse the day my sister met you." Thulina Drake, Revered Elder of the *Ahidhan*, gray of hair and humble of dress, stood upon the rock in the flume, just downstream of the white roar of the falls.

"Warbur's mind opened to the truth long ago," said Vithric. "She is not dead through any fault of mine."

"I am not grieving because she is dead." Thulina sat down on the rock. "I grieve for what she did with her life. She had a spark—you smothered it. She had reason—you twisted it."

Matthew Jobin

Vithric threw his torch into the air. "ALL THINGS ARE FIRE." The sky opened—the magic Signs spun and tilted in Edmund's mind—and the clouds rained flame. Edmund clutched his head—so this was what it felt like when the greatest living wizard got a grip on the substance of the world.

"Look out!" Geoffrey grabbed Edmund and threw him backward. A tongue of flame struck hissing in the snow, raising a cloud of steam and almost, but not quite, starting a brush fire.

Edmund got his bearings and crawled around the scorch mark. He looked down from the smoldering lip of the Harrowell, his heart in his mouth. Vithric's spell had raked the walls of the cliffs around with sheets of roving fire. It even killed a few of the bolgugs and knocked the shrikes reeling through a raging updraft. Steam rose in a pall above and below the falls. Some of the leafless trees farthest from the water smoldered—not even their coating of ice completely preserved them—but the pool below looked just as it had before.

"I thought you had at least some learning, Vithric, if no wisdom." Thulina set her sheepskin-handled walking stick on her lap and adjusted her seat among the spray. "You cannot destroy what is not really there."

"No matter." Vithric seemed not in the least wearied by his spell, though it had blown and blasted with more force than any work of wizardry Edmund had ever seen. "Hide in your no-place, old woman. You cannot accomplish what needs to be done on your own."

"Then I will wait for the one who can," said Thulina.

"Will you not see reason? We stand on the brink of a new age." Vithric's form seemed to shiver, falling through the same space of air again and again. He did not seem in the least perturbed by his condition, save that he had to shout to be heard over the sound of the wind whipping past him and the rush of the falls below. "A time when we who practice magic—even of your lesser kind—have a chance to guide the world onto a better course."

The Revered Elder of the *Ahidhan* wore a look that, from Edmund's perch high above, seemed like nothing but weary sorrow. "You know what the Nethergrim is, Vithric. Think on what you do."

"I have thought on it, Thulina." Vithric clasped his hands. He turned left and right, as though pacing about teaching, while dropping forever through the air. "A new age of the world shall dawn, a fork in the path of destiny, a chance to seize the future and make it our own. Too long have we wizards labored under the yoke of kings and nobles, men without the wit to understand the most elementary principles. We have had quite enough of that. We will use the Nethergrim for as long as we need, then overthrow and discard it. There are no limits, Thulina, to the ingenuity of men. This will be our world, a world guided by the wisest."

"This will be the Nethergrim's world, one where men and women can no longer survive," said Thulina. "You are being tricked like a country yokel on his first trip to market."

"We are doing the tricking," said Vithric. "We are doing what we must to achieve our ends."

"So says evil always."

"You know nothing of it!" Vithric reached out for the edge of the Harrowell. When he did, he winced and shuddered. For a moment, to Edmund, it looked as though his hand withered and rotted—but when he pulled it back, it was young and whole again.

"You are barred from this place, Vithric," said Thulina. "It is not only the magic you throw from the clouds that may not pass here, it is the magic you have made within yourself. The stolen lives within you will not stay with you here. Have you no other fools to send? Have all your duped apprentices died or turned against you?"

"I do not need to get in," said Vithric. "You are *Ahidhan*, nothing but a powerless hedge witch, a witless old crone who thinks magic is healing cows and putting men at peace with their hopeless ends. You cannot summon the beast of Water—and without it none of your plans can come to fruit. You need all six creatures, the chariot and the rider. If I stop you anywhere, you are undone. Where is your champion, Thulina? Where is your aid?"

Edmund backed away into the trees. He dropped into a runner's crouch, one knee in the snow.

Geoffrey followed him. "I think I understand." He knelt next to Edmund and stumbled for words. "Edmund—brother, I hope you're wrong. But if not—"

Edmund nodded. "Once I'm through, take the horse of Metal back to Rushmeet. It will obey you. Take care of Mum and Father. We might not get a chance to speak before the end." He leaped to his feet and sprinted for the edge of the falls.

Vithric heard the noise of Edmund's approach. He whirled in the air. "You? You!" He nearly choked himself with rage. He brought his right hand into the Sign of Unmaking.

Matthew Jobin

"Not just him." Geoffrey followed Edmund to the edge. He raised his bow. "Remember me?"

Vithric changed spells as quick as breath, but still only just managed to deflect Geoffrey's arrow in time. The diversion gave Edmund the chance he needed to fall through the chilly air, down in a long dive into the pool below the falls. He passed within inches of the swooping claw of a shrike, then another, then down past an abrupt change of air, beyond which his pursuers could not go. On the other side, within the echoing bowl of the Harrowell, there was no cold. The waterfall sprayed up just chill enough to prickle at his face. It did not feel so much that he was falling more slowly than he should as that he became more fully aware of the motion of time. Just before he struck water, he had a thought—perhaps if he understood exactly how each instant touched the next, he would know what eternity was, and death would have no power over him.

"WHAT MAY BE STRUCK BUT NEVER INJURED?" The Signs of Making and Water came easily to hand. He should not have had so long to speak the words—but he did. "WHO SHALL CUT THE SEA IN TWO? COME YOU FORTH, BANE OF FIRE, BASE OF BLOOD. I PLACE MY YOKE UPON YOU." He became in thought as water was, changeable without end but never changing. He would not have been surprised to find that he was a drop of water himself, falling to merge with the churning pool below. He did not fear such a fate—

—but he was still Edmund Bale, still a flesh-and-blood boy of fourteen— and one who had learned early how to dive and how to swim. Beneath, below the surface, he found what he was looking for. He grasped heavy fur that was at the same time just the motion of waves, felt it move and draw him to the surface. He rode it upward, the grip of his hands a greeting, carried on a wave to shore.

"Edmund, my dear child." The Revered Elder of the *Ahidhan* rose to greet him on the rock. "Of course it would be you. I should have guessed."

Chapter 31

The lady Helisent of Norn, only daughter of Edgar, the baron of Wolland, threw herself down in a chair. "Oh!" She reached for her shoe. "Oh, my feet!"

"This is dry." Her cousin Adelie, the thrice-widowed dame of the Droves, upended a flagon over her goblet. "Where are the servants?"

Katherine followed a train of noblewomen into a retiring room just off the main hall of the Rushmeet citadel. She did not know where to sit, so she stood by the wall. The pipes squeaked and screeched out the dance down the passage. Voices babbled to a roar.

"Whatever was that dance they were doing?" The prettiest girl in the room—or at least the one who knew best how to dress—gripped the hand of the little princess Merofled and dragged her in between the ring of cushioned seats. "It was two steps over, twine your hand and turn. Other way, then—wait, start again. Left foot—"

Helisent came to the door. "Move." She brushed Katherine over without looking at her, then leaned out. "Fetch us some wine! You, there—boy! Hop it!"

The boy that bowed through the doorway was so tall that his head brushed the ceiling. "Yes, my lady."

"And quit watering it down, this is a wedding!" Helisent slammed the door behind her. Katherine slid farther along the wall, until her shoulder brushed under a tapestry and knocked dust off the back.

"She makes for a fine statue over there," said Adelie.

"I like her hair." Helisent shot Katherine a look over her shoulder. She took her seat. "Is that how all the peasant girls do it these days?"

"You want to know how peasant girls do it, you should ask your father." The pretty girl had an accent Katherine could not place. "He has one in every village from here to Paladon."

Helisent waved her hand in Katherine's direction. "I've seen that, though, riding around, those tatty little ribbons and so on. Every milkmaid I pass is doing it now; even saw it on an old drab once—she must have been forty!"

They tittered—they all of them tittered like they had been practicing the noise. Katherine shifted her dress, making sure that the tear she had made in one side gave her easy access to the dagger she kept concealed within its folds.

"Poor old Tristan." Adelie sneered at Katherine. "He must be losing his wits, bringing *that* to a wedding feast and coronation."

"Well, he is blind—we know that much." Helisent looked the serving boy up and down in disdain. "About time. Over here first."

"Look at this—not even a proper page," said Adelie. "Balamar's such a penny-pincher. What's that outfit he's got on?"

Helisent held out her goblet. "What are you, boy, the second privy-sweeper?"

"Apprentice stablehand, my lady." Tom bowed his way back into the room, his long body bobbing as he made a careful circuit behind the chairs. "I've been hired for the day. Very sorry, I don't know where your page is." He came to Katherine last. "Would you like some wine, my—?"

"Don't you dare call her lady," said Helisent.

Katherine held out her goblet. Tom poured—mostly beeswing left. He leaned close and dropped his voice. "We're ready."

Katherine smiled. Tom bowed again and left the room.

The pretty girl dragged up another friend and made a fresh try at learning the new dance. Helisent and Adelie compared their households, listing out their many servants, each talking the other down the louder the further they got into their cups. Not one of them mentioned the terror stalking the lands to the north, not even to spare a word for the hundreds of folk camped in fear beneath the city walls. Katherine waited for them to stop trying to think of nasty things to say to her, then sidled over to the princess Merofled, who may have been the whole point of everything that was going on around her, but had still been left to languish in a corner and weep alone.

She dipped a goblet into the smallest of the great silver bowls and took her chance to approach.

"My lady." Katherine offered the goblet forth. "This is just sweet cider. Forgive me, but I think we're both too young for wine."

Princess Merofled turned—a bony little girl in a dress too grown up for her, standing on the other side of the tapestry with arms crossed at her breast. She took the goblet. "You're John Marshal's daughter."

Katherine slid in next to Merofled, concealing them both in shadow and tapestry. She held her goblet by the rim. "I am, my lady."

Merofled had a kind, rather toothy smile. "That must be wonderful, to be the daughter of a great hero. I've read all the stories I could find about Tristan, your father and the Ten, then made the bards sing the rest. You must be proud."

"I am. My name's Katherine."

"Merofled. Did they knight him, then? Your father?"

"No."

"That's stupid," said Merofled. "I'll do it when I'm queen. Are you going to marry Tristan?"

Katherine laughed. "Oh no."

"But he brought you to the dance."

Katherine saw an opening. "My lady, forgive my honesty, but I don't think folk so far apart in age should marry."

The princess played with the tassels of her dress. She shot a look across the room at Adelie, Helisent and the rest of the noblewomen. "I don't either."

Katherine followed Merofled's gaze, scanning the spangled, painted, lounging womenfolk on the cushions. "Do you suppose they're happy?"

"I know they're not," said Merofled. "All they ever do is snipe and gossip. Can I tell you a secret?"

Katherine could hardly believe her luck. The king had told her what he knew of his sister, but that was five years out of date and might well have been the rosy memories of a stolen childhood. He had said that Merofled was the sweetest, kindest girl in the world—Katherine had thought him to be playing favorites. "Of course."

"I don't think I want to get married at all." Merofled spoke as though her words were high treason—which they were, in a way. "I don't like boys very much."

Katherine laughed. "I can understand why."

Merofled stared at her silk-wrapped slippers, just visible beneath the embroidered hem of her dress. "I don't like dancing or needlework or keeping household accounts or yelling at servants or anything else a lady of the castle is supposed to do."

"What do you like, then?" Katherine shifted her hand to the rip she had made in her dress.

"I like reading," said Merofled. "I read everything I can. I like to sit in the old library at the Spire and read about the world, all the people and the places, all the things that have happened, about what life is all about and what it might be for."

Katherine smiled. "I know a boy who's just the same."

"Oh!" Merofled looked genuinely interested. "Is he noble?"

"Innkeeper's son."

"Oh." Merofled hung her head. She twitched at her embroidered sleeves. She fought with mighty effort against her tears, and almost won.

Katherine shot an appraising look across the room. Dame Adelie swatted at her servants, cursing them for errors that no one else could see. None of the noblewomen around them had the wit to understand what was happening right in front of them. "My lady, I want to show you something, but you must promise me not to cry out or say a word when you see it. All right?"

The princess nodded. "Is it a secret?"

"It is." Katherine took a deep, steadying breath. She glanced about her, then reached down into the folds of her dress—

—and drew forth a toy, a floppy, ragged old stuffed dog.

At the sight of it, Merofled's eyes went wide. Her tears flowed afresh, but from a changed face.

"Bert-face wanted me to give this to you." Katherine slipped the toy into Merofled's trembling hands.

Merofled seized the stuffed dog and hugged it tight. "He's alive?"

Katherine nodded once. "I have something to ask. If you really don't want to get married today, would you instead like to leave here?"

Merofled stared at her. "But we can't leave. There are guards."

Katherine winked.

Merofled stared down at the toy.

"My lady, please understand." Katherine could not bring herself to bluster and fool the princess. "If you don't get married, you will never be queen. You'll never sit on the throne, or have armies of men salute you or any such thing."

Merofled smiled. "I'm not such a fool as that. I'd be a dressed-up little puppet on my throne, and nothing more. I'd just be there to make sure the crown sat straight on my husband's head. Eventually, I'd even have to"—she dropped her voice and leaned close—"I'd have to *make babies* with him!"

Katherine exhaled. "Then when we go back out to the dance, stay near to me. All right?"

From the look of her, Princess Merofled had never disobeyed or done anything unexpected in her whole life. She swallowed hard, then nodded her head.

"Right, girls—up, up! You're the whole point of this do, now I'm off the market." Lady Helisent pulled at her cousin's sleeve. "Drain that later, Adelie—I'm not having you falling on your rear in the middle of the hall."

The pretty girl danced her way across the room. "To left, to right, slide hands and turn—"

"—and that's when he'll pinch you. Right there." Adelie made her squeal.

Helisent took her cousin's arm. "Can't believe this—no one even to get the door for us."

Katherine turned and opened the door. "It's not as though it's heavy, my lady."

Adelie's hiss came out sloppy. "Try not to step on my feet this time, will you?" She pushed past, seeming not to notice that the little girl she would soon curtsy to as queen stood close at Katherine's side, wearing a smile too sly and conspiratorial for Katherine's comfort.

No one wanted to stay for long beneath the covered walk past the garden from retiring room to hall. Lovely as the enclosed gardens might have been in spring, they were nothing but stick and root during Yuletide. More than that, folk seemed to be ducking away from the sky, as though some part of them knew that something was wrong with the light. Katherine found herself glancing up at it as much as she dared, while thinking only of Edmund—so much so that it surprised her just a little.

"Do you want me to help you in the dance?" Princess Merofled followed close at Katherine's side, ahead of the armored guards that shadowed the train of ladies back to the booming hall of the citadel.

Matthew Jobin

"That's kind of you." Katherine listened—the song had changed, less shrill piping and a rhythm she thought she knew. Maybe this time it would feel less like public torture.

"Don't worry, you'll be better at it than me before the day is through." Princess Merofled took Katherine by the hand. "Just hold on to me at the start, and—oh—good evening, my lords."

"Oh, Harold!" Lady Helisent tossed her apple aside—almost whole, with just the sugared parts eaten off. "My darling!" She glided up to him and simpered, there was no other word for it.

Katherine's heart beat doubly for Harry—one, to see him look so downcast, and two, to guess why. Lord Tristan stood with him in the passage. From the look of them, they had been deep in conversation.

"Do you see that, my darling?" Helisent grabbed Harry's hand. She pointed to a door along the corridor decorated in holly and flowers. "After the wedding, that's where we go—then they twine the holly across the door to seal us in for the night! Dear Harold, my lord, don't look so glum!"

Harry raised his head. "Glum?" His golden eyes flashed. He took a step toward Helisent. "My people huddle in misery outside these very walls, waiting for the stroke of doom, and you folk stand about here *dancing* . . ."

"Ah, there you are!" Lord Wolland hove around the corner, flanked by guards and led by his son, Wulfric. "My dear daughter, I'll get right to it, pull the stitches all at a go, as it were. Your wedding's off. Not much sense in marrying the lord of a burned-out ruin."

He turned a bluff smile on Harry, expecting the shaft to hit home. He found to his consternation—and to Katherine's delight—that Harry looked like a condemned man who had just been told he was to be set free.

"Watch your words, my lord," said Katherine. "We might be saying the same for Wolland by tomorrow."

Lord Wolland nearly dropped his smile. "Katherine Marshal. I told you to run while you could."

Katherine drew herself up to her full height, though she kept her hands folded in a womanly posture at her skirts. "I have never run from you, my lord. I cannot say that the opposite is also true."

Lord Wolland's deep eyes glittered dark. "We nobles have our standards, our rules of custom. You are here as Lord Tristan's guest. Once this little party ends and the crown sits on Balamar's head, you will have no such customs to protect you."

Lady Helisent found her voice. "But, Father—oh, Father, how could you?"

"No arguing, my sweet." Lord Wolland offered his arm—and since his daughter was to remain unmarried—she had no choice but to take it. "I'll find you a fine young baron when all of this is over, one with good broad lands, perhaps somewhere a bit farther in from the wilds. Coming, son?"

"In a moment, Father." Sir Wulfric lingered, waiting for Lord Wolland to move beyond earshot, then turned to Katherine with an intensity to his broad, rough features that stood her back. "I know you. I know that you plan to save the peasant folk outside the walls, whether the new king or the city watch wills it or no."

Katherine would have been a fool to admit anything of the kind, had she not in her turn come to know Sir Wulfric. "I do so plan, sir knight."

Wulfric nodded. "Good. Do not forget me, when it comes time to sound the charge." He turned away to follow his father and sister into the hall.

"What a knight he would become, if only he could free himself from his father." Lord Tristan held out his arm for Katherine to take, each of them in a different way the escort of the other. "He is one half of chivalry perfected."

Katherine would not leave Harry behind. "My lord?"

"Lord?" Harry shook his head. "Of what am I still the lord?"

"You know the answer to that," said Katherine. "Will you come dance with us?"

Fiddles and flutes fought over each other, filling the high spaces, saved from harsh echoes only by the tapestries. Those of rank whirled in an intricate rhythm before the high table, men and women together this time, passing partners at intervals Katherine could not guess. They clasped hands and turned in step, just missing each other over and again. The broad citadel of Rushmeet had been decked in splendor and smelled of spice and warmth. Lord Balamar sat in state upon a throne at the high end. Whoever his gaze fell upon stopped what he was doing and turned to bow low, some coming near to going belly down on the floor.

"Of all the nerve," said Katherine. "He's not even crowned yet."

Harry sighed. "He might as well be. There's no stopping it now."

"You should have a bit more faith in me." Katherine tugged him out onto the floor. Princess Merofled made a very fine curtsy and asked for Tristan's hand in the dance, keeping close to Katherine's side. The more Katherine saw of the princess, the more she liked her.

Harry seized Katherine by the waist, as close as good manners allowed, drawing an angry yelp from his already enraged mother, who had just flown across the room to accost a smirking Wolland. "What is it that you have come here to do?"

Katherine heard the sound she had been waiting to hear. "Just be ready. If we get separated, go behind the larder and take the second door to the left. Look around on the floor."

"Father's thunder!" Lord Balamar shot an irritated look at the grand doors. "What is that noise?"

"It is the poor, my lord, come a-wassailing for Yule." Lord Tristan held up a hand to stop the music. "You've been away from our kingdom for too long. Surely you remember that on the fourth day of every Yuletide the lord of the land hears the songs of the poor, hears them praise him and wish him a joyful new year, then distributes alms and charity."

Lord Balamar rolled his eyes. "Must we?"

Even the grim old Duke of Westry looked put out as such selfishness. "What true king would deny such a custom?"

"Very well, very well." Lord Balamar looked about him. "What sort of alms do they want?"

Lord Tristan raised his bushy eyebrows. "The poor want food, my lord. They have come for the leavings of our feast."

"Send them in, then." Lord Balamar raised a hand. "Wait—someone fetch the crown, first."

The Duke of Westry looked more than a little put out. "But, my lord, you have not yet been—"

"Oh, just do it." Lord Balamar waved his hand at a page, who scurried out of the room.

Katherine followed Harry to the side of the hall. "That changes things a little." She kept near to him despite the approach of a visibly angry Lady Isabeau. "Be ready."

"You get away from him!" Lady Isabeau came as a hissing storm. "This is your doing, you peasant harpy, isn't it?"

"Yes, my lady, that's right." Katherine nodded with a hard smile. "I raked your land with hordes of monsters to despoil your only son of his inheritance, so that Wolland would call off his wedding and I would finally have him in my fat, grubby hands."

Harry made a pleading, calming gesture. "Mother, there are greater things at stake than who I marry, or whether I marry at all."

All her life, Katherine had received nothing but insults from Lady Isabeau, but she still took thought to her welfare. "My lord." She turned to Harry. "I think we should bring your mother, too."

Harry gave Katherine a look. "That won't be easily done."

"What are the two of you talking about?" Lady Isabeau glared at Harry, then Katherine. "What are—" A burst of warbling, wailing song drowned the rest of her question.

The children who had once been slaves—no, by the law, still were slaves—crowded into the hall through the door. It would be charity of the highest order to call their singing lovely. They attacked the Yuletide songs with vigor, making jokes out of every line they could, dancing as they did up the sides of the aisles, mingling among the noble folk before anyone could say a word to stop them.

"And here we go." Katherine took Princess Merofled by the hand, just as she noticed Lord Wolland looking her way in growing alarm. She sidled back into the crowd. "This way, my lady."

"Stop!" Lord Wolland turned to shove his way through the confused revelers. "My lords, the princess! Stop them! You must—"

"Fire!" The cry went up from every side of the hall, for on cue the urchins had grabbed the torches from the sconces and flung them at the tapestries that hung on all sides. The fabric went up like tinder on every wall at once. Katherine pulled Merofled back into the covered way that led to the ladies' retiring room, but then turned in the other direction. To her relief, she found Tom and Theldry waiting for her.

"This is my friend." Katherine put Merofled's hand in Tom's. "He will lead you to your brother."

"All is ready," said Tom. "The path down into the tunnels is clear."

Princess Merofled turned to Katherine. "But what about you?"

"I'll be right behind you. I have two things to do first." Katherine tapped Harry on the arm. "Send your mother along with the princess, then come with me."

Lady Isabeau screamed at Katherine. "I will do no such thing! I will not take orders from a slatternly little—"

Harry shoved Isabeau into Theldry's waiting arms. "Don't be a fool, Mother! There's a fire!" He turned to follow Katherine back toward the hall. "What two things?"

"This is the first." Katherine ducked under the thrust of Lord Wolland's sword, just past the doorway of the hall. She could have drawn her dagger— perhaps she should have—but she would not spill blood without need. Instead she socked Lord Wolland hard in the gut, then found Harry closing in to knock him sprawling back and take his sword.

"That felt good." Harry dodged with Katherine around urchin children darting this way and that in the panic, each of them following Theldry's instructions to find the exit and safety while the nobles and their guards raced for the front door. "What's next?"

Katherine threw off her dress to reveal the tunic and breeches underneath. "This." She flew into a sprint across the middle of the hall, past guards so busy panicking that they did not mark her determined progress up toward the throne. Harry understood at once and interposed himself between Balamar and his brother Gundobad, crossing swords with Gundobad and giving Katherine the space she needed. Lord Balamar recoiled at her approach, so that the half-gold, half-stone crown of the kingdom nearly fell from his head. His eyes went wide, his wolfish face froze in fear—but Katherine had no designs against his person.

"Out the back!" Katherine snatched the cloven crown from Balamar's head, dropped her shoulder and shoved aside a smoldering tapestry. Before anyone could fathom what was happening, before Wolland or Balamar could organize the guards, she and Harry had ducked through the servants' passage, joined a waiting Tom and scurried into the storeroom where Theldry waited with Princess Merofled and a quaking Lady Isabeau. Katherine and Harry held hands all the way through the twisting sewer tunnels, but when they reached safety and Harry leaned in for a kiss, Katherine found herself turning away without quite knowing why.

Chapter 32

Tom kept watch on the guidhall steps, just past the grand double doors. His shoes still reeked from his flight through the sewers with Katherine, his mother and everyone else who had managed to escape Balamar's hall. The crowd in the square before him rolled and rumbled, a sea of bodies below a sky that hung ugly, the sun far too low and casting light that felt hollow, deprived of all warmth and throwing thin, scattered shadows, whose shapes seemed to suggest things they never quite revealed. In such light, everyone looked like an enemy, every glance hooded, every mouth curled over hard-set teeth.

"Tristan." John Marshal emerged from the back of the guildhall. He made a reverence to the boy king. "Your Grace, my lord Harold—Katherine, listen to me. What you are doing is foolish. You do not know what you risk."

"You're wrong, Papa." Katherine had prevailed on Tristan to take his sword back for the ceremony, so Tom gave her the one he had been wearing. "He is the rightful king. He must take the throne."

Lord Tristan nodded his head. "The people will see, John. They will understand. We will restore order and give the command to admit the folk of Harthingdale and Elverain inside the walls. Once that is accomplished, we will make our plans to thwart the rest of Vithric's designs, whatever they might be."

"We cannot do this." John staggered and coughed, still unsteady from his ordeal at Vithric's hands. "We risk the boy's life without need."

"John, my dear friend." Lord Tristan took on an air of firm kindliness. "You have suffered greatly these last few days. I do not think you see clearly.

Young Chlodobert is due your homage and fealty as king. It is your duty to raise him to the throne, as it is mine."

"You don't even have someone to crown him!" John stepped out under the covering portico of the guildhall as though to block them all from coming forth—but then he blinked and shrank back from the light. "You risk everything on the whim of the crowd."

Tom stepped to the edge of the circle of nobles. "Who crowns the king?"

Harry bore the half-stone, half-gold, thoroughly ugly crown of the kingdom under his arm. "The Lord Exalted Seer of Eredhros usually has that honor." He wore the colors of Elverain, belted and booted, not a hair out of place. "He is not here, though, so we must make do."

John rounded on him. "So, my lord, you think you can set the crown on the head of the king yourself?"

Harry pursed his lips. "No, Master Marshal. I shall bring forth the crown and let the king take it up with his own hands."

John snorted. "And break centuries of tradition, right out there in front of a crowd you hope will set this boy on the throne by acclaim."

Lady Isabeau had managed to find someone to fix the tear in the hem of her dress. "At least someone here remembers the proper order of things."

Katherine ignored Lady Isabeau. "Papa, he is king by sacred right!" She gestured to the boy. "The throne and its power is his to take!"

John drew his lips into a haggard line. "Very well, then." He stalked away through the nave of the guildhall, taking the side exit onto the square.

"Then you will not stay?" the boy king called after him. "You won't help us?"

"I will do all that I can for you." John shoved his way out through the doorway.

Katherine stared after her father, then sighed and turned to the royal party. "Is everyone ready?" She nodded to the princess. "My lady?"

Princess Merofled held tightly to her brother's hand. "I'm ready." She let him lead her forward to the edge of the light.

Tom followed John out through the side entrance and to the edge of the crowd. "Master Marshal? Where are you going?" He was too late—he saw no sign of John amidst the guildmen in their colors and badges, though he did spy Huddy Fuller on the side steps nearby. "Is all well below the city?"

Huddy nodded his head while pulling absently at his thin beard. "Aye, your mother and the urchins are well enough, all safe and sound, though

I've not a clue what we'll do for feeding them come tomorrow." He scanned the crowd in the square. "It's what's going on up here I don't like."

"Master Marshal said the same." Tom turned to look through the crowd, just as the first roar of recognition sounded at the entrance of the royal party onto the front steps. "What is it that worries you?"

"I can't place it." Huddy Fuller's eyebrows went up. "Hoy, did you see that? That was Clarance, way across there."

Tom craned up to look. "I don't see him."

"He was waving like a madman, then he pushed into the back of the crowd." Huddy took a few steps down. He looked back at Tom. "I don't like this. Let's go meet him."

Tom took a deep breath, then dove after Huddy. He would rather have plunged into an ice-choked lake than the swarm of city folk before him. Everyone he jostled looked him over with a wariness that often broke into open suspicion. Not a few of the men he passed kept their hands at the hilts in their belts.

". . . don't give a tinker's curse for the pack of 'em." One man leaned in loud conspiracy with another, long knives slung at their belts over thick, bloodstained leather aprons. "They wanted to live up in the hills, so if they've run afoul of some bolgugs or what have you, that's their lookout. I'm not giving up my hard-earned grub to a pack of yokel vagabonds. Is that what this is about?"

"Soon as they're inside the walls, they'll be asking for more." The second man paused to give Tom a hard look, then turned back to his companion. "We let them in now, they'll be trying to run the place come spring."

Huddy Fuller waited until he had passed out of their hearing before he spoke again. "That's the butchers' guild—you mind that bunch—they've got longer knives than anyone in the city except the watch, and aren't always so particular about where they stick 'em, if you follow." He shot a glance over his shoulder at the guildhall. "There they go, then. Hear that?"

Tom looked back to see the herald of the city raising his horn on the steps of the hall.

"Hark ye, hark ye all!" The city herald blew his horn three times from atop the platform, hard enough that he fell into a coughing fit afterward that nearly robbed him of the silence he had won. "The lord Harold of Elverain will speak!"

Harry's bearing and appearance was such that he got the attention of the crowd better than the blast of the herald's horn. "Good folk of Rushmeet, hear me! You have lived to see a momentous day, one that you will tell to your children's children. Today, here in the square of this very city, you shall see your new king proclaimed!" He held up the crown in both hands.

That got the people interested. The parade of guilds contracted in toward the guildhall. Men of substance jostled forward, trying as hard as they might to see the new king.

"Honor and hail to Lord Tristan of Harthingdale!" Harry stepped aside so that Katherine could lead Tristan forth to cheers that were even louder than those Harry had gained for himself. "And hail also to Princess Merofled, younger child of our departed king Bregisel!"

"*Younger* child?" A young man in russet with a guild badge on his arm turned to a woman much his elder. "So who's to be king, then? Where's old Balamar?"

"Maybe the wedding's off," said the old woman. "Maybe Lord Harry's to marry the princess. That'd suit me—if anyone looks like a king, it's him."

"I don't think it works like that," said the young man. "Got to be next in line for the crown, or near to that, I reckon."

The old woman laughed. "Pah, those nobles are all alike—and they're all one another's cousins, to boot—who cares which one of them rules? I'll take Pretty Harry any day."

Tom spied another gang of men lounging at the junction of an alley. These bore weapons but no obvious marks of any guild. They nodded to one another, separated and melted into the crowd.

"That bunch again." Huddy Fuller curled his lip. "They work for that wizard, don't they?"

"They do." Tom stood up as tall as he could and peered over the heads of the folk around him. "I see Clarance. This way—he's not far." He steered them through the remains of the Yuletide market, over stock and refuse and a beggar too worn out to ask for alms.

"Clarance—Clarance, hoy!" Huddy jammed his way through the remaining few yards of milling folk. What's the news?"

"The watch captain's dead." Clarance still carried his axe but was no longer wearing the livery of a watchman. He looked drained and pale. "So is Bennet, and every other man I trusted on the watch. I just saw their bodies floating downstream in the Tamber."

"Hear you all the judgment of destiny!" The city herald would never again in his life be so important, and from the sound of his pompous, straining cries, he knew it. "The Princess Merofled comes forth to acknowledge her brother as king!"

Huddy let out a low whistle. "The watch will be Balamar's pet from now on, then. Where are the rest of them?"

"Some are up on the walls." Clarance kept a hand to his axe. "They're holding the towers and gates, all of them loyal to Balamar, Wolland and the rest of that bunch."

"Where are the rest?"

"All around us," said Clarance. "They and Vithric's men, they're one and the same now."

"Hear us!" Katherine stood tall on the steps, but her voice lacked the strength to carry over the rising grumbles of the crowd. "Everyone, listen! Your king is acclaimed!"

"Nonsense!" "Rubbish!" It seemed to Tom that Vithric's men were everywhere, stirring up the crowd around them against the boy king. "We want Balamar!" "We want Balamar!"

Others in the crowd turned in angry defiance. "No! We want Chlodobert!" "Chlodobert for king!" "The elder child has the throne by right!"

"He's the son of a usurper!" "Balamar for king!" "Balamar and the Stag!" Shout countered shout, not so much arguments as challenges that sounded dangerously close to battle cries.

"As your king, I will care for all the people!" Chlodobert's voice broke in an attempt to be heard over the din. "Hear me, good folk of Rushmeet! I will open the gates for the refugees from the north! I will set the slave children free!"

Tom felt a sick, draining feeling, for after the pause that followed, the mood of the crowd seemed to turn.

"You're going to let that rabble into our city?" One of the men from Vithric's manor house, the one named Hugh, came forward to the steps. "You're going to throw our gates wide when there are monsters in the wilds? This boy wants us all killed! Down with him! Down with Chlodobert!"

Lord Tristan's voice, unlike Katherine's and the king's, could carry quite a distance. "The folk of Harthingdale and Elverain are your friends! Some of them are your kin! Do not abandon them in their time of need!"

To Tom, it seemed as though the sky itself led the answering cries. "No! Let them rot!" Neighbor turned on neighbor: "Yes! Chlodobert and mercy!" "Chlodobert and the Hound!" "Chlodobert for all the people!"

"This is getting ugly." Clarance looked left and right. "That's Caed over there, but he's not wearing his watchman's colors." He pointed at the red-haired watchman they had encountered yesterday before descending underground. "He's slipping in toward the steps—see that?"

"Oh no." Frightened as Tom was, hard as he found it, he did his best to push his way back toward Katherine and the king.

"Tom?" Huddy grabbed for him and tried to follow. "Hoy, Tom, where are you going now?"

Clarance helped Tom make a wedge. "Keep your hand on your knife, cousin."

"Balamar!" The shouts got louder. "Chlodobert!" Folk turned on one another, their anger growing under the thin sun, under the spectral shadow in the sky that Tom could feel and almost see. Harry rushed to set the crown on the boy king's head, but no one was watching.

A scream sounded from the crowd—and before Tom's blood could unfreeze, there came another.

"Murder!" Voices shouted over one another. "Someone's been stabbed!"

Clarance drew his axe with a curse. "Tom, Huddy—stay with me!"

Madness broke. Most folk tried to scatter in every direction, but death had come in too many places at once, leaving them with no clear idea which way was safe. Panic surged—the crush choked off Tom's air, while all around him he saw daggers flashing and swords held high.

"Hello, Clarance." A head of bright red hair crossed the edge of Tom's view. Clarance let out a cry of pain and slipped away from Tom's side. Huddy bellowed and charged at Caed, getting a slash across the arm for his trouble. It was all Tom could do to hold Huddy back, then hold a staggering Clarance up on his feet.

"Huddy, help!" Tom felt Clarance's weight dragging him down onto the patterned cobbles and under the trampling feet of the panicking crowd. He felt Clarance's blood seeping down over his hand. Cries sounded from all sides, from everywhere flashed eyes, panic hardly distinguishable from the hard-set gaze of the killer. A man came near, knife held low—Tom kicked out hard at him, using the force of it to shove himself and Clarance away.

Huddy grabbed for Clarance's other arm. "No, Tom, not to the steps! We'll never get through up there!" He pulled them aside toward an alley. Tom had no idea whether Clarance had already died on his arm. He shot a last glance up at the steps of the guildhall. Katherine and Harry had their swords out, but they were in retreat, beset by more than a dozen men. Tristan thrashed blindly this way and that, his sword held out but without a hope of stopping anyone. Lady Isabeau picked up Merofled and dragged her back into the darkness of the hall—then Vithric's men surged forward and drove all of Tom's friends from view.

"The king!" Tom heard Harry's cry above the din. "Where is the king?"

Chapter 33

The Day of the Wind, The Fifth Day of Yule

O n a cloud—Edmund had never dreamed or guessed that such a thing could be done. He stood on nothing he could feel, could see nothing beneath him save for puffs of rolling white. When he took a step, his feet simply stopped moving down once they passed into the cloudy bank, without his being able to feel what it was that he was pressing against. He should have felt afraid, he knew that much, but instead he simply gazed about him at the strange and shifting stars, at the hole in the sky where the moon would have been had it not been Yuletide. He felt no wind, no cold, nothing but that same feeling he had felt in the Dorwood, at Lum's Graves and the Harrowell, the feeling that if he stopped breathing, it would not matter to him one bit.

"How did we get here?" He followed the Revered Elder through knee-high cloud, toward what looked like a dome of distant mist. "How can you move us from one place to the next?" The beast of Water shadowed his steps, a great bear whose form was composed entirely of droplets and waves. The bear turned her snout, sniffing at the still, cool air. She seemed to know better than to step off the edge of the cloud, but otherwise plodded along without the least concern—perhaps just as a bear made out of water should feel in such a place. Her footsteps made no more noise than Edmund's or the Elder's—that is to say, none at all.

"These places are both here and not here." Beneath such stars the Revered Elder of the *Ahidhan* seemed not quite so old, not quite so near to tottering into her grave. "Four of the six have names, for they are places a man could reach while walking the surface of the earth. Two of them do not, for one lies below the world of mortal men and one above. These realms were made long ago by someone whose learning in each of the three schools of magic exceeds anyone alive today. The Dorwood, the Harrowell and all the rest are in truth the very same place, for those who know how to see it."

Edmund had to wonder, then, why traveling between two places that were in fact the same place had taken a whole day, though he could not help but feel relieved that the journey seemed to have taken him from one night to the next without the faintest hint of the Nethergrim's voice in his mind. He had hardly noticed the passing time, only the winding steps up from the pool, the slow progress higher and higher into mist that had enveloped and then replaced the wet stone at his feet, a long wandering in gray with neither patience nor its opposite for company. He had not known where he was going and had not known how long it would take for him to get there. Remembrance of time, though, became remembrance of self, which then became the remembrance of fear. "Is this what it's like to be dead?"

The Elder turned to him. "I have no idea." She still leaned on her sheepskin-handled walking stick, but she did not seem to need it anymore. "If I've ever died, I can't remember it."

The oddest thing about the place was the little cave, the humped pocket of cloud where the Elder led him. Not only did the cloud give the place a sort of roof, but underneath its shelter he found a bed, a chair and tables of rough, antique design—even what looked like a strange old fiddle, though one with far too many strings.

Edmund picked up a book from the table. He flipped through its vellum pages—he had never seen the ancient symbols of the Gatherers looking so fresh and undecayed. "What is this place?"

"It's someone's home, I think." The Elder sat herself down on the bed, which, it turned out, was really a layer of blankets over clouds. "They're all like this."

Edmund set the book back down on its table. There was not even the merest coating of dust to show him where it had lain before. He looked out across the clouds. "I always thought that maybe the happy dead were in such a place."

"Oh no." The Elder smiled. "When we think such things, we only show how tightly we are bound to our bodies and to the earth. We stand up alive and fall down dead, so we think that up must mean something better than down. No. The true place would be far more interesting than this."

She reclined with a sigh. "Though I must admit, this is an exceedingly comfortable bed."

Edmund tread with steps lighter than feathers, back out through the opening and over to a break in the clouds below. "There it is." Far down, impossibly far, lay the city of Rushmeet, whipped by winter winds he could not feel and draped in a white of its own. He saw more of it than he should, given the light. The longer he looked, the less sure he was of how far it really was from him. The bear of Water followed in his footsteps, snuffling down at the hole in the sky as though she might find some fish to catch within its depths.

"My friends are there." Edmund stretched out a hand—no, the city was not small and near, after all. "My family, my neighbors. I'm doing all of this for them."

"Why did you feel the need to say that?"

Edmund looked back at the Elder. "I said it because part of me wants to stay up here forever." He hugged himself, though not from cold. "Most of me, to tell the truth."

The Elder stood and approached. "Edmund, everyone in his life has cause to ask the same questions: Why me? Why now? Perhaps we should ask them aloud and, by doing so, consider what we truly mean by them."

Edmund would have felt much better to find knowing, kindly certainty on the Elder's face, but her eyes searched his as much as his searched hers. "I'm afraid," he said. "I don't want it to be me. I don't want it to be now. I want time. I want to hide, to forget, to look away from what must come. I want to be busy and distracted, held so tightly in the grip of each day that I can't see them all running by. I want to stand at the edge of someone else's grave, to pity him, but think as I walk away—not me. Not now. Not yet."

"But you say that it *is* you," said the Elder. "That it is now. Why?"

Edmund breathed in air neither warm nor cold, without wind, almost without substance. "It has to be me. Even the Nethergrim knows it."

The Elder sat down beside him, so that her legs dangled into the empty space of the hole in the clouds. "Let me play the other side for a moment.

What would happen if you just let go? What would happen if you did not fight?"

Edmund considered it. "The Nethergrim would win."

"Win what?"

Edmund looked down at the city. "The Nethergrim wants to smash us all to bits. She thinks the world is hers and that we're a nuisance to be cleared away."

"Maybe she's right," said the Elder. "What do you think Rushmeet looks like to a being who was here in the world before us? A blight on the earth, a boil, an ever-spreading sickness. Perhaps she is trying to lance the boil while she still can."

Edmund had to fight the sudden urge to boot the Revered Elder of the *Ahidhan* over the side of the cloud. "Are you telling me to stop? Are you telling me to let the monsters come in, let the sun fall, let the people I love just die?"

"No." The Revered Elder looked up at him—and, in a dizzying shift, no longer like an elder at all, instead like a delicately pretty young girl with ringlet hair and pinprick freckles. "I am asking you to arm yourself with the means to meet your end. Do not go to your death wondering why you should."

Edmund glanced about him, as though the stars, the clouds, or perhaps the watery bear could answer for him. None of them could, so he had to reach within himself. "It seems to me that if we should find a way to make peace with the world, to live in it without harming it, then that goes for everything else, too, even the Nethergrim. Somewhere, no matter how hard it is to find, there is a first harmony, a song last sung before there was such thing as sound. All the bits and pieces of magic I have ever learned— opposites, oneness, time—I feel as though they all point back to something I can't quite reach, as though I woke up just after the song ended and all I can hear is the echo. Everything good I do in this life is a way to hear that song again, to help it to be heard by everyone and everything, and by hearing it somehow everything will be—revealed. Renewed. Itself again."

The Revered Elder nodded her head. "Yes. That's why you. That's why now."

"I can do this," said Edmund. "I can try to save the lives of those I love— even the ones I don't love. It's up to them what they do with that life."

He raised his hands into the Signs of Air and Making. "What is needed by all but seen by none? Come you forth, sea of wind, stuff of breath. I place my yoke upon you."

It came as air—as air and nothing more. The stir of wind across the island of cloud raised the hairs on Edmund's arm the way summer storms always did when he watched them from the covered step of the inn. Thunder rolled in the heavens, the kind he had never heard in the midst of winter. Only by looking carefully, by trying to peer through what he saw and letting his vision spread out wide, could he see the shape of a great bird of prey, its wings but gusts of wind, its eyes nothing but a focusing of starlight. The bear of Water shifted nearer to Edmund as though to give the bird of Air space to land, or perhaps because it did not wish to get too close.

"Maybe I'll survive all this, somehow." Edmund spied his starlit reflection on the watery surface of the bear. He recoiled in surprise, for he saw himself as a man full-grown, to a height somewhat taller than he had guessed he would reach. He had a beard, one with a few streaks of gray among the blond. He looked—wise. Good and kindly, but with strength, a fire tended and controlled. "Maybe we'll have another talk just like this twenty years from now."

"Oh no." The girl Elder smiled the prettiest and most ageless of smiles. "I'll be long dead by then."

"Then you must know how it feels to be near the end," said Edmund. "What advice do you have for someone about to die?"

The Elder was no longer a girl, but was yet not old. "Say everything you ever meant to say, to everyone to whom you meant to say it." She wore her ringlet hair now bound in a veil and kept her hands clasped over a belly swollen big with child. "Speak from your heart, from the best of yourself— you will find yourself speaking only words of forgiveness and love."

"Katherine." Edmund looked down at the city. "She was never going to feel for me what I feel for her."

"I waited all my life for a love that never came." The Elder grew old again. "Or, worse yet and more honest, my love came too late, something that wounded me all the more. I wonder, though—does that make my love any less? It shaped me, that waiting. It became my prop, my knowledge of myself. I felt a longing for something. That longing made me something better than I would otherwise have been, for I held to it without grasping, cradled it without smothering it, drank from that same wellspring again and again without drowning. It wounded me, but it made me strong."

Edmund felt himself becoming smaller and younger again. "But if love is not returned to you, how do you know that it is real?"

"Child." Lines drew in deep around the Elder's eyes. "I know that a feeling is real because I feel it."

Edmund returned to contemplation of the earth below, turning from thoughts of why to thoughts of how. Something about the view of the distant city tickled at his mind, something that took a good deal of staring to understand—but when he did, it came like lightning. "Do you see that? The streets, the shape of the city!"

"We are not all blessed with a mind like yours, Edmund." The Elder peered down through the clouds. "See what?"

"The city—the whole thing!" Edmund took out the disk from his satchel. He sat cross-legged and placed it on his lap, then wound its concentric rings forward through the days of Yule. The symbols clicked together in the middle. Though new constructions had blurred them somewhat, the lines scribed in the earth by the broad and ancient streets yet matched the shape of the symbol at the center of the disk.

"The whole of Rushmeet is a symbol." Edmund passed his hand over the embossed metal of the disk. "The whole thing is a spell."

The Elder leaned over the disk with a surprised fascination that reminded Edmund very much of Tom. "What a wonder! What does it say?"

Edmund read the outlines of the streets to make sure they matched the lines that composed the central symbol of the disk. "*Courage–Upward.*"

The Elder smiled. "Well, then—I do believe that someone is trying to tell us something."

"From all that time ago?" Edmund turned the disk over, then looked up—the stars above nearly matched the positions of the stars on that side of the disk. "This thing is ancient."

"I once asked Tom whether time was a road or a river," said the Elder. "What I should have asked was whether it was a line or a loop."

Edmund stretched out his hand to stroke absently through the fur of the bear. It made his hand wet and wicked water up his sleeve, but he still felt strands to grip among the waves. He met the formless gaze of the great bird of Air. "Let's find out."

Matthew Jobin

Chapter 34

K atherine hauled her bundle in the dark, up a spiraling staircase so narrow that she could brace her back against the walls as she went. Torches sat extinguished in their sockets, leaving her with no light save for the very dimmest glow from above, some distant source of fire whose flame she could not see.

"I'm scared." Emmie clanked her tray of bowls against the inside post of the stairs. She paused at a landing hardly large enough to stand upon, through which a doorway led into a passage that ran within the middle works of the city walls. "Mama, what if I can't do it?"

"You're just here to serve the soup." Theldry came up last on the stairs. "You can do it, dear. Leave the rest to me and Katherine."

The upper turns of the stairs were somewhat easier to navigate, for there the murk was not quite entire darkness. Katherine took a glance through each arrow-slit window she passed, though there was nothing to see inside the walls or out save for a few pinpoints of fire in the camp made by the folk from Elverain and Harthingdale. Dawn had yet to come, despite all the scurrying plans she had been making and carrying out since the disaster at the guildhall. The city within the walls looked asleep, though Katherine knew better than to believe it. She adjusted her grip on her bundle of fresh watchmen's tabards—ones that she had spared a few moments to launder herself so that her ruse might have a better chance of working—making sure they draped completely around what she carried within their folds.

"All right, ready?" She turned to Theldry and Emmie at the top of the stairs, in the alcove space beside the gallery that ran along the stretch of wall above the north gate of the city. She pulled at the housedress she had borrowed from Theldry. It was impossible—she was too tall, so she had to settle for the skirts coming only halfway down her calves. She approached the heavy, ironbound door and banged on it with a fist.

"Who's that?" a man's voice rose in irritated query. "That Stick Barker out there? Not your turn at watch till dawn."

Katherine motioned Emmie forward. "We've brought your meal. From the citadel."

Eyes pressed to the eyehole in the door. "Just some womenfolk, Caed." The eyes flicked downward. "Leave it outside. We'll pick it up when you're gone."

"We've also got a fresh change of clothes." Theldry held up her mop. "And we've come to clean out your chamber pots."

Muffled argument sounded from behind the heavy door. Katherine kept Emmie front and center in the view of the eyehole, taking full advantage of her more clearly nervous and inoffensive stance.

"It's just some women, Caed—what, are you afraid of that little girl, there?" The bolts shot back. "Well, I don't care, I'm starving and it stinks in here."

Katherine kept her gait hunched and shuffling on her way into the long, narrow gallery, slipping in behind Emmie and Theldry, trying to look like the least interesting of the three. The trio of city watchmen inside paid the most attention to the stew Emmie set out on their table, hardly sparing a glance at Katherine or her bundle.

"Fine, then." Caed slammed the door shut, then shot the heavy bolts. He spared Katherine and Theldry a curt nod of his head. "Get to your work. I'll let you out when you're done."

"Now, that's more like it!" One of the other watchmen, a whipcord youth just past his boyhood, set to his meal at once. "Good stuff, good stuff—here, Caed, don't you want yours?"

"You touch my dinner and I'll chop your hands off." Caed crossed back through the gallery with torch in hand, stepping around a pile of huge bolts for the wood-and-steel ballista that faced out through a slot in the walls. He peered through an arrow slit, then set his crossbow on the seat beside it.

The third watchman was a good deal larger but only a little older than the first. "We'd never dream of it, Caed." He shot a wink at his companion, then spooned out some of the stew from Caed's bowl.

Theldry was too obviously holding her broom like a weapon for Katherine's liking. "Where's the chamber pot?"

"Can't you smell it, woman?" Caed pointed along the gallery. "Over there." Theldry shot a nervous look at Katherine, then at her daughter, then moved off along the gallery to the far end.

"Here—tall girl, come here." The first watchman stripped off his dirty tabard, showing only thick linen undershirt below. "Give me a fresh one."

Katherine unrolled a fresh tabard from her bundle, leaving what she carried within it much harder to hide. She looked to Caed. "You sure you're not hungry?"

Caed shook his head while still peering through the arrow slit. "They found the boy yet?"

Katherine handed the fresh tabard to the first watchman. "That false king, you mean? I haven't heard."

"I've got my orders about what to do if I find him." The first watchman seemed to be racing his tablemate down to the bottom of his bowl of stew. "Bring him back alive, I get ten gold marks. Bring him back dead, only two."

"They'll want to execute him in public to make sure they don't get impostors popping up in a year or two." The third watchman paused in his eating only long enough to drink. "I was on duty in the citadel before this. I heard Balamar—should we be calling him the king now?—talking it over with Lord Wolland. When they catch the boy, they'll have him beheaded in the square, so everyone knows he's dead."

Katherine caught the skinny and half-dressed watchman shooting looks her way, an appraising grin that was half an attempt to be charming and half an attempt to size her up to determine whether he should bother. She glanced aside, feigning a coy giggle—how long, Tom? How long was it supposed to take?

"Trying to show off your muscles?" The third watchman snickered at the first, then snuck some more of Caed's stew. "Shouldn't you try growing some first?"

"Nonsense! Women can't resist, once they get a good look." The first watchman flexed a skinny arm, winked at Katherine, then looked more closely. "Wait, now—you're just a little girl!"

"An awfully *big* little girl," said the third watchman. "Who are you, anyway? Never seen you around town."

"She's my cousin, from Dunston." Theldry returned. She shot a glance at Katherine and then another at Caed, who still had not touched his stew. "She came in to visit at Yuletide right before we shut the gates."

"Right, right." To Katherine's vast relief, the two watchmen at the table began to slur their words. "Lucky her, I says. Sounds like Balamar's big plan is to keep the gates shut till after Yule."

The skinny watchman shivered, then started trying to shrug his tabard over his head. "Why, what happens then?"

"Balamar's got a wizard hanging about—always coming in from the shadows at night to give him advice." The third watchman had eaten the most stew, so the effects of it hit him first. He tried to lean his hand on his jaw and missed. "Heard him saying that if he holds them monsters back till after Yule, all will come right, so he's sitting tight till then. Can't help but feel a bit bad for those folk stuck outside, though."

"Pah." Caed came back to the table. "Let 'em rot, I say. Never liked Elverain folk. One of 'em came to beg his way in a while back, offered me all the coin he had. I took a shot with my crossbow—think I winged him."

He picked up his bowl of stew and found it half empty. He lowered his bright red brows. "Hey!"

Katherine shot a look at Emmie, who took the hint and backed away. Theldry shuffled around behind Caed, sweeping the floor with her broom held tight.

Caed glared at his two friends, who giggled back at him, sweaty and pasty white. A deeper suspicion dawned on Caed's face, but too late. The third watchman's eyes rolled back in his head, then he pitched backward senseless from his chair. Katherine drew her sword from the bundle and charged.

It was over in an instant. Katherine battered Caed to the floor with the flat of her blade, then Theldry beat him senseless with her broom for good measure while shouting, "This is for my brother, you pig!" Katherine checked all three of them over—though she had no love for such men, she felt glad there had been no need to kill. "Emmie, bind them up, use the spare winch-ropes over there. Theldry, with me." She set to the winch and raised the portcullis gate, then fixed it open. She took up the watchmen's horn and blew—two notes short, one long.

"Once I'm outside, don't open this door for anyone unless you're sure it's safe." Katherine dragged all three watchmen out of the gallery. "You remember the signal to drop the gates?"

"Two long in a row." Theldry tossed the dirty chamber pot out after the watchmen. "Good luck."

Katherine threw off her housedress and raced back down the staircase in her tunic and breeches. When she reached the bottom, she found all in readiness—Wulfric on his enormous charger, Harry on a borrowed hunting courser and Indigo waiting saddled in the shadow of the gatehouse.

"Greetings, Katherine." Wulfric raised a hand in salute. "I just had a talk with my noble father. I believe I am disowned." Ranged behind him were a few dozen men of the city guilds, some on horseback but most on foot and armed with twelve-foot pikes, more than Katherine had dared to hope would come.

She clapped Huddy Fuller on the back. "Thank you. Well done."

Huddy smiled through obvious fear. "City folk are good folk, when you scratch 'em deep enough." He nodded about him. "Fullers' guild here, drovers' guild, cordwainers', coopers'—but I'm afraid the moneychangers' guild shut their door in my face and likely ran off to tattle on me to Balamar."

"Thank you, all of you." Katherine took Indigo's reins and leaped into the saddle. "We will march with pikes in close formation, while the cavalry flanks left and rides to screen." She glanced up—the black sky above had turned in the east to pinkish gray, while in the west . . . she felt a shiver.

"My lord." She turned to Tristan, who stood with a handful of men by the gates. "Draw the bolts. Keep the gates open as long as you can."

One of the men in Tristan's detachment wrung his hands around his spear. "What if the watch comes at us?"

"Lord Tristan will try to persuade them to stay their hand." Katherine rode to the gate. "Otherwise, you'll have to fight."

Tristan turned and felt his way to the great iron bolts of the door. "You have heard the stories of my brave band, the Ten Men of Elverain?" He had no more trouble finding the handle than anyone else would have had, for the feeble light had yet to reach under the cavernous gatehouse. "You have heard of the exploits of the fifty brave men who came with us to the lair of the Nethergrim? This I tell you, one and all—you will equal them this day!"

One of the men shuffled and glanced aside. "Didn't most of those men die?"

Katherine raised a hand. "When this is accomplished, you and your city will be forever dear to the heart of our true and rightful king." She rode in close to Harry and dropped to a whisper. "Any sign of him?"

Harry shook his head.

"Papa?"

"I'm sorry, Katherine." Harry passed her a spare shield. "But they weren't among the bodies left after the riot. There's still hope."

Tristan drew the bolt of the gates, then seized on the chain and started dragging the doors wide. From the walls came the sounds of growing alarm as troops of city watchmen heard the noise and guessed its meaning. "Onward, onward!" Katherine spurred Indigo to a leaping canter, slipping through the doors as soon as they had opened wide enough to admit Indigo's broad bulk. She rode out into the dawn—and for the first time, she felt what Edmund had told her he had been feeling since the start of Yule. She could almost see it, the rising hole in the western sky, the beating on her neck of rays that were not light. It felt like cold, but after all it was Yuletide and the ground she galloped across lay ankle deep in snow. No, it was something she could not name, something far worse than mere cold. She drew Tristan's great sword-of-war, then raised it in defiance to the west.

"Katherine!" Her cousin Martin stood guard at the makeshift gate left by Edmund's spell, a hundred yards from the city walls. "Katherine, they're here! Northward, look—"

An unearthly howl drowned his words. Katherine had nearly been too late—indeed, that was still a question. A vanguard of bolgugs slavered and leaped at the north side of Edmund's ditch, throwing their spears into the copse of trees while dodging the arrows fired in return, squealing in hunger at the sight of the hundreds of folk within the ring. It was only a matter of time before the creatures worked their way around to the entrance.

Farther north, beyond their position and across the bridge up the Kingsway, was a sight that reminded Katherine of her papa's stories of his last assault on the lair of the Nethergrim, something she had never quite been able to picture in her mind. A troop of stonewights cracked the ground with every pace, falling apart as they moved and yet perpetually remaking themselves from the earth below. Thornbeasts hissed along the road with the sound of a thousand brooms scraping hardened dirt. The firesprites made their own false dawn from the flames of their bodies—they had already lit a dozen outlying cottages ablaze. The shrikes swooping in from above would find Edmund's ditch no barrier.

"Cavalry, with me!" Katherine did not wait to ask whether Harry and Wulfric would follow with the rest of the riders. "Pikemen, set up with Martin by the entrance! Get everyone inside as fast as you can!" She dodged left, leaving the road and hurtling on through a field with a hedgerow for a screen. She heard the sound of hoofbeats—she caught sight of Harry riding at her side, sword at the ready.

"Katherine, we can't hew down fire or stone!" Harry cried over a wind that rose with the sun and its empty twin across the sky. "What are we to do?"

"Hit the bolgugs. Slow them down!" Katherine wheeled right once past the level of the ditch, running along behind the backs of the bolgugs who had lined up without thought to guarding themselves. She found Wulfric out in the lead, already in the fray, the full fury of his right arm revealed. There was no bluster in Wuflric, when it came to the test. Bluish-black blood flew in high arcs around him—his sword rose and dove, rose and dove.

Katherine set Tristan's sword to the work in her turn. By the time she had finished her pass of the bolgugs with the cavalry, many of the foul creatures lay dead and the rest had been forced to halt their advance around to the opening of the ditch, turning instead to defend themselves from the cavalry's next charge. Not a horse or a rider of the two dozen who had charged out with her had fallen on the first sweep, and encouraged by their success, none of them looked unwilling to make another pass despite the hundreds of spears that had swiveled to point their way. A glance across the dawn-lit snow showed villagers on the run for the open gates under a cacophony of horn signals from the confused and frightened men of the city watch. Katherine thought she could spy Edmund's family among the crowd—she was sure she saw Bella Cooper dragging old Robert Windlee along as quickly as his aged legs could carry him.

"Katherine." Harry gripped her shoulder. "Turn! Look!"

Katherine looked northward and recoiled in fright. The firesprites had burned their way across the bridge, after which the stonewights collapsed it under their combined weight and came thundering out of the river as though water was no more barrier to their progress than air. The folk of Elverain and Harthingdale streamed forth from the opening of the

Edmund's ditch, hampered by its narrow confines, some bowling others over in their panicked rush toward the city gates.

"One more pass!" Katherine spurred Indigo to the charge. "One more, and back inside! Just keep the bolgugs busy for a bit longer!" This time the bolgugs were prepared for her sweep, jabbing at horse and rider on the pass. The cavalry did much less damage and suffered some losses of their own, but they held the bolgugs in place, forcing them to defend themselves instead of charging at the villagers.

Upon rejoining the road, Katherine found that she had left herself very little space to turn and flee before the onslaught of the creatures of the Nethergrim who were impervious to the thrust of a sword. There was no screening to be done against a line of stonewights, no hacking at a creature that was nothing but an intelligent, malevolent fire. Perhaps Indigo would have stood his ground against such an onslaught, but no other horse ever born would do so. The cavalry had done all that it could, and though the refugees were nowhere near to completing their escape, there was nothing more Katherine could do but flee along with them.

"The shrikes!" Wulfric shouted in the midst of their desperate gallop back south along the road. "Lord Harold, Katherine, behind us! The shrikes are—"

Even as Katherine ducked and looked, she found the swooping formation of shrikes that had been bearing down on her thrown back into utter disarray, blown by what felt like a hurricane. Inside that hurricane—his arms and legs curled out as though grasping the neck of a flying beast she could not see—was Edmund, riding in front of the Revered Elder of the *Ahidhan*. The next thing Katherine knew, she had ridden through a squall of sleet that seemed to have come from a cloudless sky. On the other side of it, making a thunder equal to that of the advancing stonewights, came three creatures from the entrance to the ditch—a huge dog with open ribs exposed to the flame within, then a metal horse upon which rode a man in heavy, foreign-looking clothes, then last a colossal cow-like beast with horns like lances.

"Come!" The foreign man made a beckoning gesture. "*Toovhi*—riders, come between us! Ride to the city!"

Katherine spurred Indigo to a gallop, trusting his fearless nature to lead the other horses in her company through the lines of the three creatures ahead. She slowed just past the metal horse, letting Wulfric lead the riders onward to the city, where she could see the crush of refugees working with

Tristan to throw back an attempt by the city watch to shut the gates. Harry, she found to her delight, stayed with her. The shrikes wheeled in the turbulent air, thrown off their attack. The falling sleet coalesced into the shape of a great bear that took its place in the line next to the great cow-like thing. The creatures of the Nethergrim seemed to hesitate, then came on at a slow, determined trudge.

Edmund wheeled back behind the line of guarding creatures and lowered down to let the Revered Elder of the *Ahidhan* come gently to earth. "Well done, Katherine." The wind whipped his blond hair in waves. "Go inside and bar the gates behind you. Leave the rest to me."

Chapter 35

E dmund sank to one knee in the cold light of morning. The last spell he cast had left him staggering—he had been forced to draw it through the center, to give of his own life to give it shape in the world. Through the gray mist that veiled his sight, he could just make out the wild flickers of the firesprites leaping from tree to house, desperately trying to keep the flaming substance of their bodies alive in the pounding rain. One by one they wisped and winked out, drowned in the pitiless torrent from above. The spell released and winter restored itself, the rain freezing in a snap into a pool of ice on which the last of the fleeing bolgugs slipped and slid down into the channel of the Tamber.

"*Avh nu,*" as we say in my homeland." Seb reached out to help him stand. "Well done, my friend."

Edmund shivered in the renewed chill of the Yuletide wind. It had all been so terribly easy. Every spell he had ever read about had simply worked, so long as he or Seb could find the proper balance for the Signs. The five creatures at Edmund's side had done the rest. Even the desperate and eternal hunger of the bolgugs was not enough to stiffen their resolve against such an assault—after a few fruitless volleys of spears and swarming charges, the survivors had melted away under wind and thundering hooves, the rake of icy claw and the thrust of horns like lances. It was complete—the bolgugs all slaughtered or put to flight, the stonewights welded together into a helpless mass, the shrikes confused and disoriented until they had all flown straight into the ground. Even through Edmund's exhaustion, a feeling washed over him, the exhilaration of power in the palm of his hand. He came to understand that in his long, secret studies, this was the feeling he had been seeking to find.

The Nethergrim rose full and glaring in the west. **And you would trade all this for oblivion?**

"They'll be back before long, Edmund, and in greater numbers." Seb stroked the tree-trunk leg of the beast of Life. "Go within the city; do what is needed next. We will hold here."

Edmund shaded his eyes against sunlight on snow. "We've got archers up on the walls." He caught sight of Nicky Bird and Telbert Overbourne among the men holding longbows and waving from the battlements. "Bring the creatures in close—my neighbors can help protect you."

Seb got up on the back of the horse of Metal. "I do not envy what you will need to explain." He wheeled around and started at a walk toward the city walls. "We have brought your folk into the city because it is the only safe place in the north, but now we must remove the spell that does the most to protect them."

"They will still have the walls." Edmund turned and headed for the gates. "They will still have us."

And so you march onward to your end. The Nethergrim blazed in the western sky. **As foretold, as forewarned—if you carry on against me, I will be your death.**

Edmund compacted his fear into a ball at the floor of his belly. He shot a look at the mountain-cut horizon. "So be it."

A chorus of cries turned him back around just as he reached the city gates. The folk of the town of Bale were in luck. Had they arrived at the walls of Rushmeet any sooner, they would have run smack into a horde of the Nethergrim's monstrous servants. As it was, they had come just in time to have a clear run for the gates, before the monsters had had a chance to regroup and try their assault again.

"Go with them." Seb steered horse of Metal aside from the entranceway, leading the other four beasts back into the ditch-ringed copse of trees. "*Vhem tiigen*, my friend."

Edmund raised a hand. "Grandmother Bale! Uncle Aldus!" He called them out from the line of fleeing folk. "This way, follow me." He waved up to the gatehouse, and with a shout, the portcullis trundled up and the great doors drew wide. He stepped within the bounds of the city, sighing in relief as the Voice of the Nethergrim receded out of hearing. He found his father and his brother waiting just inside the doors.

"Oh." Harman Bale's face was a sight to behold. "Mother!"

"Son." Grandmother Bale looked as though she was about to push past him—but then she stopped. "You never told me about Edmund's—well, what he's turned into."

Harman scratched his neck. "We haven't talked in a while."

Grandmother Bale peered more closely at Edmund's father. "You're looking poorly."

"Nearly killed by a wizard, a few months back," said Harman. "All things considered, I'm lucky. There's been worse than that going around lately."

Uncle Aldus turned around to gape. "Is that Lord Tristan shutting the big doors there?"

"It is I," Tristan answered. He held out a hand for Edmund to take and lead him near. "A good job for an old man with his sinews but no sight. Who do we have here, Edmund?"

"The folk of the town of Bale, my lord," said Edmund. "Just beside me is my grandmother and my father's elder brother."

"Ah, more of the clan!" Lord Tristan ignored all show of deference from Edmund's family, coming forward instead to fumble and clasp hands with a blustering grandmother Bale. "Will you come with me? We have camps set up in the square for the newcomers, and where it is safe, many city folk have opened their doors to give shelter. I will make sure you have a roof above you, my dear woman—we elders must look out for one another."

Edmund left Lord Tristan and his father to guide the folk of Bale within the city. "Geoffrey!" He raised a hand in happy greeting to his brother.

"Edmund." Geoffrey bore the bow that had once been Edmund's own, a quiver of arrows and a long knife. "Good to see you." Edmund would have given anything to wipe the battle-weary hardness from his little brother's face.

"What's the news?" Edmund followed Geoffrey up the road toward the guildhall, where a makeshift headquarters had been placed. "What about Balamar, Wolland and the watch?"

"There's been a battle inside while you had yours outside," said Geoffrey. "We've beaten them back to the citadel. Tristan tried to start a parley, tried to explain that we were all on the same side whether we like it or not. He nearly got stuck full of arrows for his trouble."

"I hope they work out that they're not our enemies soon," said Edmund. "We could use the help."

He looked his brother up and down. "Where'd you get the armor?"

"The armory," said Geoffrey. "Where armor comes from."

Edmund stepped around a gang of city folk on their way to man the walls. "It's too big on you."

"Shut your face," Geoffrey snapped out, then seemed to check himself. "Well, you were wrong. We've gotten a chance to talk again. I haven't told Father what you're planning to do, not yet. Tell me why I shouldn't."

"Just don't." Edmund waved back at some folk from Dorham who recognized him and shouted a hail, but did not stop. "Just let what is to be happen."

Geoffrey grabbed at him. "They're your parents. We're your family. We won't just let you die!"

Edmund stopped at the junction of the streets. "Look up. Look east, then west. Can you see it yet?"

Geoffrey looked. "The sun is low. It's—cold somehow and . . . there's something funny about the sky in the west."

"That is the Nethergrim." Edmund dropped his voice, though he hardly needed to do so among the cacophony made by people and livestock around him. "She is there, in the sky, and every day she orbits closer to the sun. Tomorrow she will reach it and blot it out. After that, only her rays will shine here, only her sort of world will be possible. A new age will dawn, or maybe an old age will come again—same thing, in the end. People like you and me, Geoffrey, the people you see around you, Mum and Father, Katherine, Tom, everyone—we'll become like ghosts, like half-imagined stories of something that could never be. Do you remember the ritual we do on the eve of every Yule?"

Geoffrey nodded. "That chariot, with the funny beasts and the boy with the candle on the back."

Edmund nodded. He looked up at the wan, weak sun.

Geoffrey's sorrow took him so hard that it looked like rage. "If you go, how do you know you won't come back?"

"It's the sun, Geoffrey. It will burn." Edmund had no idea how he could say it so calmly. Maybe the Nethergrim was right. Maybe he still did not see death for what it was.

"Geoffrey." He nodded to the girl he saw approaching. "Could you leave the two of us alone? We'll speak again before tomorrow, I promise."

Geoffrey did not want to leave Edmund just then, but he could not seem to think of what to say in reply. He stormed away, red in the face, as though Edmund had said something mean to him. Edmund would not leave it there—no, not for the rest of Geoffrey's life—but he had precious little time and there was someone before him to whom he must speak. Even there, though, even there on the brink of his end, he felt a blush rising and found a closing lump in his throat.

"Edmund!" Like Geoffrey, Katherine had found some armor, but unlike Geoffrey's suit of boiled leather, she wore a shirt of chain mail that came down just past her hips. She had bound up her hair and wore Tristan's sword. "I still can hardly believe what I just saw. Poets will be singing about you in a hundred years and more!"

"That was mostly Yuletide." Edmund had expected—dreaded—finding Katherine with Harry, but she seemed to be alone, on her way toward the gates. He felt a little happy swell—she had come to find him. "There's something I must tell you."

"That makes two of us," said Katherine. "So much has happened. I need your help—I'm afraid I've made some terrible mistakes and I'm still not sure—"

"Wait." Edmund stepped closer. "Please. I know there's a lot to plan, much to be done by tomorrow, but before it all starts, please, just hear me."

Katherine's dark eyes—oh, such eyes—searched his face. She wore a look that told him that she knew what he was going to say.

"I love you." Edmund found it much easier than he had feared, there amidst the refugees shouting for their families, the troops of men handing around what weapons they could find, the droves of oxen being led off to a makeshift and noisy slaughtering ground across the square. "Please understand what I mean. I dreamed of marrying you. I dreamed that one day you might kiss me."

Katherine responded almost as though Edmund had told her the very opposite, as though he had spurned her and proclaimed that he had always hated her. "I know. I've known for a long time. Maybe there is something wrong with me, that I—"

"Please don't explain," said Edmund. "I'm not telling you because I want you to answer. I'm telling you because tomorrow—"

"Katherine!" The familiar voice cut across the noise of the square. "Edmund!"

Edmund hung his head. He felt the urge to laugh—Tom, getting in the way, one last time.

"Oh, Tom." Katherine brushed a tear aside as she turned, a tear Edmund thought he would go to his grave remembering. "Oh no, is it Clarance? He was looking so poorly. I'm sorry if—Tom, what? What is it?"

"Oh, Katherine." Snot poured from Tom's nose, mingling with tears that ran in streams down his cheeks and off his chin. His face was contorted in a grief that made him shockingly ugly. He was covered in blood. "Katherine."

Edmund had not the faintest idea what had been going on in the city. He had not seen either of his friends in days. Even still, the look on Tom's face told him what was wrong like the leap of thought to thought, some vicious magic that forced the truth into him and would not admit the slightest hope that he was wrong.

Katherine broke into a run, led by Tom back to the guildhall. Edmund found himself thinking, as he charged after them, of the night when they had all sat together in Athelstan's field and dreamed of some great change that might steer them away from the dreary lives about to unfold before them. If he could go back to one point in his past and make a change, he thought, he would go right there. Peter Overbourne would not be murdered, the bolgugs would not steal away the children and drag them to their deaths, the Nethergrim would not rise again and he would live out his days as first the innkeeper's son and then the innkeeper, putting his father in his grave and carrying on brewing ale and serving meals to his bumptious, ignorant, kindly, decent neighbors. Maybe he would have married Anna Maybell. Maybe he would have gotten fat and been happy enough. He would trade everything, in a heartbeat he would trade everything he had learned and gained for that.

Just like that night, the night when Emma Russet had screamed from atop Wishing Hill, he could not keep up with the long-legged strides of his friends, so he came last to the scene. He hurtled through the door of the guildhall to the sound of Katherine's scream. The fond dream of the safe, small world he had once so despised vanished, leaving him with the broad, reaching cold of the world that was.

They were not too late for the very end, but too late for it to mean much of anything. Edmund did not know what John Marshal saw with his last sight, whether, in his final throes, pale and bloodless, his guts trailing out upon the guildhall floor, he knew that his daughter was clutching his hand, crying his name, telling him she loved him and begging him not to go. Edmund was not sure whether anyone heard his own voice shouting out to move the dying man outside the precincts of the city, so that some desperate spell might put John's ruined body back together. It was over too fast. The hand in Katherine's lost its grip, the eyes looked nowhere—death.

"Papa." Katherine knelt at his side. "If you can hear me yet, I love you. I know you cannot stay. Your daughter loves you."

Edmund staggered back. His knees nearly gave out. He felt long, thin arms around him.

"I tried." Tom laid his head on Edmund's shoulder. He shuddered and shook, slick down his front with John Marshal's blood. "When they came in, I tried everything. I tried."

"He saved me." The boy king sat on the floor on John's other side. "With each and every breath, with everything he did, he saved me. He saved me even when he was dying himself. He brought me here with the last—his last . . ." He put his head in his hands.

The world started up again around Edmund. People who had been there all along came out of the echoing noise he had ignored on his entrance. A woman Edmund did not know kissed Tom's forehead, then Katherine's. Harry hurried in late, startled back in real grief, then fumbled for just the wrong sort of mealy, pointless words.

The world went on, closed up around a death and walked away. With every breath Edmund took, he took one more breath that John Marshal did not share.

"Is this what you meant?" he said, without knowing whether the Nethergrim could hear him, said it knowing he would not hear the answer. "You won't change my mind."

He approached John's body and did what Tom had once done for Peter Overbourne. He closed John's eyes—dark eyes just like Katherine's.

"I swore to you that I would watch over her and see her safe." Edmund said it quietly enough that not even Katherine could hear, though she had collapsed to the floor just behind him. "With my last breath I will do it."

He knelt there for a while. He felt the ache of his knees on the stone, wanted them to ache even more. Tristan came in, led by Geoffrey—the aged hero was nearly as hard to console as Katherine.

"Nothing they could do." Some other stranger hovered near, just out of the circle of misery. "Can hardly believe he even made it this far."

The folk of Moorvale came in from their posts and shelters. Their sorrow came like waves that broke and broke.

Martin Upfield held Katherine in a bear hug. "You've still got kin. You've still got me."

"The best of us." Lord Tristan tore at his beard. "The best of all of us."

The Revered Elder of the *Ahidhan* came in on Rahilda's arm, her walking stick tapping on the stone floor. She creaked down beside John and piled his guts atop his belly. No one but the princess even noticed their true and rightful king sitting there on the floor. After a while Edmund turned to the boy, for he had been sitting next to John all the while, grasping his other hand.

"Your Grace, whatever happened to bring you back here, we must make sure that John did not make this sacrifice for nothing." Edmund knew how stern he sounded, how much he wanted to hear that John was dead by some fault of the hunched, uneven-featured boy before him. "We must see this through to the very end."

The king let go of John's hand. "Death is not so very bad. Time can't catch him now."

The world walked on and stupidly on. Horns sounded—Jumble raised his head to bark at them. Before long, a man came bursting into the guildhall—youngish, with a thin, short beard. The woman next to Tom reached out to embrace him—he stared down at John Marshal in shock, for that was not why he had come.

"The monsters are back—they're pressing to the walls." The man searched out and found Edmund in the crowd around John's corpse. "You're the wizard who brought those other creatures, aren't you? Well, they're under attack."

Chapter 36

T om had no trouble catching Edmund on his dash through the streets of Rushmeet. First, he could sprint almost double Edmund's speed. Second, though the shops and houses still seemed to leer and loom at him, he had been there long enough to know one street from another. Third and last, Edmund was walking while holding out the strange metal disk, looking down at it and then up at the lanes and alleyways around him, as though the one were telling him something about the other.

"How could you say that to Katherine?" Tom stopped short of grabbing Edmund by the shoulder, but he still raised his voice louder than usual. "How could you tell her to just march back up onto the walls? Her father only just died!"

"I'm saying it because it must be done!" Edmund took another bearing with his disk, then strode away, shouldering through a group of folk from Moorvale and Longsettle without returning their hails. "Those creatures outside with Seb must be defended, and after that, the whole city will need to be defended. There will be time for funerals later!"

A bellow that resounded from over the city walls doubled and redoubled through the alleys, freezing everyone around in their tracks. Tom shot a look northward, up at the walls. He spied the makeshift levy of men who had replaced the city watch all staring outward, as though something beyond the walls had drawn their full attention. Among them stood Wulfric, his azure surcoat rippling in the wind. Katherine appeared from the staircase below. It was too great a distance for Tom to read her face, but she moved with purpose—moments later, the men of Moorvale had drawn a volley and fired at something Tom could not see.

"If any one of those creatures dies, the Nethergrim reclaims the world." Edmund rushed south, then west, then stopped. "We need them all, all alive, or we are lost—and everything John ever did, everything he ever worked to save will be gone, too. Is that reason enough to stop crying and act?"

Tom forced his sorrow down. "What do you need?"

Edmund looked down at the disk, then around him. "I need older streets, the oldest in the city."

"This way, then."

Tom led Edmund down toward the river, toward Tumble Bridge, the docks, the stink of fish and refuse. Even in the worst of their panic, the incoming refugees from Elverain and Moorvale had avoided the place, so rather oddly, it was the only part of the city that looked more or less as it had when Tom had first seen it. The only differences were the lack of folk on the streets, along with new boards hammered across the windows of the hovels, as though that might provide some defense against what was coming.

"Yes." Edmund stared at the disk. "Yes, this is more like it. You might not believe this, but these streets were once the grandest in the city, many centuries ago."

Tom glanced behind him, then around. "Edmund, I think we're being followed." He was nearly sure he could see shadows flitting between the alleys alongside, keeping pace with him. "We should have brought more folk with us." Jumble let out a growl, his hackles up.

"Too late—can't go back." Edmund seemed to have gained a much better idea of where he was going. He steered Tom right, then left, then left again, veering down alleys so narrow that the broken-down and leaning houses above seemed nearly to meet. Even there, down in what felt like the city's rotting bowels, the light—the Nethergrim's light—shone hard and empty, casting a second shadow that Tom knew he was not seeing with his eyes. The sun, the real sun, the sun Tom had known all his life, seemed to be shrinking in the sky as it fell toward the west. From the distant city walls rose the sound of many men's voices raised as one—a cheer? A cry of terror? Tom could not tell.

"Here, Tom. Over here." Edmund led Tom into what once would have been a square. The hovels within were decayed to the point of falling onto one another. Even in the hard cold of Yule, they stank. It seemed almost as though Tom had to wade, at the end, through an impossible tangle of junk and refuse, but then Edmund stopped and kicked frozen mud from a simple flat stone set in the earth.

"This is it. The center of the glyph, the very center of the old city." He placed the disk atop the stone. They were just the same size, and though years of weathering had erased almost everything on the stone, what remained looked like it was made to fit the disk. "Grab Jumble. Stand back."

Tom took hold of Jumble and pulled him away behind a dung heap. "What's about to happen?"

"I honestly don't know." Edmund went still, as he often did just before he started a spell. Tom wanted to say something, to tell Edmund that magic would not work inside the city; but before he could do so, the shadowed shuffling nearby resolved into a face—and then a smell which replused him more than all the city garbage in the world could ever do.

"Well, that was a merry little chase." Gwarin the slaver stepped from the cover of the nearest hovel, dagger in hand. "Been told to look for your friend here, give him a nice welcome when he reached the city."

Tom looked upon the slaver. The light of two suns, one true, one false, fell on him—and Tom knew.

"You've been causing me some trouble." The oil in the slaver's beard no longer held it in as neat a point. "Cost me years, taking my goods away."

"They're not goods," said Tom. "They're children."

The slaver curled his lip into a smile. "I've lost my men, too, tracking John Marshal back and forth across the city. He dropped my best blades— but I got him good. He won't get far."

"You failed," said Tom. "The king is safe with us again."

Edmund knelt and placed his hand on the disk. If he knew that the slaver was there, he did not show it. His hands moved, fingers working rapidly along the disk.

"No matter." The slaver advanced, sword in hand. "If I get this boy here, I've been promised enough gold to set me up like a lord. I'll be a slave-monger no more—no, the folk who step and fetch for me will be my own servants."

Tom came forth from the shadows, Jumble at his side. He drew his sword.

The slaver curled his lip. "Don't try it, boy. You've got no idea who you're dealing with."

"Oh yes, I do," said Tom. "Father."

The slaver's eyes went wide in surprise, suspicion, then recognition. He brought up his blade a little late, but he was too wily to be thrown off for long.

Tom wished he had let Katherine train him with the sword. He ducked and wove, slashing madly at the slaver to the rising chant of Edmund's spell. He reached, he slashed—he overbalanced, tipping himself into the dung. He snaked this way and that, his sword out of reach, then felt the stamp of boot upon his leg. Jumble tried to stand over him and got kicked, yelping, aside.

"My son, eh?" The slaver leaned in, blade before him. "Afraid this will be a short reunion."

The blade raised—then it turned, driving in toward the slaver's own chest. It was only after it had been driven home, after the slaver had stared past Tom in surprise before pitching over, that Tom understood that Edmund had been chanting out another spell.

"No time." Edmund picked up Tom from the ground and pulled him back from his twitching, dying father. "No time to think. No time for anything. Run. Run back to the gates. The five creatures with Seb must be allowed back in. Do you understand?"

Tom seized Jumble, checked him over for injuries, then looked at Edmund. "How did you save me? Magic can't happen here."

A rumbling sounded from deep beneath the earth—then another and another. The refuse-littered ground bulged, twisted and burst. Before Tom's eyes, a cube of mortared stone rose to the surface. Its walls crumbled, leaving only a roof supported by four columns at the corners—and revealing the chariot within, along with the gang of frightened children blinking in the sudden light.

Sibby stumbled forward, then recoiled from the sight of Gwarin, the slaver. "He's dead." She clutched the littlest boy. "He's dead!"

The littlest boy ripped from Sibby's arms. He came forward and aimed a kick at the slaver's body.

"Tom!" Edmund grabbed him. "You've got to go now! Tell Katherine she has to get the five creatures inside. I will stay and guard the chariot."

Tom stared at the stone structure. "How did this happen?"

"The spell is broken," said Edmund. "Magic is possible here now. The creatures can come in, come here to the harness. Tom, hurry—now! If I can make magic in the city, so can Vithric."

That was all Tom needed. He turned to bolt, leaving Edmund and Sibby to gather the children. He had been told, in his life, that he was a good sprinter—in fact, Katherine had once told him that she had never seen anyone who could match him. To that raw talent, he could now add his knowledge of the streets, for as much as the place gave him shivers, its winding form was less of a mystery than it once had been. He had call to draw on both speed and wit, for he very nearly ran smack into Lord Wolland, Lord Balamar and the other nobles of his party, moving in armor in a determined-looking gang toward the north gate. He outdistanced them with ease, losing them in a crowd of people who fell back from them in sullen anger, looking ready to attack them if they could only think of how. He found his way back to the wide run of Market Street, flew past the guildhall and started shouting long before he reached the foot of the gatehouse.

"The gates! Open the gates!" He found space in each heaving breath for the shout of just a few words. "Katherine, Tristan, it's Tom! Open the gates! Let Seb and the creatures in!"

Katherine saw him from above. She believed him—she shouted the order. No one seemed willing to gainsay her; by the time Tom had reached the heavy wooden gates, they had already swung wide to let her out on Indigo, followed by Wulfric, Harry and a host of desperately charging men. Tom stopped at the doors, heaving for breath.

"Who is that?" Lord Tristan held his heavy hands to the rings. "Tom? Stand with me, I need a pair of eyes."

Tom felt at his side—he had left his sword back by the chariot. He peered out at the land just beyond the walls. The sight turned his legs to jelly. All the old stories of the fury of the Nethergrim in days long past had to him just been stories, things in which he had believed without understanding. He came to understanding then, came to know what Edmund had meant when he said that all the world hung in the balance. Everyone there, every man on the walls from noble knight to village bowman—they all saw, they all knew.

"Be ready!" Tom shouted upward at the gatehouse. "Mama, it's Tom! Be ready to drop the gates again!"

The wizard called Seb rode upon the horse of Metal, arms out wide, a rippling wave of earth throwing the tide of bolgugs back behind him. Indigo bucked and kicked, Katherine wove and slashed—then Tom lost sight of her amidst the unearthly fray.

"Here they come!" Tom reached for Tristan's shoulder, pulling him aside from the charging hurtle of the dog of Fire. The folk within the city who had come to stare in horrified fascination scattered this way and that at the sight of it, many of them crying out that all was lost, that the enemy was within the walls and doom had come. Next through came the foaming bear of Water, then a sweep of wind announced the great falcon of Air. Seb and Katherine charged through, side by side, Harry gripping Katherine's waist and crouched on Indigo's rump behind her. Last of all came the great beast of Life, her every step a crack of thunder.

Theldry needed no signal. The portcullis came down behind the last of the beasts—then shuddered at the impact of a horde of bolgugs. Murder holes opened in the gatehouse, and the city men dropped flaming oil on the creatures of the Nethergrim, burning them squealing to cinders. Lord Tristan heaved and shut the doors, then drew the bar across it.

"My son." Lord Wolland approached from the midst of the city, striding ahead of Lord Balamar and the other nobles. "Where is Wulfric? Where is my son?"

"He fell in battle." Katherine helped Harry dismount. "I am sorry. His valor may have saved us all."

But, no—no. Too late. Tom felt hot fluid on him, rushing down across his back. He turned in shock, hearing then the rumbling, hopeless groan. The beast of Life had been pierced in her chest, deep enough that her heartblood was coming out in torrents. She swayed—everyone scattered—she made a desperate, crawling movement, as though she meant to go deeper into the city, maybe to the chariot. Then she fell with a boom that sounded like the end of everything.

Katherine fell to her knees. "We failed." She put her face in her hands. "Oh, Papa. We failed."

Tom strode forward. "Give me your sword." He held out his hand to Katherine. "Give me your sword!"

Katherine looked up at him, shaking and hopeless. She let her sword slip from her hand. Tom took it up.

He passed by the huge, staring eye of the great beast of Life. He touched a hand to the heavy fur. "If you can still feel pain, I am sorry." He found the place and plunged in the blade.

Chapter 37

Days of war are not as are days of peace. In days of peace, the shock of a loved one's death might throw someone down for weeks, might run a family to tears night after night, might throw a pall of hopeless gray over days of plowing, of harrowing and sowing, of the carding of wool and the bringing forth of lambs. In days of war each body topples on another, and all that those who have yet to fall can think is how to live to see another dawn. In time, perhaps, there might be tears, there might be time to sit in the garden and wonder, to ache and to miss. There might be time to see the world without the dead, to see it going past and wonder whether this was how everyone gradually steps out of the stream of life, tied ever more to what was and is no longer. In war, though, at the very test of things, there is no time at all.

"She will live?" Katherine stepped forth from one of the towers that flanked the gates, then over the mound of boards and stones piled up as a barricade. The stars had twisted and fallen into unfamiliar shapes. The wind whipped screaming through the streets. She felt the bite of cold, but at the same time did not feel it.

"It's a he." Tom stood with the infant beast of Life, the one he had cut forth from its dead mother's womb, scraping frozen bits of birth fluid from its fluffy coat. Three times had the creatures of the Nethergrim hurled themselves against the walls of Rushmeet, walls no longer stiffened by the spell that had once kept them out. Three times had they been thrown back, but each time at a greater cost and by a narrower margin. There had been precious few chances to arrange the dead: Horsa Blackcalf, whose fiddle would never sing again; Gilbert Wainwright, leaving behind his wife and infant son; little Harbert from Roughy, who had survived being dragged to the lair of the Nethergrim that autumn only to be killed today, a few months later, carrying water to the men along the walls. The Duke of Westry had proven himself better than Tristan's words, dying in an assault to retake the northwestern tower from a storm of fleshy, sticky, wall-climbing creatures for which Katherine had no name. No one cried for the brave dead laid out in rows at the foot of the walls. With such cold, there was no fear that they would rot before a moment could be found to bury them. Katherine's father had been moved to lie among them, waiting for the chance to be carried to his grave, should there be anyone left to wield the shovel.

Katherine felt at the bruise on her side where a bolgug's spear would have killed her had she not been wearing the armor she had found. She took Tom's offered waterskin and drank without thinking of anything but thirst. For all the valor she had seen that day from knight and common man, she had no illusions—the city still stood because of Edmund and Seb. There was nothing arrow or sword could do to creatures made of stone or living flame. Without the two wizards to throw them back, such creatures would long before have undermined the walls and set the houses within ablaze. Edmund and Seb stood side by side next to the five creatures of the magical Signs, leaning on each other—one fair, one dark, but both of them somehow looking equally pale.

"Where is Vithric?" she said. "Everyone says that he's the greatest wizard of this age. The binding spell on the city is broken. He is free to do what he pleases—if you two can do what I have seen today, then what can he do?"

"Anything he wants, more or less." Edmund's voice came out cracked and weak. "More than me and Seb put together, that's for sure."

"Perhaps he waits." Seb sounded somewhat stronger, but he was full grown and fully trained. "Powerful as he is, he is yet a mortal man. There are many ways for him to get what he wants. He awaits the appearance of the best and safest."

Edmund shuffled aside to admit Thulina Drake and Lord Tristan into their circle. "All Vithric has to do is kill one of the six creatures or destroy the chariot or kill me—early, that is—and he has won."

"Edmund, must this be?" Katherine felt another squeeze in her insides. "Must it be you?"

"Who else?" Edmund shot sidelong looks left and right, though, in the torchlight Katherine could see no one but her friends and allies. "Vithric could easily be listening to us right now. There's almost no limit to what he can do while Yuletide lasts."

"Then what are we to do in return?" Katherine looked to Tristan, to Thulina, to all the living folk she had thought would always know what best to do next. "If Vithric might know what we are doing and can do almost anything to stop us, how can we possibly defeat him?"

Lord Tristan stepped forth to answer. "We must keep trying for as long as we can." Though Katherine could have guessed his words before he spoke them, she still felt the better for hearing them said. "We are not yet beaten, thus we must continue in the attempt."

"We cannot let those who died for us die in vain." The boy king had stayed at Katherine's side—as though he were in her charge, almost acting like her squire. He seemed to be speaking to no one else among their number but Edmund. "Nor those soon to die."

Edmund looked about to the widening circle—no one even so much as blinked at the arrival of Lord Wolland among their number. "The sixth creature," he said, "the creature of Earth, must still be found and retrieved at midnight, at the beginning of the sixth day. If that can be done, if the team can be assembled and harnessed, then tomorrow we might bring the sun back to life and some of us might then see it rise the morning after."

"So that's what it's down to, then." Martin Upfield had done as much as anyone to defend the city that day. He had held a postern gate in a tower shut by his own strength against the grasping pull of creatures whose aspect Katherine thought it too terrible to recall, for long enough that men could come down and shore it up with rock and timber. "We're fighting to have a tomorrow."

"Yes, cousin." Katherine turned to walk up the street toward the guildhall. Lords and knights, wizards, villagers, creatures of the magical substances—the true and rightful king, all followed her. "It's down to that."

She found Harry waiting for her at the edge of the market square. "Lord Balamar will not come forth from the citadel." Harry pointed to the crossbow bolt in his shield. "He has barred the doors and has his men fire on anyone who comes forth to parley."

Matthew Jobin

"More fool he, then." Lord Wolland's sword, to his credit, was flecked from tip to crossguard with blue-black blood. "There's a time to argue over who is king. This is not that time."

Katherine restrained herself from turning a quip on Wolland. After all, though she could hope to bury her father on the morrow, he could not hope for a chance to bury his only son, for Wulfric's body lay outside the city amidst a swarm of eternally hungry bolgugs. Between all the folk that gathered there before the guildhall of Rushmeet, a strange concordance had arisen. They were no longer their ranks in life, beyond what those ranks had taught them that were of use. They were only what they could accomplish in the last defense—and their resolve to accomplish it. Martin Upfield was not a peasant, he was a strong, brave man. Lord Wolland was a man in armor with a sword. Seb was a wizard, Thulina was a healer—now, what hope could they make from what they still had?

"We do not know where Vithric will strike." Katherine mounted the guildhall steps so that everyone could see her. It looked to her as though even the dog of Fire was listening, ears up and haunches down, behind Lord Tristan. Impressive as the creature was, she preferred the wet nose and kindly eyes of Jumble, who met her atop the stairs and snuffled at her wind-chilled hand. "Some of us must form a defense of sword and spell. Others must keep holding the walls, while yet others must find and retrieve this last creature for the chariot, the beast of Earth."

"I will go below, to summon the creature of Earth." Seb looked about him. "That is, if we know where to find it."

"There a number of us who can help you," said Thulina. "I will come with you, as will Tom and his mother. Between us, we can hope to escort you to the chasm that runs beneath the city."

Edmund turned to Seb. "It will be dangerous. Vithric might choose that as his target."

"My friend." Seb clearly meant the word. "I risk death this day. You go to yours with certainty."

"Place me where you want me," said Lord Wolland. "Give me space to have my revenge for my son, that is all I ask."

"Then would you lead the men upon the walls, my lord?" Katherine no longer wondered at making plans with the man she had bested in battle two months before. "We must hold the city until the chariot flies, or all is lost."

Though Wolland nodded his assent, his words were never heard, for a shrill, pained exclamation cut across them.

"Edmund—Edmund, there you are!" Sarra Bale elbowed Wolland, Seb and the Revered Elder of the *Ahidhan* aside in her rush to reach Edmund with Geoffrey and Edmund's father in tow. "Son, you stop this nonsense. You stop it right this instant!"

"Mum." Edmund looked oddly bashful. "There's no other way."

"There's got to be." Edmund's father looked, if anything, worse than his mother. "Geoffrey can't be right—this can't be true!"

Geoffrey still bore his bow, but his quiver was empty. "I'm sorry, Edmund. I kept it from them for as long as I could."

"Mum. Father." Edmund let them hector him, browbeat him, plead and weep before he spoke again. "It must be done. Someone must take the chariot into the sky and relight the sun tomorrow."

Edmund's mother seized him, shook him, held him. "But why you? Why you?"

"Isn't that what everyone asks eventually?" Edmund let her hold him without squirming in the least.

"You're just a boy." Sarra Bale moaned. "You're my boy."

Katherine felt Harry drawing near. She would not let him slide his hand into hers. He looked at her, uncertain. She could not tell him why.

Edmund broke free of his mother. "Listen, everyone, please. There is still much to do. The chariot is exposed, out and aboveground by Tumble Bridge. Let us bring all five of the creatures to it, as soon as we can."

Lord Tristan wrinkled his brow. "All in one place? But they are Vithric's targets."

"Yes." Katherine thought it over. "Yes, Edmund's right. If Vithric can win by striking at any link, we only weaken ourselves the more by keeping those links separate."

Edmund turned to Tristan. "My lord, will you stand with us at the chariot?"

"I will be glad to do so," said Tristan. "But I do not see how I can aid you."

"Vithric was once your friend," said Edmund. "Maybe, if it comes to it, you can talk to him."

Tristan seemed momentarily as ready to weep as Edmund's mother. "I would wish, should this be the last test, that I might stand beside you all with sword in hand."

"Then take mine." Edmund unlaced his belt and drew it around Tristan's much wider waist without asking permission to touch the person of a lord of the realm. "I don't really need it."

Tristan's hand slid down to grip the hilt. He sighed, his milky, sightless eyes straining at nothing. "I thank you. It will at least remind me of old days. That will be a comfort."

"Mum—Father, Geoffrey." Edmund turned to his family. "Will you stay with me tonight?"

"Son, anything." Harman Bale held a spear and wore bits of leather armor that did not quite add up to a full suit. "You just tell us what you need."

Katherine turned to grip Harry's shoulder. "We all have parts to play. You are needed on the walls."

Harry looked like he had expected much more than a touch on the arm. "I want to stay with you."

"But you are needed on the walls," said Katherine. "Protect us. Protect me."

Harry's golden eyes flashed. "We might never meet again."

"Make sure that we do." Katherine could not resist the kiss—just one, but on the cheek. She turned south. "Edmund, my lord Tristan, with me. Tom—Tom, come here before you go."

She gathered Tom together with Edmund, the three of them together, perhaps for the very last time. "My friends. No one can replace either one of you in my heart. None of the folk around us understand what we are."

Edmund, pale and drawn as he was, still found a smile. "If we succeed, there will be days for folk to live past tomorrow. Think of that."

"If we succeed, it will be because of us more than anyone." Katherine placed a kiss on Tom's forehead. "Go with speed, my friend. Do not fail."

Tom clasped her arm, then left with Seb, his mother, Thulina Drake and Jumble. Harry, Wolland and most of the armed and armored folk marched off in the other direction. Edmund cast a wry look at Harry's shadowed, departing form.

"Will you walk with me awhile?" Katherine led Edmund—helped him, really, for he must have drawn his spells through the center a dozen times that day—south through the deserted square along Market Street. Edmund's family followed at a distance, leading Tristan and the boy king and looking like they were already walking in procession to Edmund's grave.

Katherine hurried Edmund just a little, waited until they had gained some space from the others. "I know what you were thinking, back there."

Edmund flicked a look at her. "I'm sure you don't."

"Yes I do." Katherine drew a deep breath. "And I'm going to fix it."

Edmund let her bring him to a stop under the awning of a market stall. "Fix what? Now I'm sure I don't know what you're—"

—and she took him in her arms and kissed him. Not just a little, either. Partway through it, she began to wonder something. Perhaps, just perhaps, she was not just doing this to grant a last wish to someone about to die, for she found that once she started, she did not want to stop.

She did stop, after a while, if for no other reason than that Edmund's family had almost caught up to them. When she let go, she half expected Edmund to splutter or giggle or say something silly. Flushed as he was, shining as were his eyes of harebell blue, he merely nodded, with that same kind, sad smile on his face she had seen him wear so much of late.

"Thank you," he said.

"There's so little time in this life." They continued walking, Katherine near to him, still holding him up. She could hear herself starting to talk faster than she should, to cover thoughts that wheeled and spun in her. "Papa's gone—I don't know if he heard me. I never got to tell him . . ."

"He knew." Edmund without his sword looked like a beggar, or a prisoner on his way to the gallows, his tunic hanging like a smock. Every glance Katherine took at him made her ache the harder. Many of them, perhaps all of them might die by tomorrow, but he was bound to a coming death with the certainty of falling water. He had to die for her to live.

"Why do you love me?" she said. "I'm not at all like other girls."

"Maybe that's why." Edmund paced on, looking up at the stars. "Love can be selfish, it can be picky and unfair, but it asks us to give ourselves for others. The more it's felt by everyone, the more . . . well, it's like a song, you see, and . . . I'm sorry. I explained this better to Thulina."

Katherine could have wished for a more easily defensible position than the dockside lot where stood the chariot, as well as one that did not look quite so squalid. The former slave children had been hard at work, from the looks of things, clearing away the piles of trash from around the chariot and

Matthew Jobin

setting up posts of watch that Katherine never saw until an urchin leaped out to ask who passed in the night. The dog of Fire was the only source of light they had or needed, its open ribs casting bars of shadow around its ever-burning heart. There was as yet no reason to hitch the five creatures to the chariot, so they were allowed to range as they liked around the harness. The infant beast of Life, though as large as the others, still made piteous cries for its dead and absent mother. It tried to nuzzle the horse of Metal—no good—then the dog of Fire, which resulted in an unearthly growl and some singed fur. In the end, it had to content itself with Geoffrey, who petted its legs and buried his head in the ruff of its neck, trying without success to stop his own sobs from carrying in the quiet dark. Lord Tristan did his best—and his best was quite something—to comfort Edmund's parents, but no one can truly console the mother of a boy about to die.

"You will be a knight in my service." The king broke in on Katherine and Edmund as they were about to kiss again. He did not seem to notice the flush on both of their faces or the way they jumped apart just in time. "I don't care that you're a girl. I will knight you and make you one of my household."

Katherine bowed to her king, as any knight would do. "My liege."

"And you?" The king followed Edmund around to the back of the chariot, though he did not seem to wish to get too close to the skeleton laid in state between the wheels. "Edmund Bale, what can I do for you?"

"Look after my family." Edmund pointed to Geoffrey, to his mother and father. "Look after my neighbors. Their homes are gone—their lives must be rebuilt. Should you gain the throne, in truth, Your Grace, do not look away from the north."

Katherine smiled in the teeth of the wind, in the cold that seemed to descend on everything. "Oh, I would not let him."

Edmund turned to look over the chariot, the grand wheels and ornaments, the intricate carvings on its bronze sides. He looked down at the blue gem in the forehead of the skeleton, then up at the matching gem in the forehead of the king.

"It's me," said the king. "Dead of old age, long ago."

Edmund's thoughts seemed to leap from beginning to end with a speed that still amazed Katherine. "You will go backward in time, then, Your Grace. Into the past."

The boy king scratched his gem. "So it seems."

Katherine blinked. "Backward in time? You mean, like going back down a road?"

"Not at all like that." Edmund touched the gem in the skeletal forehead. "If you go back down a road, you are really going up it again. This is different."

The boy king stepped away from the chariot. "Yes. I think I must go back—someday, somehow."

"Back into the past." Katherine forgot her misery for a moment. "I wonder what you will do—or, what you did, I suppose."

"He will found this city." Edmund turned to the king. "This place is yours. You made this place, you grew in power in all three paths of magic, you fashioned the streets into a spell that blocked all other spells until I broke it."

The boy king looked down at his own corpse. "But why? Even if I learned how to do that, what was I trying to do?"

"The same thing you were trying to do when you made this." Edmund pulled out the strange metal disk and placed it on the floor of the chariot.

The boy king gaped. "I made that?"

"Yes." Edmund smiled. "Centuries before you stole it, you made it—so I guess you didn't really steal it after all."

The fog in Katherine's mind began to clear. "If the king will go backward in time, then he will go—has gone—backward to help us win." She made a reverence to the king. "You must have spent your whole life trying to make sure we can succeed today."

The boy king did not seem to want her acclaim. "But how? What was I trying to do?"

"You were trying to send a message." Edmund turned the wheels of the disk until the symbols joined. "The last day of Yule, the sixth day, the Day of the Tower, a day not seen in so long that we had forgotten it could happen. The symbols join, and—here."

Edmund held up the disk and pointed at the symbol in the middle. "It reads *Courage–Upward*. He stepped around the side of the cart. "You sent the message, Your Grace—I hear and heed it. I will not falter. I will not fail."

Katherine followed Edmund. She wanted to kiss him again, right there in front of the king, in front of everyone. She wanted to do much more than kiss him. Perhaps she should. She took his hand—she thought that he would turn her way at once—but instead found him examining the pattern of slash marks around the rim of the chariot.

"I thought that was strange, when I first saw it." Katherine ran her fingers along the marks. "They're arranged in a pattern—numbers, you see?"

"I do." Edmund counted left to right. "Four, one, two. Three, six, five."

"More stuff to do with time, I think." The boy king looked in from the other side. "If I made this chariot, then those numbers must be part of the message."

Katherine bent her thought to what she saw before her. "There are six days of Yule."

Edmund swept back his hair, one hand pressed to his forehead. "Six numbers—six days, but out of sequence." He looked to the king. "Your Grace, instead of just going backward in time, can someone go—sideways?"

The boy king nodded. "There are legends of such things, passed down by word of mouth in the lightless halls of Eredhros, but I have never known if it was truly possible. The very greatest of the *Eredh* could go backward in time. There are only rumors about other directions."

"Other directions?" Just the thought of it made Katherine's head hurt.

"Four, one, two," Edmund repeated the pattern. "Three, six, five. Katherine, didn't your father say those same numbers?"

"He did," said Katherine. "Papa started saying them back when we first met the king, when he was angry at me for no reason, before he was caught by Vithric and forgot everything for a while."

The shock that came over Edmund seemed almost to lift him from the ground. He grabbed Katherine by both hands. "Go. Go now. Go find your father!"

"What?" Katherine shook her head. "Edmund, Papa is dead, remember? He is laid out waiting for his grave. Why would you—"

"Go!" Edmund pushed her. "Go to him. Now!"

Katherine cried the whole way up the streets—for confusion, perhaps; for loss, for the falling stars. She passed folk who hailed her, asking for aid or advice about the defense of the walls. She passed others in a tooth-clenched revelry, a chilly last debauch on the edge of time. Someone had set fire to a house just to dance in the warmth of the blaze. The cobblestones pounded at her feet, the ice that coated them nearly turning her sprint into a tumble over and over again. She hated Edmund, hated him. Why would he make her do such a thing? She hated him, hated magic, hated all the world.

"Oh, Katherine." Her cousin Martin stood at the edge of the line of corpses laid out beneath the city walls. "I wish you hadn't come yet. I'm still looking."

"Looking?" Katherine could hear the shrill bite of her own voice, hear the bounce of it against the broad expanse of mortared stone. "What are you searching for?"

Martin shook his head. He leaned on Nicky Bird—an easy thing to do, considering their difference in height.

"Folk are saying this is the very last night in the world," said Nicky. "We thought—we had a bit of time off the walls, so we thought we'd come say what we could for the dead, just us Moorvale folk. When we got here, though, we—Katherine, I swear that we laid your father out right here, next to Horsa Blackcalf, and now he's—we've looked everywhere, everywhere, but he's—"

Nicky trailed off. He stared, parchment white, at something over Katherine's shoulder. Martin did the same, then fainted dead away, his heavy form coming down with a thud in the snow.

Four, one, two. Katherine felt the hairs on her neck prickle high. *Three, six . . .*

She turned around.

Five.

Matthew Jobin

Chapter 38

The Day of the Tower, The Sixth Day of Yule

"Hurry." The Revered Elder's voice rose just above a whisper. "We must hurry!"

Theldry turned this way and that in front of Tom, her lantern held up before a face grown frantic in her long and fruitless search. "I'm sorry, everyone. Everything's different down here now. The tunnels have all shifted around. I can't work out where I am."

"We've been down here for a long time." Tom felt a carving on the wall that he was nearly sure he had seen at least once before. "It must be past dawn by now. What happens if the creature of Earth arrives but there is no one to summon it?"

"That's not what I fear." The Revered Elder looked left, then right, then straight—then down smaller passages leading off between those directions. "What I fear is that our enemies will reach the place first, summon forth the creature and destroy it."

Tom's hand leaped back from the wall, for it rumbled and bounced, as though some force from above had shaken it. "What was that?" Dust descended, along with cobwebs and flakes of stone.

"That was Vithric." Seb coughed and waved the dust aside. "He shakes the earth. The walls of the city can no more hold him back on this day than a castle made of sand can hold back the tide."

Theldry grabbed Tom's arm. "Huddy—the children!"

Tom leaned back against the wall, despite its damp chill and its coating of dust. It was almost too much to be borne. In the city above him waited his friends, his neighbors, the people of the north, the whole world—the rest of his family. For all he knew, many of them were already dead in the assault that he could hear renewed even far as he was below the earth. If he did not find and retrieve the creature soon, he might as well jump into the chasm when he found it, for the world above, indeed all the world, would soon be gone.

"I found the way there after going down from Vithric's manor." He raised his head. "My mother knows—or at least she knew—every nook and cranny of these passages. If she can see what I saw, maybe she will know where to look."

Theldry shook her head. "How can I see what you saw?"

Tom looked to Seb.

"Yes." Seb beckoned them in together. "Yes! Such magic is possible. It is easily possible now. Come, come—boy and woman. Each of you, look into one of my eyes. Tom, the left eye. Theldry, the right."

Theldry stood shoulder to shoulder with Tom—and put one hand on the small of his back. Tom stared into Seb's dark, sharp eye.

"It will help if you stop thinking about what you are trying to accomplish." Seb raised one hand, moving a finger back and forth in front of Tom and Theldry with the strange grace Edmund often had when he cast a spell. "Do not try to remember anything in particular, do not think about these tunnels or what you fear will happen. It is best, in fact, if you do not think at all."

Tom found the request an easy one. He had been training himself not to dwell on fear and pain all his life. From the sounds of it, from the catch in her breath and the number of times Seb repeated his chant and moved his fingers, it took Theldry somewhat longer to reach the same state. When she did, though, and the spell took hold, Tom found himself far, far away from the catacombs indeed.

Mother. He did not know whether she could hear him, or even whether he was truly speaking. Theldry loomed above him, so very large, so very young. *Mama.*

"Baby." Theldry shivered—not from cold, for it was summer. "My baby, my own. Someone, someone somehow, please watch over him, please protect him."

Tom stared up at her, then past her to the stars. His arms did not work very well. When he tried to move them, to reach out for his mother's face, he found himself weak and clumsy. When he tried to speak, all he could do was gurgle. His legs were bound in a swaddling of rags.

"I will not name you. I have no hope that anyone will know it." Theldry leaned down to place a kiss on Tom's forehead. "I love you. I always will. My baby, my own." She trembled; she could not make herself leave—then a door swung wide nearby, letting forth the rumble of revelry and hard laughter, driving her to flight down the alley.

Tom tried to reach for her, but his arms did not work. *Mama.* He could not move. The laughter died; booted footsteps came nearer.

Seb's voice cut in, booming down from the sky. "That was perhaps too far." The world spun, the sun wheeled.

Tom was seven; he pitched hay and birthed lambs in spring. Theldry stole bread, stole coins, stole brooches from the merchant's wives right off their fine cloaks.

Tom was nine; he would not let the puppy die, no matter what his master said, so he held a tiny, starving Jumble in the crook of his arm and fed him goat's milk though he knew he would get a beating for it. Theldry got caught, got hauled before the worthies of the city and sentenced to the pillory.

Tom was eleven; he felt the lash of his master's whip again and again, until he could no longer feel anything. Theldry felt the touch of the slaver— Tom's father. She had suffered it for so long that she could not feel anything either.

"My baby, my own." Theldry lay starving and awake below the city, little Clarance curled in fitful sleep at her side. "Are you still there?" Of course not—her baby was dead. Every punishment, every cruelty in her life came like a judgment.

"I am sorry—we have no time to dwell here." Seb's voice cut in again, dragging Tom and his mother out of their severed pasts, pulling them onward—Tom plays with Katherine and Edmund in secret after dark on Wishing Hill; Theldry tries to steal from a young Huddy Fuller only to find him ready to give her freely what she had hoped to take—toward the present. "There. Tom—Theldry. Do you both see it?"

Tom did not know how to make sense of what he saw. He only knew that he saw it. "That's the place. That's the scar in the earth I crossed with John Marshal." He felt another ache at the memory of rescuing John from Vithric's torture, only to see him lying gutted and dead a day later.

"I asked for a protector," said Theldry. "I got my wish."

Tom looked up the passage in his memory, the one that led past Vithric's secret study under the city. "There. Mama, do you see?"

Theldry let go of Tom, turning out of the spell before Seb could end it. "Yes—this way! This way, hurry, while my memory lasts!" She moved at a shuffling run, quick enough that Tom had quite a deal of trouble supporting the Revered Elder at the same speed.

"A subtle cost for such a spell, but a steep one." Seb took up the rearguard. In the light of Tom's torch, his face looked wracked with sorrow. "I'll be carrying those memories for the rest of my life. Always the same question—why is there so much pain in this world?"

Tom had neither time nor breath to answer. He followed his mother on her darting course through the tunnels, tapping Tristan's shoulder when it came time to duck. Theldry stopped and looked about her many times, confused by the changes wrought by the raising of the chariot, but she never paused for long, eventually finding her way on a long route through the oldest and most unchanged of the passages, inward on what felt like the twisting run of a spiral—inward, inward until . . .

"There!" Tom stepped within the realm of the chasm, feeling just as before that he had stepped into another world. "This place—it felt like it was part of a spell, even when I found it before. How can that be, if the city would not allow magic within it?"

"This is too far down in the earth for the spell that bound the city to reach." Seb stepped to the foot of the bridge and looked down. "I will do this best in my own language. Stand back from the edge, everyone."

Tom did not know whether he needed to do so, but he still drew his sword and turned to guard the entrance. He heard Seb's voice take on strange, overlapping echoes, then he smelled the smells of earth, the damp of good topsoil turned over for spring, rain on rock, sun on sand.

Seb ran the back of his hand across his sweaty forehead. "The beast of Earth approaches."

Matthew Jobin

Tom felt a rumble under his feet. He steeled himself for the shock—anything might be coming up from below. He put himself between the chasm and both his mother and the Elder, standing as he thought Tristan might stand. The rumble grew, forcing Seb to back away from the edge of the chasm. A shape emerged, two paws, small eyes that drowned the torchlight and a long snout.

"Of course." Tom lowered his sword. He did not wait for Seb's word to run his hand through the fur of the great badger of Earth.

The rumble had not come from Seb's spell. The ground rippled beneath Tom's feet with a violence that nearly rolled him over the lip of the chasm. His mother seized him by the back of his shirt—Thulina lost hold of her walking stick, but Seb caught her before she struck the ground.

"What is that?" Tom gained his feet only for another rippling wave to throw him down again. Rocks and clods of earth fell from above, breaking against the floor all about him. "What is happening?"

"Tom." Seb helped him stand, bringing him together with Theldry, Thulina and Jumble. "Look."

Vithric stood at the edge of the chamber, in the passage down which Tom and the others had come. He extended two fingers and spoke a single word—the shock wave that followed tumbled Tom on top of his mother. The great badger let out a hiss, its long jaws open to show its teeth, but it could not seem to decide whether to attack or retreat. Jumble did just the same, his black-and-white coloring making him seem like a miniature of the great beast, though Tom knew that his whining growl spoke of nothing but fear.

"He followed us." Seb threw out a hand to grasp the footing of the bridge. "He could not find this place until we did."

"You are both a clever and a supremely foolish young man, Seb." Vithric looked no older than Seb did, save for his eyes. "You sat with me in my chambers through month after month of lecture and dispute alongside the wizards and apprentices of the Clave. You never once raised an objection to our plans to remake the world, to use the Nethergrim to create a new age—but all along, you and your little clutch of friends plotted against me. You and I are rational men. If you tell me why you betrayed me, perhaps I will find some reason to be merciful."

Seb struggled to his feet. "You were wrong, Vithric, always wrong. You said that the reach of man is boundless. You told us that we could grip the very stars. The urge to power without limit is a sickness."

Vithric sighed at the Revered Elder. "Is this your doing, Thulina? I have always said that the teachings of the *Ahidhan* were like a poison to the mind of the young wizard."

"Young Seb sees farther than you ever could, Vithric." Thulina struggled up, braced on her walking stick. "So does Edmund Bale. The answer is harmony, not control. If you reach out to grasp the stars, you will only find yourself set aflame."

"My dear old girl," said Vithric. "One of the things I look forward to most in the age to come is ensuring that there are none of your kind left to babble such nonsense." He chopped with his hand—it seemed as though the very air shuddered and came near to ripping apart.

Thulina seemed to take the brunt of the shock—without Tom to hold her up, she would have collapsed. "You could not reach us at the Harrowell, Vithric. You are barred also from this place."

"Oh, I don't need to get inside." Vithric clapped his hands again. The cavern shook, then an unearthly cracking noise turned Tom's head. The chasm behind him had grown wider. The bridge that spanned it could not stand the strain. It broke in the middle, blocks falling down into the void below. There would be no escape in the direction Tom had fled with John Marshal.

"This is the sixth day of Yule, the day between the ages, harbinger and herald of the coming time when my kind hold sway over all the world," said Vithric. "You will find me unbound today by even that which constrained me at the Harrowell."

Seb stepped forward. "Then you will find me equally unbound, Vithric. Perhaps you will also find me not so easy to overcome."

"Spare me your empty heroics." Vithric raised his hands again. "There will be no final contest between us. When I crush this realm, I will crush you inside it." When he brought his palms together, it felt as though the air around Tom grew thicker in the blast that came from all sides.

"What is he doing?" Tom advanced with his sword held in both hands, but the ground would not stay still beneath his feet. The great badger of Earth dug its claws into what had once been a floor but had been churned up into a clutter of broken tiles and bare earth. Theldry clung to its fur, holding Jumble in the crook of her free arm.

"Vithric is separating worlds, making the realm we are in impossible." Thulina kept her stick pressed point down to the shuddering earth. "I am

Matthew Jobin

trying to keep them bound together as one, but Vithric is too strong. I cannot hold out against him much longer."

Tom lost hold of his sword—it bounced and slid into the pit behind him. The ceiling ripped and started to come down, the closing lid of his tomb.

"Mama." He curled down, then tried crawling to the last place he had seen Theldry. "Mama, I wanted more time with you."

"Tom!" He felt a hand on his shoulder—not his mother's. "Do you remember how it felt when you came near to death? Remember when you met me in the other place?"

Tom could hardly see the Revered Elder through the dust. The memory was not hard to summon up, there in that place of fast approaching death. The Elder's sister, Warbur Drake, had poisoned him. As he lay dying, he had met the Elder in a place that had felt like a dream—a forest, then a waterfall beside a pool.

"Do you understand, Tom?" Thulina had to shout to be heard. "The other realms, the Dorwood, the Harrowell—you have been there! You can go to them!"

Tom stumbled down again. He looked up—through flying dust and falling rock he saw Vithric's face, lit with giddy power, looking very much like his former master did when he readied the whip. Tom's mother cradled Jumble, held from tumbling away and forever down only by the grip of the great badger's claw.

"Go there!" Thulina spun Tom around to stare at her. "Take the beast of Earth, take everyone you can and go!"

Tom felt the shock of the collapsing realm all the stronger through the Elder's hand. He could feel her trying to keep the space where they stood bound to the world, while at the same time could feel Vithric snapping its connection ever faster. "How?"

"You know how!" Thulina turned away from him. "Remember what you felt, when you found me by the waterfall." She set her walking stick on the ground, but the ground buckled and the stick broke.

Seb made a sign with his hands, then barked forth words in his own tongue. Stones picked themselves from the ground and formed themselves into thin, shaking pillars, bracing up the crumbling roof of the cavern above. "We will hold him for as long as we can. Tom, you must leave now!"

Tom did not have any idea what to do—and then, all of a sudden, he did. "Mama." He took her hand. "Jumble. Come with me." He reached down to touch the ragged coat of his dearest friend. The great beast of Earth blinked its oddly tiny eyes at him, as though it knew his thoughts inside out.

"Where?" Tom's mother ducked out of the way of a falling chip of rock from the ceiling. "Son, come with you to where?"

Tom breathed in air cool and sweet with the scents of pine and the flowers of the glade. "Here, Mama. Right here." The secret was simple—there was nothing to do. He had only to dream and he was there.

Chapter 39

"**F**ather. Oh, Papa, Papa."

Katherine knelt, weary beyond all thought. She could do nothing but stroke Emmie's shoulder for the briefest instant, then grasp her by the back of her dress. "He died to defend you. Please— move! Use the life he gave you!" She picked up Emmie's bawling, terrified little brother from the ground and set him in her arms.

It had started with the fall of the walls—all of them, all at once, with hardly a chance for the screams to subside before the unearthly baying of the charge. The servants of the Nethergrim struck at first light, fire and thunder assaulting the wounded city from all sides, bolgugs slapping their wide bare feet over rubble almost before it had settled from the crash. Hands with too many fingers had reached from the earth, gripping at the panicked, fleeing defenders. Clouds had blown in, red beneath the bitter dawn. They rained fire that Edmund could only keep from setting the whole city alight with a desperate counterspell that had toppled him over, white and senseless. The sun rose—everyone, everyone could see what rose across from it—everyone could see and feel the Nethergrim at last.

"Up!" John Marshal seized Emmie bodily from the ground, pushing her onward through the streets. Katherine did the same for Edmund, who seemed to have fallen into a delirium, crying his defiance to the western sky. There was no time to make sense of anything—her father somehow alive, but death, death everywhere. She left the corpse of Huddy Fuller lying sprawled on the street, the foul creature who had skewered him butchered in turn by the thrusts of John Marshal's sword. The only thing to which she could cling was the next step, the next breath, the hope that if they reached the chariot and held the space around it for long enough, then Tom might return with the sixth creature and they just might have time to sacrifice Edmund's life to save everyone else's. So dire had things become that she could not spare a shred of remorse for it. She rushed forward, holding Edmund's hand—what she felt for him amazed her with its strength, yet she had to make sure that he did not live to see the sunset.

The boy king never once left her side. He could do little of use with the sword in his hands, but his power to see the branching paths of the future saved Katherine's party more than once since the fall of the walls, directing them away from the worst of the city and finding a path through twisting streets choked now with bolgugs, now with nameless things, now with knots of folk who had been fighting on past the death of all hope. Little Princess Merofled had found a horn, somewhere—she blew it for all she was worth at the sight of every man, woman and child Katherine's party came across. Folk clustered, weapons drawn, heeding Katherine when she cried out, "With me! For the king!"

Come what may, she would not die crouched and cowering, though the Nethergrim blazed up the back of her neck with a heat that was cold and yet burned. Reunions came fierce and quick—Rahilda and some Harthingdale folk, Lord Wolland with a band of cloth tied on one leg to stanch the bleeding, the Twintrees with Miles running out in the lead to seize Geoffrey hard about the waist. The precincts of the city sprung ablaze, the ring of ruin tightened—onward, onward.

Death upon death—Nicky Bird, the town crier, the Hollows brothers. The men of city and countryside had given their all, then done so again with their wives and sisters at their sides, wielding the weapons dropped by their dead friends and kin. Old men who should have lived out their last years in peace by the fireside fell in defense of their grandchildren. Edmund's family had somehow clung together, Grandmother to Geoffrey, Sarra to Harman, with Edmund's uncle Aldus trailing near, guarding them all with a makeshift club made from the leg of a table. Katherine's cousin Martin bled from both arms, cut again and again when he had seized bolgugs wriggling and snapped their necks. Another horde of foul creatures fell across Katherine's path despite the king's best efforts to guide them—Geoffrey had arrows in the guts of two of them before Katherine could close to striking distance. Her

Matthew Jobin

father came with her, the two of them moving through a dance of blocks, thrusts and parries that had been part of their life together on the farm back home; though now instead of facing each other in sporting practice, they turned the fullness of their skill upon the foe, their rage at the fall of their home, the gore and waste, the death of the sun channeled out through the points of their swords. May the world fall that day, may the sun come smoldering out of the sky—onward, onward.

Every time Katherine rushed into the breach, she found herself coming up against creatures that no sword, no axe, no pull of Martin's arms could ever hope to bring down. Every time she rushed in to buy her family, her neighbors and her king the distance of one more street down which to flee, she knew that without Edmund all was lost. Each and every time, Edmund rose to the clash with a fury that would have frightened her, had there been any space left in her heart for fear. The beams of houses exploded, thrusting themselves out to impale huge beasts of putrid flesh. Rain fell on stonewights, then froze, then melted and froze again, the ice spreading cracks in their towering forms that widened with each flash of warm and cold until they fell into heaps of stone no more alive than the rubble of the city walls. Each time Edmund drew forth a miracle, Katherine looked back to see whether the effort had killed him. Each time, he seemed to grow a little weaker, each time his spells seemed to cost him more, but on he went, clutching his brother's arm—onward, onward.

"Papa." Katherine leaned upon her sword, for no will in the world could force her farther on before she caught her breath. She looked upon her papa, whose dying hand she had clutched but hours before. "Please, I do not understand. How—"

"Not now, child." John Marshal bore less trace of shock and pain than anyone else she had seen that day. "Now is the time for hard deeds."

He took the lead of their party, striding on with sword raised high. Katherine caught her breath and followed him, knowing that this, more than anything, was what he had trained her to do, to walk on when every part of her screamed for rest and sleep, so that the folk behind her would find it in themselves to follow.

She caught up to her papa at a turn that led eastward and down toward the river. She felt the blaze of the Nethergrim on her back, could hear Edmund's yelping replies to taunts she could not hear. Horrible beyond measure though things were, she wondered how this morning must feel in the rest of the world—Paladon, Westry, Mitilán and farther places she did not know. All the world awoke that morning to a dying sun, woke to the Nethergrim glaring through their windows, their world lit by a light that somehow made it darker. The old year had ended, but the new year had not come.

"Katherine!" The voice was her papa's. It snapped her awake, making her understand that she had fallen into an exhausted inward trance. She looked up to see her father charging forward, her cousin Martin following.

"By the cloven crown." Harman Bale stared ahead of him. "No saving him, I'm afraid."

Farther down the street, pressed up against the wall of a dingy tanner's shed, was Harry, making desperate lunges to keep at bay a closing circle of the sewn-together things Katherine had last seen making an attempt to scale the walls. Katherine found her strength—she flew to a sprint, outpacing her father and cousin despite their head start—but Harman was right. The sound of coming help would be the last thing Harry would ever hear. The sewn-together things—limbs and heads and trunks of men and animals, stitched without the slightest regard to sense—closed in.

Edmund's voice rushed past Katherine like a gust of wind, powerful enough to stir her hair. "YOU ARE ALL UNDONE!"

The monsters surrounding Harry turned to regard Edmund. Before Harry even had time to bring his sword back up into guard, the stitches that held the monsters together popped, and in a spray of gore, every one of them fell apart.

"Katherine." Harry got up, then slipped, covered head to toe in blood. He struggled up again at her approach, then stumbled down again. "Katherine, have you seen my mother? She—"

"Will you be good to her?" Edmund had caught up to Katherine. He pushed past her and seized Harry by the shirt, almost by the throat. "If she pledges herself to you, will you love her always? Will you stay with her and never leave her? Upon your honor, do you swear it?"

Harry spat out some blood—to Katherine's endless relief, not his own blood. His gaze drifted from Edmund to Katherine, then, with eyes wide, to John Marshal.

"Look at me!" Edmund loomed over Harry. "Do you swear it?"

Harry stared at Edmund, golden eyes locked with blue. "I swear it."

Edmund let go. "Then marry her. Love her. There is no time in this life for anything less." He left Harry and Katherine together, staggering away with his brother's help.

Katherine helped Harry to stand. "What were you doing out here?"

"Trying to get a warning back to you." Harry pushed back his blood-caked hair and followed Katherine to the front of their party. "Katherine—your father . . . how?"

"I don't know." Katherine ran her hand along Harry's surcoat, swiping away the worst of the gore. "I don't care."

The sight of Harry brought a cheer from the folk of Elverain. He raised his sword and fell into step behind John Marshal. "Onward! For the king! Hope yet lives!" He glanced at Katherine and dropped his voice. "It does yet live, doesn't it?"

"What sort of warning were you trying to bring to us?" Katherine pulled a shield from the body of a fallen watchman on the road, able to do no more than whisper her thanks to the dead before handing it to Harry. She rounded the next corner to find her father halted.

Harry heaved a sigh. He pointed ahead of him. "That."

"Give us the boy!" Lord Balamar stood in a tight knot with his remaining men on the low and refuse-littered street that led toward the docks and the river. Beyond their ranks, Katherine could see the chariot, the creatures, Lord Tristan and the children on the raised platform of the chamber that had once lain beneath the city.

"Still only five creatures." Edmund coughed and swayed next to Katherine, leaning on his mother's arm for support. "Tom, Theldry, where are you?"

Lord Balamar wore chain-mail armor with plate pauldrons and greaves. "Give us the boy and we will let you pass." He bore a mace and shield with the insignia of the Stag. "Otherwise, you will have to come through us."

"You accursed, benighted fool, Balamar!" Lord Wolland limped out in front of John. "Look at the sky! Look upon our folly, then stand aside, curse you!" He got a volley of crossbow bolts for his trouble, two of which thunked into his raised shield.

Katherine looked to a sky that seemed to be melting. "The sun is rising. So is the Nethergrim. Their paths will cross at noon—Edmund, what happens then?"

"The end." Edmund's eyes rolled back in his head, which then bobbled and swayed. His legs buckled.

Katherine seized him. "Edmund, what's wrong?"

"Too many spells too fast. Drawing through center. Can't . . ." Edmund slumped senseless against his mother.

John strode forth, his shield raised. "Boar's snout, Katherine."

"Boar's snout." Katherine looked about her at the nobles in her party. "Understand?"

"Aye." Lord Wolland took his place beside John Marshal and a step behind. "Boar's snout." Katherine did the same on her papa's other side. Harry followed a step behind and beside Katherine. Another volley of bolts flew—there were thankfully only a half-dozen crossbowmen in Balamar's party, so their shots were absorbed by the shields at the front.

"Anyone without bows, follow our pattern—make a wedge." Katherine looked behind her. "Geoffrey?"

She need not have asked. Geoffrey had the archers lined up at once, child, woman and man. "Everyone, volleys on my signal! Arc them high, drop them on their heads. Draw, aim—fire!"

"Charge!" John Marshal moved under the shadow of the falling arrows. Katherine took a last chance to glance aside before the clash. The wedge held tight, its formation solid enough despite the fact that only the tip consisted of those who had ever trained in such a maneuver. Martin had third position on the opposite wing of the wedge, barreling forward with a shield in one hand and a poleaxe in the other that most men would need two hands to wield. Behind and beside him came Henry Twintree, then after him Hugh Jocelyn and then Edmund's father. She felt a burst of pride for her home— then she locked eyes on the man in the enemy ranks before her and raised her sword.

The crash of the snout drove back Balamar's men, cutting their ranks in two, but their training and better armor blunted its power before it could rout them completely. John and Katherine rounded back after punching through the enemy lines, each of them taking the opposite side without exchanging so much as a glance to sort the matter out. They pressed hard at the backs of Balamar's force, seeking to whittle them away before their own lines broke, but from the panicked shouts coming from their own force, Katherine found her worst fears coming true. Most of Balamar's men had survived the charge and now pressed outward, driving at the wings of

Matthew Jobin

John's wedge where the weakest and least-armored parts of his own people had been stationed, chopping and shoving toward the unprotected archers, the mothers carrying their babies in slings across their chests—and the king.

"Scatter them!" Katherine clashed shield on shield with one of the city watchmen who had thought Balamar's service his best path. "No quarter—scatter them!"

Martin bellowed and swung. Harry ducked, thrusted and wove. Blood sprayed, gushing from someone's neck. The back lines of John Marshal's wedge wavered, then broke, leaving John, Katherine and the best trained of his force on the opposite side of their enemy from their enemy's ultimate target.

"You!" Balamar sprang to a clanking charge. Princess Merofled screamed and tugged at the boy king. Balamar came on with his mace swinging up in an arc, his wolfish face straining with thirty years of hunger. Katherine shoved with her shield to knock the foe before her aside and made a desperate rush to reach him, knowing all the while that she could never catch him in time. Balamar swung back—

—and fell with Geoffrey Bale's arrow sticking out of one eye. Katherine closed the distance to finish him off, half from mercy and half to make sure.

"Your lord is dead!" She whirled to scream the words while standing over Balamar's corpse. "You have lost—stand aside! Stand aside and we will let you live!"

Balamar's men, with no one left for whom to fight, backed up to each side of the street, weapons held out to parry and shields to block. To their great credit, none of Katherine's party took a blow out of vengeance. They let their enemy melt away through alleys and doorways, leaving open the path down the noisome street that led to the cleared old lot, where stood the chariot, the children, the five creatures and Tristan—

—and Vithric.

"No." Edmund let go of his mother's arm and staggered forward as Vithric alighted from the air between him and the chariot. "No—stop him!" Katherine found another reserve of desperate strength to make yet another lunging charge, rushing with her father down the street toward the chariot, only to find that when she approached it she somehow whirled and ran in the opposite direction. Geoffrey called for a volley at Vithric, but he and his archers had to duck and scatter when their arrows flew straight back at them from the tops of their arcs. Edmund tried a spell—Vithric countered it as though swatting a fly off his arm. He tried another, then another—then collapsed.

"This world is not really made for happy endings," said Vithric. "You may stand there and watch, if you wish." He turned his back on them all.

Chapter 40

If you carry on against me, I will be your death. The Nethergrim rose to its zenith over Edmund, a light that somehow made all the world darker. **It is written in the stars, graven in the earth. The rivers mutter it when no mortal is listening. The choice is yours.**

Edmund gripped his hand around the lock of Katherine's hair he kept wrapped around his finger. Katherine fell to her knees beside him.

"Have we lost?" She did not seem to notice the gash on her arm, right below the hem of her chain-mail sleeve. "Is it over?"

Edmund ripped a strip from his own shirt. "I don't know yet." He took her arm and bound the wound. "Hold on—just a little longer."

John Marshal led another wild charge toward the chariot, only to find himself rushing back away again, turned around by the dizzying effects of Vithric's spell. Geoffrey and the archers did not dare try another volley, for a number of them had already fallen, pierced through by their own arrows. All around, baying, squealing, shaking the earth, the creatures of the Nethergrim closed in, flattening houses and setting the rubble aflame, erasing the stamp of man from the earth.

This is my world. The spell Edmund used to guard his mind could no longer stop the Nethergrim's Voice from leaking in. **You and your kind are a blight upon it. When I am finished with you, it will be as though you never were.** All Edmund could hope was that the spell could stop the Nethergrim from seeing into every corner of his mind for just a little longer.

"Hold them!" Edmund stood up and shouted to the desperate, wounded, unutterably weary folk strewn about at the limit of Vithric's spell. "Turn and hold the monsters back, just a little longer!"

Hold for what? The Nethergrim mocked him but, at the same time, queried him. **What can you possibly hope for now?**

Hope. Edmund gazed across the debris-littered stretch of ground toward the chariot. That was all he had left, but in truth, it was all that he had ever had.

"Tristan." Vithric strode forward until he was just out of range of the five creatures harnessed to the chariot. "I am glad to see you. There were things I wished to tell you before the end."

The five creatures strained in their harness, but locked together as they were, they could not turn to do much to threaten Vithric. The urchin children sat huddled behind the chariot, all their heads down as though wishing to be ignored.

"Vithric?" Tristan felt blindly outward with his hands, his eyes pressed tightly shut. "You sound so young, just as I remember you."

Edmund whirled at the sound of braying bolgugs on the street behind him. "Hold them!" He worked a spell to throw up a simple earthen rampart all around him, caring nothing for the cost he paid, which would make every garden in the city barren for a year. "Hold them back for just a little longer."

John Marshal asked no questions. He rushed to the edge of Edmund's new redoubt, mounting it just in time to skewer the lead bolgug and throw its twitching corpse back upon its fellows. With a shout that told of the grief within his rage, Martin Upfield followed, then Lord Wolland, then Rahilda—kin, friend, neighbor into the fray, one last time. Katherine seized Edmund and kissed him hard, though Harry stood nearby to gape at it. She took up her sword and charged to the rampart, shield high, sword higher.

Edmund, can you truly not understand? The Nethergrim's Voice blotted out everything when it spoke, leaving Edmund gasping and blinking in the pauses. **You are destined to lose. I have already seen it.**

Edmund looked over his shoulder. Vithric stood but a few yards from Tristan, one hand raised into the Sign for Unmaking—but then the curl of a vicious smile began on his face. He dropped his hand and approached Tristan. Edmund breathed out, the flame of his hope not quite extinguished.

"We have not spoken in some years, Tristan." Vithric looked young enough to be Tristan's grandson, everywhere but in his hard, bitter, spiteful eyes. "It seems fitting that we should have one more chance."

Tristan felt forward with his hands, stumbling over the refuse-littered ground between him and Vithric. "My old friend, has it really come to such a pass? Can this truly be what you wish upon the world?"

"I will survive what is to come." Vithric shot a bitter smirk up at the Nethergrim. "I alone, in fact. All dies, but I live. That is all that matters."

"Why, then?" Tears welled forth from Tristan's closed eyes, running out along the lines of his cheeks and into his white beard. "My friend—you stood with me against the Nethergrim for years. Why did you turn?"

"Once, long ago, you tried to save my life," said Vithric. "Do you remember?"

"I gave you my horse," said Tristan. "I told you to take him and flee, so that you might survive the coming of the servants of the Nethergrim."

"But I came back." Vithric took another step closer to Tristan—closer, closer. "Do you know why?"

Tristan kept his huge arms crossed, his hands far away from the sword Edmund had given him. "You said that you wanted to return the gift I gave you."

"And you thought it meant do a kindness for a kindness." Vithric came closer still to Tristan. "No—I came to throw it back at you, to show you that I would owe you nothing, that no one could change my life by giving me a gift I could not return."

"But you fought at my side," said Tristan. "You were a hero."

Vithric shot another sneering glance up at the Nethergrim. "I lay long plans, Tristan. Very long plans."

"Then there is no hope," said Tristan. "No mercy."

"No." Vithric stepped nearer. "No, Tristan, there is none."

Tristan waved his hand in the direction of the children. "Not even for them?"

"No, Tristan. For no one." Vithric glanced at the children—then looked closer. The children looked back at him, but really, just near him, for every single one of them stared about with milky, sightless eyes.

Tristan heaved a sigh. "So be it." He opened his eyes—clear and dark blue. They focused on Vithric.

"No—" Vithric had time only to raise his hands to his waist before Tristan's sword was out of its scabbard and driven through his ribcage. Tristan used all of his reach and all of his strength, aiming the blow to make sure of the kill. Edmund had no idea whether anything else passed between the two men in that last instant. If so, it was nothing but a look.

Vithric's spell broke at the rattle of his final breath. Edmund grabbed the king by the arm. "Follow, Your Grace!" He rushed forward, though it felt as if the glare of the Nethergrim would melt him into the ground.

"To me!" Tristan charged past Edmund and on toward the rampart, his borrowed eyes alight with the flame of war. "For the king! For the sun!" His cry drew Edmund's gaze for just a moment—there was no one like him, not Katherine, not John, no one could compare. He leaped over the rampart just as its defenders began to waver, taking the place of a fallen Harry and driving back a dozen bolgugs with a fearless, unmatched skill. There simply was no telling where his blade might go before it thrust; there was no way for any foe around him to read his movements before they resulted in the killing blow. The servants of the Nethergrim fell howling back.

The world will end the same, whether you fight me or not. The Nethergrim, so far as Edmund could tell, was starting to sound rather worried. **You will struggle and strive, then fail and fall. You are mortal. I am not.**

"Here, Your Grace." Edmund brought the king up to the chariot. "I need your help. You cast the spell that created the six realms of the Signs, placing one of them in each direction. You prepared all of this, long ago."

The boy king blinked at him. "What do you want me to do?"

"Undo your other great spell," said Edmund. "You made one to block magic in the city. You made another to create the six realms around it. You don't remember it because you haven't done it yet—but it still happened in the past. You are a disciple of the *Eredh*, you should understand." ·

The boy king nodded. He walked around to the back of the chariot and looked over his skeletal corpse. He touched the gem in his forehead with one hand, then the gem in the forehead of the skull before him. It did not work like Edmund's magic, like *Dhrakal*. To Edmund, nothing seemed to happen— but then things suddenly were as the king had always intended.

"I simply reminded myself to set the ending of the spell for right now." The boy king turned a smile on Edmund, while all around them the Dorwood, the Harrowell and all the places of the Signs merged together.

Edmund breathed another sigh of hope. He had guessed right—Tom was still within those realms, along with the great badger of Earth, so when the boy king merged the lands, he left Tom, Jumble, and the beast standing in some confusion at Edmund's side.

"My friend." Tom seized Edmund close. "Does it have to be this way?"

"Go, Tom." Edmund clasped his hand one last time, then bent down for a final stroke of Jumble's fur. "Defend us, just a bit longer."

Edmund stepped around to the front of the chariot, the great badger of Earth at his heel. The badger bent his head for the harness, taking his place next to his opposite, the falcon of Air, which was so hard to see it was as if its harness straps simply dangled free, blown back and forth by gusts of wind that no one there could feel.

Come, then. The Nethergrim scowled above him. **Come into the blankness. Come into the void of death.**

"Do you really think you can scare me with talk like that?" Edmund shot a hard look up at the place where the disk of sun and Nethergrim were about to converge. "You've been warning me about this since we first met. I know what you think death is, or at least what you want it to seem to be. Maybe you can't understand, because you are not mortal like us. We know we are going to die, so the only thing that matters to us is how we meet it."

Fool. Come, then. Your end awaits.

Edmund bent down at the back of the cart. "Your Grace, by your leave." He hauled the king's old bones out of the chariot and laid them as gently as he could upon the ground. He looked around him—he noticed John Marshal standing near the rampart, in what seemed to be a lull in the fighting. John stared across the open ground toward the chariot, his back turned to the rampart as though the monsters behind him somehow did not matter.

The boy king stood with Edmund like an honor guard, or perhaps the closest thing Edmund would ever have to someone who spoke over his grave. "Edmund, your family."

Edmund looked over at the rampart, where his father stood with a spear, his brother with a bow, and his mother doing her best to guard them both with a makeshift club. "The best thing I can do for them is waste no more time. If I go now, they might survive." He stepped onto the chariot and grasped the reins.

The boy king shuddered. "You go to die for my sake."

Edmund nodded. "So did John Marshal—though I still do not know how." He cast another glance at John, who was staring fixedly back at him, or perhaps both him and the king at once. A tickle formed in his mind—was something wrong?

No. He lit the torch he would carry into the sun. He was trying to persuade himself not to die. "Look after them, my king." The horse of Metal had the lead position on the right—it swiveled its head, waiting on his word. It did not look like the contraption with its bizarre collection of beasts could fly, but he knew that it could.

I shall enjoy watching you burn. The Nethergrim seemed to seethe above him. **I have never truly hated any mortal being before—but, Edmund, I do hate you. On your way to your death, you might take some comfort in that.**

Edmund took the reins in a firm grip. The horse of Metal let out a trumpeting neigh, the wheels of the chariot began to turn—

"No. Wait. Edmund, wait!"

Edmund looked back, feeling strangely annoyed. If the axe was to fall and sever his head, he did not want to wait and listen to it being sharpened any longer. "Your Grace?"

The king stepped forward, white and trembling. "It isn't you. I'm a coward, such a coward. Edmund, it isn't you. It's me."

"What?" Edmund pulled on the reins to stop the team. "Your Grace, what are you saying?" He felt a sudden flare of nothing-light above him, a glaring glow of—rage, fear. The Nethergrim was afraid!

"The disk, Edmund. The Darknot. Bring it out." The king took it from Edmund's hands and turned it to the end joining the symbols on the sixth day. "You said this symbol means *Courage–Upward*. I made this, Edmund. I made the spell. You said that this thing is called the Darknot, a loop in fate. I made the loop! Don't you see—it's a message I sent to myself!"

Edmund stood stunned—then he looked up over the head of the king as the creatures of the Nethergrim redoubled their assault upon his rampart. He came to understand that until that instant they had been holding back the fullness of their fury.

The king set the Darknot on the floor of the chariot. "You are so good, so ready to give yourself up, that you never saw it. It's me. This message is for me, sent by myself. You are about to go on into the sun—but you will fail there, after which I will be sent back into the past to try again." He looked over his shoulder at John Marshal. "That's why I had to be kept in Eredhros, that's why I had to be preserved until this day. It has to be me."

"But the Nethergrim is taunting me," said Edmund. "Telling me she will be my death."

"And you believed her," said the king. "She is a liar and always was. This was her last defense. If all else failed—if her creatures and her wizards could not kill me, could not stop the six creatures assembling or destroy the chariot—then the wrong rider would lead the team into the sky. It has to be me."

Kill them! The Nethergrim no longer spoke to Edmund, and that, in its way, was proof enough. Her commands radiated outward on the shafts of her horrible light. **Kill! Stop them! Stop them now!**

Katherine let out a battle cry that was more than half a cry of terror. She leaped to the top of the rampart to meet the onrush of the creatures of the Nethergrim, who came in full wild fury, devoid of even the primitive cunning they had yet shown. Bolgug, quiggan, boggan, stonewight—they all hurled themselves at the rampart, compelled by the dark rays above them to crush the defenders by the sheer weight of their numbers.

"Go!" The king pulled Edmund bodily from the chariot. "I command it!"

Edmund paused for the briefest instant to kneel. "Hail, King Chlodobert!" He leaped up and raced full tilt toward his friends, kin and neighbors. His feet had never felt so light upon the ground.

"Fight on!" John Marshal saw Edmund join them. "Fight on. Heed me, everyone, there is hope!"

Edmund came on in a storm—in truth, a storm—rolling over family and friend and then descending on the foe with lightning in his hands. The sixth day of Yule granted his every wish; it occurred to him, while in the midst of drawing lightning from the sky at the cost of ruining every stick of firewood for fifty miles around, that he might just possibly be the most powerful wizard left alive in the world.

"Edmund, what is happening?" Katherine pulled him back over the lip of the rampart and out of the way of the countercharge of the remaining bolgugs. "Why didn't you go? I can hear the Nethergrim screaming in my head."

"Look up," said Edmund.

Katherine turned to look—so did everyone—for the battle fell to a strange, waiting pause. There was something pathetic about the

Nethergrim's screams; the great king upon his chariot, pulled by his six harnessed beasts, had easily outdistanced her shrikes and risen past the last of her defenses. Her rays slackened, leaving her creatures to fall back and scatter. She pulsed, focusing her rays upon the king, perhaps to tell him some deadly secret. To no avail—the chariot got smaller and smaller still, hurtling into the heart of the sun. The scream of the Nethergrim rose until it could be heard by everyone, until for an instant it blotted out all other sound. The next thing Edmund knew, he was lying on the ground, dirt and snow in his mouth—breathing, alive.

"Katherine." He picked himself up from the ground, then helped her do the same. "Look up again."

Everyone did. They all cried out as one.

"The sun." Geoffrey leaped into the air. "The sun!"

Winter though it was, the sun shone anew, its rays the rays of the dawning year. The Nethergrim fell from the sky, burning as she came down, her cries ever more terrified and yet fainter, then fainter, then—

"Gone." Katherine dropped her sword. "Is she really gone?"

Edmund did not answer, since he did not know. He turned to look left and right, making sure of the field of battle around him. The remaining servants of the Nethergrim broke and scattered, fleeing through the burning, ruined lanes of the city.

"Tom!" Theldry took him in her arms. The wind swept chill across the city, for it was yet winter, but that only made the embraces all the warmer.

"We won." Geoffrey threw his bow into the air. "We won!"

"We did." Lord Tristan—his eyes a blind milky white again—returned from the rampart, led by Martin Upfield. "I thank you, Edmund, for ending your spell, now that it is not needed."

"I didn't end it, my lord." Edmund laughed. "Yuletide is over—I can't do spells like that anymore."

The light of the noonday sun broke full upon the eyes of the urchin children huddled around the place where the chariot had once stood. They struggled up, all together, still unsure of whether they should melt away into the rubble of the city. Tom and Theldry made sure that they did not.

"You are ours, now—all of ours." Theldry gathered the children together. "You are the future of the north."

Hugh Jocelyn had survived to throw down his spear with the look of a man who never wanted to pick one up again. "So who will be king now, then?"

"Who cares?" Harman Bale had not only survived but, from the look of his spear, had done great deeds of war. He knelt among the fallen. "Tom—Tom, come here. Lord Harry's alive!"

Edmund did not feel the slightest trace of annoyance at it. Maybe Katherine would get married to Harry, or maybe Harry would come to his senses and marry himself to some noble girl. No matter, no matter—he was happy to see Katherine's happiness, happy to see her run to Harry's side and cry that he had only been knocked senseless, a broken rib or two, nothing more.

"You knew." Edmund turned John Marshal. "You knew that it had to be the king, but you didn't say it."

John slid his sword back into its scabbard. "He had to choose of his own free will. No one could make him do it."

"We won." The flood of feeling broke on Edmund. "My friends. We did it! We won!"

"Yes, we did." Katherine returned. She kissed Tom on the cheek—then Edmund on the lips.

Harry came near. "Katherine?" He stood back again, unsure.

"My lord." Katherine curtsied to him. "I am pleased that you are well."

Harry wiped the gore from his face, then clutched the goose-egg bruise on his head and walked away.

"Now, Katherine." John Marshal came to stand among them. "Tom—Edmund. I have the honor to say, one last time, that you have done it. You thwarted the Nethergrim, yet again, this time perhaps for good. A new age of the world can begin because of what you have done."

"Oh, Papa." Katherine seized him tight. "And you are here. It was so—it doesn't matter. You're here now."

John looked over Katherine's shoulder at Edmund—and Edmund understood. He drank in John's face, tried his best to fix the image of it in his mind. If he could learn to live so that the same look set itself on his own face one day, he would know that he had lived well.

"Now, John." A new voice broke in from nearby, approaching along with unsteady footsteps in the snow. "All is accomplished. It is time."

Tom spun around. "You. I saw you before, back at Master Marshal's farm."

"Four, one, two." The old man took off his wide-brimmed hat and tried his best to swat down his shock of white hair. "Three, six, five, yes? That was the pattern?"

"It was." John turned to the old man. "Must this be?"

The old man nodded down his head—almost a bow of reverence. "It must be."

Katherine let go of her father. A shaking horror overcame her, dawning with her understanding.

"You are the Lord Exalted Seer." Edmund turned to the old man. "You were the king's teacher, master of the *Eredh*."

The old man nodded again. "I am."

"You are the only one of your kind skilled enough to send someone backward in time," said Edmund. "Or sideways."

The old man seemed to stare at Edmund more through the diamond in his forehead than through his two eyes. "You will do much, Edmund Bale of Moorvale. The paths of the future beckon you onward. The life you have dreamed about approaches. Use it well."

Edmund knew the answer, but still he had to ask: "Can I trade it to stop what you are about to do?"

The old man shook his head. "You cannot."

Katherine let out a scream. She grabbed for her father and cried out: "Papa." She spoke his name again and yet again, softer and softer, until she merely grasped his neck. Edmund had a vision—he did not know if it was a true—John carrying a tiny Katherine around while she wept, hugging and hushing her until the tears stopped.

"Katherine." John grasped her hands. "My daughter, please. It has to be, or we would never have reached this day. Do you understand?"

Geoffrey came then, over from the place where Edmund's family stood together—together, whole, alive. "Edmund? What's happening?"

Edmund's resolve broke. Sorrow seized and shook him, so that he could hardly speak the words. "John Marshal has to go now."

"Go where?" Geoffrey looked about him—Tom had been swept into John and Katherine's embrace. "What's happening? We won!"

"We did," said Edmund. "Now we have to make sure that it happened this way."

"Tristan—Tristan!" John called out over Katherine's shoulder. "Someone bring Lord Tristan to me."

Lord Tristan came alone, feeling out blind until Edmund took his hand. "John? My old friend, what is wrong? There should be joy, joy beyond all measure! Folk have died, yes, but their sacrifice has bought all the world a new dawn!"

"You speak more truth than you know," said John. "I lived these last six days out of step with time. The first day of Yule was my fourth, the second day my first and so on."

Understanding seemed to age Tristan into his dotage all at once. "Oh, my friend, my dear friend—you died yesterday, but you are alive now. A twist in time. You died to save the king, so that he could have a chance to survive to die for us today."

"I did." John held tight to Katherine's hand. "I bought this day—now I must pay for it. Will you take my daughter into your household, when I am gone?"

"My dear friend, the first and best of us all." Tristan was as overcome as Tom and Katherine. "She will be forever cherished in my home, this I swear."

Katherine had never been stronger, never been more worthy of Edmund's love and admiration than in what she did next. She stopped crying. "Papa. My blessed, beloved father." She kissed his hands. "Thank you."

"But why?" Geoffrey clung hard to Edmund. "We won. Why?"

"The same reason I would have given, if it had been me." Edmund let his brother hold him close. "I would have done it for you."

John let go of Katherine, though it made her tremble and reach out into the space between them. "We all of us pass into and out of this world. That cannot be changed." He stood alone—perhaps, in the end, as it should be. "What we can do is make something beautiful out of time, to stitch and weave its pains and joys into a tapestry lovely beyond all words."

"A tapestry for whom?" said Edmund. "Who are we making it for?"

John turned a smile upon them all that Edmund would remember all his life. "That is what we all get to discover."

Edmund left his brother to come stand shoulder to shoulder with Katherine and Tom. The sun shone noon high, arisen into the new year of a new age of the world. The Nethergrim had spoken of a void, an endless blankness—the Nethergrim was a liar.

John turned to the seer. "I am ready."

Made in the USA
Las Vegas, NV
27 September 2021